CINDERELLA SOLDIER

A Glass Slipper Adventure Book 2

Allie Burton

Allie Burton

Cinderella Soldier

A Glass Slipper Adventure

Copyright © 2020 by Alice Fairbanks-Burton

All rights reserved

CONTENTS

Introduction   V

1. Chapter 1   1

2. Chapter 2   10

3. Chapter 3   17

4. Chapter 4   25

5. Chapter 5   36

6. Chapter 6   48

7. Chapter 7   61

8. Chapter 8   73

9. Chapter 9   82

10. Chapter 10   90

11. Chapter 11   100

12. Chapter 12   112

13. Chapter 13   122

14. Chapter 14   130

15. Chapter 15   138

16. Chapter 16   148

17. Chapter 17   157

18. Chapter 18 — 164

19. Chapter 19 — 177

20. Chapter 20 — 190

21. Chapter 21 — 203

22. Chapter 22 — 216

23. Chapter 23 — 228

24. Chapter 24 — 240

25. Chapter 25 — 251

26. Chapter 26 — 260

27. Chapter 27 — 271

28. Chapter 28 — 279

29. Chapter 29 — 289

Cinderella Spy — 298

Snow Wicked White — 301

A Note from Allie Burton — 304

Also By — 306

About Author — 308

INTRODUCTION

Chapter One

Sharp steel pressed against my neck. "This is the way to win, princess."

I sucked in a bitter breath, and not from the closeness of the blade. Perry Moss couldn't know the truth, few did. Because princess wasn't just a taunt, it was a title.

My title.

Locking gazes with him, I glared at his attempt to best me. His silver eyes flashed with what looked like hatred, and then went hard and cool. Cute, but a total stranger and one of my new classmates. Had he forgotten we were on the same side training for a real battle? To be soldiers in the fight against Regent Theobald and his cronies?

The blade pressed harder against my throat. Perry was one of a few students who chose to spar against me. His long, dark hair had been braided away from his forehead. His thin, angular face always appeared in a superior pout. "Concede, Ellery."

Why did it sound as if he was asking me to give up more than this fight?

"No." I wrapped my fingers tighter around the coiled carbon lasso, a connection of magical notches that did my bidding. And its own. The weapon had found me on my first adventure.

My weapon whipped forward, wrapping around the hilt of his blade. The blade clattered onto the weapons training ground in a puff of dry dirt.

Perry scowled and backed away, disgust written across his face. "You're using magic, not skill."

He seemed to feel the need to best me in weapons and in magic class. It was as if he needed to prove his superiority in every aspect of fairy training. Which I didn't doubt. I'd received my fairy magic a few months ago when I'd turned sixteen. The weapons training was completely new.

And yet, I held my own. Real battle experience counted for something.

My chin tilted up and power thrummed through my veins. Yanking the whip back, I took a deep inhale. I coiled the shiny rope with care and held it at my hip. "We're fairies. Magic is what we do."

I was only half fairy. A fact the other students consistently pointed out. Snickered at. Talked about behind my half human back. They didn't know the truth about me yet. I'd known for a week and couldn't accept the truth.

I was a princess. A fairy princess.

What would these kids say when they learned?

I remembered the moment Commander Gardenia, also my fairy godmother, had first told me. We'd returned from destroying the auraguillotine under the human palace and had been escorted to Queens Academy. It had taken me awhile to process the ridiculous statement. Actually, I still didn't fully comprehend it.

I'd stuttered the word. "P-p-princess?"

"You're the lost princess, Ellery." Gardenia twirled a large ring around her finger. I'd never seen her nervous before. "Your mother was a third princess. When she fell in love with your father, her mother, the queen, let her live the life she wanted. The queen had two older daughters who would have children of their own so there was no reason to keep your mother bound to the realm. The two princesses died before they had children." Gardenia's calmness belied the havoc she'd created inside me.

My head whirled, making me dizzy. The churning dropped to my belly and I felt sick. My lungs struggled to take a ragged breath.

I had a grandmother—who was the queen, and aunts whom I'd never meet and who had died.

She placed a flat palm on my shoulder. "You became next in line for the throne."

The havoc ramped up and twisted similar to a tornado. Everything I'd known or understood became uprooted like my family tree. The limbs of what I'd believed to be true crashed to the ground, metaphorically blindsiding me. I sank to the floor.

I was pulled in two different directions, both against my will. "No. No. Noooo."

How could I have gone from being a servant in my stepmother's home to being a princess? By coming to the fairy school, I thought I'd gotten rid of my shackles. Being a princess would mean a new set of restrictions, handcuffs made of diamonds, or whatever fairies put on their crowns. I wanted to fight in the war on the side of the majiks, not be pampered and protected. I did not want to be forced into a role I didn't want to play.

"You need to learn how to fight without magic. That's what weapons class is about." Perry stepped forward and swiped at his blade, bringing me back to the present.

He was right. If I wanted to prove my worth, I'd need to become the best fighter in school. To show Gardenia I was meant to be a soldier, not a princess. I'd known Queens Academy would be worse than human school. And then Gardenia had thrown this entire princess thing at me.

Battle training had been combined with magic training—because I needed help with my newly-forming powers—and she'd added on fairy etiquette and history. I didn't need the last two to win a war.

The weapons training ground resembled a large sports field, but this wasn't a game. Not to me or to my opponent. The smell of grass and dirt stuck in my nose and I found the earth scent comforting. Natural elements were attractive to fairies and since coming to the academy my fairy side dominated.

"Weren't you beneath Regent Theobald's royal palace where magic is suppressed?" The strange twist in conversation showed Perry had heard rumors about my mission the night of the royal ball.

Many of the students had. They didn't know the truth, the full scope of what I'd been through, and I didn't plan to enlighten them. If they couldn't like me for who I was, why should I give them the information they sought?

"No comment." Swiveling away, I strolled to the portable arsenal and perused my choice of weapons.

He had a point about learning to fight without magic. Not that I'd admit it. There'd been times under the human royal palace I'd wished I'd had access to my malfunctioning powers. The humans had developed technology to contain majiks' magic, and grit and determination had been our battle weapons.

I fingered the notched coil whip—my favorite weapon. It understood what I needed and anticipated my enemy's next move. The humans couldn't suppress the magic in the entire Kingdom of Alandaska.

This war would be magic versus technology.

Why study the ancient arts of fighting and weaponry when we had magical power deep inside us? Now that I was learning to control my magic, I didn't see the need to use other weapons.

Still, I picked up a sabre and ran my gloved hand over the blade. Perry wanted a fair fight with no magic, so I'd give him one.

I slashed the weapon and a zing traveled through my arm. Pivoting, I faced my opponent. *"En guard."*

"Allez." He lunged, his blade glinting with sunlight.

I feinted to the right.

He lunged again, and our swords clashed.

The impact shattered up my arm and shook my spine. The weakness and fear brought me to a different place when I'd been feeble and unsure. I wasn't that person anymore.

I charged forward.

He attacked with intent, as if relishing the need to hurt or embarrass me. To make me lose this fight. My muscles hardened. Most of the kids at the academy treated me differently. They were suspicious or downright hated me. Nothing I hadn't dealt with in my past.

"Not so confident without your magic." Smirking, he parried, forcing me to take several steps back.

A guffaw shot out of my mouth. If he had seen my use of magic a week ago, he never would've made the statement.

"Fairies have magic. You have magic. We should be able to use it." A new attitude for me.

I might've agreed to fight without my powers this time, but I believed in using everything at my disposal to win. When I first received my powers, my magic misfired whenever I attempted, and sometimes when I didn't. Since starting at Queens Academy one week ago, I'd been learning and studying. I'd gotten better.

"You should learn the hard way." Perry jabbed at my chest and I jumped, withdrawing into the shadows formed by the academy's balcony. "Then, when you use magic it's easy."

He arced his sword down in a smooth move showing how simple it was for him.

I wished I'd been trained in fighting since birth, not washing dishes. But I hadn't and I'd learn to live with it. Or die trying.

Blocking his sword with my sabre, the clanging of metal rang in my head. Sweat formed on my upper lip. Even though the day was chilly, I wished I'd worn a single layer of clothes. I was about to wish the outer jacket away when I remembered his challenge.

No magic. I could do this.

He swung at me again and I ducked.

This wasn't a friendly bout or practice. This guy was going for me. Which was okay. The hard training would exhaust me, and I'd forget...

Don't think about the prince. Don't think about the prince.

I hadn't heard if Prince Zacharye, or Rye as I called him, had survived the one night we'd spent in the palace dungeon. My heart shattered and tears burned my eyes as I remembered the explosion. I had to pull myself together.

Perry's assault continued, blow after blow.

Panting, I kept maneuvering further and further back. He had me pinned against the balustrade.

A dark shiver passed through me. Perry didn't like me, wanted to best me. However, he was the only one who'd train with me and I desperately needed training. Would he take the contest too far and cause injury? He'd come close minutes ago.

My opponent conjured a second sword from mid-air.

My heart raced and the sweat on my lip formed a thin layer of ice. "You said no magic."

"I said *you* should learn the hard way. I've learned. Now it's your turn." His wings spread, adding to his strength.

The fluttering of his brown and gold wings distracted me. Glittery gold lined the edges and pulsed from the iridescent veins. His wings gave him leverage to fight.

My head spun, and my gaze tried to follow the swirls of his weapons. I pressed against the concrete of the balustrade and my weapons hand fell to my side. Defeat set in. No wings, terrible magic, average fighting skills. Would I ever be good enough to become a soldier in the queen's army?

"Why did you have to come back?" Perry's almost inaudible whisper was followed by a slash. His blade came at my face.

I twisted my head, but I was too late. The blade sliced my cheek. Pain radiated from the wound. The spot felt tingly and sticky and numbed my body and my mind.

He raised the weapon to strike again.

Bracing my foot against the balustrade, I pushed out and into him. Adrenaline surged through my bloodstream. I wouldn't sit back and let him injure me. My chest bumped into his and he faltered. I raised my sword, ready to do damage.

His expression showed shock at my attack, and maybe a little admiration.

"Perry," a high-pitched female screeched. "Commander Gardenia is looking for you."

His skin went pale as if he'd suffered a wound. His lavender blue eyes appeared dazed and then refocused.

My shoulders slumped, and I let out a long, slow sigh. I pulled the blade back. Saved by my fairy godmother again.

Another reason the kids hated me. The commander had singled me out for special attention since I'd arrived. They didn't know she was my fairy godmother. When Gardenia spoke, fairies listened.

Including Perry because he retreated. "Sorry about the scratch. Adrenaline got the best of me."

Adrenaline, huh? I knew the other fairies hated me. I didn't think they were out to kill.

He shot a glance at the person who'd interrupted our battle. He scrunched up his upper lip, showing he didn't like her either. "I'm on my way."

Huffing, he tossed his weapon down and spun on his pointed boots, hurrying inside the castle-turned-school. He wore tight brown breeches and a leather vest similar to most of the male fairies. A take on the regular male school uniform.

I lifted my hand to my cheek. Liquid warmed my fingertips and I pulled my hand away. Blood. Had he truly wanted to hurt me? His hatred had been palpable.

"He tried to kill you." The high-pitched voice reminded me I wasn't alone. "Are you okay?"

She'd saved me as much as Gardenia because the guy had hatred on his face and a sword at my neck.

The student fairy was taller than me, which was unusual. Long, curly blond hair accented her heart-shaped face. Her skin appeared smooth and perfect and her lips were a bright red. It didn't seem natural, which was rare for a fairy. Her wings held at a stiff angle. Her breasts popped out of the sleeveless green and purple plaid vest. The pleated skirt stopped high on her thighs.

I'd altered my uniform, making the plaid skirt longer and wearing a white blouse under the vest. Other fairies needed room for their wings. I didn't. Another way I stood out.

She hurried toward me. "You're bleeding."

Leaning away, I swiped at the spot on my cheek. I'd seen worse.

"I've got fiddle leaf in my bag." She dug in a small bag, taking several seconds to root around before she pulled out a bright green leaf.

I took a step back. Why would one of the students want to help me?

She quirked her head. "The fiddle leaf will stop the bleeding."

I snatched the leaf from her hand and pressed it against my bleeding cheek. Another thing I needed to learn, natural healing methods. For whatever reason, I came in contact with injured majiks a lot, or I became one.

"Thanks." My tone wasn't quite thankful because I was suspicious of anyone being nice.

"I'm Bee." She held out her hand.

Narrowing my gaze, I examined her hand for any tricks or magical devices. "Ellery." Slowly, I placed my hand in hers for a quick shake.

"I'm new to the academy. I enrolled late because when my powers finally manifested, my parents were away." Her expression appeared open and honest and her bright green gaze flashed. "Any advice on how to get along here?"

"Stay away from me." I spoke through gritted teeth.

"What?" She pursed her lips, showing her offense.

I'd been rude, and I didn't want her getting off on the wrong wing like I had.

"The students don't like me so if you want to have friends, you should probably stay away from me." My cheeks heated as I rushed through the words. Mortification had become my constant companion.

"You can hold your own." Her chin nodded at the spot where I'd battled Perry.

Embarrassment exploded and I fisted my hands to keep from physically lashing out. Perry struck me, caused blood to trickle. "Do you need glasses?" I let my mouth run.

Her head quirked and her brown eyebrows arched in question.

Of course, a fairy wouldn't need glasses. She probably didn't know what they were. Eyesight could be fixed with magic by a parent or fairy godmother. A sour taste filled my mouth. Not that I'd know because my fairy godmother hadn't shown up in my life until a few months ago.

"Perry had me cornered. He drew blood. I was going to lose." Or die.

"He used magic to get the second sword. You didn't." Her head quirked again. "Why not?"

"Because he chided me into agreeing not to use magic."

"He *lied* to you?" She emphasized the word lied.

"Fairies can't lie." As a half fairy, I could. Normally, my human abilities weren't helpful in the fairy world. In this case, I enjoyed having the ability to lie.

Bee smirked. "There are ways to get around the truth."

The truth always found you though. I'd learned that lesson the hard way.

Chapter Two

The bell rang, signaling the end of lunch period. Students flooded the hallways, talking and laughing. They all took a wide berth around me.

"She's the one who got Bim killed." Flying past me in the hallway, the girl's wings spread wide and grazed off my covered shoulder, taunting me. She wore the school uniform in perfect regulation from the length of her plaid skirt to the width of the vest.

My head pounded. Bim, the fairy she talked about so casually, had been a hero. He'd sacrificed himself to save me and my friends and was rewarded with gossip.

Another girl hurried to stroll beside her, shoving strawberry pudding into her mouth. "I heard an elf died, too."

Keltie. The dead elf's name thudded in my chest.

"Can you believe the half breed befriended an elf?" The first fairy visibly shivered for effect, knowing I walked behind them.

The stinky smell of fairy perfume and teenage hormones burned my nostrils, adding to the pounding in my head.

"What kind of fairy name is Ellery?" A guy joined the blabbering group. He didn't wear a shirt and let his wings have free reign across the corridor.

I knew Queen's Academy would be bad. Between the rumors, the ostracism, and my own guilt, I hadn't expected to be popular. I wasn't here to make friends.

Why bother when they either left you or died?

Keltie and Bim had died. Arbor, my best friend, had left on a secret errand. Hokima and Tos had returned to their homelands. Stone had disappeared after escorting me to this school. And I didn't know if Rye, or should I say Prince Zacharye, was alive or dead.

My heart squeezed and I struggled to take a fractured gulp of air. I'd begged Gardenia to send spies to find out what had happened to the prince. She'd said I should concern myself with the fairy kingdom and leave the humans to rot.

To this day, Rye still didn't rule the Kingdom of Alandaska, yet Regent Theobald hadn't crowned himself king. When he did, war would break out between the humans and majiks, and I planned to fight, even with the pesky royal thing.

I bumped into something. Someone.

The girls who'd been gossiping had stopped in the middle of the hallway.

"Watch out, half breed." The guy snarled the words.

"Sorry, I..." I was thinking. Something they probably didn't do very much.

The girl with the dessert twisted her lips in an awkward smile. She lifted her cup of pudding and smushed it into my chest. The attack resembled a messy grenade. The red-colored mush soaked into my new school uniform and slid down my shirt, leaving a bright red stain.

The three of them laughed. Their chuckles hit me in the gut, harder and messier than the pudding. My cheeks heated, and the warmth slid across my face and neck. Using my hand, I swiped at the blotches of red, probably making the stain worse. I hated these school uniforms anyhow.

"Oops." She fluttered her wings.

I clenched my fingers into fists, refusing to be pulled into some petty squabble. These kids didn't understand the stakes of the upcoming war. They didn't understand the evil in the human palace, the cruelty I'd seen against majiks. I'd fight with my life for the cause, not for popularity.

Trudging through the ornate hallways, my feet left marks on the flat pavestones of the floor. Moss grew between the large, flat stones continuing the nature-meets-castle décor. Stained glass windows lined the corridor bringing the light in from outside, except this was an internal hallway. Nature and magic provided the ostentation. It was so different from the human palace of crystal and glass, where technology superseded everything, even underneath.

Veering to the left, I opened one side of grand double doors made of intricately carved wood depicting a forest. The shortcut would take me through the ballroom and avoid other students. I slipped inside and pushed the heavy door closed.

Leaning against the door, I sighed. I'd met Prince Zacharye in a ballroom, though we'd never danced. I'd fallen in love. My heart throbbed. I'd never told him.

Glass walls and ceilings framed the ballroom. It was an atrium for fairies. Tall trees with bright flowers grew outside the walls, casting colorful splashes of light onto the floor. Green and purple, red and yellow, blue and pink. It was a kaleidoscope of color. Doric columns held up the glass. Green vines with purple grapes wrapped around the pillars.

The fairy ballroom wasn't used for dancing anymore. It was used for training and meetings. The fairy castle had been turned into the secret school when majiks were no longer allowed to attend human schools. Living rooms had been converted to classrooms. Bedrooms had been converted to dormitories. The library had stayed a library.

Forcing myself off the door, I hurried across the vast marble floors toward the stage where a single royal throne sat. The throne floated on a cloud stationed between two large trees. The branches of the trees glowed, matching the chandelier hanging above. The night sky was visible even though it was daytime.

I couldn't imagine sitting in the uncomfortable chair with hundreds of people staring. I'd crack under the pressure and the politics. I hoped I'd never have to take charge.

Pushing aside a curtain, I entered the back offices for the queen. Commander Gardenia had one of the largest offices with the best access and the best view. Silver Birch, her assistant, sat at a desk outside the closed office door. She waved me in.

I pushed the door open and halted.

The room had been transformed from the fairy commander's study with magical orbs and fairy wands lying about into a utilitarian office with a metal desk, matching chairs, upholstered sofa, and a coffee table.

My gaze swung back to the woman sitting on the sofa.

Sybil, my stepmother.

Her red hair was grayer than before. Her face was more lined. She wore a wrinkled blue dress with a lowcut neckline.

My stomach dropped, and nerves sprang to the tips of my fingers. What was she doing here? *How* was she here at the magical Queens Academy?

I zeroed in on Gardenia pacing behind the couch and reeled back.

She wore a boring black suit, trying to pass as human. Her pursed lips and narrowed gaze told me the truth. My fairy godmother must've brought my stepmother here. She'd stabbed me in the back and the sharp slice stung. I thought I'd left my human past behind. I didn't miss it and wanted nothing from it. Well, almost nothing.

"Hi, Ellery." Ingrid waved from the side of the room. "Do you know how to connect my celltab? I'm not getting a signal."

My head angled toward the girl. I hadn't noticed her or Ilana, my other stepsister, with the shock of seeing Sybil. The girls' hair appeared a brighter, faker red. Both of them wore a lot of makeup, emphasizing their eyes and high cheekbones.

"Really? How can you run a school without connectivity?" Ilana sneered, the beauty mark above her lip becoming more prominent. She inspected the filled bookshelf that hadn't been there a day ago. Boring titles like Technology Science, Human Genealogy, and Shakespeare. No magic books or sorcerers' spells.

I squeezed my eyelids tight, hoping the scene would disappear. It didn't. And neither did my stepfamily.

"What is all over your shirt? You're a slob and a disgrace to the Milford name."

Sybil's criticism smacked and my cheeks reddened with re-membered embarrassment. I'd forgotten about the pudding in-cident. Forgotten my clothes were a mess. Forgotten how cruel my stepmother could be. What this woman thought didn't matter anymore. She always criticized me whether it was warranted or not. What mattered now was finishing my training so I could become a soldier and fight. My stepmother would not interfere.

Gardenia's mouth opened, shocked by my stepmother's slur.

"What're they doing here?" I tried to keep my voice calm and in control. Showing emotion fed my stepmother's ire.

Gardenia fluttered her hand similar to how she fluttered her wings. "They're your family."

"They're not family." *Thank the wood spirits.* And why was she defending them? She'd wanted me to leave them and come to the academy.

Sybil got to her feet and her expression screwed up like a carp. "How dare you!"

I ignored her and took a step toward Gardenia. "You said it your-self, Sybil made me a slave." I hated to admit my fairy godmother had been right. "She's not a blood relative, and neither are Ingrid and Ilana. They are not fairies."

It had taken so long for me to accept my fairy self. I'd planned to pretend to be human for my entire life until my best friend, Arbor, had been arrested for magic that I'd done, and Gardenia had sent me to the royal ball to kill Prince Zacharye. Except I'd fallen in love instead. He'd helped me navigate the tunnels beneath the palace, and I'd met my majik friends who'd fought by my side.

Pulling my shoulders back, I stuck out my chest. I was proud of what I'd gone through in order to come to the realization of who I was. "I'm a fairy. And I won't claim a relationship to them."

Sybil stepped toward me.

I refused to back down. I was no longer under her control or afraid of her blackmail.

Her cheeks were a bright red and her eyes glared. Her hand reached up and she slapped me.

My cheek stung, but not as much as my pride. I froze, not sure how to react. I was trained to fight and had magical powers. I could demolish her. Then, I'd be stooping to her level.

My stepsisters gasped.

Gardenia's business persona disappeared. Her wings sprouted, and her fingers twitched, grasping her wand. "Lady Milford, that's no way to treat a princess."

My stepmother's expression was carved in stone. She didn't move. Shock must've set in.

I didn't know whether to laugh or cry. To my stepfamily, I'd been a servant. When all along, I'd been royal. My secret was out and to people I disliked more than the mean girls in the hallway.

Sybil's cheeks puffed. Her lips wiggled in a strange action, similar to a fish puckering and unpuckering, as if she tasted something sour. "A what?"

A nervous giggle built in my lungs. I pinched my lips together, trying to hold in the chuckle.

She swiveled toward Gardenia and the pronouncement. "What princess?"

Gardenia's mouth hung open, and then she snapped it shut. She puffed out her cheeks and closed her eyes. Her gaze swung up, searching for an explanation. "Ellery is a princess. A princess from the Royal House of Kunglig. A fairy princess."

"You're not real royalty like the regent. Just a lowly princess in this zauber world." Smirking, Sybil advanced toward me.

I sucked in a wheeze. Zauber was the worst way to say majik. The insult assaulted my already low opinion of myself. Poor magic. No friends. Fell in love with the wrong guy, possibly a dead guy.

Gardenia swirled her wand and circles of sparkles wrapped around Sybil, putting her in a magical bind. Ingrid and Ilana openly gaped. Their shocked gasps echoed around the room.

Tension filled the office. It was a battle of wills and I already knew who would win.

Gardenia flicked her wand and my stepmother fell back on the couch, resembling a beached whale.

"Imagine Elle being a princess," Ingrid whined with a touch of wonder. "She could meet and marry Prince Zacharye."

The name jolted me out of my shock. "He's alive?"

"Why would Prince Zacharye want to marry a fairy?" Ilana scoffed.

I waited on tenterhooks, holding my breath. "Is Rye—Prince Zacharye—alive?"

"Why would you even ask such a ridiculous question?" Ilana sneered as if I was stupid. "Of course, he's alive."

Joy spread through my veins, tingling against my skin and lighting my soul.

"He signed a law classifying majiks as state subjects without citizenship rights."

The tingling stopped. The joy morphed to nausea churning in my stomach. He'd taken away our rights? How could Rye do this?

"Did you see him on a news vid signing the law?" I needed visual proof. Regent Theobald had lied about so many things. Had lied to Rye and the kingdom.

Sybil struggled to sit up. "If Elle's a fairy princess, the prince will want to kill her, not marry her."

Her gleeful declaration caused the earlier backstabbing knife to twist through my heart. I wanted to stand up and defend Rye, except I couldn't let my sinister stepmother find out the truth. There'd be questions and consequences.

Like how Rye had fought for majiks under the palace. How I thought he'd died. We were of a similar stature now. I wasn't a half breed servant, I was a princess, I'd be his equal.

And his enemy.

CHAPTER THREE

"Why did you bring my stepfamily here in the first place?" I'd wanted to keep this world separate from my past. I wanted to blend into my new environment, not stand out—my motto since my father died years ago.

"They're here to discuss ownership of Milford house." Gardenia had magically bound the three of them and we'd left them in the office to talk in the corridor.

My pulse pounded. The main reason I'd pretended to be human was knowing I'd inherit the house. "My home?"

"Those humans need a place to live and you've disappeared into the fairy homeland." Gardenia shrugged, suggesting the decision would be easy.

"No." I shook my head back and forth and air leaked out of my chest. I suffocated with panic. "They can't have my house."

The house had been in my father's family for generations. I was the last Milford. The home reminded me of happier times with my dad, and it held the trunk with my mother's belongings. The house had been the reason I'd put up with Sybil and her blackmail.

"You don't need a simple human house when you have a castle." Gardenia waved her arms to encompass the arched hallways filled with the echoes of nature.

Birds tweeting, crickets chirping, a river flowing.

The sounds should've been relaxing. Air wheezed in my lungs. I'd never thought of the perks of being royal, only the panic. "And I suppose I have servants and guards and jewels and a crown." I grabbed my hair and yanked. "Oh, my wood nymphs! I'm already a freak. Can you imagine me with a tiara?"

"Princess Ellery." Gardenia's stern tone jerked me back to the moment.

"Don't call me that."

"I won't in public. We'll need to keep it secret for awhile."

"Why?" Was she embarrassed of me? I glanced at my dirty shirt. Of course, Gardenia was embarrassed. "I can't be a princess. Look at me."

I was a mess. Untrained and unliked. My magic misfired. And I hadn't been part of the fairy world until very recently. I was still learning the rules.

"We will discuss this later, after the humans leave."

Sucking in a large breath, I gripped Gardenia's arms. "They know I'm a princess. Sybil can't keep her mouth shut."

She had a SCUM, Security Collectors of Unique Magic, boyfriend. The SCUM arrested majiks who broke the strict laws. And even those who didn't. Sybil would tell her boyfriend, and he'd tell his commander and he'd tell someone higher up. My stepmonster and stepsisters would find a way to take advantage of me. They always did.

"We can alter Sybil and your stepsisters' memories." Gardenia removed her arms from my grip and twiddled her fingers. A celltab with an official document on the screen appeared in her hand. "What do you want to do with Milford house?"

My eyes burned. What were my options? I'd need a degree to prove my humanity in order to inherit and take control of my home. After saving Arbor and learning of the atrocities happening to majiks, I'd abandoned human school and enrolled at Queens Academy. Going back to Milford House, to the human world, didn't appeal. I wanted to fight for what was right. The burning in my eyes intensified. All my memories were there. But I'd make new memories. I already had. Arbor would return and I'd make new friends.

"With the new rules you can't go back. It's not safe for you." Gardenia pointed out the newest law.

The law signed by Rye.

Here, I'd been worried about whether he was alive or dead, and he'd been signing laws against me and my kind. I couldn't take Prince Zacharye into the equation.

"Once the war begins, there will be a clear demarcation line. No one will be crossing it. Humans or majiks." She pressed her point.

My gut roiled with thoughts of the battle to come. Humans and majiks dying. Friends dying.

"When the majiks win," her voice rose with pride, "you will be at Queens Castle to rule."

My stomach clenched, stopping the roiling and making me nauseous. I wasn't a ruler. I barely survived leading my friends through the dungeon of the human palace. I'd just saved Arbor. And lost Bim and Keltie during the quest.

"I understand you're not ready to accept who you are. Yet." Gardenia patted my shoulder. "And I hadn't meant to shock by announcing your status in front of anyone, but that woman..."

Understanding Sybil's effect on people, I slowly exhaled. I remembered the time she'd given me a long list of chores to complete before the royal ball or the time she'd made me clean the stone wall around the garden at Milford House.

"We need to send those humans on their way. There will be less questions about your disappearance if the house is settled in their name."

A numbed pain surrounded my heart. It was only a house. I understood my real place was with the fairies, whether fighting or on the throne. Yet, I couldn't agree. "My mom's trunk is in my attic bedroom and it has fairy items inside."

A risk that couldn't be left behind.

"I've already sent someone to retrieve the trunk."

My eyebrows rose. She'd known about the trunk left to me when my mom had died. Sometimes the woman knew too much.

"There are a couple of things I want of my dad's, too." And I wanted to see the house one last time.

"It's too dangerous for you." She shook her head slowly, already regretting her response.

I took a long, slow pull of air. The thought of never returning to my home hit me hard. One more thing I'd do for the cause. "Okay. I'll sign." I gripped the thin stylo between white fingers. Biting my lower lip, I signed my name.

Gardenia gave the celltab to her assistant. "Please alter the memories of the humans and send them home."

I waited for sadness or loneliness to overwhelm me. When it didn't, I understood I'd never thought of Sybil, Ilana, or Ingrid as family. Not seeing them again wouldn't bother me. I wished them happiness without me to boss around. I no longer had a family, except...

"What about my grandmother? The queen." My lips numbed on the word.

"What about your grandmother?"

"I want to meet her." My single living relative. I'd been here a week and had been afraid to ask. She was a powerful and busy queen.

"She's very ill." Sadness poured from my fairy godmother. "We should go right away. Right after I take care of...them." She waved at her office.

Renewed sadness caused my legs to weaken. I'd lost my mom and dad, two aunts I hadn't known, and my house. But I was gaining a new world, one I was willing to fight for.

After sending my stepfamily back to their home, Gardenia whisked me down corridors that became grander and grander as we walked. Stained glass made up the walls with images of fairies frolicking and flying in the woods, of using magic to help each other and humans. Light shined through the windows, making the colors bold and beautiful.

I couldn't appreciate the beauty. My thoughts swirled in turmoil. I hadn't had time to prepare to meet a queen, my grandmother. There was so much I didn't comprehend, rules and etiquette, and I had so many questions.

Two liveried servants stood outside double doors bigger than the ones leading into the ballrooms. The servants were dressed in the royal colors of green and purple and they were tall. Their build reminded me of Stone, who was half giant.

Gardenia made a sign with her hands too quick for me to catch. Another thing I didn't know.

The servants opened the double doors wide and we passed through without waiting a second.

The babble of rushing water greeted me. A massive waterfall fell from between stone arches two stories high. The water crashed into a small pond where it gurgled down a stream, circling the interior of the room similar to the moat on the outside of a castle.

Following Gardenia, I crossed over the water on an invisible bridge, holding my breath in case I fell through.

More liveried servants hurried around the room doing chores of some sort. They didn't even glance as we approached the canopied bed. The bed was bigger than any room in Milford House and floated on a cloud, like the throne chair.

My gaze widened.

Butterflies, lightning bugs, and birds flew around the bed adding to the naturalness of the room. It was comparable to being in a beautifully carved cave with the stalactites and stalagmites as decoration.

My nerves flitted like the butterflies. This was real. I was meeting Queen Dahliadew and she was my grandmother.

Gardenia climbed the steps to the platform surrounding the bed and moved aside the netting.

The tiny queen lay in the center of the huge bed. Her head was propped up on pillows made from flowers. Natural scents of mist and citrus circled around me. The heavy blankets, resembling moss, lay over her small frame. Her skin was so pale it looked opaque. Her huge mossy green eyes peered at me.

The butterflies in my stomach morphed into hummingbirds and beat their wings just as fast. Do I bow or curtsy? What do I call her? I didn't know royal protocol.

"Queen Dahliadew." Gardenia made an elaborate gesture of spreading her wings and tucking them in at the same time she bowed at the waist. "I'd like you to meet Princess Ellery."

I jerked my head to stare at Gardenia, not used to being called a princess.

The queen craned her neck. "Are you sure?"

I blanched at the question. Even the queen didn't think I was royal material. I pressed my hand against the stain on my shirt, trying to cover it from view.

Gardenia nodded. "Lily's daughter and your granddaughter."

The queen twirled a finger. "Where are her wings?"

Her magic took hold of me and I spun around, showing the queen my back. Losing my balance, I stuck my hands out to keep from falling, which made me look even more foolish.

"Her wings haven't manifested yet." Gardenia tugged on my arm and spun me back around.

I felt like a BarbBob doll and just as confused. Wings? I didn't think I'd get wings because I was half human. Every other fairy at school had them and I'd accepted not having wings would be another way I was different. "I, um—"

Gardenia shook her head at me in disapproval.

I wasn't allowed to speak to the queen? She was my grandmother. I wanted to talk to her, get to know her, learn from her while I could. A yearning tugged me toward her. I needed this connection like a mighty oak needed its roots.

"Ellery." The queen said my name as if it was a foreign word. "Can we change it?"

"No!" This time I didn't wait for Gardenia to quiet me. I wasn't changing my name. My parents had given it to me. I really didn't want to be a princess anyhow.

Queen Dahliadew slipped on a smile. "Opinionated. I enjoy that."

"And stubborn." My fairy godmother shouldn't be speaking bad of me in front of the queen.

"Finally, we meet." The queen held out her hand.

I glanced at Gardenia before taking the queen's papery thin hand in mine. "It's, um, nice to meet you."

"Is it?" The queen might be ill, but she was shrewd. "You resemble your mother."

My initial nerves settled, and I beamed. I liked being compared to my mom now. When Arbor had said something similar in the past, I'd gotten angry.

"Give me your other hand."

At the queen's command, my other hand jumped into hers. It wasn't magic this time, only the ultimate authority in her tone. I would never hold that authority. I could never rule.

The queen held my hands tight, rubbing her fingers up and down as if sensing me. Come to think of it, I felt a niggle in my brain. Something was trying to get inside. Was she trying to see my thoughts? Was it possible?

I shut down any opening and smashed my lips together. Making no noise, I hummed in my mind, using Mother Earth's gift to block the invasion.

"You think about the human prince." Queen Dahliadew's raspy voice interrupted my internal humming.

My eyes widened. I'd tried to keep my mind blank.

"Regent Theobald will never give up the throne as long as he lives." She spoke as though she knew, although she didn't see that in my head.

Did the queen use a crystal ball, or did she have more spies in the castle?

"You are strong on the inside." The queen released my hands. "You will need strength on the outside."

Ha. I felt weak. Perry had beaten me soundly today. Almost killed me.

The queen's eyes closed.

My chest clutched. She couldn't die yet.

"Is she...alright?" I peeked at Gardenia and she signaled to step away from the bed.

"The queen is sleeping," she whispered. "She sleeps more and more every day."

"What's wrong with her?" Surely, the fairies had medicine and healers to cure the most important person in our world.

Gardenia took my hand and patted the top. "The queen was poisoned. The reason you need to be extra careful, Ellery."

Chapter Four

*P**oisoned.*

Queen Dahliadew had been poisoned.

The phrase repeated in my head and echoed in my heart as we left her bedroom. My chest seemed to open in a gaping wound. I'd just met my grandmother, the queen. She couldn't die now.

Gardenia's statement arrowed through me as I stared at her. She didn't want people to know I was the lost princess. Why? Because I was in danger too? The blood in my veins stagnated and then rushed forward. Would someone want to poison me? Kill me?

There'd been murder in Perry's gaze when he'd attacked. If Bee hadn't interrupted, who knows what he would've done. I slumped onto one of the chairs in the hallway outside the queen's room. I'd thought he didn't like me similar to everyone else at this stupid school. But maybe he wanted me dead if he knew my secret.

Was I going to be constantly under attack once everyone knows the truth? Was this the type of life I wanted? Did I have a choice?

Gardenia knelt beside me and spoke softly. "For your protection, you need to keep this a secret."

"Who would I tell?" I raged with hurt and loneliness. I had no friends here. No one to share confidences or gossip. No one to protect me.

"If it gets out you're the lost princess, you'll be put under twenty-four-hour protection." She patted my knee to get my attention. "Do you understand?"

I understood. The fresh air, the roar of the waterfall, the smell of nature from the queen's bedroom suffocated instead of soothed.

If word got out, I'd be a prisoner in my own castle.

Was it too late to return to my human life? I cringed, remembering the mean tease in Arbor's voice when she'd been arrested. I didn't want to go back to my stepfamily and my old life. I didn't want this new life either. Plus, I'd signed away my home.

Once dismissed, I hurried toward my room. The walls of the castle seemed to cave in on me. I struggled to breath even though my feet had slowed to a crawl.

Suffocating responsibilities. Political enemies. Royal etiquette.

I didn't want to be a princess, and certainly not in a castle where fairies might want me dead. Death by poison. Gardenia would become even more protective. She'd never let me fight in a battle. She'd probably give me a royal guard.

Like Stone.

My pulse quickened. He'd been guarding me under Regent Theobald's palace. I missed him. And my best friend Arbor. And the other friends I'd made on my journey. I wished they were here now, and I could confide in them. My lungs heaved. I had this incredible, awful news and no one to share it with.

And then there was Rye.

I let out a sigh. He was alive and I was happy, and yet he'd signed that terrible law. Had he learned nothing under his own palace? Had he felt nothing toward me?

Taking the next turn, I peeked around the corner. My nerves were on edge and I couldn't help wondering if I'd encounter an assassin. *Huh.* Something I was familiar with. The dark corridor was gloomier than most of the hallways. Granted, night had fallen. A storm raged outside. Rain pounded on the windows and thunder echoed near and far.

I circled around slowly. I must've taken a wrong turn. This was my castle and I didn't know how to find my way around.

A flash of lightning lit the corridor and I jerked. A dark silhouette showed in the distance. Thunder rumbled and another flash. The person disappeared.

I gasped. Nothing to worry about. I'd find a familiar space and figure out how to get back to my room. Puffing my lips, I took in a slow breath and surveyed behind me. My thoughts continued to run on. I'd been a servant and now I was a princess. I took another puff trying to slow my pulse. The kids already hated me because I was a half breed and would never listen to me if I became queen.

I didn't want to be a queen. I wanted to be a warrior.

A scraping sound scratched at my ears.

I jumped and rounded my shoulders. Yeah, some warrior I'd make. A tiny noise scared me.

Skreetch. Skreetch.

Steadying myself, I slipped my hand around the coiled whip at my waist. I was determined to be brave. To show everyone I'd be a good warrior. Who cared about the princess stuff?

Skreetch. Skreetch.

My body tensed, my senses at the ready. I wouldn't run, I'd defend myself. I'd prove I could fight and win.

"Whatcha doing?"

"Aiea!" Adopting Keltie's infamous scream, I pivoted.

Bee stood in front of me.

My hand holding the whip pressed against my chest. "I almost had a heart attack."

"Sounded like it too with the weird scream." Bee snickered. "Nice way to greet a friend."

The description of herself jolted me. Did she consider herself my friend? My skin warmed and I wanted to reach out. I needed a friend right now. "Sorry. I didn't know who was there."

"Cause I'm so scary-looking." She bared her teeth and curled her hands into claws in a bad imitation of a bear.

Giggles erupted, more nervous than anything. Arbor used to make me laugh. Where was she when I needed to confide? "Well, when you've been told—" I slapped my hand over my mouth.

"Been told what?" Bee's unnaturally green eyes glinted.

I'd piqued her curiosity by nearly spilling my secret. "Nothing."

"Now, I know you're keeping secrets from me." The upset in her voice struck a chord. "That's no way to treat a friend."

There was the friend word again. Was she?

I understood how it felt to have someone close keeping secrets. Rye kept secrets when he hadn't told me he was the prince. Stone kept secrets when he didn't admit he worked for my fairy godmother. Gardenia kept secrets about me being a princess.

Emotion swelled in my midsection. Those secrets had hurt. It would be nice to have a new friend at this school and I didn't want to upset my new friend. It would be a relief to finally share my news with someone. To get their advice. I licked my lips as indecision flickered inside. Gardenia had told me not to tell anyone and I'd just met Bee.

"I'll tell you a secret first." She bumped her hip against mine. "I heard they've located the lost heir."

The blood drained from my head. "What?"

"Not what, silly." Her lighthearted tone told me she was sharing information, one friend to another. "Who."

"Who?"

"You sound like an owl." She bumped my hip again and her smile brightened. "This is top secret stuff. I overheard the teachers and they said the princess was here at Queens Academy."

My knees knocked together. I didn't know what to say. "Why do you care?"

She shrugged in an offhand gesture. "I don't. I thought it was interesting gossip. Since you said you didn't have any friends besides me," she winked, making me relish being a co-conspirator, "We could make this our secret project. Find out who the heir is. Wouldn't it be cool to know before anyone else?"

I leaned away trying to figure out what was in her mind. "Once you discover who the lost princess is, what would you do with the information?"

"Tell you, of course." She placed a hand on my arm and squeezed a little too tightly in her enthusiasm. "I'd rather *we* discover who she is together. We'd keep it a secret. We could be all superior, knowing before anyone else."

If I told her I wasn't interested in becoming a sleuth, would she be angry at me? Would I lose our budding friendship? And if I didn't help, would she continue to dig? Would she discover the truth on her own and know I kept the secret hidden?

"You wouldn't tell anyone?"

"Why would I?" She flung her hand not caring about the answer, only curious. "I don't owe the other students anything. They haven't treated me well on my first few days."

I could relate.

"What if knowing something they didn't and telling them, would make you more popular?" Human girls at my last school traded gossip to become more popular. I'd been one of their targets.

"I don't care about being popular." Bee shook her head, appearing impatient. "I want to hurry up and finish my studies as quickly as possible so I can go out and fight."

Her goals aligned with mine. I didn't care about being popular. I wanted to fight too.

I bit my lower lip. "Wouldn't you be wasting precious study time searching for this lost princess?"

"True." Bee hooked her arm through mine and started sauntering, dragging me along with her. "But we'd be searching together. It would be fun."

A grin slipped onto my face. I hadn't had fun in a long time. Not since starting my crazy adventure and admitting to my fairy self. Of course, the entire search would be a waste of time. Precious time I needed for my extra training and tutors. If I didn't help Bee, would she ask someone else? Become better friends with another fairy leaving me with no one to talk to? And what if the clues led back to me?

I gulped. Wouldn't it be better to confess to being the princess and let Bee help me hide the fact?

All those questions zinged and bounced around in my brain as our feet treaded on the marble floors. Gardenia told me not to tell anyone. Except Bee already knew the princess was at the school.

She tugged me in tighter, our linked arms becoming a bond between us. "Come on. I told you a secret. Now you tell me one. It doesn't have to be a big secret, just something to show you care about me."

Her statement hung between us. Not a threat. More of a challenge.

I needed a friend at the academy. Someone to confide in and trust. Bee promised not to tell anyone the information about the lost princess. She could help me keep the secret.

A test first to see how she reacts. "I'm half fairy."

Her chin tilted toward me. No hatred or disgust showed on her face. Her brow was smooth, and her lips stayed shaped in a small smile. "Really? That's why you don't have wings. I'd wondered. What's it like?"

Holding my breath, I waited for the other wing to flap. No insults. She kept a tight grip on my arm. She appeared more curious than shocked which made me comfortable with answering. "Well, it's why a lot of the kids don't like me."

"Too bad for them." She pulled on me with a friendly tug and we walked a little faster. "I like you. Who cares what they think?"

She'd stick up for me. "There's more..."

"Don't tell me your other half is siren because I'd be jealous."

"No. My other half is human." My cheeks heated, embarrassed to admit it. Which was so different than weeks ago. Before, I'd tried to hide my fairy half. But I'd learned being a fairy was nothing to be embarrassed about.

"Maybe that explains why the other kids don't like you. Maybe they think they can't trust you." Her reasonableness told me she didn't care what my other half was comprised of. "We will be fighting a war against the human league."

A definite possibility. "Do you trust me?"

"I told you my biggest secret." She waved her hand in what was becoming a familiar action. "Of course, I trust you."

Confidence filled me, and I made my decision. Bee was a fairy and couldn't lie. She was going to become a good friend, maybe my best friend if Arbor didn't return soon. Bee had taken my being half human well. She didn't hate me because of it. I needed to talk to someone about what was happening. I'd been bottling it up since learning the truth. And now, I had the additional pressure of the danger of being royal.

If I didn't tell someone, I was going to burst.

Taking a large inhale of air, I blurted, "I'm the lost princess."

Bee slapped my arm. "Yeah, right. That's a good one."

She thought I joked.

"No, really." I halted, and she came to an abrupt stop because of our linked arms. "My mother was Lily Kunglig, third daughter of Queen Dahliadew."

Bee's smile flattened. Her eyes grew as wide as tree knots. Her chin dropped. "Oh, my wood spirits!"

No one else could hear. "Shh!"

"Oh, my wood spirits," she whispered this time. "Incredible."

I was glad she came to acceptance so quickly. It had taken me a lot longer.

"Is it?" I hated the fact.

"You're a princess." Her arms reached around to hug me and stopped. She dropped into a curtsy.

Horror scraped through me. "No. Stop."

I glanced around again, worry catching at my throat. No one could witness her royal protocol.

"Think about it." She grabbed my arm and squeezed tight again, shackling me. "You can tell these other kids what to do. You can order the teachers around. You can lord it over everyone."

"No!" I didn't want to be a princess and didn't want anyone else to know. "You can't tell anyone."

"What?" Her incredulous expression was emphasized by her large eyes.

Worry gnawed at my insides. I never should've told her. "You can't tell anyone. It has to stay a secret." I should've executed a binding promise before I let the news out.

"Why?" She truly didn't understand. Nothing nefarious at all.

"Commander Gardenia thinks it's dangerous for people to know." I gnawed my bottom lip again, worried I'd bite right through.

Nodding, Bee's expression went serious. "I can understand. I mean, they kept your existence a secret forever. Only rumors."

"Exactly." I wasn't going to tell her about the danger to my life. I'd already shared too much.

"And, you're half fairy so fairies might have a harder time accepting you."

Another strike against me.

"Not that I care." She linked our arms again. "You'll show them. You're a princess and you'll get to lead the charge on the battlefield."

"If Gardenia even lets me fight."

After seeing the injustices majiks had suffered under the leadership of Regent Theobald, fighting was the one thing I wanted to do.

"This is so cool though," Bee squealed.

Which was great, confirming I'd made the right decision to share my news.

But nothing else about this was cool. The fact I'd broken my promise by telling Bee. The fact I was the lost princess. The fact someone wanted me dead. The fact I really didn't want to be a princess at all.

⇝ ⇜

The following morning, I rushed to meet Gardenia in the throne room before her meetings started. Since Queen Dahliadew was ill, my fairy godmother—as commander—had taken over some of the queen's duties. Pushing the door open, I paused.

Last night, after Bee had led me back to my room, I'd spent the night tossing and turning. I couldn't sleep. As the lost heir, I didn't want to be assassinated. I didn't want to sit in the floating chair and rule.

The cold marble floors infiltrated my shoes, chilling me to the bone. The school uniform felt tight, constricting. The stage with the throne chair had seemed formidable before, today the cloud was black. I shivered. Fairies had ruled their realm before the pact with the humans, before the Kingdom of Alandaska had existed. Something I'd learned in my private tutoring with Professor Woods, an ancient fairy with ties to the ruling class.

Gardenia paced in front of the stage. Her normally shimmering clothes had lost their shine. Her light tread clattered heavy on the wood of the stage. Her face creased with worry as though she debated quietly in her head. The war planning must not be going as expected.

Ruling a kingdom or realm would always be difficult. During times of war, it took its toll on the leader.

"How are the negotiations going with Regent Theobald?" After seeing Gardenia's worry, I could guess the answer.

The man still had control of the throne and the crown and the power. Rumors about his rampaging to stop majiks and steal their magic were whispered from fairy to fairy. Even I'd heard the gossip.

And yet, the gossip about the prince was minimal. Why?

"Not well. Regent Theobald is a majik-aphobe. He won't even meet with our representatives. He sends lower-level negotiators. What did you have on your mind, Ellery?" Gardenia's face wrinkled in concentration. "I haven't learned anything else about Prince Zacharye, if that's why you're here."

I tried to keep my expression controlled even while my thoughts ran around in a panicked swirl. I'd given Gardenia the pertinent facts of that fateful night when I'd gone to rescue Arbor and destroyed the auraguillotine, an instrument of torture. I couldn't bring myself to confess my feelings about the prince. How I'd met him not realizing who he was, how we'd forged a friendship and what I thought was a deeper connection. I hoped Rye would have influence over the regent. I hoped he could be an agent for change.

Those were the reasons I'd decided not to assassinate him, not because I was crushing on him. The magical dagger had agreed with me.

And then in the battle, he'd been crushed—literally, and I hadn't known if he lived or died.

Stretching my neck, I tried to shake off my nerves. I'd thought about it all night. Seeing the throne floating before me had sealed my decision. "I've decided not to be a princess."

Her brow smoothed showing surprise. "It's not a decision. It's a birthright."

"Even so..." I tried to sound steady and sure. "I want to be a warrior and fight. Not sit on a throne."

"Royalty does not only sit on a throne." She slashed at the chair. Her lips pinched together in disapproval. "They have responsibilities and decrees."

I crossed my arms. If I was so important, people needed to listen to me. "And my decision is not to be royal."

Gardenia blew out from between her tight lips, making a whistling noise. She took hold of my hand and squeezed. "There's nothing to be afraid of."

I slipped my hand from hers. I wasn't afraid, not really. "I want to fight, not be coddled."

"Good. Because as the princess of the fairies, you have an important task to complete."

My head whirled and my stomach clenched. I was supposed to be rejecting the princess gig and now she was giving me another assignment. "No more genealogy tests or studying etiquette."

Her laughter tinkled. "No. It's a mission."

The last time she'd given me a mission I'd been in way over my head.

"While I don't want to take more tests, I haven't mastered my magic or my fighting skills. I have more to learn." I hung my head, hating to admit these weaknesses.

She waved her hand, indicating my objections were baseless. "No worries. We can train you before you leave."

More than I had on my last mission.

Grabbing my hand, she squeezed harder. "Before the war commences, we need to get possession of the Divinity Orb."

The name of the item struck in the center of my chest. An important majik artifact. I'd heard about the orb from Professor Woods. Learned of its powers. "The Divinity Orb forecasts the future."

"And so much more." The awe in Gardenia's tone set off my nerves and my doubts, similar to twin warning bells.

I'd been tricked by her before. "If this orb is so important, why send me?"

Chapter Five

"You must go because you are royal. Mother Morningmist, *your great-grandmother*, will give you the Divinity Orb." Gardenia's face grew shadowed. Her lips thinned. "No need for any silliness."

"Excuse me?" I stumbled. "Did you say great-grandmother?"

"Yes."

I reeled back. "You mean Queen Dahliadew's mother?"

"Correct. Queen Morningmist, or how she's known now, Mother Morningmist."

A thrill tingled through my bloodstream. I had another relative. Someone who could share how to be royal and fairy ways. Someone who could tell me stories about my mom. "She's alive?"

"Alive, retired, and living in peace."

"Where?"

"She's the High Priestess of Aristos Sanctuary."

The priestesses of Aristos were a secret sorority who lived an isolated life high on Drage Mountain. They wore long, red robes to hide their identity and could fight the best of our warriors. They were ninjas who studied the ancient arts. "Why send me?"

"Your familial relation. Your royal connection. Your..." Gardenia hid her expression, possibly hiding what she was about to say. "You will have help."

"You?" I couldn't see my fairy godmother going on a mission. She had too many duties at the castle assisting the queen.

"Others."

My breath caught. I didn't trust anyone else at this school. I had no friends except Bee. No one would help or defend me.

Gardenia clapped her hands twice and the large double doors swung open. Standing under the archway were Tos, Hokima, and Arbor.

My heart swelled and leapt with love and enthusiasm. These were my friends. Majiks I could count on and who believed in me. Squealing, I ran toward them. "Oh, my sprite!"

"Ellery." Arbor, a smoke sprite, fluttered about with her usual excitement. Unusual for her to use my more formal name.

Her appearance was different. Her multi-colored, tufted hair had been tamed into a close-cropped, pink bob. The radical clothes she normally wore were gone, replaced by something more uniform. Camouflage, almost.

She landed on my shoulder and I patted her tiny feet.

The brownie, Tos, stood taller and wore fine clothes. When we'd first met, she'd worn rags and had a rip in her pointy ear. "It's so great to see you!" She wrapped her arms around my leg.

I bent down and hugged her.

Hokima, a troll, seemed the same, although less grumpy when he flashed a pointy-toothed grin. Under the human palace I don't think I'd ever seen him smile. Of course, we hadn't had anything to smile about. He also wore a nice tunic with a green sash around his neck with odd-shaped medals. "Good to see you."

"I can't believe you're here." I hugged him and he took it.

Tears filled my eyes and overflowed, dripping down my cheeks, as we greeted each other. I didn't realize how isolated and alone I'd been. These were true friends. Majiks I could count on and confess my worries.

But not my secret. I'd already shared with someone and the doubts clung to me like mist.

Gardenia clapped her hands again and the doors slammed shut. There was a slight upward twist to her lips. She enjoyed seeing our reunion. "We need to finalize the plans to get the Divinity Orb."

This was huge. The Divinity Orb would be essential during the war. We could know what Regent Theobald's plans were, troop movements, and weapons.

My arms dropped from around my friends. Their expressions hadn't changed. They'd known why they were summoned to Queens Academy. Did my friends believe we were capable of retrieving the artifact? My gaze narrowed watching them. Obviously, they'd had time to ponder the situation. Why were they told before me? I was the princess after all.

"They allow admission to young nobles of a certain birth and her companions and guards." Gardenia pinned me down with a stare.

I tilted my head and stuck my chin out. "I thought we were keeping—"

"You will *pretend* to be royal." Her interruption had me clenching my fists. "It's the reason I've had you taking special classes on etiquette and peerage. I've been preparing you for this mission, Ellery."

I froze. She wanted me to keep the princess secret from my closest friends. Friends who'd risked their lives for me. Friends I trusted. I crossed my arms. Arbor was my best friend and we didn't keep secrets from each other. I'd already blown the princess secret by telling Bee so I should tell Arbor. Except, I needed to prove to Gardenia I was trustworthy.

"To gain entry into Aristos Sanctuary, you must be royal." Arbor flew around in circles.

Gardenia ignored my angry body language. "Tos, Hokima, and Arbor will be your companions and servants."

Gulping air, I realized how strange it was to have things turned around, even if we were pretending to pretend. I had been pretending not to be royal to keep my heritage a secret. Now, she wanted me to pretend to be royal, even though I really was the princess.

Hokima raised his hand slowly. "Will the priestesses accept us? A half fairy, a smoke sprite, a brownie, and a troll?"

"They will accept Ellery, so they will accept all of you. They don't have a choice." Gardenia's voice brooked no argument.

I wasn't so sure and searched for other objections.

"The mission will be dangerous. We're acting as spies." My stomach roiled. My friends had already been through so much when we'd ventured beneath Regent Theobald's palace. What if I screwed up, or my magic misfired, or I let them down? "I think we'll need more help."

"One of the school's guards will be joining you on your quest." My fairy godmother firmed her lips, waiting for a negative reaction from me. She must realize my protests were about my confidence, not her plans. "He will be your personal guard. He was wounded in a recent skirmish."

She clapped her hands and another door opened, revealing Stone.

My chest squeezed tight and my pulse went into overdrive. He wasn't a nameless school guard. He'd been with me under the human palace, too. At the end, after the destruction of the auraguillotine and our escape, I had no idea what had happened to him. We'd arrived at the academy and he'd disappeared into the healing center. I'd wondered if he'd been punished or demoted for my failures.

Or maybe he'd asked to not be around me any longer. He'd known I wanted to save Rye, even though my mission had been to assassinate the prince.

Stone ducked under the low—for him—doorway, wearing a uniform of the Fairy Royal Protection Unit. The green color with purple accents complimented the greenish tinge to his skin—which I originally hadn't noticed because we'd been underground. His broad shoulders stretched the material tight against his chest and the loose pants couldn't hide the thickness of his thighs. The highly-trained regiment guarded my fairy godmother and others of importance in the realm.

I wheezed. I was one of those important ones.

His long, blond hair was scraped into compliance. His face was clean-shaven, making him seem less rough. His two blond brows rose, showing amusement at my intimate inspection. The rascal.

"Stone!" my friends chimed in synchronization.

I ran to hug him and slapped him on his muscular arm. "Why didn't you tell me you were here?"

He yanked me into his arms and held me a little too close. His scent of evergreen wound around me. "You missed me. I knew you had a crush on me."

His taunt had me breaking the hold.

"As if." I said it loud enough for everyone to hear.

While I could admit Stone was good-looking, I liked Rye. Stone had protected me from the moment we met. Gardenia's words clicked through my head. "You're a guard at the school?"

He'd been here this entire time and never visited. Without thought, I grabbed the whip strapped to my side and casted out. The rope coiled around Stone, tying him up. Just as he'd tied my emotions in knots with the flirting and the kiss.

"I know you missed me, but we should do this in private." His whispered words shot a flame through me.

My cheeks heated, and I couldn't stop myself from taking a swing at his square chin. He ducked and laughed. Loudly.

"Ellery!"

Gardenia's disapproving tone had me fisting my hand at my side. I could hear her voice in my head. *Princesses don't punch.*

Hunching my shoulders, I tamed my wild emotions. This man infuriated me and caused me to lose my control. I was already hanging by a thin spider's web with the changes and revelations occurring in my life.

Stone snapped to attention and saluted Commander Gardenia. He pivoted to the others in the group and winked. Flirtatious as ever.

I had to remember it wasn't me he was attracted to, any female in the vicinity would do. He couldn't stop the smarmy bones in his giant body. Or half giant. Another thing we had in common.

"We need to get serious and plan." Gardenia pulled out her wand and pointed it at my heart. "Do you accept this mission?"

I'd practically begged to join the fight. If I did well on this quest, she'd have no excuse not to let me go into battle, princess or not. And I'd meet my great-grandmother.

Glancing at my friends, I gauged their expressions. Serious and curious. They probably understood more about the challenges of the mission than I did, yet they were here, which meant they were behind me.

To be together again, fighting on the right side, had my chest swelling with their devotion and friendship. "Yes."

"You have three days to prepare and train." Gardenia's brows drew together in concentration. "I want to emphasize that your mission is a secret. Only the queen, me, and your team know the true purpose."

Another secret.

The thought dropped into my stomach and filled me with dread. For a group unable to tell lies, why were fairies so secretive?

⇢⇉ ⇇⇜

"Nice room." Arbor flew around the perimeter of my large suite.

The ensuite bedroom I'd been brought to when I first arrived had seemed too nice for a half fairy who didn't want to attend Queens Academy. The room had been another reason for the other students to resent me.

If Gardenia didn't want anyone to realize who I was, why treat me differently?

Stone, Hokima, Tos, and Arbor had walked out of the room and Gardenia had kept me back, reemphasizing the need to not tell anyone I was the princess. That being royal meant being discreet. I didn't enjoy keeping secrets from my friends, especially those risking their lives. Guilt wound inside me, pulling my muscles taut. I'd already spilled my secret to someone I'd recently met. I wanted to smack my forehead. I'd been alone and desperate to talk to someone. I fell back on the excuse.

Arbor landed on the four-poster bed centering the room. Twinkling lights swirled around the posts. Her green skirt and shirt blended into the natural environment. So different from the clothes she'd worn in the past. Her single-colored hair, the first thing I'd noticed about her, was cut shorter and groomed to her head. Not a hair out of place. Had something happened to make her change?

I noticed her studying me and cleared my thoughts and my throat. "Much nicer than the attic at my old house."

"I've brought something for you," she screeched, unable to contain her excitement, again reminding me of our past.

She'd brought me simple gifts all the time. A robin's egg when she'd told me the story about how the birds helped fairies locate lost things. A rock with a direct connection to Mother Earth. The yearning for a simpler time choked me. For my sixteenth birthday, Arbor had given me a stick she'd shaved to a fine point. She'd joked about how it would be my wand until I received an official one. At the time, I'd used it to stab her, saying it would be more effective as a weapon because I didn't have magic.

How wrong I'd been. About many things.

"I'm glad you're back." I hugged her tiny body, demonstrating how much I'd missed her. Since arriving at Queens Academy I'd been so lonely, and now I had my friends together again. And one new one, Bee.

"On my way back, I stopped at your old attic bedroom." She hadn't told me where she was going or when she'd be back.

Crossing my arms, I wanted to ask about her disappearing act. Where had she been? What had she been doing? If she kept secrets, so could I.

"Why?" Had Arbor been there while my stepfamily had been at Queens Academy?

"To get this. Ta-da!" She flew to the closet door and swung it open, revealing a trunk.

My mother's trunk.

I dashed to the closet. The trunk was the one thing I had left of my mom. I sank to my knees and skimmed trembling fingers across the etched carvings of a forest scene filled with magical creatures. Fumbling with the lock, I lifted the lid. The scent of musty perfume wafted from inside and filled my head with emotions and memories.

My mom's emotions.

This was my special gift and the last connection with my mom. When I touched her things, I felt her emotions from when she last used the item. I reached in and wrapped my hands around an old-fashioned bound journal and a rush of emotions jumbled into my head. My mom had written her thoughts and emotions in this book. And living in the fairy world, her memories would have so much more meaning.

"Thank you, Arbor."

"You're welcome." She gave a jaunty salute.

I shut the lid with care and sat back on my haunches, contemplating what I'd lost when I'd given away my house.

"What's wrong?" She flew onto my shoulder. "I thought the trunk filled with your mother's things would make you happy."

I patted her tiny foot. Trust Arbor to understand exactly what I was feeling. "I love having my mom's things, I just wish I had something of my dad's too."

She tapped her foot on my shoulder. "The things in the trunk are fairy artifacts and couldn't be left behind now that you're not inheriting the house."

So, the gift hadn't been all about doing something for me. She'd brought the trunk because she didn't want humans getting their hands on fairy artifacts. "You know about my house?"

"Gardenia mentioned what happened with your stepmother."

I twitched and Arbor flew off. I wasn't sure how I felt about her and Gardenia becoming chummy. If my fairy godmother told her about the house, had she told Arbor I was the princess? And if so, why didn't Arbor say something?

"I know," Arbor interrupted my thoughts with her loud enthusiasm. "I'll go back and get something of your dad's. What do you want?"

What did I want? There were his T-shirts I used to wear, although I couldn't wear them at fairy school. There was a photo of the two of us, a pocket watch passed down in his family for generations, and a flutter disc we used to play with. "I don't know where anything is located."

My stepmother had kept most of his things when he'd died. It would be nice to be able to go to the house and pick the items I wanted myself. To look around the home one more time and say my final goodbye. The recent memories with Sybil and my stepsisters weren't great, but I'd had wonderful times with my father.

Pressing the palms of my hands together, I twisted to face Arbor. "What I really want is to go to Milford House one more time."

"Well, um..." Her strange hesitation caused my senses to go on high alert. "I don't think that's wise."

"Why? No one would know. We could pop in with your smoke and be back a short time later."

"What about the mission? We have to train and prepare."

"A couple of hours won't be a big deal." Excitement shimmered down my spine. A final time to look around, grab a couple of things, and say goodbye to my old home. I jumped to my feet. "Let's do it."

"Right now?" Avoiding my gaze, she buzzed toward the door.

"Why not now?"

"You've got training with Tos and Hokima in a few minutes. They need to learn the fairy ways if they're going to pretend to be your servants."

"Right. I forgot." I snorted. "Can you believe me with my own servants?"

Arbor jerked back and recovered. "I know." Her voice was quieter than normal. "You better not get spoiled."

"As if."

A tense silence fell between us as we walked toward the training ground. I couldn't remember a time when we were awkward around each other. It seemed she was hiding something from me. And I hid something really important from her. We were both keeping secrets.

A crowd gathered around the upper balconies of the training ground. Mean chuckles and jeers filtered down from the fairy students who'd taken time out of their schedule to watch a brownie and a troll train, suggesting they viewed this as a circus or a bloodbath.

I shifted away from their nasty glances.

Tos held a sword bigger than her body and wore camouflage pants and shirt. She stood in a defensive stance and waited for my attack. Her face furrowed in concentration.

With an even longer sword in hand, I faced Stone. "Why did you choose me to be her opponent?"

I wasn't the best fairy fighter, not by a longshot, as Perry had proven. If on our mission we were confronted, I wanted my companions to be at their best.

Stone leaned into me and his lips twitched. "Would you rather go hand-to-hand with me?"

The flirtatious tone had been a constant every time I was in the same room with the half giant. Flummoxed, I stood gaping. I never knew how to respond. Did his flirting even mean anything?

I huffed. "I meant there are others who are better equipped to train a brownie."

"I don't trust others." He stepped closer to Tos and showed her how to hold the sword properly.

His comment made me feel better yet didn't answer my question.

Entering the fighting ring, the crowd's murmurs increased. They would probably rather have a brownie win a fight than me.

"Ready?" I held up my sword.

"*En guard*." Before I could respond, Tos whipped her blade toward me.

Just in time, I blocked the swing. "You're supposed to wait until I say *allez*."

"In a real battle, there won't be niceties." She stepped back and immediately propelled forward with a jab.

I fell back a step, not expecting such strength from the small brownie. "True."

She took another jab and another. The clanging of our swords rang above the booing of the crowd. Surprisingly, they were rooting for me.

Would the fairies be on my side when they found out I was the princess? If I proved I could fight and win against a brownie, they'd be loyal to me. Wishing I had my magical whip, I took a broad swing at Tos' feet with renewed energy.

She jumped high, higher than my head. My eyes widened, taking in the sight. She had hidden skills.

"Slice the brownie in two," the crowd of fairies yelled. I'd been wrong about who they'd cheer for.

Their cruel tones cut through me and my will to win at all costs ended. This wasn't a fight to the death. Tos and I weren't enemies. We were friends.

She parried and thrust, barely missing my padded chest. "Fairies stick together even though majiks are supposed to be allies."

"You know I'm not like that." I counterattacked, whipping my blade back and forth and clashing with hers. "You're my friend."

"And yet your other friends," she waved her sword at the crowd before attacking me with relish, "wish me bloodied."

Knowing the different kinds of majiks had a lot of work to do to learn and respect each other, I didn't respond because she was right. No one would be injured today. Our purpose was training. And yet, most of the students hadn't seen me fight. They refused to battle against me. This was my opportunity to show them I could fight with the best of them.

And maybe lead.

I thrust my sword, taking Tos off guard. She stumbled and lost her footing. Taking advantage of her being off-balance, I attacked swinging my sword back and forth and back and forth. With each thrust, I took a step closer and she retreated. The crowd went wild. I worked her toward a short stone wall. She no longer had the space to parry with strength and I used my position to back her into a corner. I held my sword at her heart. The bout ended, and I had won.

Breathing heavily, I waited for her to say she conceded.

"Kill it!" someone shouted from the crowd. "Brownie lives don't matter!"

The angry words slashed at me as if I'd been struck by my own sword.

"Brownie lives don't matter!" The crowd repeated the mantra in a chant.

The chant hammered in my head. These were my people, students at my school, future subjects. The hammering turned to pounding.

Tos' expression went bleak. Her frown dipped into more of a question of *what was I going to do?*

Of course, I'd release her. Should I let her go and take a bow in front of the bloodthirsty fairies? Or did I defend her and alienate the crowd of future subjects?

Chapter Six

My conscience ticked. Defend my friend or prove myself to the chanting fairy crowd.

Brownie lives don't matter.

The hateful words drilled into me and anger spiked. Staying silent was almost as bad as killing Tos. The fairies needed to understand the other majiks were our partners, not our enemies. Not our inferiors.

I lifted my sword off Tos and threw the weapon to the ground.

The crowd stopped chanting, stunned by my actions. They were about to be more stunned.

Staring down the angry crowd, I held my hand out and helped Tos to stand.

Her eyes went wider. Her scarred ears wiggled as if unsure of what to expect.

"Tos is my friend," I yelled at the crowd, trying to be heard over their shocked murmurs. "She protected me under the human palace. At risk to her own life. She's here to help me again."

She dipped her head shyly and then tilted her chin to glare at the crowd. Her lips lifted at the corners showing her pointy teeth in a bright grin.

My chest lightened. I'd ignored Arbor's friendship in the past. I would never ignore any true friend again. I'd never treat the other majiks as inferior. The fairies needed to learn this wasn't about one brownie.

"All brownies are friends. They are majiks, just like us. And they are going to fight against Regent Theobald in the upcoming war."

The crowd went silent. They peered at both of us with suspicion. Angry murmurs grew louder and louder. If they erupted into violence, I couldn't take them all on. I wouldn't take them on. They were supposed to be my people. Not that they knew.

Stone clanged a sword against a big metal gong getting everyone's attention. "Ellery is right." His commanding voice held them. He put his muscular arm around my shoulders and lifted Tos in the palm of his other hand. "Brownies are our partners. So are trolls and ogres and giants and all other majiks."

The crowd listened. Would I ever gain similar respect?

My body relaxed, the tension easing out. Stone was good to have on my side. I smiled at him in gratitude.

He winked back.

My stomach fluttered, and I slipped from under his arm. I hadn't meant anything by my smile.

"It's time for all of you to go to class." His announcement was met with grumbling from the students. He set Tos on the ground, took a spear, and tossed it to Hokima.

A single shriek came from the other fairies. More high-pitched murmurs of fear. They were afraid of one troll having a weapon. Another kind of prejudice.

Huffing, I fisted my hands, ready to defend him too.

Hokima gripped the spear in both hands and charged toward the crowd.

The fairies scattered, half running and half flying from the balcony and into the school.

Hokima and Stone chuckled. I joined in for I could see the humor in the situation. One troll against dozens of magical fairies, and the fairies ran.

"You need to do a better job of training those young whelps." Hokima stabbed the spear in the ground. His rough clothes of too-short pants and ripped shirt didn't fit in with the uniforms at Queens Academy. "We're going to war."

I swiveled to Tos, who hadn't joined in our laughter. "Sorry about defeating you." If I'd lost, I'd be totally humiliated.

"I'll get you next time." Her enthusiasm soothed my worry. She moved by Hokima to consult with him.

If we could work together, why couldn't all majiks? I had to keep that goal in mind. My friends were different sorts of majiks. The only full fairy was Arbor. Glancing around, I noted she'd left sometime during the fight. I frowned. What urgent business did she have now?

"Thanks for standing up to the fairies for me." I approached Stone, knowing I needed to give him more than thanks. "You've always got my back."

His hard lips slipped into a seductive smile. "I want more than your back."

The suggestive tone sent a thrill down my spine. I pushed against his carved chest. How could I be attracted to him when I was crushing on Rye? Maybe because Stone was here, and Rye wasn't. Maybe because Stone and I were both half breeds. Maybe because Rye had signed the law against us. Maybe because I'd never see the prince again.

I took my displeasure out on the fairies. "I can't believe they're treating allies this way."

"I can." Stone's voice deepened into sadness.

What had happened in his past to make him so cynical? Could it be his half giant status? I'd been treated badly by my steps because I was half human. I could relate to him. Maybe that was the reason for this chemical attraction. I understood him. Staring into his green orbs, I wanted to reach out to comfort him. To kiss him?

"Reporting for mission training." Perry spread his wings wide and flew from the balcony, gracefully landing on his feet. His wings flapped with his entrance. He was clearly showing off.

"Mission?" My pulse drubbed, and my gaze swung between him and Stone. "My mission?" I lowered my voice, even though I wanted to shout. "My *secret* mission?"

Stone nodded, appearing okay with the intrusion. "Commander Gardenia believes Perry will add to our team."

Perry gave me a superior smirk.

The ground was yanked from beneath me. "But—"

"Gardenia has her reasons." Stone wouldn't let me state my objection. He didn't question Gardenia's orders.

I did.

Gardenia didn't know Perry had tried to kill me.

⟶⟩⟩⟩ ⟨⟨⟨⟵

The human house attic, once my bedroom, was now just an attic. No mushy bed. No nicked dresser filled with overly large T-shirts and ragged jeans. No evidence I'd ever slept here.

"What happened to my things?" A little lost, I whirled around the small space, confirming my initial suspicion.

"Well..." Arbor flew around my head making me more dizzy. "When you signed over the house and left the human world, the best way to explain it was for you to never have lived here."

"What!"

"Keep your voice down. They'll hear."

"Who will hear?" I still wore the dirty leggings and long tunic from my earlier training.

"Your stepmonster and stepsisters." Arbor always called Sybil my stepmonster and imitated her, too.

"They're here?" I tiptoed to the door, curious about how they lived their lives without me to do their dirty work.

"Yes." Her gaze darted around looking a little paranoid. Her outfit resembled a modified uniform. "We didn't have time to find a way to make them leave."

"They believe I never lived here." The thought punctured a deep hole of depression. All my servitude, all my efforts to play nice, hadn't mattered.

"Gardenia needed to do powerful magic to erase your existence." A tinge of pride wrapped around Arbor's words.

It wasn't the time to think about how she felt toward my fairy godmother. I'd been erased. My entire childhood gone. I'd given up the rights to my home and now to my very human existence. "What about getting my dad's things? If I never lived in the attic, the stuff I kept of his was never here."

"I didn't think about that." Arbor's wings flapped, and a stream of yellow smoke came from her tiny body. "We should leave."

Why had she suddenly changed her mind? It had been like pulling teeth to get her to agree to bring me. She'd delayed and delayed. And now, she wanted to leave before I'd gotten what I wanted in the first place.

"No." Standing firm, I glared. "We came all this way against Gardenia's wishes. I need to get something of my father's."

I peered out the small door in the floor and down the electric ladder leading to the main part of the house.

"What're you thinking?" Arbor used a warning tone.

She'd always been bossy. Now, she acted more like a guard than a friend.

"I need to go through the rest of the house and find something of Dad's." I remembered a family heirloom watch my grandfather had given to him.

"You'll get caught." The only other time she was the cautious one was when I'd performed over-the-top magic in this very house, and she'd been arrested for the crime. She was usually game for anything. Something had changed.

"You stay here." I didn't want her to be seen. I could pass for human. "I'll go by myself."

Her smoke morphed to more of an orange. She snapped her tiny fingers. "I'll create a distraction."

"Good idea."

She flew out the attic window. Pressing the button, the ladder I stood on extended down to the next level where the three bedrooms were located.

Ding. Dong.

I froze. Someone was at the front door. Possibly Arbor's form of distraction.

"I'll get it." Sybil shouted, sounding put out.

Probably because she'd always ordered me to answer the door. Except she wouldn't remember because she doesn't remember me. At least I knew where she was in the house.

I snuck past my stepsisters' rooms and creaked open the master bedroom door. Slipping inside, I closed the door behind me.

Pink carpet covered the entire room, and pink paint had been splashed on the walls. Not enough paint to cover the cracks. The metallic headboard on the bed glistened and the hyperbaric lid hanging above the mattress hummed, indicating it had recently been turned off.

Even more gaudy like Sybil. What had my father seen in the woman?

A moving image of him sat in a frame on the bedside table. At one time the frame held a photo of me and him. Now, it was him and the steps—a constant vision of their happy life together.

A sour taste swirled in my mouth. I understood the reason for making them not remember me. I hated that I was the only person with memories of my early life.

My gaze landed on Sybil's jewelry box. She asked for the large monstrosity for a wedding gift from my father. She'd believed he'd be giving her jewels to fill it and been disappointed. Swiftly, I shifted to the third drawer of the bureau where my father had kept his watches.

I slid the drawer open and found the gold pocket watch. He'd planned to give the watch to me. Sybil had told me I'd get it when I obtained the house. Now, I'd never inherit.

Lifting the fancy timepiece out of the drawer, I remembered the intricate design. The watch kept time and date. A historical piece most humans wouldn't have even kept in this digital age.

The bedroom door creaked open and Ingrid stood in the opening.

My feet glued to the spot. I couldn't think, couldn't move.

Her red curls bounced when she came to a sudden halt. Her eyes widened, and her mouth opened. "Thief! There's a thief in the house!"

I wanted to run and hide beneath the bed like I used to when one of the stepsisters tattled. At least she was the nicer of the two. "No. It's me, Elle. I'm not a thief."

"Help!" Ingrid swung around and slammed the door shut. Her loud shouts came through the thick bedroom door. She'd tell her mother, and Sybil would call the authorities.

The SCUM.

Tremors rocked down my back. I shoved the watch in my pocket and dashed toward the door. Flinging it open, I checked the hallway and found it clear.

Commotion came from downstairs. Screaming and running. I couldn't go out that way. Hopping on the electronic ladder, I pressed the button and the ladder hauled me back to the attic.

"Arbor!" I glanced around the room and didn't spot her. I ran to the open window overlooking the backyard. "Arbor!"

"She was here, Mother. I swear." Ingrid's declaration carried up through the attic opening.

"People don't disappear." Sybil's disbelieving tone sent a shiver of memory through me. "Just zaubers do."

I gasped at the slur. She'd used the insulting word in the fairy commander's office. She must now use the slur all the time. I'd used it in the past to try to fit in with the humans. I hadn't heard the word much since leaving the human world and had forgotten how much it hurt.

"It was a girl. What about up there?" Ingrid must've stepped closer to the attic opening because her voice was louder. "The ladder's up. The thief is trying to escape through the attic."

"This better not be one of your ridiculous tales," Sybil trilled with an edge of laughter. "Remember the one about going to a fairy castle and meeting a princess?"

My knees went weak and I leaned against a box to hold myself up. For some reason, Ingrid remembered our last meeting. I should tell Gardenia so she could fix the gap, except she didn't know I'd come to Milford house.

"Call the ladder down." Ingrid urged her mother.

I shot to a standing position. I couldn't get caught up here. Rushing the ladder, I grabbed a small metal rod and jammed it into the mechanism.

"It's not working." Sybil must be pressing the button.

"Like everything else in this house." Ingrid's announcement acidified.

I was the one who'd kept the house together, cleaning and repairing things. Without me, the house would've fallen apart. Now it was. I should've felt exultant or triumphant. Finally, I'd shown them I'd been an important part of their family. My shoulders dipped and I only felt sad.

"Fix it!" Sybil pounded on the bottom of the metal ladder and it rang in my ears. That was how she used to yell at me.

"I don't know how." Ingrid sniffed. "Ask Ilana."

I was sorry Ingrid took some of the abuse I used to endure. I didn't have to worry about lazy Ilana coming to the rescue.

"I'll call my boyfriend. He'll fix it." Sybil must've smiled because she sounded happier.

While my emotions headed in the opposite direction. Her boyfriend was SCUM, a member of the Security Collectors of Unique Magic. And by collectors, I meant killers. They'd arrested Arbor. They tortured and killed majiks without a trial.

I couldn't stay put in the attic. I couldn't wait for Arbor.

Hurrying to the window, I threw one leg over the ledge.

"What're you doing?" Arbor flew right at me. "Do you want to get caught?"

"Where were you?" I couldn't stop turning the question into an accusation.

"Ringing the doorbell. Helping you." Her snotty voice should've put me in my place.

I was too worried. "Ingrid saw me. We need to get out of here."

Arbor bowed slightly before puffing an obscuring smoke around both of us. "As you wish."

Something about her tone bothered me. I couldn't put my finger on it. Before I could think, she helped me apparate back to Queens Academy.

"Where have you been?" Bee said the moment she stepped into my room minutes after I'd returned from my old home.

Arbor had flown off the second we'd gotten back. More mysterious actions by my best friend. Was everyone acting different or is it because I now saw the world differently?

"Well?" Bee's accusation put me on alert. She wore the school uniform, except the buttons were in the wrong holes as though she'd gotten dressed fast.

Shaking my head, I thought of what to tell her. I'd been sworn to secrecy about the trip home. I sighed. Another secret to keep.

"I mean, I've missed you and worried about you, especially after I saw you training with a brownie and troll." Bee clasped my shoulder expressing comfort. "What is Commander Gardenia thinking?"

I shook off her touch. Bee must have the same attitude and prejudices as the other fairies at school. I thought she'd be more understanding. "The brownie and troll are my friends."

"That's not what I meant. Not at all." She grabbed my hand and tugged me closer. "What I meant is you're already not the most popular girl in school—"

"An understatement."

"And by forcing you to train with a brownie and a troll, by showing your friendship, the other fairies are going to disapprove of you even more."

She appeared earnest. I'd hoped Bee would be understanding because she accepted the fact that I was half fairy. Keeping her friendship meant a lot to me because she was another student at the school. When Tos and Hokima returned home and Arbor disappeared for another odd reason, Bee would still be at Queens Academy.

"I don't care what everyone thinks." Which was sort of true. I wanted it to be true.

"So, where were you?"

Biting my lip, I wasn't sure what to tell her. I didn't want her mad and I wanted Arbor and Bee to become friends.

I slipped the watch out and held it in my palm. "I went to get this."

"Ooh." Bee poked her finger at the gold timepiece. "It's beautiful. It's a watch, right? A human watch."

Her appreciation and interest warmed me. "It was my father's."

"That's so nice you have something of his." She smiled. "Where did you get it?"

I smashed my lips together, debating what to say. She understood my longing to have something of my father's and appreciated the beauty of the object. "I went to my old home in Lindenhamn."

Her jaw dropped even further. "That's dangerous."

Especially for me.

I cringed. "We almost got caught."

"We? Who did you go with?" Speaking casually, she trailed a finger across the quilt on my bed.

"I went with an old friend. A smoke sprite named Arbor."

Bee's expression didn't change which proved she wasn't prejudiced of what used to be termed lesser fairies. "I wish I could've gone with you." Her sadness plucked at my heartstrings. "Now that your old friend is back, what happens to me?"

"What do you mean?"

"I thought we were going to be best friends." Hurt tinged her statement.

Tilting my chin, I realized she'd become attached to me quickly. I wanted to be friends but hadn't expected an instant bond on her side. I wasn't used to having multiple best friends and didn't know how to juggle the expectations. "We are good friends."

A satisfied grin landed on her face. "I'd enjoy getting to know Arbor."

Returning her smile, I appreciated Bee wanted to get to know my best friend. They could become friends, too.

She picked up the watch with a gentle touch. "Your dad was human, right?"

Again, she didn't sound disgusted or prejudiced. She accepted me with my odd friends and associations. I wished both her and Arbor could've met my dad. They would've liked him, and he would've liked them. He wasn't prejudiced. I remember one time when he helped an ogre pay for the skywalk.

Nodding, I giggled, remembering Ingrid's expression. "You should've seen the expression on my stepsister's face when she saw me with my hands in her mother's jewelry box."

"Ooh! Adventurous and exciting." Bee chuckled. "I need more adventure in my life. School is boring."

"Maybe too exciting." I sobered, thinking of the consequences if we'd been caught. "I escaped into the attic where I would've been trapped if Arbor hadn't returned."

"You're so brave." Bee jumped to sit on the tall bed. "I'm proud to call you my friend."

"Thanks." Hanging my head, I scuffed the floor. I wasn't used to friends calling me brave. Rye had called me that once. Huffing, I needed to put thoughts of him aside.

"I saw you training with Stone, the school guard." Her voice went soft and she blinked in an exaggerated fashion. "He's dreamy."

"He's annoying."

Flirting. Bossing me around. Flirting. Telling me how to fight. Flirting. Telling me how to behave. Flirting. Telling me what he wants me to feel. And flirting.

She fanned her face with her hand. "He's so tall and handsome. His muscles bulge beneath his clothes. The first time I saw him I almost fainted. Except if I had fainted, I couldn't have asked him to perform CPR."

The image caused me to giggle. The laughter lightened my spirits and reminded me how Arbor had once made me happy. Unfortunately, we hadn't spent much time together since she'd been back. Because of it, I felt out of sorts with her and myself.

"What's the reason you need special training? With Captain Handsome and other majiks?" She leaned toward me. "Is it something to do with you being a princess?"

Wiggling my shoulders, I debated whether to tell her about the mission. I'd already told her my biggest secret, and about going home to retrieve the watch. Telling her one more thing wouldn't hurt anyone. Plus, if she knew, she wouldn't be jealous about the time I spent away from her. She'd understand and stay my friend while I was gone. She was a regular, one hundred percent fairy. If she liked me, others would too.

I leaned toward her. "I'm training for a secret mission."

"Awesome!" She bounced on the bed, jiggling me off balance. "Is Captain Handsome going? Who else?"

"Yes. And Tos, Hokima, and Arbor."

"Your best friend." Jealousy edged Bee's words. "It will be a party."

"Not exactly." I didn't want her thinking this was going to be fun and games. This was a serious quest. "Perry Moss is coming, too."

Her shock showed in wide eyes and open mouth. "The guy who was about to kill you when we met?"

"That's him."

"You need me to come along to protect you from him." She nodded with emphasis. "No one else knows how much he hates you."

The strong sentiment reeled me back. I knew he disliked me. Thinking it and being told from an outside source was much more impactful. "I don't know if he hates me." Of course, why else would he try to kill me.

"Oh, he does." She grabbed my hands and squeezed. "The reason you need me to come with."

"I don't know if I can ask if you can come along."

"You're the princess, surely you can demand I be put on your team." She sounded so reasonable and confident.

I was the princess. And I hadn't asked for anything. I didn't even want to be the princess. Maybe I could request one thing. It would be nice to have another friend along on the trip. A friend who would stay by my side when we returned to school.

If we returned to school. "It might be dangerous."

"Eating in the school cafeteria is dangerous." She had a point on many levels.

"Alright. I'll ask."

Chapter Seven

"What were you thinking?" Stone's low yell carried farther than a scream.

I paused near the wall leading to his office. The fact he had an office on the grounds pissed me off. He'd never told me he was nearby, let alone was important enough to have an office in the castle-turned-academy. There were so many things I didn't know about Stone.

Curiosity had me moving forward at a slow pace. If I listened by accident—okay, eavesdropped—I might learn more.

His office was located at the front of the barracks where the troops were housed. The rough stone building stretched around the outside of the training grounds, which meant he could have easily found me in the tower or in any of my classes. He could've seen me training, and yet he'd never come to say hello.

"I was there to protect her." Arbor's respectful voice spooked me. "I'm her friend, too. What else was I supposed to do when she insisted on going back?"

Why was Stone yelling at Arbor? He had no right to punish someone who wasn't under his command. She must be getting in trouble because of me. Been there, done that. She was my friend and I'd defend her.

I charged forward and slammed open the wooden door to the office. "Why are you two arguing?"

The cramped office had a desk and a shelf filled with weapons. A small stone fireplace had been swept clean, although the smoke smell clung to the room. No personal items sat on his desk. No framed photo or anything indicating he had family.

Arbor flew above the desk, while Stone stood mid-step, suggesting he'd been pacing the room.

"We're not arguing." He undid the top button of his shirt.

"Nope." Arbor shook her head back and forth. "Having a disagreement about how *friends* help each other." She flew to me and landed on my shoulder. "I was explaining how badly you wanted to go to your house and grab a few things, and as a friend, I took you."

I patted her tiny arm. "She's right. This was my fault. I had to go back one last time."

"It was dangerous for both of you." His tone rose and his gaze narrowed.

"You're not my pretend guard until we start our mission." Just because he'd saved me once didn't mean he was responsible for me always. "Mind your own business."

His blond brows furrowed, and his lips pursed into an angry pout. He actually growled. I would've been scared if I didn't know him and how he'd protected me in the past.

"Arbor, I need to have a word with Ellery." He waved his hand at the door. "Do you mind."

The statement should've been a question. It sounded like a command.

Arbor's wings fluttered, mimicking a nervous hummingbird. She glanced at me and back at Stone. A silent communication passed between them. Did he normally flirt with her, not yell? They seemed to know each other, even though they'd recently met.

"I've got to get packed for the mission. We leave in the morning." She didn't argue or stay by my side. She nodded and flew out of the room.

Waiting for her to be gone, he marched closer, boxing me into a corner. "It is my business to know where you are at all times."

The gravity of his words dug deep into my soul. "You're pretending to be my guard." I took a step back and bumped into the wall. "For the mission." I gulped. "And since the mission hasn't started yet..." I shrugged, bringing me closer to him.

He tilted toward me. His hard lips were inches from mine. To make his point or to kiss me? He'd kissed me before. After he'd rescued me from prison and before we'd decided to destroy the auraguillotine together. And then he'd disappeared on our return here, leaving me alone.

That kiss had been different from Rye's. The prince's kiss had been intense, but gentle. Our connection had been more than physical. Or so I thought.

"If that's the case, if I'm not acting as your guard right now..." His voice dropped lower, more sensual, causing tiny shivers to cross my skin. "I'm free to do this."

His lips plummeted to mine. Hard, bruising, punishing.

The force caused my lips to move, to open my mouth and welcome him. The only reason. Not because his mouth became warm on mine, less punishing and more persuasive. Or because his tongue danced against the seam of my lips, tempting me to open. Or because the kiss spread heat through my body. Unexpected heat, heat inducing my toes to tingle and my head to swoon.

Giving a final nibble, Stone backed away. His eyes held a sparkle. High color on his cheeks showed he'd been as excited. His lips were plump from the kiss.

My head cleared. He couldn't go around kissing girls. "How dare you."

"I dare." The corner of his lips lifted. "I dare you to tell me you didn't enjoy it." His brows rose, waiting for my denial.

My heart throbbed and my ribcage resembled a prison cell. I couldn't deny the chemistry between us. And yet, I loved Rye. I had since the moment I met him. Or maybe that had been foolish love. I had to remember the prince had betrayed me by signing that terrible law. Maybe it was time to forget the prince and contemplate the future.

Stone's superior smirk told me he knew there'd be no dissent. Except there were reasons nothing could happen between us. And I bet he knew the most important one.

Quirking my chin in a haughty angle, I glared. As a guard, he was taught to follow the rules. He knew my true status. "How dare you take liberties *with a princess?*"

The color left his face. His hard lips firmed into a straight line. There was no surprise or shock. He'd always known I was a princess. And he was a guard. It didn't matter to me. To him and his rules, it would. So, the big question: was he using this attraction not because he liked me, but to trick me?

He took a step away. "That's a secret you're not supposed to share."

"But you already knew, didn't you?"

He'd even called me princess as a tease once.

I stepped into his space and poked a finger into his hard chest. "You knew I was a princess before I did." I poked him again. "You knew when we were together under the regent's palace, and you know now, when you initiated a kiss."

Doubts rubbed against my heart leaving the exterior raw and vulnerable. I had to wonder, was Stone attracted to me or my title?

⇥⇥⇥ ⇤⇤⇤

"I can't believe he kissed me." I tossed an extra pair of socks on my bed. "Kissed me!"

The frustration I'd experienced all evening came out in the haphazard way I packed for my trip. We were leaving on our mission tomorrow, but the one thing I had on my mind was Stone's kiss from earlier this evening. He'd kissed me before in the heat of a battle with adrenaline coursing through our veins. This time, he had no excuse.

"He assumed I'd enjoyed it." Words burst from me, even though I was alone in my room. I'd admit there was attraction, basic chemistry. Any student could explain combustion. He didn't know what my true emotions were. And I didn't know how he felt.

Then there was Rye.

What about him? My conscience teased.

Prince Zacharye would be ruler of the humans. He was making new laws and decrees that punished majiks. He wasn't thinking about me. I'd probably imagined our connection. We'd never see each other again. There was no reason for feeling guilty about enjoying a kiss from another guy.

Enjoying?

I reeled back. I had enjoyed the kiss. It wasn't the toe-curling kiss I'd shared with Rye, but that had been my first kiss. I'd probably blown it out of proportion.

Add on the rumors. Regent Theobald and Prince Zacharye were preparing for war against the majiks. Against me. More atrocities were credited to them every day. Rounding up innocent majiks. Ambushes in the homelands. The rebuilding of the auraguillotine to steal the power from every majik possible. Maybe his uncle had swayed him to the dark side.

Rye and I each had a duty to our own kind, and Stone fought on my side. With me, not against me.

I sank onto the mattress filled with clothes. The obligations and responsibilities weighed me down. I had no time for romance. I was already at a disadvantage as the fairy princess. A half breed with no wings. No one would accept me having a relationship with a guard, who was half giant as well.

The realization hit harder with my admittance to myself. Since learning of my royal ties, I'd tried to push it away, to forget. It was real. When others found out, my life would change forever.

Dropping my head into my hands, I squeezed my eyes shut, trying to hold in a frustrated scream. I needed to accept my life would be different. That I'd be bound to the castle once everyone was informed.

A knock at the door startled my thoughts. "Come in."

Silver Birch, Gardenia's assistant, opened the door, holding a set of keys. Her dark, glittery hair was in a stark bun. "You're awake."

"I couldn't sleep." I would not tell her why. "You know, I'm excited about the mission."

"Gardenia has sent for you." The assistant's gaze became hooded and she didn't respond directly to my comment.

"In the middle of the night?" This couldn't be good news.

The assistant glanced back into the hallway. "Queen Dahliadew has taken a turn for the worse."

My heart squeezed tight. "Oh no."

"Come with me."

Jumping up, I dropped the shirt I'd been holding and followed her out of the room. My thoughts whirled as Silver Birch led me toward the queen's silent corridor. My eyes burned when I thought of never getting to know the woman who was my grandmother.

Two solemn guards let us into the queen's chambers. The smell of nature and incense blended in a peaceful harmony. The ladies' maids hovered nearby to act at the queen's slightest need. Gardenia stood by the headboard, her expression grim.

My legs trembled as I approached the bed. My dad had died in an accident while on a trip. My mother had died from a long-term illness. Neither had died from poisoning.

Slow murder. Purposeful murder.

Murder because of who she was. I swallowed a terrified lump.

"Princess Ellery." Queen Dahliadew sounded quieter and weaker than she had a day before. She'd lost the royal tone and it saddened me.

Bowing my head, I again wished we had more time together. Time to form a close relationship, time for her to teach me what I needed to know. Holding in a sniff, I clasped my fidgety hands together. I didn't want her to die because she was my grandmother. I'd be alone in this environment.

"Queen Dahliadew." My rough voice scratched at my throat.

"There are important..." She coughed, and her chest lifted in the silk nightgown. "Important things you should know about ruling the fairies."

Panic shredded my lungs. I wasn't ready. I'd just accepted I was a princess.

"There are hundreds." Gardenia's harshness interrupted my sadness and fear.

It was as if she wanted me to be mad at her instead of sad about the queen. Is that how she built character?

"Gardenia can teach you most of what you need to learn. She taught me." The queen's chest rose again. A cough sputtered out of her mouth and changed into hacking. Her entire body spasmed as the cough overtook her small frame.

My gaze darted to Gardenia. Was she fairy godmother to all the royals? How old was she? Hard to tell with a few wrinkles and a wise gleam in her eyes.

"Some things only a queen can pass down to a queen." The queen's superior-royal tone was back.

I'd never have the resonance and I couldn't fake it. I'd tried with Stone earlier.

"Take my hands," Queen Dahliadew ordered in a stronger demand.

I took hold of her thin hands in mine. Her skin felt smooth and papery, like a fine parchment. Whatever she was about to impart was going to be big and I wasn't ready.

My fingers started to prickle. Warmth spread across the palm of my hand and filtered through my bloodstream. My wrists charged with electricity. My arms heated.

Queen Dahliadew's eyes closed, and she had a dreamy expression. Her lips parted in a small, satisfied smile. The hands in mine vibrated. Her body convulsed.

My chin dropped, and I glanced at my fairy godmother for her reaction. What was going on? Gardenia nodded, indicating she'd expected this.

I'd expected royal information or the keys to the castle or even another fairy secret. Not this shaking and gyrating connection. Not her soul. Licking my lips, I opened my mouth to protest. I didn't want to kill the queen by taking whatever she was giving.

Gardenia shook her head sternly.

The vibration calmed to a din. Prickles spread inside my entire body giving me an internal glow. The prickles reached outward, it couldn't be seen. "What is this sorcery?"

Because it had to be magic the queen had transferred. Would my powers now be stronger? Did I steal her magic?

"Let the queen rest." Gardenia separated my hands from the queen's, even though I felt a tug to not let go. "I'll explain everything and teach you in the morning."

That would take time. Hours, even days.

"I leave on my mission tomorrow." I shook my hands at my sides. They felt as though they'd fallen asleep and wouldn't wake up. I didn't know what had happened. I knew it was major. I hoped I hadn't killed the queen in the process. "She's not dead, is she?"

"It's late. She's tired." Gardenia looked tired too. Deep shadows hung below her eyes like crescent moons. "We'll discuss the mission and other things in the morning."

That didn't sound good. The mission needed to be completed and they needed my royal status to be accepted by the priestesses so Mother Morningmist would give me the orb. If Queen Dahliadew was about to die, how could I leave? Leave my grandmother to die without family by her side?

Blood pounded through my veins as my thoughts pounded through my head. If she died, I'd become queen. I'd be imprisoned in the castle and treated as if I was made of glass. I'd never get to fight, never get another quest.

The ladies' maids bowed to me as I passed.

My feet stumbled, and I glanced at Gardenia.

"The servants closest to the queen know who you are."

Whaaat? They hadn't bowed last time I'd visited the queen. The one thing different was the queen's health. She could die sooner than expected. Imaginary shackles clamped around my ankles and I stumbled again.

"What about my mission?" Presumably, the quest would be my last bout of freedom.

"I said, we'll discuss it in the morning." By her tone, she must mean she'd be canceling the mission.

I needed this mission. I needed it to prove to the fairies I'd make a good queen. I needed it to prove to myself I was worthy of the title. "But—"

"Now's not the time." Gardenia pivoted back toward the queen's chambers. "Goodnight, Princess Ellery."

The weight of a tiara sunk onto my head. If the fairies learned who I was now, they'd never respect me. I remembered the taunts from the kids in the hallway. They'd never agree to be ruled by me. We were entering a war. I needed loyalty and respect. The way to get it quickly was to conclude a successful mission.

I rushed through the empty corridors, needing to get back to my room and bury my head under a pillow. No, I needed to escape before the shackles grew tighter.

But there was no escape.

"What're you doing running around the castle so late at night?" Bee stood by my door. Her uniform had been replaced by black pants and top making her blend into the background. The servants wore something similar.

"I could ask you the same thing." My breathing came fast as if I'd run a mile instead of a few hallways. I unlocked my door with a spell and walked inside.

"I was looking for you." Bee followed me inside.

The room was as messy as I'd left it. Nothing had changed, and yet everything had changed. "I'm sorry. I never got the chance to ask Commander Gardenia if you could join our mission."

Bee's expression turned wary and she closed the door with a heavy thud. "There's not going to be a mission."

"What? Why do you say that?" My head swirled with the news and my reeling emotions. Arbor's elusiveness. Stone's kiss. The queen's health. Gardenia's reticence to talk about the mission.

"I heard a mission to go to the Aristos Sanctuary has been canceled." Bee heard rumors before anyone.

I hoped she didn't spread them. Uneasiness filtered through remembering how she'd wanted to discover who the lost princess was and how I'd decided to confess. "Where did you hear it? How did you hear?"

"Servants were talking in the laundry room." She picked up one of my shirts, folded it, and put it in my bag. "They were washing clothes for someone who was going."

"Our mission was supposed to be secret." I'd decided to pack only a few clothes because I had the Necessary Bag which provided anything I needed, even clean underwear.

Gardenia hadn't said anything about the mission being canceled, only that we'd talk in the morning. The way she'd said it though, how she'd cut me off when I'd asked, had been a hint. She hadn't wanted to tell me yet.

If Bee had heard through gossip the mission was canceled, maybe she knew why. "Why is the mission being canceled?"

"You're too important now." Bee sat on the bed, making herself comfortable. "Not sure what's happened in the last few hours, but it's what the servants said."

My ribcage constricted, putting pressure on my lungs. I knew what had happened in the last few hours. I shook my arms again. If the queen died, I'd become…I'd become… I couldn't even think it and I couldn't say it out loud. The queen's health was a state secret. Just like me.

"If I don't go on this mission, I'll never get the chance to prove myself to the other fairies." I heard the whine and didn't care. I'd never get to meet my great-grandmother, the one other member of my family.

"What do you mean?"

"The fairy kingdom doesn't know who I am. They won't respect me as princess or queen." I knew I'd have to give up my freedom once word got out of my royal-ness. I thought I had time. Time to prove myself.

"I thought you didn't want to be princess."

"I don't." I clenched my fists. "But I am, and there's nothing I can do about it."

"There's a male heir." Bee slipped in the tidbit.

I gasped and my mind swirled. An inkling of a memory came to me. Someone had told me about a male cousin, from Mother Morningmist's brother's line. Could this unknown distant cousin be a way out? "I thought succession went through the female line."

"It does. But when no one knew of your existence there was talk." And Bee would know about gossip and rumors.

"They still don't know of my existence." I cringed, thinking about how the students would react to the news. "The students hate me. They'll hate me more when they learned they have to bow to me."

She shrugged as if my world wasn't crashing down. "The fairies won't have a choice."

"I've been reading up on fairy history." Not because I wanted to. "And there's been succession issues in the past, people contesting who should rule. Not during the Kunglig line."

A shiver ran up my spine. Fairies could protest my ascension. The last thing needed during a war was an internal conflict. I couldn't force the issue on the fairies. I had to step up.

"Are you thinking someone might contest your succession to the throne?"

Bee's question made me think about the possibility.

"Too bad the mission's been canceled. All of you have trained so hard." Her sympathetic voice had an edge, a pushing of boundaries.

"We have worked hard."

Tos and Hokima had traveled here and learned fairy etiquette and rules and fighting. I'd practiced until my muscles ached.

"It's not fair." Bee slammed her fist on the four-poster bed.

"It really isn't." The unfairness of life whipped through me.

"You've trained, and you've planned." Bee took a pair of pants and shoved them in my bag. "You're practically packed."

"True."

"You're so ready, you could leave right now in the middle of the night."

Her words struck a fire at my feet. "We *could* leave now. We could sneak out and start our mission before it's officially canceled."

Before I'm locked inside the castle like a prisoner and not a princess.

CHAPTER EIGHT

B ee's magical messaging system had worked. She'd quickly taught me how to use Mother Earth's gift to send fireflies to each member of my team. The fireflies spelled out the note with their light.

Now, Arbor, Tos, Hokima, Stone, and Perry stood in my bedroom looking disheveled and half awake, carrying their hastily packed bags. Only Stone appeared perfect, suggesting he hadn't been sleeping. My gaze narrowed. What had he been up to? And with who?

"Why are we up in the middle of the night?" Arbor yawned and ran fingers through her short, straight hair. She laid on the center of my pillow.

"Is this part of the training?" Tos appeared grumpier than Hokima. She'd plopped on my bed, too.

"Not training." I rubbed my hands together, worried about their reactions. "This is the real deal."

Stone stretched his arms above his head and the edge of his T-shirt rose revealing carved abs. "What's going on, Ellery?"

Don't stare at him. Speak to everyone.

"There's a change in our itinerary." I'd planned to ask Gardenia to replace Stone as my pretend guard at the same time I'd ask to let Bee join the team. I hadn't gotten the chance.

"What change?" Perry stood at attention, wide awake and interested even if he was wearing baggy pants and a long shirt. He leaned against the closed bedroom door, as if afraid to come further into the room.

My stomach churned. This is where my human ability to lie would come in handy. I paced around the bed, looking at no one. "The weather report says snow is coming. We need to leave now."

Perry sniffed. "I don't sense a snowstorm."

My gaze darted to Arbor, who'd never explained fairies had abilities to sense the weather. I certainly didn't. Bee said she could conjure snow. "Weather changes."

"Can I talk to you in private?" Stone grabbed my upper arm and dragged me to the small sitting area in my room. This was where I'd originally planned to have the meeting, not around my bed. I couldn't even control a meeting. How was I going to control a country? "What's really going on?"

"Nothing." The defensive, automatic response discharged, knowing he'd be the most difficult to trick. "If you don't want to come along, that's fine. We'll go on our own."

He growled and gripped my arm tighter. "I'm your personal guard. I'm not letting you out of my sight outside the castle. Not again."

Guilt wallowed in my churning gut. He was referring to Arbor taking me home without permission. "You're my *pretend* personal guard."

"I'm your guard. I'm not going to argue semantics with you."

"Good." I shot him a saccharine smile. "Because I'm leaving now, with or without you."

He opened his mouth to protest, but I strode away back to the others. He wouldn't dare tell them my most important secret.

The door smashed open and Bee stood in the entryway carrying a small pack. The bag appeared small, similar to my Necessary Bag. She wore traveling clothes, loose pants, and layers on top.

"What are *you* doing here?" Arbor flew off the bed toward Bee's face.

Her welcoming grin faded. "Elle invited me."

All heads swiveled toward me. Arbor's mossy green eyes sharpened, blazing with hostility. Was she jealous of my new friend? Tos and Hokima's glared, a questioning distrust. Perry's gray eyes were clouded with anger. He remembered how she'd stopped him from killing me. Stone's gaze pierced the deepest. He didn't approve of the addition to the team.

None of them did.

I squirmed beneath their inspection. As the leader of the group, I needed to get used to unpopular decisions. This was my team. I marched to Bee's side and put my arm around her shoulders. "Bee is coming with us. She's taking the place of the healer."

"What?" Perry's single-word response said so much more.

Disgust and distrust. Angst and anger. Fear and frivolity.

He believed my decision was bad. I brushed off his opinion. He didn't matter.

"You don't have to come if you don't want." I forced myself not to smile. I didn't want him coming with anyhow.

"I'm coming." His glare spoke volumes.

"Why is *she* coming?" Arbor's question showed her mistrust.

She didn't even know Bee. How could the sprite make a snap decision about someone?

I couldn't take crap from my team, or my friends. I needed to stay strong and positive. "Because she can add to our team." I wouldn't accept dissension. Bee was my friend and someone I could count on. Good enough for me. "If anyone wants to pull out, now's your chance."

I stared at Stone, expecting him to protest. He glowered, staying silent. I regarded Arbor. She smirked, but her gaze stayed narrow. Hokima's eyes were closed. Maybe he'd slept through the exchange. Tos shrugged and put on her normally happy face. Perry's wary gaze darted between Bee and me. He didn't trust either of us.

"No objections?" When no one said anything, I carried on even knowing there was silent resistance. I peered at my father's timepiece. "Good. Let's go."

Arbor fluttered above the pillow. Tos jumped off the bed. The others started to shuffle out.

Shaking my hands, I knew I had to address one more issue before we left. Maybe the fairies in the room were used to the secretive ways, but they weren't used to lying. "One more thing."

I glanced at Bee and she nodded, instilling confidence. She'd helped me come up with the plan.

By not telling them the real reason we were leaving early or that I was a princess, I was lying to them. I swallowed the lump in my throat. "You can't tell anyone about our early departure. Especially Gardenia. No messaging or notes as we head out."

"Why?" Arbor sounded hurt. She realized I'd made important decisions without her input.

"Commander Gardenia has enough to worry about." A half-truth. She did have a lot to worry about. But that wasn't the reason I didn't want her to know. "In the morning, when she finds out we've left, she'll be glad we got out before the storm."

"But she's in charge of the mission." Hokima's objection surprised me. He was normally cooperative.

"I'm in charge." I needed to be clear. "Plus, she's my fairy godmother and I think I know her better than anyone."

Perry stopped mid-stride. His body stiffened, and his expression became dazed.

"You okay, Perry?" I'd never seen the guy anything less than confident.

He jerked his head down and swept out of the room.

The others accepted my answer and filed out, too. Arriving in the courtyard, I assessed everyone. "Ready?"

My vigilant gaze traveled among my team and above their heads toward the dark recesses. I'd expected one of them to tattle, Stone or Arbor being the most likely subjects. Stone worked for Gardenia, and Arbor seemed to respect her.

No guards hid in the alcoves or came out to confront. Relief relaxed my limbs. We were ready, they were listening, and no one stopped us.

At their nods, I headed toward the gleaming metalloid podship readied for our departure in the morning. Windows lined the sleek vessel and the door lifted with a whoosh. The podship would take us to the base of Drage Mountain. Since Tos, Hokima, and I couldn't apparate anywhere, this was the quickest way to the base. We'd hike from there.

Drage Mountain was a holy place and no fairy could apparate beyond the base. Professor Woods explained the journey was part of the experience and should be relished. The hike took an average of four days, with our inexperienced group it might take longer.

Stone let me go first. He must be planning to act as my guard from this point forward even though it wasn't necessary until we arrived at Aristos Sanctuary.

Holding my shoulders straight, I ignored the annoyance buzzing inside me.

Gardenia had told my team I would be pretending to be a royal, but not about being the lost princess. The High Priestess, Mother Morningmist, would know my true identity.

Slipping into the podship, I tugged on Bee's hand, so she'd sit beside me.

"Come on, Arbor." I wanted her by my side as well. Picking a seat near the back, I shoved my bag under the seat. I wanted to be as far away from Stone as possible in the cramped space.

The leather chairs were fitted with shoulder harnesses and other safety features. This podship was different from the one I'd taken to the ball, the one Gardenia had created from an orange colored chair. This podship was a troop carrier and an instrument of war.

Hokima carried Tos, and he picked a place on the other side of Bee.

Her body tensed for a second and I glanced her way. "Something wrong?"

"For a second I thought I forgot something." She rummaged a hand in her bag. "I'm good though."

Of course, she hadn't been upset about Hokima sitting next to her. She wasn't prejudiced.

"You did make us pack fast," Hokima grumped.

Arbor flew over my shoulder, not willing to take a seat yet. "It's not as if we can't conjure what we need."

"Maybe *you* can." Squeezing between Bee and Hokima, Tos reminded us of our differences.

Brownies and trolls did not have the same powers as fairies. It was one of the many reasons the different groups didn't get along. The other majiks believed fairies would take advantage of them because of our magic. In the past we had, according to my history lessons.

Frowning, I thought about the various times in history where royal fairies had behaved badly. I wasn't going to act that way.

Perry and Stone were the last to enter and took seats up front. The metal door lowered on its hinges. Stone punched in the coordinates. Lights flickered on the control panel and the engine hummed with a slight vibration. The podship lifted and proceeded forward.

My stomach scooped with the movement. Out the front windshield, I spotted the highest point of the old castle.

My legs fidgeted against the seat. This was it! Enthusiasm, excitement, and adrenaline exploded inside my veins. I was doing something important for the fairies. I'd make it to Aristos Sanctuary and be given the Divinity Orb. I'd return home a hero, and maybe then I'd be willing to admit my princess status. Maybe everyone would accept me.

The podship came to a screeching halt.

Grabbing the seat, I kept myself from slipping off and landing on the floor of the transport. Everyone else had managed to stay in place.

"What happened?" Arbor flew toward the front.

Stone jiggled a couple of buttons. "We were stopped by the castle perimeter security system."

"What? Why?" I didn't realize the castle had a perimeter system. "I understand trying to keep people out. Why would Gardenia want to keep people in?"

"To keep the students safe." Perry spoke with authority. "Transports scheduled to leave have a programmed password for a specific time. Since we're leaving early, I'm betting our exit wasn't scheduled."

Maybe he was an authority.

Which begged the question, why would he need to be? And why wasn't I? I should know these things.

"Castle guards approaching." Stone used a button and a window opened. He shot me a told-you-this-was-a-bad-idea look.

My mouth went dry. I should've asked more questions or done more research before making a snap decision to leave early without even discussing it with Gardenia.

I scurried to my feet and sidled up to Stone. "What're we going to do?"

"Now you ask?" Tilting his head, he wiggled his eyebrows in a tease. "Stay calm. Let's see what they want."

Darn him for staying serene in this situation. I was the leader.

Two fairy guards fluttered toward the podship. They wore dark helmets and uniforms bearing the insignia of their rank. They resembled the human SCUM.

Military. Authoritative. Controlling what I wanted to do.

My belly quivered, but I refused to show fear.

Stone flashed a bright, confident smile. "Can I help you?"

"This is a non-scheduled exit." A guard with a scar running down his cheek checked what resembled a human celltab. "You need authorization to leave Queens Academy grounds."

The quivering traveled from my midsection and burned up my throat. "Why? Aren't the students free to do as they please?"

Stone's dark glance told me to be quiet.

"We're leaving earlier than planned. Before the snowstorm." Perry smirked across at me. He used my reasoning even though he didn't believe it.

I glared at both guys. They thought they were so smart.

The guard took his celltab device and pointed a stream of light through the window. The light circled the small cabin beaming on each of us. "This podship is transporting other forms of majiks."

The burning grew hotter, heating my entire body. I'd had my DNA scanned before. The invasion of privacy had left me vulnerable.

"I'm Captain Stone Vitor." He attempted another grin. "I'm half giant. It's in my records." He nudged me with his elbow.

"Um, I'm Ellery Milford, and I'm half human." I didn't know if the information was in my records or not. Gardenia probably hadn't put the other truth about me in anything official. Not yet.

The guard stared at his device. "Not the reason. You're transporting a brownie and a troll."

Their scanning was that accurate? Tos and Hokima sat at the back of the vehicle. The guard hadn't even peered inside.

I cleared my throat. I needed to prove my leadership by defending my non-fairy friends again. "Tos and Hokima are guests at the academy. Check your information. They both arrived a few days ago as guests of Commander Gardenia."

The guard frowned. "Let me check it out." He crossed toward the small guardhouse by the gate.

If nothing else, my fairy godmother was good for scaring people into action.

"Maybe we can take off while they're checking," I whispered to Stone.

"They have a lock on our equipment." Perry pressed his hand against the control panel. "We can't go anywhere until they give the okay."

Our tiny cabin went silent. My breathing puffed in and out, releasing carbon dioxide while sucking up all the oxygen. Biting my lip, I tried to control the raggedness in my lungs.

You are the leader. You need to stay calm.

The guard headed back our way. Each step he took seemed to slow.

He slapped the open edge of the window, making me jolt. "The non-fairies check out."

I sagged against the console. "We can go?"

"Not without the password."

The request punched me. "What?"

The guard's expression stayed the same. "If the exit is non-scheduled, you need the correct password to leave."

Glancing at Perry and Stone, they didn't appear surprised and peered at me expectantly, believing I'd planned and knew the password.

But I didn't.

CHAPTER NINE

T he mission would end before it began.

My entire body wilted, as though it had already done the long trek up Drage Mountain to Aristos Sanctuary. The adrenaline swoosh took a left turn in the wrong direction. We weren't going to get out of the castle, and if we waited, I wouldn't be allowed to go.

"Silver Maple Timberland," Bee yelled from the back of the podship.

I swung my head to look. Why was she shouting out random words? Stone, Perry, and everyone else spun to stare at her, too.

The guard tapped on his celltab and nodded. "Confirmed. You're free to take off."

The adrenaline shot right back through me. A smile exploded on my face.

"Thank you." Stone pressed a button and the window closed. He rotated back to the controls.

"Way to go, Bee!" Clapping my hands, I was so glad I'd invited her. If not, we would've been stuck here until we were caught.

My new friend knew things. She heard gossip and other news. Why wouldn't she know the password?

The podship lifted and I hurried to the back and gave Bee a big hug. Squeezing back into my place, I noticed the surprise on everyone else's face. They questioned bringing her along when she hadn't trained.

Arbor landed on my opposite shoulder. I angled my chin to whisper to her, "See. Bee's already adding to the team."

"Yeah, about one hundred pounds." Arbor's snarky comment buzzed through me. "What I'd like to know is how she knew the password."

"Yeah. How did you know the password? It changes every day." Perry swiveled in his seat up front to analyze every slight muscle movement in Bee's face.

He didn't trust her either. Well, I didn't trust him so we were even.

I squirmed as the stare down continued. She must've heard the password from the servants where she learned everything else. Why had she been paying attention to passwords? I'd just decided to leave early. Coincidence? Or should I take what Arbor and Perry believed more seriously?

Except Arbor was jealous, and Perry didn't trust anyone.

Bee slumped back into the seat and crossed her arms, appearing defensive and scared. "I heard it from the laundry guy. He goes in and out of here at all hours and isn't on a regular schedule."

Sounded reasonable. Through servants' gossip, she'd learned about the lost princess and she'd also heard about the mission being canceled. Having ears close to the servants was important and a lesson I'd have to remember if I ever became queen.

Reassuring her, I put my arm around her shoulders. "You saved our mission. That's all I care about."

I glared at Arbor, a warning for her to drop the subject. Bee was my friend and I believed in her.

Arbor huffed and flew to sit on Stone's shoulder.

Firming my lips, I knew I had to stick up for Bee. She was part of the team and had been helpful. I'd explain everything to Arbor later. Her and I had been friends for a while, and she'd understand.

The tiny sprite sitting on the half giant's shoulder looked odd. When had they become friends? The scene of him yelling at her flashed in my head. They hadn't met until the very end of the battle under the human palace. What was their relationship?

We flew above the top of Queens Academy. Turrets struck into the sky. Moss grew on the few flat surfaces of the roof. Segmental arches curved around windows and doors. Balconies hung over the edges of the walls. And a covered bridge went from one building to the next. A sense of pride and belonging skimmed through my veins. This castle would become my home.

I noted the bright lights coming from the rooms in the highest tower, where Queen Dahliadew's chambers were located. The queen must be awake. Or her condition was worse.

Leaving the dying queen, basically disobeying Gardenia's orders, had my stomach twisting. Technically, she hadn't called off the mission. But by her tone and expression, I'd had a strong feeling the mission would be canceled, and Bee had confirmed my fears.

The mission would give me time to accept my new position and show the fairies I was worthy. A good enough reason to proceed without orders.

Or so I kept telling myself.

The quiet mood in the cabin continued, making my thoughts deeper. Doubts about the journey poked in my mind. It was too late now. I had to stay the course and at least pretend I knew what I was doing, that I had leadership skills.

"This is as far as the podship will go." Stone maneuvered the controls and the podship landed with a gentle thud. He pressed a button and the door of the transport vehicle slid open.

Shaking my head, I stood and waited for everyone else to disembark. The podship would stay here until we returned. Unless Gardenia came searching for the transport, and for me.

Alighting from the vehicle, I noted the tall trees. Black spruce trees with branches hanging down and holding large pinecones. Wolf pine trees with narrow trunks and green canopy above. The tree scent reminded me of Stone. The ground had lichen and fallen leaves. A narrow trail led up the first hill and bright streaks of sun peeked over the horizon.

"Doesn't look like snow to me." Perry adjusted the weapons at his side and stretched his wings.

I ignored the taunt, giving Bee a glance. They wouldn't believe my lie much longer and would question my orders. Question my leadership.

My head spun again with the doubts about my abilities. I had to push on.

Bee gave me a reassuring smile, understanding my silent plea. She said she could help with the weather. I was beginning to rely on her and her judgement.

"Everybody ready?" Stone stood at the start of a clearly marked path. The pilgrimage to the Aristos Sanctuary was once an annual event. "We'll take this path until we reach halfway to our campsite. We'll take a break there."

"How many hours?" Hokima grumped.

"Depends how quick we are." Stone gave a short grimace. "Perry, you take the lead."

"Why can't we use our wings and fly?" The complaint in the fairy's question was a shot to the heart.

I froze because he was making fun of me and my wingless state.

"Because we have majik guests with us and they don't fly. I don't fly." Stone was referring to Hokima and Tos, who followed behind.

Nothing was said about me. Inside, my stature shrunk. I didn't have my wings and being half human, I would probably never get them.

Hokima carried Tos on his arm. I wondered how long they'd last together.

"Ladies." Stone bowed.

Arbor buzzed onto the path. Bee stuck by my side. She didn't complain about not flying. Stone brought up the rear. He was taking his duties seriously.

Twisted vines crisscrossed the dirty trail, ready to trip up a hiker. Even though the sun rose higher in the sky, the thick tree canopy covered the lighter blue, leaving the forest in perpetual darkness. I rubbed my arms even though I wore a vest and a jacket. Because of my snowstorm forecast, I'd had to dress in thick layers.

The trail climbed upward, and I found myself huffing. The steep incline never flattened out. It went up, and up, and up. Of course, we were climbing a mountain. Until recently, I was more used to manual labor on my stepmother's behalf, not physical activity. I found myself tiring easily.

"When the sun..." Tos sung in a beautiful voice.

Mesmerized, I slowed my pace.

"Do you want to announce to every creature we're here?" Perry's sharpness cut through my enchantment.

Tos stopped singing and the atmosphere tensed.

It took me a second to put his meaning together. "What do you mean, *every creature?*"

I knew the dangers of the Mork Forest before we reached the tree line. Normal animals like elk, wolverines, and bears at the lower level. Those creatures I expected. We had weapons in case we were attacked. I shifted my hand to touch the coiled whip at my side, taking strength from its presence.

"He means trolls and ogres." Hokima had moved at a steady pace without huffing or puffing. He was large and used to the mountain air.

"No offense." Perry cut in.

"None taken." Hokima appeared fine with the insult. "Don't forget dragons. Although we'll need to get higher to see any of those."

I shivered, remembering the dragon I'd encountered in a cage at the royal ball. The heat of its flames and its large teeth.

"There's also the unique fairy animals." Tos' excitement showed in her smile. "I've heard stories about them."

My dream of unified majiks was farther off than I wanted. We were so different. And yet, most everyone in our group was getting along. Now, if I could get Arbor and Bee to become friends.

I noticed Bee swatting at Arbor. "Bee, stop."

"Your friend keeps buzzing by my ear." She waved in front of her face as if Arbor was a bug.

What was up with Arbor? As soon as I got the chance, I was going to talk to her. About her actions and how she treated Bee. About Arbor's jealousy and her relationship with Stone. About why she defended Gardenia more than me. I didn't even know my best friend anymore.

"How am I supposed to listen for animals and creatures if I can't hear anything except Arbor?" Bee stomped her foot as she walked.

I huffed, tired of playing referee. "Arbor, why don't you fly ahead? You can tell us what to expect."

"Great idea." Bee smirked.

Arbor grimaced into a snotty expression, tilted her chin up, and flew by Perry.

Now that they were separated, I could worry about other things. "What kind of fairy animals? What else lurks in the woods?"

I considered each tree differently. Knots became hidden places for things to hide. The vines became treacherous snakes. The leafy green vegetation became shelter for animals. Birds chirped, shouting a message.

"There's nothing to worry about." Stone's deep proclamation came from behind. "I'm here."

I swiveled my head. "I should know what to expect."

"There's the Voyeur Vulture. It's about the size of a falcon and has huge teeth." Bee shifted her hands to show the size of the creature. "And the Strangler Snake, which can slither for hundreds of miles using their sense of smell. They strangle majiks for pleasure."

My foot got tangled in a vine. Panic bulleted through me and I yanked my leg, trying to get untangled.

"You okay?"

"Fine. Fine." At least I hadn't tripped.

"The Clustered Red Waxy Cap is this cute little animal with teeth resembling a gopher," Bee continued.

I glanced back at Stone again. He stood straight as he marched, while my spine sagged and sweat formed down the middle of my back. Was he listening? I turned to stare straight ahead. Perry marched in front. He kept pivoting back and forth, expecting an attack.

Arbor flew between Perry and Hokima. Tos skipped beside him. I wished I could skip. I could barely put one foot in front of the other. My half human part was slowing me down.

Bee pointed into the woods. "I'll be right back."

"Don't go too far off the path." Stone guarded everyone.

We'd been hiking for several hours. I wanted to ask for a break, but no one else was slowing. Adjusting my pack on my shoulder, I pushed harder to catch up. Stone followed behind. He'd never leave my side.

"Look." Bee came out from behind a tree and pointed further up the path. "It's snowing."

She winked at me and I was grateful she provided the promised storm.

Stone stepped between us. "Why don't you take the lead, Ellery?" Because he wanted me to pick up the pace, I was sure.

Stomping ahead, I tried to go faster. Snow fell, cold crystals hitting my cheeks. The wind picked up its pace. And the bite in the air made me shiver. Maybe snow had been a bad idea.

"Are you sure you want me leading? You disagreed with leaving early." I didn't hold back my surly tone, taking my frustration out on Stone.

"If you lead, I can watch your...backside." Did he mean in a protective way or was he saying something more?

I could practically feel his stare on my butt, which made me self-conscious of every wiggle. My gait became stiff, slowing my step.

"And a nice backside it is." He chuckled. "If only it would move faster."

"Oh." I tugged down the back of my jacket and picked up my pace.

I'd show him. Show him I could hike fast. Show him his flirting didn't bother me. Show him I could take the lead, hiking and in the group.

The snow crunched beneath my boots. Ice clung to the edges and my footstep went deeper and deeper into the snow. My earlier sweat chilled my back and I rubbed my hands against my arms. Several times, I felt Stone's body heat as he closed the space between us.

He almost bumped into me again. "If you don't pick up the pace, your backside is going to meet my front side." The tease in his voice curled up at the end.

He thought the situation was funny. He knew I was tired and cold and totally unprepared for the journey. He believed he was in better shape. And he insinuated with his tease that he could keep me warm with his body alone.

Remembering the last time we'd been close, I knew it was true. All of it.

"I could sweep you off your feet."

I wasn't sure if he meant the love expression, or literally picking me up and carrying me. Glancing back, I analyzed his smirk.

"I've already been swept off my feet by Rye." I used an uppity tone and turned my back to Stone, continuing to march forward.

"You mean the leader of our enemy?"

My chest tightened at the unfair claim. "Rye's not the enemy. His uncle is."

"So, says you." Stone rarely mumbled, and I took advantage of it and pretended not to hear.

But I'd heard, and the claim stabbed through my heart. I stumbled. Rye had signed the law, not his uncle. Had he also signed the end of my love for him?

Chapter Ten

Hours later, at the point where I didn't think my frozen feet could take another step, Stone said, "Let's break for lunch." He must've read my mind.

I collapsed onto a fallen log, not caring about the two inches of snow piled up. My cheeks felt numb and snow crystals clung to my eyelashes.

The others took off their packs and cleared the snow off nearby rocks or other logs. Rocks circled in a ring and in the center was a dark spot from a fire. The small clearing showed the stormy sky above us.

Shivering, I slipped off my pack, wishing I could reach in, take out my Necessary Bag, and pull out a fire. "Too bad it's so wet we can't make a fire."

The downside to Bee's magical snowstorm. Besides the cold.

"You've lived as a human too long." Perry brandished his wand and made a few elaborate sweeps. He mumbled unintelligible words, probably not wanting me to learn.

A homey campfire popped up in the middle of our circle. Bright orange flames crackled, and I held my hands to the heat. A handy trick. I needed to learn how to do that. Maybe Bee could teach me.

Perry pulled back his shoulders in a superior stance. He peered at me with condescension, thinking he was better. Knowing he was better. Why had he agreed to come on this mission if he hated me so much?

Shaking off the curious thought, I knew I needed to use this downtime to learn more about the upcoming meeting. I had no idea how to handle the situation with the priestesses and I didn't want to go in blind. Gardenia had planned to give me important information and instructions before we left. We'd gone early, and I didn't learn anything. Cringing, I wished I would've thought this through. I'd been panicked and Bee had pressured.

Starting simple, I asked, "Why do the priestesses wear red robes?"

"I've heard it's the simplest color dye to make." Arbor flew back and forth above the fire, drying her wings.

"It's how they hold in their magic." Bee spoke with authority and Arbor stuck out her tiny tongue.

Another thing my two friends didn't agree on.

Tos took off her tiny hiking boots and set them closer to the flames. "Why do they live in such an isolated place?"

"And why is the sanctuary protected so fairies can't apparate in?" Hokima caught the nutrition pouch Stone tossed him.

Handing each of us a pouch to consume, Stone stayed standing on constant alert. If he wanted to be the guard dog, I'd let him.

"The purpose of the Aristos Sanctuary is to keep ancient secrets." Perry ripped open his pouch. "Because of the need for additional security an enchantment was cast on the entire mountain so random fairies couldn't apparate in and out. It's similar to the shield over Alandaska."

"There are cracks in the shield." Bee sucked on her pouch and avoided everyone's gaze.

My brow furrowed. How was that even possible?

"Where did you hear that?" Stone stopped his circular stalking.

She shrugged and took another sip from her pouch. "Somewhere."

"Servants, again?" Arbor fluttered in front of Bee's face. "That's become a convenient excuse."

I'd noted the same thing. It was her go-to explanation.

"Why do you hang around the laundry room and the servants' quarters so much?" Perry leaned forward aggressively.

Bee kept her head low and murmured something.

"What?" Arbor badgered.

My new friend shot to her feet and bumped into Arbor, shoving the sprite over the fire.

"Ouch!" Arbor swerved toward me. "Bee made me burn myself on purpose."

The action and accusation were a double whammy.

"I'm sure it was an accident." It had to be. My one friend wouldn't hurt the other.

Bee dashed into the woods, clearly upset.

My pulse raced. "Bee, wait!"

Stone charged in her direction.

"No. I'll go and talk to her." I scrambled to my feet. Following her tracks, I hurried toward the sound of crying. Glancing back, I noted Stone stopped at the edge of the woods watching. No, guarding.

Both comforting and annoying.

Bee stooped, leaning against a tree trunk. Her shoulders were hunched, and she tugged at the gloves on her hands. Her tear-stained face spoke of her upset.

Sympathy washed through me. She knew the others didn't want her here. I placed a hand on her back and rubbed. "Are you okay?"

"They accuse me and don't believe me." She sniffed, refusing to raise her head.

Biting my lip, I tried to approach the subject delicately. "You do tend to say you heard things from the servants a lot. For example, the news about the lost princess."

She whipped her head up. "About you. And I've not told anyone your secret."

"I know, and I appreciate it." I waved my hand at where the group gathered. "They don't understand how trustworthy you are."

"You do?" Her head tilted, and her eyes glared with accusation. "Enough that you don't want to know why I'm with the servants?"

I was curious and tempted to ask. Sensing this was a test, I rubbed her back again. "I don't need to know. I trust you."

Uneasiness shot through me. Or was that the cold?

Her gaze dipped down and then she raised her head toward the sky, as though searching for the right answer. "I hang out with the servants because...I am one."

I choked. "What?"

"In order to pay tuition at Queens Academy, I have to work. It's why I hear things I probably shouldn't."

I sagged against the tree. Her situation was so similar to my own past. I'd become Sybil's servant so I could stay in human school and my home. My sympathy grew. I understood the difficulties she faced.

"You won't tell anyone, will you?" She asked me to keep the secret, just as she kept my secret.

"Of course not."

"And Elle." She stood tall and wiped the tears from her face. "The reason the priestesses are so secretive is because they're made up of former royals and noblewomen and hold tremendous magical power."

Like my great-grandmother.

The afternoon wore on as did the blisters on my feet. I'd asked Bee to stop the snow and bring out the sun. Now, we trudged through slush. The mud clung to my boots, making them heavier and causing my steps to slow. Or so I told myself. This was only the first of four days, and it seemed like a week already. By the time we reached the priestesses I wouldn't look royal, I'd appear like a beggar.

"Let's set up camp for the night." Stone picked a spot shielded by a cliff wall with a grassy space for our tents. The hills had ended, and we were definitely in the mountains. The hard climbing would start in the morning.

Stone pulled a tiny packet from his bag and tapped on it. The packet popped open to make a tent large enough to hold his bulk. Arbor picked a leaf and dragged it to a spot right next to the wall. She flew around and around, pulling the leaf's edges until she formed a comfy cone for her to sleep in. Hokima picked sticks up off the ground and balanced them against each other. He spread a tarp over the top. Tos used sticks also and layered small leaves across the sides, coming to an angle at the top. Perry used his wand and spun an elegant tent with colorful streamers for a door.

I stood watching, stunned. I didn't have the skill or the magic to make a habitat as competent or fancy as any of theirs. I'd planned to pull a sleeping roll out of my Necessary Bag.

Perry added twinkling lights around the edges of his tent before glowering at me. "Do you think because you will be *pretending* to be royal, you don't have to do any work?"

The way he said pretending was a slap in the face. He must be digging for information. Did he suspect the truth? Searching the darkening sky, I tried to think of a good excuse. I didn't want to admit my magic sucked.

"We're going to share a tent." Bee came to my rescue. "I wanted to gather some fireflies for light before we decided what type of tent we wanted."

Arbor stood at the edge of her leaf tent and glared at my friend.

Discomfort swarmed in my gut. My old friend didn't seem to understand my magical problems. Bee did.

"Yes, fireflies." I reached in my Necessary Bag and pulled out a glass jar. "Let's go catch some."

Bee hooked her arm through mine, and we headed away from the campsite.

"Don't go out of sight." Stone's warning sent a chill through me. "Perry, you take first watch. I'll nap and take most of the overnight shift."

"Stone is such a worry wart," I whispered to Bee.

"I think he's crushing on you." She giggled.

"No." I hadn't told her about our shared kiss, didn't want to acknowledge it. "He doesn't think I'm capable." Imagining what Perry would say if he learned I didn't know how to do basic spells would crush my tender ego. He'd make fun of me even more. And poor Bee. "Can you teach me how to conjure a tent?"

"Sure." She pulled apart from me. "It will be harder without a wand."

"You don't use a wand." In fact, I didn't think I'd ever seen her do magic. Well, except for the snowstorm. If she could conjure a weather incident, she must be powerful.

"First, you need to connect with your magical source. Have you been taught that yet?" When I nodded, she continued. "You have to picture what you want to happen. And last, you have to say the enchantment words." She repeated the words to me twice. "Got it?"

Closing my eyes, I thought of my magical source, I noticed the tingling start inside my body, almost as strong as when I'd held Queen Dahliadew's hand. The tent needed to be bigger and better than Perry's.

"Can you picture the tent?"

"Yes."

"Give it a back door."

Odd request. "Okay."

"Great. Wait until we get back so you can show them what a great fairy you are."

I appreciated how Bee thought. She understood my need to prove myself. Fingers crossed, I could actually conjure the tent.

⤙⤙⤙ ⤚⤚⤚

"Wake up, princess." Stone's deep tone sent awareness shooting through me.

Hating this unwanted attraction, I curled deeper into the air mattress and blankets. I couldn't even think about liking a guy. Any guy. I had too much to prove. And of course, there was Rye.

Stone tickled my cheek with a rough finger. "It's time to go."

I groaned. From head to toe, my entire body ached. Last night after conjuring the tent, Bee had kept me awake talking. She told tales about the priestesses and about other animals in the woods. After her stories, I found it difficult to sleep and I'd tossed and turned.

"Come on, princess."

I jolted at the nickname that wasn't a nickname.

"Everybody else is up and ready."

Springing into a sitting position, I glanced around the tent. Bee was gone, and her things were packed. Stone was dressed in a heavier jacket and thick, lined pants.

I shivered and pulled the blanket up to my neck. "You shouldn't be in my tent." And neither should I. They were going to think I was lazy, sleeping in.

"It's a campsite, not a nunnery."

A nunnery was where we were headed. Or as the priestesses called it, a sanctuary.

He stood and opened the tent door. Frigid wind blew through the opening. "Dress warm. It's freezing, and the weather will get colder the higher we climb."

After he left, I grabbed my clothes and got dressed under the warm blankets. I added layer upon layer, knowing the restrictive clothing would slow me down even more. Once dressed, I peeked outside. Stone had spoken the truth. Everyone else was packed and dressed. Their tents were gone, and they stood around chatting, waiting for me.

I wanted to kick my lazy butt. I should've set an alarm. Or Bee should've woken me.

"Good morning, sleepyhead." Arbor's friendly tease dug into me.

What my friends didn't know was I hadn't slept the night before last because of the late visit with the queen. Guilt walloped in my midsection for leaving without notice. "Sorry. Someone should've woken me sooner."

"I volunteered." Perry's brow scrunched with annoyance. "Stone wouldn't allow me to make your tent and bedding disappear, so you'd find yourself flat on the dirt."

Arbor, Tos, and Hokima chuckled. They thought Perry's joke was funny. I didn't because I sensed his suggestion was more than friendly banter.

"There's food on the fire. I'll get it while you finish up." Bee stood to prepare my breakfast.

"She's not a queen." Perry's frown deepened, and he became more watchful. "Let her do it herself like everyone else."

Uneasiness slid up my spine. He'd teased about being royal yesterday as if he knew.

I needed to distract him from the topic. I might be royal, but I certainly didn't smell like one. "I'm not a queen. I do need to go take care of necessities, however."

He blushed, and I went into the woods to take care of business.

When I got back, the fire was out, and everyone milled about, ready to go. I wolfed down the oatmeal, and we were on our way.

My stiff muscles complained an hour into the hike. The bright sun did little to dispel the cold or the darkness of the forest. By noon, we reached the montane forest level. The trees thinned and the frigid, howling wind increased. My teeth chattered. When the sun began to set, I was ready to toss down my bag and fall onto the hard ground.

Everyone else had kept pace. I'd been consistently behind. Arbor had fluttered back and forth, trying to keep up my spirits. Tos had hummed quietly, setting a soothing atmosphere. Bee had been too nice, asking if I needed help or wanted to rest. Hokima and Perry would go ahead to scout and report back to Stone. They'd traveled twice the distance.

Stone had become the de facto leader of this group because of his capability and experience. No one reported or looked to me to make decisions. If they had, we would've stopped at lunch and not started hiking again. It would've taken weeks, not days, to get to Aristos Sanctuary.

I had to try harder, hike faster, and make practical decisions. And rely on those with experience.

"Let's camp here," Stone announced at a spot where tall trees protected a small space. He dropped a few pieces of timber onto a pile in the center of the spot. Pieces he'd picked up as he'd hiked.

Overachiever.

I dropped my bag and it thudded to the ground. "Thank the wood spirits."

"Hokima and Perry scout the perimeter." Stone started issuing orders to do things to keep us safe. Things I never would've thought of.

My shoulders rolled in. So much for being in charge. How could I take control when I didn't know how to do any of this stuff?

"Bee and Tos, head down to the small stream we passed for water. Arbor, fly up high and check out the vicinity." Stone ordered and everyone listened.

Maybe if I watched him, I'd learn to be a leader. His deep voice rung with authority. His strong features expressed his determination. His manly lips kissed fiendishly. Heat flushed my cheeks. *Stop, just stop.* Watching him was dangerous.

Perry took out a small dagger from the strap on his leg. "Maybe Elle would enjoy a nap while we do the set-up."

Hurt and humiliation stirred into anger. My ears pounded, and my vision clouded. "I can help."

The entire team went still, watching this play out. If I failed, I'd embarrass myself even further.

Standing on shaking legs, I squared my shoulders, trying not to show my insecurity and uncertainty. My pulse thrashed, and my throat went dry. I searched for something to do. Most of the tasks had been assigned.

"I'll start a fire." I'd watched Perry yesterday. How would they trust me to lead, to rule, if I couldn't accomplish this simple task?

Narrowing my gaze, I stared at the spot where the fire would go. I focused on what I wanted to happen, how the flames would ignite and warm the area.

"Any day now." Perry's disparaging comment distracted, and I lost focus.

What if I couldn't start the fire? What if my magic sizzled? He'd tell the fairies back at school and I'd never be respected. Having a wand would make the spell easier. Except you didn't get a wand until you got your wings and I didn't know if I'd ever get my wings. Not with my half status.

Narrowing my gaze even more, I glared at the spot. I imagined the fire. I murmured the enchantment.

A spark ignited. Pride burst inside me. I focused harder. The blaze grew and began to catch on the wood. I'd done it. The campfire was blazing at the perfect level. A burst of unusual energy sizzled through my entire body. Could it be whatever power the queen had instilled in me or something different?

Flames combusted, lighting up the night sky.

Horror etched across my skin. Shivers followed sweat. I couldn't control the blaze. My arms shook and I rushed through the reverse enchantment. It wasn't working. The fire was growing.

The fire burst upwards, catching the surrounding trees, igniting the leaves and branches. Embers dropped to the scrub on the ground catching the dry plants on fire. Smoke surrounded us, and I started to choke.

The inferno was out of control.

The inferno I'd created.

Chapter Eleven

The fire exploded around us.

The detonation blasted through me and I stumbled backwards.

Heat seared and the smell of burnt *everything* filled the atmosphere. The out-of-control inferno scorched the earth and the trees and everything.

Covering my mouth, I crawled on the ground. Tiny rocks dug into my skin and the smell of dirt, which usually brought comfort, suffocated. A fiery tree limb crashed to the ground. I jerked. The bark crackled and tiny spurts of fire burned through the dry wood.

The fire was uncontrollable.

Panic had me digging my elbows into the dirt and dragging my body away. I took in a shallow wheeze and choked on the smoke-clogged air and my guilt. I had to think of a way to put this fire out.

Was there a fire-stopping spell? I wracked my brain. I couldn't recall one. Waves of heat overtook me. My mouth went dry. We were going to die or be injured. Or even worse, be returned to the castle.

This wasn't about me. I firmed my backbone. I had to do something to stop the fire.

Flames licked the covered ground. We couldn't let the fire burn the entire forest.

"Rain!" The idea hit similar to a much-needed storm and I searched for Bee. She'd created a snowstorm, rain should be easy.

She stood by the edge of the forest, her feet facing in two different directions, trying to decide whether to help or flee. Her terrified expression told me she felt the same as me, but we needed to stop the fire, not run.

"Bee!" I yelled over the thunder of the flames, and she snapped her panicked expression in my direction. "Rain! Make it rain!"

She shook her head, her eyes growing even wider. Petrified, she didn't move her body. She was too scared to help.

My shoulders drooped. I'd come to rely on her, maybe too much. I needed to learn how to do things on my own.

Tos and Hokima were beside each other, tossing handfuls of dirt at the burning edges of the forest. They were trying to stop the fire without magic. Their efforts were heroic.

Using the canvas of his tent, Stone smothered flames as he stalked toward me. He used his strong giant's breath to blow out a section and pushed forward. Sometimes the cold air worked, other times it fanned the blaze. His gaze flicked to me again and again, checking even while he couldn't get to me.

The chaos of the scene unfolded like a vid. I sucked down a smoky breath and coughed. Smothering with canvas or covering with dirt wasn't going to work. The fire was too powerful, too overwhelming. Too magical?

Flying around the fire, Perry pulled out his wand and waved. He probably knew a spell to stop my fire mistake.

My throat constricted, and my blood pressure rocketed. I wanted to tell him I could stop the fire. Except this was more important than my pride. If Perry knew how to contain the inferno, he should do it. I wished I knew a rain spell or even a Mother Earth rain dance. I glared at the spot where the fire began. The focus of my uncontrolled magic. What had been the source of the unusual burst of power?

The wind picked up, blowing leaves and small twigs. My hair blew around my face. A mini tornado inside the fire gathered strength. I tried to think of a spell or enchantment, anything that would help.

Arbor flew above the smoke storm. The fire tornado whipped higher, catching her in its draft. Fire singed her wings and arms. She started falling to the ground.

"Ahhh!" Her anguished scream seared me as if I'd been burned.

My heart leapt into my throat, causing my air passages to become blocked. I rushed forward. I had to save her.

Arbor's tiny body fell *down, down, down*. She hit a wooden log and flopped to the ground.

My pulse strangled out a beat. I reached her and carefully scooped her up. "Arbor?"

Her wings were blackened from the intense fire. Her skin darkened red with ugly white welts. I bent over, protecting her from the nearby flames.

Perry's brown wings spread out wider. He fluttered above the fire and waved his wand, trying various enchantments. None seemed to work. His movements became sluggish and less smooth.

My jaw dropped and my scorched lungs tried to suck in a surprised inhalation. Did he not know how to use magic to put out the fire or was the magic I used different from others? Was I different?

"Rain, Perry." I shouted as loud as I could. It didn't matter that he'd be the hero. Arbor was injured and there was nowhere to run. Plus, damaging nature wasn't something fairies did. "Make it rain."

He glanced at me and nodded. Swiveling his body, he spoke words I couldn't understand.

A single drop of rain hit my head. Then another and another.

I looked up.

Dark clouds gathered overhead. The droplets of water turned to pouring rain. The rain changed into a downpour, soaking my clothes, the ground, and most importantly, the fire.

The flames morphed to smoke. Stone used his breath to blow the smoke away.

Perry saved the day. My eyes stung, even so, I kept my chin up. I hoped he could save Arbor.

What was left of her wings lay flat on the ground. Her clothes were gone, torn, or melted against her skin. The ugly white welts grew bigger. Blisters formed across her entire body.

I sniffed. "Arbor? Are you okay?"

She didn't respond, lying lifeless on the ground.

Panic welled inside my chest. I gasped. "Arbor!"

Anguish rent my body, leaving me weak. I couldn't lose another friend.

"Arbor! I'm sorry. So sorry." The tears came freely now, running down my cheeks to mix with the soot on my face. I had to do something. But what? I wasn't trained in first aid and I'd proved my magic was terrible. Someone else had to do something.

Stone, Hokima, Tos, and Perry continued to put out hot spots of the fire. Bee was closest.

"Bee! Help!" I didn't know healing magic. "You have to do something to save her."

She stood frozen. She hadn't helped with the fire either because of what I thought was panic. Her expression still showed fear. Was she not good with the sick and injured?

"Bee?" Just because my one friend didn't approve of the other didn't mean they shouldn't help each other. They were both my friends and we were a team and needed to behave like one.

"I...I...I can't." Bee hung her head and twisted her hands together. "I don't know how."

Gasping, I gaped. She'd made it snow. She'd said messing with weather was one of the hardest spells. Perry had made it rain. I regarded him.

"Oh, for sprite's sake." Perry slipped his wand into his belt and flew over. Kneeling down beside Arbor, he examined her. "Move back."

If he could help Arbor, I'd do anything he asked. Arbor meant everything to me. She'd known me before I'd accepted my fairy self, when I'd been a servant in my home. She'd taught me things and made me laugh. While she'd been gone, I'd blamed her for my loneliness. I was wrong.

Bee, Stone, Hokima, and Tos watched from a short distance away, forming a semi-circle. Their serious expressions told me they understood the horrible situation.

I wrung my hands.

Perry stretched his arms and waved his wand similar to a conductor. His wings fluttered behind him. He focused with an intensity that brought wrinkles to his brow and puckered his lips. His mouth formed words I'd never heard before, speaking what was to me a foreign language. He knew what to do and how to help. He was a strong fairy with excellent magical and fighting skills. I'd been skeptical of him joining my team, and I'd been wrong. I needed to apologize for the way I'd acted.

Arbor mumbled something and thrashed on the ground. Her raw burns were less red and her skin flaked instead of slithering off her body.

Joy sung through my heart. "She's alive."

"No thanks to you." Perry collapsed, his energy spent. His anger was on full display by the hard tone.

Hanging my head, I knew I deserved his fury.

"Perry," Stone warned with an edge in his voice.

"I'm sorry I doubted having you on my team, Perry." After giving my apology, I bent closer to Arbor. Her breathing was erratic, and she moaned. The blisters weren't growing or bursting, but they were still present and appeared painful. She wouldn't be able to fly or walk. "She'll need a healer's care."

"I wanted a healer to join our team, and you brought her along instead." Perry lifted his head to glare and then glowered at Bee.

I winced. The priestesses limited the number of servants and they had healers of their own. I thought we could survive four days without the need of a healer. The healer Gardenia had wanted to come with us was one of her cronies. I didn't want the woman reporting back my every action, especially when we'd left earlier than expected.

Bee seemed to pull into herself. Her shoulders hunched, and her chin tucked in.

She'd been helpful to me from the moment I met her. Saving me from Perry, telling me about her search for the lost princess, and the cancelation of my mission. She'd created the snowstorm to assist in my machinations. She'd been my friend, and good for my ego. Although, she hadn't helped with the fire.

I deflated inside. Deciding what was best for the team, not my ego, would've been a better choice. I needed to defend her though. "Bee knew the password. We never would've gotten out of the academy grounds if she wasn't with us."

Stone kicked a large, burnt tree branch out of the way. "Maybe that would've been a good thing."

What did he mean? I told him he didn't have to come. "If you know something, say it."

The air zipped with tension, as well as smoke. Perry was still mad, and Bee was still scared. Tos and Hokima went silent, watching us argue. They must think we're terrible majiks.

I wanted to throw up my hands. Never again did I want people to think poorly of fairies. Or half fairies.

Stone scrunched his lips together as if he had more to say. Maybe it was something that couldn't be said in the group. I'd wheedle it out of him later. Arbor was more important.

"Perry, can you do anything more to help Arbor with the pain?"

He knelt beside the smoke sprite to examine her. "If we can find some fiddle leaves, I can compress it and put it on the burns. She won't be able to continue the journey. Between the burns and the damage to her lungs, she can't handle the altitude."

"I can pull a healing ointment out of my Necessary Bag." Finally, I could be of assistance. Thinking of what I needed, I put my hand in the bag, pulled out the tube, and handed it to Perry. It wasn't my magic, it was Gardenia's. My spirits sank lower.

Watching Perry apply the gooey ointment, I couldn't stop the worry for my friend. The need to continue the quest was stronger. "We can't leave her here alone."

"No, we can't." Stone started setting up what was left of his canvas tent.

The once enormous shelter had been reduced to the poles and bottom layer. The top of the tent had been completely burnt with ragged edges and large holes. The side panels were gone.

"Let me use magic to repair your tent." If I could. I mean, I had magic but clearly, I wasn't perfect. Not even very good. I was learning how to control my powers.

"No, thanks."

Guilt stuck in my throat. His sleeping situation was my fault. Arbor's injuries were my fault. I needed to step up and be the leader I was supposed to be. This was my quest. Not Perry's or Stone's. From this point forward, I'd be a strong leader. Decisive and brave.

Perry might be more powerful and better trained in magic. He might be a better fighter. I could learn those things. The fire I'd started had been strong. I'd experienced an extra surge of energy I'd never felt before, which worried me. Powerful energy.

I considered Perry. Had he injected his magic into mine to make me appear a fool? Was he trying to sabotage the mission? Or was he spying for Gardenia?

What did I know about castle intrigue?

"Since Perry has healing talents, he should stay with Arbor," I said decisively.

My mission. My decision. My way to get rid of him.

I might admire his skill. I didn't trust him. Didn't know if he spied for Gardenia or someone intent on evil.

He jerked his head up from where he was applying the ointment to Arbor and scowled. He didn't like my suggestion.

Stone shook his head. "We need Perry for his magic and his strength."

Tos couldn't protect Arbor and herself. We needed Hokima in case we encountered mountain trolls. There was one sensible choice and she was going to hate it. "Bee is the best candidate to stay with Arbor then."

"Me?" Bee's face crimped in disgust.

I angled back, realizing how much she disliked the smoke sprite. "Bee, you're the best person to take care of her and protect her. Once we arrive at Aristos Sanctuary, we'll send a healer to help mend Arbor's lungs and you can join us later." I held my breath knowing it was the best option, hoping she'd agree without a fuss.

Bee turned to me and grabbed my hands. "But...I'm your friend and I need to go with you." She sounded more desperate than loyal.

I appreciated her loyalty and needed to take advantage of it. This wasn't about me. It was about what was best for the mission. "As a favor to me, I'm asking you to stay and take care of Arbor."

Bee smashed her lips together and an angry flash gleamed in her eyes. Her stubborn chin protruded before it slowly came down in a nod. Her agreement should have made me feel better, more comfortable. For some reason, it threw my thoughts into a tizzy of confusion and uncertainty. Did I trust her with Arbor?

"Decision made." Stone stretched his arms. "Let's make Arbor comfortable, and then everyone get some rest. I'll take the first watch."

Perry stood and perused each one of us. His gaze lingered on me. "I have something to say."

"Is it really important, Perry?" Bee fake-yawned. "It's been a long day."

"It's important you know why I'm really here."

He was a spy. My suspicion was correct.

He cleared his throat and puffed out his chest. "If the lost princess hadn't been found, I'd be the one ruling once Queen Dahliadew dies."

His declaration reverberated in my soul. The vibrations shook me to my core. Putting a hand out, I leaned against a tree, needing strength. I'd expected subterfuge. I'd expected court intrigue—look what happened between Rye and his uncle. I'd never expected to be facing my competition.

Bee had said something about a male heir waiting in the wings. The male heir was Perry. That's why he'd almost killed me. That's why he hated me so much.

My stomach dropped. Which meant he knew who I was. He must.

And Gardenia had forced him to be part of my team on this mission. She must've known who he was too. A test then? See who would be best to inherit the throne? Him or me? Did she believe he was a better choice?

I'd thought Gardenia was on my side. Sure, she'd tricked me with the plot to assassinate Prince Zacharye. I believed it had been a scheme to get me to see the fairy side of myself. And it had worked. What if it had actually been a plot to get me killed or another test?

Was Gardenia trying to overthrow me?

Stone watched my every facial tic. He'd known about Perry. Bee twisted her hands together. She knew his background, too.

I ogled Perry, my competitor for the crown. He didn't appear anything like me. "How is that possible?"

"My great-grandfather was Queen Morningmist's brother."

I sucked in a sharp, slow breath. We were traveling to meet Queen Morningmist, my great-grandmother. And apparently Perry's great aunt. "You are the male heir?"

"Yes." He pulled his shoulders back and stood proud, resembling a prince. Someone who'd known his identity his entire life, who'd been trained to be royal, who understood the politics of court life. "And I would make a much better ruler than—"

"Perry." Stone's interruption demonstrated his desire to keep my identity secret if Perry did know the truth.

Stone knew who I was, and he didn't want Perry telling anyone else in our group. Too late. Bee knew too.

"We'll talk about your right to rule later, and in private. We're under Commander Gardenia's orders to work together to make this mission a success." Stone reminded Perry of our oath and our mission.

If Perry had known about me, why would he accept this mission? Why help his rival? My thoughts swung back to the idea this was a test. A test for both of us? Maybe he'd had suspicions about who I was and had wanted to journey with us to discover the truth.

Well he had, and he'd almost divulged it to everyone.

⊷⟫⟫⟩ ⟨⟨⟨⟨⊷

"Elle, wake up."

I groaned. Had I overslept again? At least it wasn't Stone or Perry waking me.

"Wake up." The urgency in Bee's tone had me reassessing.

Everything had contributed to my exhaustion. The hike, the magical mistake, Arbor's injuries, Perry's disclosure.

I opened my eyes and noted the darkness. "Is it time for my night watch?" I'd insisted with Arbor injured, I'd take her shift. I didn't want to be treated like a princess.

"The castle guards are here, and they plan to take you back to Queens Academy."

"What? Why?" I scrambled from beneath the covers and crawled to the doorway of the tent. "What're they doing here?"

"Shh! Don't let them know you're awake." Bee started shoving things into her bag.

I put my ear to the tent flap.

"We've been tracking your group for the last two days," an anonymous female voice spoke. She must be a castle guard. "The fire gave us your exact location."

Another negative thing my fire had caused. I couldn't catch a break.

"Ellery has permission to travel to Aristos Sanctuary from Commander Gardenia." Stone must be on night watch. That meant it wasn't late. "Why take her back now?"

He questioned the guard's orders, proving his loyalty. My mood lightened. I had good friends protecting me.

"Your mission was canceled. You were never supposed to leave," the female guard said. "We realize you've had no way to communicate on Drage Mountain. The cancelation order went through shortly before you left the castle grounds."

I winced. I'd been caught. Stone would discover I'd lied. Glancing at Bee, I noted her guilty expression. She took part of the blame.

"The team will be upset about the change in plans." Stone's delivery had a rough edge.

"The rest of you can continue on." The female guard didn't bend.

Perry would complete the quest. I would fail, and he'd get the Divinity Orb and the throne. Maybe that would be a good thing. I never wanted to be a princess. And yet, a male had never been in charge. Uncertainty about succession would make our fairy force weaker. We needed to be strong going into a war.

"I'm assuming traveling back can wait until morning."

Bee nudged me with her elbow at Stone's comment.

"We'll make camp with you for the night." The female guard issued orders to whoever was with her. "And return Ellery to the castle in the morning."

The imaginary shackles grew tighter around my wrists and ankles. They circled my neck and choked off my oxygen flow. I was going to be a prisoner in the castle sooner than expected. Or if Gardenia wanted Perry to ascend to the throne, maybe I'd become a prisoner in their dungeon.

"We have a severely injured smoke sprite. You can take her back to get healing treatment."

I respected how Stone thought of taking care of Arbor.

"Of course."

After agreeing, the female guard must've assisted the other guards in setting up their tents. The clatter of their work melted into a distant haze as I sank back on my haunches. Had the queen died? Is that why Gardenia sent them to come for me? If the queen was already gone, she couldn't instill any royal guidance. The only relative I had left was the head priestess, Mother Morningmist.

And Perry.

I didn't see him being much help. I'd done nothing auspicious for the fairies and all they knew about me was the rumors they'd heard. Or, had Gardenia somehow heard about the fire and my mistakes? Maybe she wanted Perry to complete the mission on his own and become prince.

My heart jumped and stamped with my decision.

I wanted to be the princess. My heart pumped hard once. I wanted to rule the fairies. On my terms and when I was ready. My heart pumped again.

The realization had crept up on me until this final moment. Between Gardenia's lectures and the professors' teachings. Through Bee's enthusiasm and Arbor's support. Amidst my improving magic and knowledge of the fairy world. I wanted to take my role and be a leader to the fairies.

"Pack your things." Bee's movements were a flurry.

"What?"

She wanted me to go with the guards, even helping me to get packed.

"Didn't you hear Stone?"

I'd heard him. "He agreed to let them take me back to the castle in the morning."

"No, silly." Her indulgent expression confused me.

"I heard him tell the castle guards they could escort me back in the morning." My eyes burned. He hadn't stuck up for my mission.

Bee shoved a jacket into her bag. "He bought you time to escape."

CHAPTER TWELVE

D *id he? Did he really?*

I pondered Stone's response even as I packed my small bag. Did Stone want me to run away? He'd been overprotective from day one. He knew I was the lost princess. He worked for Commander Gardenia, who'd ordered my return. Forcefully if necessary, by the statements of the castle guards.

Swallowing, another thought occurred. My pulse skyrocketed. What if they weren't castle guards or what if they were castle guards but not working for Gardenia? Queen Dahliadew had been poisoned. What if this unknown force was coming after me now?

"Do you really believe Stone wants me to sneak away in the middle of the night?" Like a coward.

"Stone knows you're the lost princess, doesn't he?" Bee fiddled with the back wall of the tent.

"Yes."

She groaned. "I thought so." She stood up and waved her hand. "Can't you see why he's helping you? He understands you need to prove yourself."

I'd never discussed my misgivings with him, and yet he did seem to always understand my needs. For example, when I'd told him I wanted to destroy the auraguillotine, he'd come along with me. To help. Against Gardenia's orders.

Or had it been to protect me? Did he realize these guards weren't legitimate and truly bought me time? It was just a theory, but with the danger at the palace it could be true.

"What about Arbor?" I hated leaving my injured friend.

"She's injured and wouldn't be able to make the rest of the trek. Now the guards are here, she'll be returned to the castle so she can have a healer's attention."

And Bee wouldn't have to stay with her, the thought teased my mind. Except this wasn't about the animosity between Bee and Arbor. This was about me not being taken against my will back to the castle. I wasn't ready to go yet. And if the guards were here to harm me, running away was the right thing.

"Okay." My voice quivered. I'd barely survived the trek so far with an entire team. Bee and I out on the mountain alone was another story entirely. I needed to take one step at a time. Focus on practical things. "How're we going to get out of the tent without being seen?"

Stone and Perry were discussing something outside the tent door. Mumblings from a few of the castle guards could also be heard. They'd see us leave.

"Through the back door." Bee knelt by the wall again and tugged apart two panels.

She'd asked me to put a second exit in. How could she possibly have known?

She waved me out. "Make for the hidden path to the right."

With my small backpack and the Necessary Bag inside, I headed into the dark night. Everything smelled of smoke. The trees appeared darker, spookier, probably because of the fire. Blackened skeletons in the night sky.

"Which way?" I couldn't find the path.

"This way." Bee must've scoped the area out when we first arrived. Good thing one of us knew where we were going.

"What was that?" A guard swiveled in our direction.

I froze and Bee hid behind the trunk of a tree.

After a second, the guard pivoted back around.

Bee hurried through a hedge of bushes similar to a jackrabbit, and I followed. Flinging her bag on top of a rock, she scrambled—an expert climber. I'd never seen her move so fast. She hadn't displayed these skills in front of the team, always hanging back with me. Why did she hide her talents? That would've proved to the others she belonged on the quest.

I stuck my foot in a small crevice. Using my core strength, I pulled myself up the rock. I grabbed a tree root and tugged myself the rest of the way. It was difficult to see in the dark. Smoke blocked the stars.

Bee climbed like a mountain troll, leaping from flat rock to flat rock, not using her wings to fly. Her speed was amazing, yet her movements were jerky. She would've been able to escape the guards no problem. She was already getting far ahead of me. I couldn't let her down.

Pushing myself, I ran faster keeping up with her speed.

We climbed short cliffs, skirted edges with scary drops, and jogged steep paths. My lungs hurt, my legs trembled, and my feet throbbed. I pushed on. The air became thinner and colder. The wind blew stronger. There was no protection.

Reaching a flat piece of rock, I bent, trying to catch my breath. I raised my head and took in the view. The clear night sky shined brightly with stars, the mountain behind us a foreboding shadow. A trail circumvented around the cliff we'd climbed and led down into the valley. Smoke sat on top of the valley in a heavy fog.

Probably caused by my fire.

Squinting, I tried to make out our campsite. I could imagine Arbor asleep in Tos' tent, and Hokima or Perry or Stone standing guard. If it was Stone, I wondered if he knew I was gone. And if so, whether he was staring high into the mountains trying to spot me.

The sensation of being watched felt so real I shivered and wrapped my arms around myself.

"Here." Bee handed me what resembled human binoculars with a strap to attach the object to your head.

"What're these?" I examined the strange equipment.

"Night vision goggles." She adjusted her own set on her head.

"Human tech?" I was surprised a fairy, one who'd lived among fairies her entire life, would have this type of equipment.

Shrugging, she peered at the ground while tightening the straps. "We'll need every advantage to win this war, including using the humans' technology against them."

I'd believed the war would be magic versus technology. The fairies would have an advantage if they used magic *and* tech. Humans didn't have magic. Unless Regent Theobald found another way to steal majiks' powers now that the auraguillotine was destroyed. Maybe they'd already built another one.

Putting on the goggles, I noticed how the world colored an eerie green glow. The trees had ghostly outlines and the stars had glaring silhouettes. I adjusted my goggles and followed her. She'd been prepared for any possibility. The back exit in the tent and the night vision goggles. The hairs on the back of my neck wavered. What other surprises could I expect?

⇝⇝ ⇜⇜

At daybreak, Bee announced it was time for a short rest.

Her take-charge attitude picked at my conscience. I was supposed to be leading this expedition. Originally, I'd given up leadership to Stone, and now I was giving it up to Bee. Yet, she was more prepared than I. She was helping me. A good leader surrounded herself with good people. Bee was good. There'd been no reason for her to run away in the middle of the night except to help me.

Cringing at the last sentiment, I plopped down on a rock and took off the night vision goggles. We'd reached the tree line and the wind howled. I put my hand in my Necessary Bag and pulled out another jacket.

Bee handed me a nutrition bar. "We can't risk making a fire."

My cheeks heated. "I can control my magic."

"It's not that." She donned a gray coat, almost disappearing into the cliffs in the background. "We don't want the guards tracking us."

"You think they will?"

"You're the princess." Her harsh tone cut into me. "They were sent by Commander Gardenia to bring you back. Of course, they'll search for you."

I bit my bottom lip, hating the doubts about sneaking out without informing Stone. Bee was my friend and I could express those things to her. "Maybe if we went back, I could explain to the guards the need to go to Aristos Sanctuary."

Bee's raw laugh had the ring of cynicism. "You think they'll take your word over the commander's?"

"I am the princess. Next in line to the throne, and all." I tried to make light of my status.

"Ha!" Her expression went stiff and cold. "Commander Gardenia has been in command for so long, she believes she's the rightful ruler."

My stomach dropped almost as far as we'd climbed. I'd joked with Gardenia about that very fact. Had I struck closer to the truth than I'd realized? And here, I thought Perry was my biggest threat.

"What I mean is, she acts like Regent Theobald. And we hate what he's doing, don't we?" For some reason, Bee didn't sound convincing.

How could any fairy, any majik for that matter, respect what the regent had done?

"When Prince Zacharye takes control of things, it will be different." The need to defend Rye jumped to my lips. I still believed in him, didn't I?

I'd spent a few hours with him and believed I'd known him. We'd had a connection. Or was it only me? He'd lied from the beginning until the very end when I'd discovered he was the prince. I'd lied to him too though, and then made my escape from the exploding portion of the castle.

"The prince will never get control." Bee's vindictive tone sent shock through my system.

"How do you know?" I glowered until she squirmed.

"Even if he does, he'll adhere to the same policies." She seemed so sure.

While I was unsure. Unsure about Rye and his beliefs even though he'd signed the evil decree. Unsure about Gardenia. Things were being thrown at warp speed and I needed time on my own to figure things out.

Rest over, we headed up a steep path where rocks tumbled down as we walked.

I shouldn't have run away. I should've confronted the royal guard and told them to take a message to Gardenia. And yet, she'd championed adding Perry to the team. He also had royal blood so he could get in with the priestesses. If I didn't accomplish my goal at the sanctuary, would he get the chance to complete the quest?

And if he did, would that win him the fairy throne?

I grabbed a rock jutting out and pulled myself up. "Do you think Commander Gardenia would prefer Perry to ascend the fairy throne over me?"

"She forced you to take him on the mission." Bee tossed me a serious expression. "She knows who he is, and she knows he tried to kill you."

My pulse ticked upwards. "I didn't tell Gardenia about the training session where he almost killed me. I didn't know who he was at the time."

Bee scoffed even as she hurtled around a large boulder. "Commander Gardenia knows. She knows everything."

Except apparently whatever Bee had planned.

My belly churned. I'd trusted people in my past and they'd betrayed me. If I questioned her tactics now, would she turn on me? Leave me stranded on the side of a mountain and fly off on her wings? How could I ask without asking?

"When and where will we sleep?" If I could catch up on sleep, my mind wouldn't be fuzzy. I was physically and mentally exhausted.

"We've got to stay ahead of the guards." She mounted a boulder and jumped down on the other side. "We can rest when we get there."

With Stone, we'd had a day left of hiking. I gripped another outcropping and struggled to get to the top of the rock. My hands were raw. "Get to the Aristos Sanctuary?"

Bee jogged around a corner, not answering.

Of course, we were going to the sanctuary. It was the purpose of the trip.

Pushing my muscles into action, I followed. The route became steeper and every one of my limbs ached and my bones creaked. The barely discernible gravel path became narrower and more treacherous. My feet slipped on the rocks. We were climbing straight up, not taking the winding trail I remembered from Gardenia's maps. Maps I'd studied. My breath became labored, leaving me gasping and wheezing.

I tapped Bee's arm when I finally caught her. "Is this a shortcut?"

She breathed heavily as well. "Y-y-yes. The original plan was to take the roundabout trail because the climb wouldn't be as arduous for everyone. We're going straight up to be quicker."

My forehead scrunched and I glanced at my father's watch. "It's late morning. If this is a shortcut, shouldn't we be able to see the sanctuary by now?"

She swiveled quickly and lost her step. "We're approaching from the backside."

"Even so—"

"You ready for a break?" She dropped her bag on a small outcropping of rock.

"Yes. For sprites sake, yes." My sore body protested every movement. "Aren't you tired?"

"Exhausted."

So, I wasn't in terrible shape.

"Snack?" She thought of everything.

My mouth salivated. "Yessss."

Bee must be the most prepared fairy ever. She tossed a packaged-and-ready meal to me. Stone had meals similar to this stored in the safe room we'd used hidden inside Regent Theobald's palace. High in protein and nutrition. They were the best way to refuel a depleted body.

"Thanks."

She was as prepared as Stone when he'd been a spy in the human palace. I ripped open the pouch and started sucking down the tart apple taste. Pondering the comparison, I continued to eat to keep up my strength.

After finishing her snack, she used her backpack as a pillow. Light snoring signaled her sleep. I sized her up. She'd saved me from Perry and wanted to be my friend, not knowing who I was yet. When I'd told her about the princess thing, she'd kept my secret. She'd begged to come on the mission. She supported me. And she'd definitely been prepared.

Why?

Doubt niggled in my brain. I wished I could peek inside her backpack and learn her secrets. Although she'd shared her biggest secret. She was a servant in the castle while attending school. And I could totally relate.

I must've drifted off with my thoughts because a noise woke me.

Pounding or marching or something.

I blinked. Fairy-shaped shadows shaded the spot where I slept. Not just fairies. Royal guard fairies.

My heart pounded, matching their marching feet. Scanning around, I searched for Bee. She was gone. She must've run off when the guards approached even though she had nothing to run from. The guards were after me.

The pulse at my wrist went into panic mode, flittering and fluttering. Blood rushed to my head, making me dizzy. I'd relied on my friend too much. It was my chance to argue or fight.

I scrambled to my feet and grabbed for the whip at my waist.

Two guards rounded the turn, tucking their wings behind them. Their hiking boots appeared to be mostly clean. They'd flown while Bee and I had hiked and hurried and climbed and crawled. Had Bee's shortcut been a long-cut? A way to shake the guards from our tail?

One male and one female wearing castle guard uniforms of mostly green with purple accents approached. They must be advanced scouts.

I hid the whip behind my back. "Can I help you?"

I spoke with an accent, trying to hide my true identity. Did they know who I was? That I was the one they'd been ordered to take back to Queens Academy? Maybe these weren't the same guards.

"Ellery Milford?" the clean-shaven male guard asked.

The blood racing to my head dropped to my stomach with a heavy thud. I'd been caught and now I'd have to hike down the stupid mountain. "Um, who wants to know?"

"I'm Captain Briarhop." The female guard gave a slight bow. "And I'm under orders from Commander Gardenia to escort you back to Queens Academy."

Twisting my hands together, I refused to go along with them. I didn't know if Gardenia was for me or against me. I didn't know if these guards were working under her orders even if they said so.

"Do you know who you're talking to?" I dropped the ridiculous accent and mimicked the queen's uppity tone.

The male guard held up a celltab which had a photo of me on its shiny surface. "Ellery Milford."

"And do you know *who* I am?" Was I going to have to tell him I was the princess, or did he already know?

He gave a confused look to his partner. "Ellery Milford."

"Yes, I know I'm Ellery Milford." Firming my lips, I tilted my chin in an attempt to glance down at the man. "Do you know *what* I am?"

Their confused expressions didn't change. They must not know I'm the princess. Had Gardenia kept it secret for my protection, or for hers and Perry's?

"We're under orders to escort you back to the castle," she repeated, treating me as a slow-minded idiot.

I huffed a frazzled breath. "I won't go back without a fight."

"Your wish is my command, Your Majesty." Bee jumped down from above, wielding a glinting sword. "En guard."

Chapter Thirteen

Before I had time to react, Bee was taking on both guards. Swords clashed and the guards fluttered their wings.

I gasped. I didn't mean fight fight. I meant a discussion or an argument. They were probably my own castle guards. I wanted to explain to them how important my mission was, or to order them, if needed. I was their princess. Of course, I didn't know if they'd believe me.

Bee's weapon flung with un-fairylike speed as she overpowered the two winged guards. She'd come from a position of strength between the surprise attack and aggressive maneuvers. Her sureness with the blade signified she was a trained fighter. She'd never told me.

The guards fought from defensive positions. The first guard jumped toward Bee and followed with a lunge.

I sucked in a jagged wheeze. "Stop!" I didn't want anyone getting injured. We could talk this out. Skirting back, I believed the guards wouldn't harm me, just arrest me, and keep me in custody. They had no need to hold back on my friend. I had to help her.

Drawing my whip, I fiddled with the end, waiting for an opening. I didn't want to hurt them or return to the castle with them. Bee had given me an opportunity to carry on my mission.

"Don't kill. Only defend or injure." I whispered to the whip and sent the notched rope flying.

The whip wrapped around the male guard's legs and tugged tight. He fell to the ground.

A short thrill went through me at my success. I retrieved the whip and struck again while he lay on the ground. The whip wrapped around his arms and shoulders and held him down. The man could do no harm.

A lightness filled me at the completed job, but this battle wasn't over. It was Bee against the female guard.

"Stop, fighting!" Everything hammered inside my ribcage.

Bee didn't listen. She performed a stop hit, an advanced move where the second guard came at her and she counterattacked, changing it into an assault on the guard. She had hidden skills I wasn't aware of. Apparently, she could've fought off Perry when we'd first met. Why had she hidden her prowess for fighting?

She lunged, and the guard parried. She lunged again and brought her back foot forward in an awkward action.

Twisting my hands together, I watched with horror. I didn't want anyone to die.

The guard pushed Bee back. She renewed her offensive action. Her blade whirled and clattered.

She left an unprotected space by her chest and I squealed. "Watch it!"

Unflinching, she let the guard parry into her space, and she feinted. She used the guard's irregular position to go for the blade.

The guard's sword went flying.

I let out the breath I didn't know I'd been holding.

She pressed the edge of her blade to the guard's throat.

I remembered that feeling of utter helplessness. "Bee, no!"

These guards were loyal to the crown. A crown I would wear in the future.

She snarled, her lips twisting in an ugly pout. "We can't let them go. They'll follow us or return to the group and tell them our location."

A good point.

Biting my lip, I tried to think of a solution.

While holding the second guard in position, she fiddled with something in her pocket and pulled out a round, shiny disc.

The object looked familiar.

Releasing the fairy she held, she tossed the disc between the two guards.

An explosion combusted and echoed off the cliffs.

The deafening blast set off a low hissing in my ears. My heart slowed, pushing the blood through my veins in huge proportions, and then burst. The sensation was familiar, and yet the opposite of something I'd experienced before when Stone had saved me from the human guards in the palace. When Bim had died.

Bee held her head, experiencing the same agony as I was. The guard she'd fought collapsed to the ground. Her chest stopped moving. The guard I had wrapped in my whip's cord quit struggling.

My racing pulse screeched to a halt and continued at a more normal pace. "What happened?"

She helped me untangle the whip from around the guard. "The guards are dead. We need to get out of here."

"Dead?" I stumbled. Affected by the noise or the deaths I wasn't sure.

She tugged on my hand and pulled me away from the scene. "The blast is going to bring every guard, fairy, and troll to this area."

My whip dragged behind me like my spirits. Touching my forehead, I tried to pull myself together. The fight. The deafening blast. The death. How could a loud noise kill them? My mind whirled while I tried to process. How could I process something so terrifying?

Bee continued dragging me up the path. I didn't resist. I was too dazed. My friend was more loyal to me than the queen, and I wasn't sure if that was a good thing. Her determination to help might be taking me in the wrong direction.

"Why did you kill the guards?" My voice strangled. "Against my orders."

"They were going to take you to the castle." She didn't let go of my hand, tugging me uphill. "I thought you didn't want to go back."

"I didn't, but they were *castle guards*." A silent scream rent through my chest. I appreciated her friendship, except she'd gone against our own side. Gone against what we were fighting for. "They were contained and were on our side."

"They were from the same contingent of guards at our camp."

"We didn't kill those guards. We ran away." Which I felt bad about, and now felt ten times worse.

"It's war." Her frigid tone came across as callous. "Humans and fairies, trolls and brownies, ogres and smoke sprites are going to die on both sides."

Rage filled adrenaline spiked through me. Why didn't she understand? "We aren't fighting against the castle guards."

Pausing in her rapid hike, she glanced back. Her cold and calculating gaze told a different story. She blinked, and the coldness was gone.

The rage twisted into panic at what we'd done. "We need to go back. Maybe they're alive." I couldn't be part of this.

"They're not alive." She tightened her grip around my wrist and pulled me harder. "That was a UNAD, Unnatural Acoustic Discord."

My jaw dropped. I angled my head to stare at the back of hers. "I know what a NAD is. It kills humans."

It was the device Stone had given to Bim to attack human guards. About a dozen of them had died from the blast. Stone and I had been affected because we were both half human. It hadn't killed us. The sound had been the opposite of natural white noise and intense enough to kill.

The torment in my head had been the exact opposite of what happened this time. "The castle guards were full fairies so the NAD shouldn't affect them."

"This device, the UNAD, kills majiks." Bee yanked on my arm to hurry me up. She showed no sympathy for me or the dead guards.

Stone had explained how the NAD was dangerous to me because my half human side would be affected and experience the pain. This device must've affected my half fairy side. The agony had been as intense as before. This time it was my half human side that had kept me alive.

"The fairies invented the NAD to kill humans. Why would the fairies invent a second version capable of killing their own?"

"Where do you think the fairies got the idea from?" Her superior-knowing tone sliced through me.

I jerked to a stop, pulling her to a halt. "You're half human."

She lifted her head and didn't say a word.

I was right. "Why didn't you tell me?" I'd confessed to her the same secret.

It was another thing we had in common. She understood the conflict I had within myself. It's why I'd felt an affinity toward her from the moment we'd met.

Shrugging, she pivoted forward and started to walk. "I don't know."

My ribcage expanded. "It's why you wanted to become my friend. You understood me more deeply than anyone else." There were more half majiks than I'd thought. Stone, and now Bee. There had to be others. "Is that why you don't have any friends at the academy? They know you're half fairy, so they hate you."

She didn't respond, just kept going.

If the other students hated Bee because she was half fairy, they must hate me more for other reasons. "I thought they hated me because I'd lived in the human world and tried to pass as human. If they hate you and you've lived among the fairies there's a deeper resentment."

My thoughts continued to go wild with the revelation. We trudged up steep inclines and scrambled over rocks. I barely noticed because my brain was in a whirlwind. There were more of us halfs. There had to be. What did that mean for me though?

I kicked at a rock and it went sailing off the edge of the cliff. I knew it meant one thing. "The fairies will never accept me as princess."

Bee whirled around. "Quit making this about you."

The vehemence in her tone cut me in half. She was right. We had more important things to consider, for example why we hadn't reached the sanctuary yet. And, how she'd killed two castle guards and I was an accomplice.

She rolled up her fists and pretended to wipe her eyes. "Poor me. I'm a princess."

"I don't sound like that." Hurt vibrated to my soul. I thought she was my friend. Why was she making fun of me?

"You do." She scrunched up her face and mimicked. "*Nobody likes me or will accept me. I was a servant for my stepfamily. And I'm not going to tell anyone about what happened under the human palace. Let them speculate. My magic will become stronger once I'm trained.*"

Her mimicking scraped a raw nerve.

"They will accept me." Everything firmed inside me. I had to believe. "And it's not all about me."

"Could have fooled me and everyone else on this trip."

My lips pursed. "You wanted to come along on my mission."

"*My* mission." She mimicked me again.

Maybe her and Arbor would've gotten along if Bee knew Arbor did impressions too.

"*My* magic." Bee backed up toward the wall of the cliff, away from me closer to the edge. "*My* future role as princess." She took another step back. "You only think about yourself!"

The accusations stabbed in my chest. Is that what she really thought? I wasn't all about myself, was I? The oxygen in my lungs leaked out. I did think about my problems a lot. Worried what people were thinking or their impression of me. Concerned about how they'd react to me being half human, and royalty. Tormented by what they said behind my back.

No wonder my impact at school had been negative—first with the humans and now with the fairies.

"*Skreeeep. Skreeeeeeep. Skreeeep.*"

My gaze darted to the sky. A Wyvern flew overhead. A monstrous, fire-breathing dragon willing to kill anything.

The solid thoughts I had vanished from my head. Terror scraped down my spine.

The dragon swooped closer. Its shadows casted a dark pall. Fire shot from its mouth and the air fouled with the smell of rot.

Bee scrambled against the cliff face. She scooted into a small crevice and blended into the rock. There was no space for me to hide. Plus, after what she said about me, I had to prove it wasn't all about me by saving her.

The dragon passed between me and the drop on the other side of the cliff. Its large orange snout barely missed me, and I shivered. Its luminescent scales shined with the sunlight. Its teeth were bigger than my hands. The creature was scary and beautiful.

Ducking down, my heels almost slipped off the edge. Small rocks tumbled over. The *clink, clink, clink* of the stones foretold my fate if I fell.

I had nowhere to run. Nowhere to hide.

Grabbing my coiled whip, I stood to face the threat. I didn't whine all the time. My spine went ramrod straight. I wouldn't be cowered by a dragon.

The dragon blasted another flame. The heat from the fire was more intense than the forest fire I'd started. A different heat burned inside me. The heat of horror.

I kept my glare on the animal, refusing to express fear. There wasn't a place to hide and I couldn't jump down. So, I'd fight.

I'd show Bee I wasn't a complainer. Show her I'd gotten past my history of being a servant. My heart skidded. I'd never told Bee about my stepfamily.

Glancing back, I studied her. How had she known?

"Skreeeep. Skreeeeeeep. Skreeeep."

No time to consider my friend's information. I jerked back around to face the dragon. Everything slowed down.

The dragon's claws shaped in a curled position. Its shadow overcame my own leaving me in darkness. The dragon was right above me.

Every part of me shook. My shoulders curled trying to become smaller. My body quivered. I grabbed my whip and cast it back.

Sharp talons pierced through my clothes and skin. The stinging pain didn't dull my fear, only enhanced my terror. The dragon had me in its clutches.

The whip's tip dropped down from the wind created by the dragon's wings.

Alarm scraped out of my throat. "Help!"

Bee's eyes went wide. Her expression of horror multiplied my own.

The dragon would rip me apart and kill me. I already smelled blood. I glanced at my left shoulder. My blood. Trying to lift my arm to cast the whip, agony shot through my shoulder and my arm fell to my side. Something was damaged. Gripping the whip, I realized I had no defenses. Terror charged and scratched up my throat and I screamed.

The dragon flapped its long wings, creating a breeze. Its hot breath and rotten smell made me sick.

My feet lifted off the ground and the dragon carried me away.

Chapter Fourteen

Gasp upon gasp rushed out from between my numb lips as the dragon carried me higher.

My lungs shrunk and I couldn't breathe. Freezing wind hit my face, numbing my skin. Excruciating pain ripped through my shoulders where the talons pinched my skin. Blood seeped through my clothes.

The world pulled away as we flew high in the sky. My gaze and mind went fuzzy. The mountains didn't seem so majestic from up here. The snowcapped peaks resembled ice cream sundaes and the tree line circled the edge like a bowl. The trees blended, and the paths looked similar to a child's scribbles.

I must be delusional. Panic gripped me, sending icy tendrils through my veins as I returned to reality. Maybe I'd already lost too much blood and was dying a slow death.

Kicking my legs, I struggled to get free. Yet, if the dragon dropped me, I'd die from the fall. My body went limp and I let my legs dangle. Was this going to be my end? To be eaten by a dragon? Why hadn't the dragon eaten where he'd captured me? He could've eaten Bee, too. Although, I was glad she wouldn't suffer the same fate as me, even though I was mad at her.

I scraped in another panicked gasp.

A second dragon, with the same orange coloring, flew to the side. Smaller, but just as deadly. The young dragon had fire-red pupils and sharp teeth. Its wings weren't as big as the dragon carrying me, but they were powerful enough to create a backdraft as it circled around.

The little dragon flew closer. Quirking its head, its red gaze inspected me. Maybe the small dragon had never seen a fairy before. Maybe I was going to be this one's lunch. Could be why the big dragon hadn't eaten me on the spot.

"Eeep. Eeep." The squeak seemed familiar.

The squeak sounded like... "Drago?"

The red eyes widened, and his mouth opened in what my delusional mind thought was a smile. If he was Drago, he'd gotten big. Last time I'd seen him he'd fit in my purse.

Crazy laughter bubbled out. I really must be imagining things. Of all the mountains in all the kingdom, what were the chances Drago would be here? I'd tried to rescue him when I'd been under Regent Theobald's palace. Then again, every dragon came from this part of Alandaska. If Drago escaped the palace, it would make sense he'd return to where the other dragons lived.

Hope built, lightening some of the torment. "Drago?"

His expression didn't change. Were dragons even able to change expressions? I didn't know. I hadn't taken the dragon class.

The large dragon sped up.

I tried to twist my head back to see Drago. Pain shot through my shoulders and neck. My throat choked with bile. The possibility of the small dragon being Drago was miniscule. And even if it was, would he save me because I'd saved him?

The small dragon buzzed around the top of the big dragon. The small dragon's wings fluttered. Determination shone in its gaze.

The larger dragon shook its head.

I flopped one way and the other. "Ahhh!" I stiffened as stabbing agony ricocheted through my body. I sucked in a sharp breath. Not from the pain. From the fear of being dropped by accident and falling to my death.

The dragon stopped shaking and I went limp. Increasing its speed, it flew straight for the top of a rocky ledge high on a mountain. My stomach revolted.

I tried to search for the little dragon. Drago. It had to be him.

Drago's wings flapped back and forth in an excited motion. Did he think I was about to die too?

The mountain loomed closer. It was about fifty yards away. I could make out the crags in the rocks. The muscles in my body tightened. Afraid to see my own demise, I squeezed my eyes closed. Was I going to be rammed into the side of the cliff or was the dragon going to eat me? I wasn't sure which would be worse.

My legs rammed into what resembled concrete. Agony burst from my feet and up my calves. "Ahhhhhhhh!"

Forcing my eyes open, I glanced down. My feet hung limply from my ankles. They must've hit the edge of the ledge we'd flown over. My feet had to be broken. Throbbing radiated up both my legs. They were scraped and bleeding. I'd never walk again.

If I lived.

The dragon's claws eased from beneath my skin. Fresh blood flowed, soaking more reddish-brown into my shirt and jacket. My head felt dizzy.

And then the dragon released me.

Breath whooshed out.

I fell and fell and fell.

The dizziness multiplied. My eyes dropped to the back of my head. I was going to plunge to my death, or at least severe injury.

And the dragons would eat my bloody carcass.

I hit the ground with a *thump*.

My body flopped from the impact and agony shot through every part of me. Laying there, I analyzed my core and each limb. I was in too much torment to be dead. Death would be a welcome oblivion. Struggling, I peeked.

The big dragon was gone. The small dragon hovered watching, presumably checking to see if I was alive. Our gazes made contact. Who-I-believed-to-be-Drago flew off.

My throat thickened, and tears burned. I should be relieved the dragons didn't eat me, but I felt bereft. The two dragons could come back. An exhalation shattered through my lungs, torturing my aching ribs. A vulture could come to investigate. I should hide.

I tried to move, sit up, crawl, anything. Pain rocketed through my entire body. Everything hurt—from my eyeballs to my toes. Bleeding, broken, and bruised. And the worst part: I was alone.

All alone.

I struggled to open my eyes. An agonizing convulsion shot through my body and radiated in waves of pain. My dry mouth craved water. My head pounded and I shivered.

The low sun in the sky told me it was evening. I must've blacked out. Hours must've passed. I was alive, not eaten by dragons or vultures. Worry threaded across my skin, pulling tight. For how long?

I tried to move. Misery overtook me. Groaning, I did my best to get my broken body to curl into a fetal position. The night would get colder. Hypothermia was another way to die.

A bright light floated toward me. The luminescent glow reminded me of an Air Fairy. The light circled around and around showing me the way. I wanted to reach for the light. To touch it and embrace it.

The lighted orb grew bigger and came closer. I wasn't going toward the light as if I were dying. The light was moving toward me. Relief swooshed through me. I wasn't ready to die. I needed to help the fairies win the war.

Colors flashed and swirled in a round orb. Shapes formed.

Stone standing in the forest, a grim expression on his face. His emotion came off him in waves. Desperation and sorrow. He yelled something at a group of soldiers. They were searching for something. Someone.

Me.

I jerked awake. The dark night enshrouded me. The vision had been a dream.

I was still injured. Still alone.

The hissing of a vulture sent a chill down my spine.

I didn't care much because I was freezing. My teeth chattered and the goosebumps on my skin were as high as mountains. My stomach growled. Hunger was a good sign. It proved I still cared about eating. Except I didn't have any food or water or anything.

The orb glinted in front of me. The light was filled with gold. Gold cloud. Gold trees. Gold throne.

The throne room at Queens Academy where everything had changed to gold.

I glanced up and saw the night sky shining. Was I back home? Stone must've found me and brought me back.

My spirits rose. "Hey! I'm here."

No one came at my call. I could see but no one saw me. Or heard me.

A crowd gathered around the floating cloud with the throne chair. The fairies ranted and shouted. Not shouts of celebration, but of anger. Their faces were snarling and fierce.

From behind the chair, Gardenia emerged. She'd aged since I'd gone on my mission. Her hair was gray, and wrinkles formed on her face. Her eyes had lost their sparkle.

"Boo! Boo!" The crowd jeered my fairy godmother.

"Silence!" She cast a spell over the fairies, and they quieted.

I couldn't believe what I was seeing. She'd been loved and respected. Why did they hate her now?

"It's time to crown the new ruler of the fairies." She revealed a crown made of heavy gold.

It wasn't the tiara that Queen Dahliadew had worn. If they were crowning the new queen, which would be me, then Queen Dahliadew had died.

Sadness because I'd never get to know her, never get to learn from her, pierced my heart. Leaving without permission had been a mistake.

Gardenia bowed to a shadow behind the chair. "Let me introduce your new king."

King?

"King Perry."

I jolted awake. Panting, my ribs pulled, and pain radiated out.

It had been a dream. Only a dream.

More like a nightmare. If Perry became king, that meant I...

...I died.

Probably here on the side of this mountain. The glacial night would freeze me to death. The vultures would pick my bones clean and no one would know what happened to me. I wished the dragons would return with their flames. Burning and being eaten alive would be quicker than freezing to death.

The moon was high in the night sky. I stared at its golden glow. My eyes flickered.

The now-familiar orb showed a different palace. One I'd been to before, except not this location. This view came through one of the tall glass spires. If I were dreaming, how would I know what the human palace looked like in places I hadn't been? My mind created details it didn't know.

The sleek hallway with winding glass steps going up and up and up. This was the tallest tower in the palace, and I didn't know its purpose.

"Stop. I'm the rightful ruler."

My heart leapt hearing Rye's voice. A raw and strained voice.

Two men wearing black came into view. In between them, they carried Rye.

Swooning, I didn't think I'd ever get to see him again. My gaze swallowed him up.

His long legs and broad shoulders. His bruised mouth—

My gaze stopped. His kissable lips were swollen. One eye was black and blue. His head wasn't wearing a crown, but a bandage seeping with his own blood.

Horror rose, as did bile in my throat.

"I'm Prince Zacharye. You should be loyal to me." He twisted and fought against his captors.

"Orders of King Theobald."

"My uncle is not the king!"

One of the men slapped Rye across the face. "He will be soon. Better get used to it."

Rye glared, refusing to show pain or cowardice. He was a fighter.

"Or not." The second man laughed. "You won't be around to see the coronation."

Agony stabbed through my chest and shot through the rest of my body. My eyes flickered open. Were these dreams or nightmares? Visions or warnings?

If I survived this, I'd come back stronger and fiercer. I'd fight for the fairies and my crown. I'd send spies to find out what was happening in the human palace, and I'd help whoever assisted the majiks in their quest.

Forcing my eyelids to stay open, I fought to stay awake. If I slept, I'd be giving up. And I wasn't going to give up again.

The light of dawn broke. I'd made it through the night. The torture inside my body paralyzed me. Everything was broken or torn or bruised. I couldn't even assess the internal injuries. I couldn't move. How was I going to get out of here and find help?

A shuffling caught my attention.

Shifting my head, I stopped myself from screaming out in pain, and then fear.

A troll stood a few feet away. The toes on its large feet curled and stuck out, resembling claws. Its thin legs exhibited dirt and wrinkles. The shift and coat it wore had holes and stains. Its smell wafted my way and I felt nauseous. Its enormous head was highlighted by a humongous mouth with pointy teeth and a bulbous nose. The eyes bulged from their sockets. Hairy eyebrows curled into horns.

Trolls weren't bad. I had a friend who was a troll. But rumors of what trolls ate, or should I say who, trolls ate curled in my stomach. This troll stomped toward me, holding a sharp spear.

Cold sweat broke out on my back. My pulse ticked as if I was about to explode. I wouldn't die of hypothermia, or be torched by a dragon, or eaten by a vulture. I was going to die by the sinewy hands of a troll.

Willing my hand to my side, I fisted my fingers around my whip. The weapon had created miraculous things in other fights. Hopefully, it would come to my aid.

The handle hummed between my fingers. I used my mind to communicate. *Defend.*

The whip lay limp in my hand. Uselessness clung to me. I'd vowed to fight a dragon. Now, I couldn't defend myself against a troll.

The troll paced forward. Its hunched body leaned on the spear. Its gaze analyzed me.

"Defend." My voice was weak, raw, barely above a whisper.

Frustration and fear spiked in my head. My stomach tied in knots. I was too feeble, too injured, to fight or even defend myself.

The troll raised the spear, ready to attack.

I sucked in a sharp breath. The whip wasn't working, and I didn't know why. This could be my end. "What do you want?"

"You."

Chapter Fifteen

I woke up to darkness.

Not the darkness of night though. I was deep in a cave. Blankets surrounded me, keeping me warm as I laid on a soft bed. My body hurt, except it wasn't the all-consuming agony I'd felt earlier.

Assessing my situation, I struggled to keep my eyes open. First, I wasn't dead. A good thing. Second, the pain had lessened, although I didn't understand why. Third, someone had carried me into the cave and taken care of me.

Flames flickered near the front of the cave. A dark shape bent over, tending a fire.

My body started to shake. Fear tried to grip me. I couldn't find the strength. I couldn't remember anything since the troll had approached. It hadn't attacked though. I remembered the spear coming towards me, and curving away, coming forward and curving away—a pattern drawn in the sky.

On instinct, I grasped for the whip at my side. The weapon was gone.

"The Silver Snare is safe." The troll spun around in a slow shift. "Your whip."

My whip had a name? How did the troll know I'd been reaching for something?

"I know because I do."

I stiffened. Was the troll reading my mind?

"I'm not reading your thoughts." The troll sounded old and feminine. A female troll? "I know because that would be a normal thought process."

Nothing about this situation was normal. How would a troll know what I thought? What a human or a fairy would think? I frowned. I'd never been prejudiced against other majiks. In the past, it was only the fairies I didn't want to be a part of. My friend Hokima was a troll. He'd loved and lost and was brave and trustworthy.

I swallowed and my dry throat burned. "Where am I?" *And what are you going to do with me?*

The troll poured a steaming liquid from a pitcher into a cup. She wasn't wearing the rags I remembered. The clothes she wore now appeared snug and flexible. "You're thirsty."

Licking my lips, I wasn't so sure I believed she wasn't a mind reader.

"This will help with your injuries." She held the cup to my mouth, and I took a sip.

The liquid soothed my throat and my mind.

"Dragons." I jolted and tried to sit up. The dragons had attacked me and Bee. What had happened to her? "My friend—"

"You're in no shape to rescue anyone." The troll pushed me back onto the bed and covered me with a blanket up to my shoulders. "If your friend was attacked by a dragon, either she survived, or she didn't."

The troll seemed nonchalant. Apparently coming across someone who'd been attacked by a dragon was an everyday occurrence. Maybe it was for this troll. My gut roiled. What about my other friends? Where were Stone, Perry, Tos, and Hokima? Were they searching for me or did they believe I was dead?

"I won't hurt you. I'm Watu." She lowered her head suspiciously like a bow. "And you are?"

My lungs closed up. I wasn't sure what to say because I didn't want this stranger knowing the truth. Several truths. I was half fairy and half human. I was the lost princess. I was completely lost. I didn't know if I could trust her, even if she had saved my life. I didn't know which side she was on, whether she'd give me to my enemies. I didn't even know who my enemies were at this point.

"You don't know? You can't read my mind?"

"I'm not a mind reader. I'm observant." She helped me with another sip. A longer sip. A sip calming my panic.

If I told her I was a princess, would she treat me differently? Use me as a bargaining chip? "I'm Elle."

"Welcome...Elle."

Did the strange pause mean something? Could Watu sense I'd left so much out?

"This will make you feel better." She helped me with another sip.

"Are you a doctor?"

Quirking her head, she watched me. "You are half human."

I choked on the liquid. "How did you know?"

"Humans use the term doctor."

Normally, trolls didn't spend any time with humans. How would she know this fact? I continued to sip. The drink didn't taste specific. It could have been anything from hot water, to broth, to coffee. The liquid flowed down my throat and spread warmth throughout my chest and midsection.

"I've studied the healing arts."

Worry knotted inside. "Do you know what my other half is?"

"Fairy, of course."

I furrowed my brow. She was so positive I was half fairy. "How do you know?"

"When I cleaned the wounds on your back, I saw the pedicles where your wings will come out."

"My what!" My roiling belly churned and burned up my throat. I tried to twist around. Realizing that was stupid, I flailed my arm, trying to touch the middle of my back. Pain shot from my shoulder and I collapsed onto the bed. I didn't know I had pedicles.

"This is a new development for you."

"I didn't think I'd ever get wings." My voice went high, part thrill and part panic.

"Fire Fairies develop magic late. Since you are half fairy, it makes logical sense your wings would sprout later than most."

My spirits flew. I could get wings. That didn't change the fact I was terrible with magic. For example, the fire and the damage it caused Arbor. "Doesn't matter. I'm a terrible fairy."

And a terrible friend. I'd abandoned Arbor, Stone, Tos, and Hokima to sneak away with Bee. I didn't know what had happened to her. And a terrible princess because I'd disregarded the queen's wishes and Gardenia's orders and went on the mission anyhow.

"Training and practice are needed."

"You sound like my fairy godmother."

The commander's comments stuck in my head. Gardenia was the one who'd ordered the troops to bring me back. My friends were probably headed back to the castle. I held in a sob. Or Perry was leading the mission because I'd deserted them.

I tried to sit up. The pain had me lying back down again. "What's wrong with me? What's broken?" Because surely, I had more than one broken bone. "How long will it take for my injuries to heal?"

"Impatience is not a virtue." Her strange rhythm of speech clicked through my brain.

"My friend might've been attacked by dragons, too. No one will search for her."

No one on my team would care. I didn't understand why Arbor and Stone and Perry distrusted Bee.

Watu took the empty mug and turned away. "You can do nothing to help your friend now. Rest."

My eyelids felt heavy.

"Dream." More command than a suggestion.

My eyelids slammed shut and I couldn't force them open.

"Conquer."

The last word whispered into my consciousness and everything went black.

When the colorful orb appeared to me, I knew I'd follow its light.

Arbor lay on a bed in a hospital. It wasn't a human hospital with medical cyborgs attending her. Healers, not doctors, floated around her small bed. Birds sung a beautiful melody and the buzzing of bees harmonized.

My heart squeezed. Was this helping her or was she already dead?

Angling closer in the dream, I tried to see Arbor's chest moving or her eyelids flicker.

Jerking awake, I slammed my fist onto the mattress where I lay. If I had to have these terrible dreams, then I wanted to see what I wanted. I shivered. I didn't know if Arbor was alive or dead.

Tears burned and it wasn't from pain. The torture from my injuries had lessened even more. That couldn't have happened in a few hours. How long had I slept? I didn't know what time of day it was or even *what* day it was. Confusion rattled my brain. Leaning on my good arm, I tried to peer toward the front of the cave.

Nature was calling. And so was escape.

I inched my feet toward the edge of the platform bed. My legs got caught in the large shift I wore.

"Asking for help isn't a crime." Watu spoke in her strange lyrical tone.

Guess I wasn't going to get away and find my friends. "I need to relieve myself."

"Of course." She shuffled over, her large feet dragging in the dirt, and handed me a stick. "For balance."

Peering at my feet, I noted the purplish bruises, red lacerations, and swelling. "My feet—"

"Will be tender and painful."

"I thought they were both broken." The way they'd smashed into the side of the mountain and dangled from my ankles.

"They were." She helped me to stand.

Dizziness swarmed my head. It took weeks for broken bones to heal, even with modern technology. "What? How?"

"I told you I was a healer."

"A gifted healer."

Leaning heavily on the stout stick, I took a small step. Pain throbbed around my feet and ankles, but I was standing. And if my feet were fixed, I could walk away, make my escape. Except I didn't know where I was or how to get back. I needed to dig for information.

Her lips lifted in a knowing smile. "This way."

Had she read my thoughts or was paranoia setting in? She'd taken care of me and helped with my injuries. My ribs were bruised. My shoulders burned and felt sticky under the cloth shift she must've dressed me in.

My gaze darted around, looking for my clothes and my whip. The Silver Snare.

The pallet I laid on was built into the side of the cave. The flat stone of the floor had been swept clean and coldness infiltrated my bruised feet. A small fire burned with a tripod balanced above, holding a metal pot. The smoke from the fire drifted lazily out a small hole in the roof of the cave. Old trunks lined the walls. Bright light came through the cave entrance blinding me.

When we reached the doorway, she directed me to a small covered area with a bush. "You can't walk too far."

I took care of business and she helped me back to the pallet and covered me with blankets. My limbs trembled from the exertion. The little bit of exercise had exhausted me. My spirits sagged. No way could I take off on my own.

"Where are we?" I'd asked once before and hadn't gotten a straight answer.

"Terrenholm Cavern."

I'd never heard of the place. "Are there other trolls nearby?" Maybe one of them knew Hokima.

"No. This place is high above Aristos Sanctuary."

If Watu lived close, maybe she could get a message to them. "Do you know the priestesses?"

"I know of them." She carried another steaming mug to me. "As you do."

"Surely, you know more than me." I knew barely anything. Sipping from the mug, I let the hot liquid soothe my body. There was something relaxing about the drink. "Thank you."

Her mysterious smile set me on edge. "Surely, you know more than you think."

I let the strange comment sink in. I did know more now than I had a few moments ago. "How far is it to the sanctuary?"

"Depends on your strength and your will."

Another puzzling response. Did she not give straight answers?

"How many feet? Yards? Miles?" My frustration crept higher in my tone.

She frowned, clearly disappointed. "Your feet cannot take you there."

The frustration tied into a knot in my stomach. Was she going to keep me a prisoner? "Why?"

Her gaze roved up and down my body, stopping at my face. She examined me, as if trying to find my soul. "You are not ready."

"Ready for what?" The knot tightened and tore, similar to my anger. I was tired of the riddles, tired of the pain, just plain tired.

I blinked several times. My lids were heavy as a podship. I'd already slept for what must be hours, possibly days. I couldn't be sleepy so soon. Sniffing the steam coming off the mug, I smelled chamomile and a dusky scent like valerian root.

I tossed the cup to the ground. "Are you drugging me?"

Watu's lips twisted into an impish smirk.

I slammed into oblivion.

The colorful orb floated before me again. It had become my guide in this dreamland.

The city of Lindenhamn was laid out below me. Drage Mountain, the human palace, the winding streets of the old part of the city edged into the rigid block pattern of the new parts of town.

I zoomed closer. Into the shantytowns where humans lived among the majiks. Where multiple families lived on top of one another. Where there was poverty and sickness.

A little girl with dirty blond hair sat in a mechanical chair. Her legs were being straightened by old fashioned braces and her skin was charred red. Tears ran down her cheeks and her clothes were too small and torn.

My chest welled up. Who was this poor little girl and why was she in my dreams?

When I awoke next, the cave was empty. I couldn't see or smell Watu.

I didn't know the troll's plans for me. I did know how to get out. She might've saved me from the dragons, vultures, and elements and brought me here, but she spoke in riddles and drugged me. There was no other reason for why I'd fallen asleep so quickly after drinking her potion.

Sitting up, I closed my eyes, waiting for the dizziness to pass. My muscles tensed. I needed to get to either the sanctuary or find Stone and my team. Then, I needed to send out a search party for Bee.

I grabbed the stick by the side of the pallet and gripped it tightly. Using my arm strength, I pushed myself to a stand. My shoulders throbbed with the effort. Huffing raggedly, I took my first step. Agony speared through my legs and I winced.

Maybe escape wasn't the best option at this point. Still, I could search the cave for my clothes and whip. Maybe find provisions for when I was able to leave. I limped to the first trunk and rested. Opening the lid, I searched inside. Mostly clothes, a lot of red. Things I could use to layer my body from the cold. I went to another chest and peered inside. Cookware and dishes. Moving along the wall, I rested, searched, and continued on.

Hobbling further back in the cave, I spotted a strange glow. The entrance of the cave was in the other direction. I understood this light was unnatural. Felt the tug to continue forward.

I struggled down the uneven tunnel. One cave led to another and another. There were no lights or decorations or even household items in the passageway. If I hadn't seen the glow, I would've assumed nothing else was back here. I came to a wide opening and halted.

Watu stood in the cathedral portion of the cave. The top opened in a small circle letting light in. But this wasn't the light drawing me.

A crystal orb floated above her outstretched arms. The orb flashed colors of blue and orange and purple and green. Images formed on the surface of the orb and disappeared, forming into something else.

I'd seen this orb before.

My mind clicked through memories trying to distinguish one from the other. Trying to remember. Closing my eyes, I brought the visual to mind.

I sucked in a tortured breath. The orb wasn't anything I'd seen in person.

This was the orb from my hallucinating dreams.

Peering at the vision, the bright colors hurt my eyes. The orb must know I shouldn't be here, shouldn't see what I was seeing. Guilt trickled through my system.

I had a right to know. This involved me somehow, otherwise it wouldn't be the same orb from my dream. I peered closer.

Two ninjas dressed in red fought a close battle. The facets of the orb fractured the scene into small pieces. A flash of a sword. The glint of defense. The red swashes of their garments as they fought.

The dramatic sword fight intensified. I could feel the emotions from one of the combatants swirling inside me. Determination. Fear. Bravery. Hate.

One of the fighters spun and seemed to look directly at the orb, sensing a presence.

My presence?

The green eyes bore through me. The intensity rocked internally, as if she saw my soul.

I gasped.

The combatant was me.

Chapter Sixteen

T he orb vanished.

I staggered back and slid against the side of the tunnel to the ground. My body drained of the little strength I possessed.

Slowly, Watu pivoted. Her deep frown and narrowed gaze told me she was not pleased.

I wasn't pleased with her either. I knew I didn't have the energy to run. "Who are you? *What* are you?" I'd thought she was an ordinary troll living an isolated life like many trolls.

"You know *who* I am." She stepped around the small pool and moved toward me. "Are you ready to understand *what* I am?"

The challenge in her voice scared me. My body trembled. "Am I?"

"That is the question." She gripped my arm and helped me stand. "Your mind is willing. Your body is not."

Her answer confused me more. "What do you want from me?"

"I will not hurt you." Which, of course, wasn't a straight answer.

"You drugged me." I yanked my arm away and tried to walk on my own. The spasms spread from my belly to my chest and back.

"Medicinal herbs will heal and help you sleep. Which also heals." She shoved the stick, which I'd dropped on the ground, at me. "Will you run away from me? Run away from your destiny?"

She knew? How could she not be a mind reader if she knew I was contemplating escape? And why would she think staying here was my destiny?

"I'd be running toward my destiny." To prove myself.

My pulse slowed and my shoulders dropped. Knowing the mission was about to be canceled, I'd gone anyway. Was that running away? When the guard came to escort me back to the castle, I'd snuck out. Had that been running away too?

Look where those decisions had gotten me. Maybe running away wasn't a good thing.

An especially sharp spasm went through my stomach and I bent over. Grabbing my torso, I had to wonder if the pain was from an injury or the tea she gave me.

"May I help you back to the pallet?"

I liked that she asked instead of ordering. Admitting I needed help was a big step for me. "Yes."

Leaning on her, I limped to the pallet. She helped me lay down on the bed and covered me with blankets. Swiveling toward the burning fire, she poured a steaming mug and brought it to my side.

"How did you do that in there?" I jerked my chin toward the back room. "Why was I in the vision?"

She pressed the cup into my hands. "Not good to see a possible future path."

I startled. "Future path? My future?"

The image of the two ninjas fighting played again and again in my head. Hate stabbed my chest. I didn't hate anyone that much. Sure, I didn't like people. I disobeyed and disagreed. But hatred so strong had to come from a dark place. Could I have construed the orb's images and the emotions wrong?

"Do you trust me?" Watu pointed to the mug and made a gesture to drink.

There were many reasons why I shouldn't trust her. She was a troll and a stranger. She'd drugged me, although she said it was to heal. She had strange powers and foresight normal trolls didn't possess.

She'd saved me. She spoke in riddles that were honest answers. She seemed knowledgeable about me and my future. And Hokima was a troll and my friend.

Mulling my answer, I took a long sip. Right now, I didn't have a choice. Being diplomatic and showing respect was the right way to go. "I trust you."

Her pointy teeth stuck out as she smiled. "The first step to being accepted and becoming a great leader is to believe in yourself."

Her words swelled in my lungs. She was right. I thought I needed to be successful on this quest to prove myself to the fairies, but I really needed to prove myself capable. Except if Watu didn't know I was a princess, how did she know my greatest desire?

Or did she know exactly who I was?

***

"All great leaders rely on counselors," Watu said as we sat around the warmth of the fire. "Mentors and friends."

Gaining strength by the day, I was strong enough to sit by the fire and go for short walks. My dad's watch kept me abreast of time passing. I'd been in her home for eight days.

Our conversations were never casual gossip. The troll asked deep questions and taught me more about myself than I'd ever known.

My original perception of her with the hairy eyebrows and horns, the large mouth with pointy teeth, and bulbous nose had changed. Her wide, flat nose was beneficial for living at altitude. Her horns appeared regal. Her large mouth gave the biggest smiles.

"Friends." I held back a sniffle. "I don't know if I have friends anymore."

Bee could be dead. Arbor could be permanently injured. Stone would be angry I'd left. Tos and Hokima would believe I'd abandoned them. And Gardenia would be furious.

"If they are true friends, they will be to the end." Watu's sage wisdom gave me hope.

"Is there a way to get a message to someone?" I remembered how I'd used fireflies to communicate with my team.

"I have no way of communicating with the outside world."

"How do you survive living here? Isn't it lonely?"

"I have your company." Her serene expression sent a wave of peace my way.

I wondered if otherwise she'd be alone. Always alone. "I was an unexpected guest."

"Were you?"

Her response sent my mind reeling. "You knew I was coming?"

"I had an urge to hunt in the area where I found you. I knew this wouldn't be the average hunt for food." She'd said she didn't read minds. Could she know the future from the orb?

"Can you see the future?"

She chuckled. "No one can know the future."

"You said... when I saw the orb...you said it could be my future."

"Could be." She used a stick to stir the fire. Smoke rose in tiny tendrils. "Could be not."

Holding my hands up, I warmed them by the fire trying not to pull them into fists. Her puzzling expressions and half-answers ground into me. I wanted answers. Real answers.

"Before you can have any future, you must heal. And you must learn."

"Learn what?" I'd hated studying at the human school and at Queens Academy. "I'm more of an action fairy."

Her smirk challenged. "Show me. Make this fire bigger."

My chest tightened. The last time I'd tried to make a fire it had exploded and burnt part of the forest. The raging inferno had injured my best friend. "You don't want me starting a fire, believe me. Let me try something else."

Something not so dangerous.

"I do believe you. I believe in you." Her steady gaze and confident tone put a bit of grit and spunk into me. "Fire."

Licking my lips, I thought back to the moment of the fire. How something extra had jolted through my spell. If I could control that, I could spark the fire higher without letting it blaze. I huffed and focused, imagined what I wanted to happen, and said the spell in my head.

For a second, the image of the uncontrolled fire flashed in my mind and how it had brought the queen's guards. My breathing went ragged. Or the time I started a fire at human school. I caught Watu's confident expression and relaxed.

The fire flared higher. The flame scorched the roof, yet I never lost control.

"Excellent." She bowed her head. "Now, I can heat the evening meal."

Laughter bubbled out. I hadn't felt this happy in a long time. Watching her cook our meal, I flexed my feet and tested other injured points in my body. The swelling was down in my feet and the bruises less visible. My shoulder lacerations hadn't become infected and hurt less. My internal injuries were healing because when I moved, I just ached. The scrapes and burns had formed into scabs. The pain was down to a dull roar.

The only thing increasing was the itch in the middle of my back. Excitement and worry sent my stomach tumbling. Was this some strange reaction to Watu's potion or was something happening with my wings?

⟫⟫ ⟪⟪

The next day, we were outside the cave on a clear and crisp morning.

Sitting with my legs crossed, I tried to meditate as Watu had taught. To think of nothing and go deep. It was difficult to concentrate when the itch in my back grew more and more intense. The uncomfortable sensation had kept me tossing and turning on my pallet throughout the night.

"I sense you are having difficulty concentrating." She broke her focus to study me. "Let's continue on."

She sensed my concerns and tribulations. She'd become more than my rescuer. She'd become my mentor and possible friend. Standing, she started the stretching and yoga practices of the Asian arts. She wore leggings and a long shirt, identical to what she'd given me to wear. Except on me, the shirt and leggings hung loose and baggy.

Lifting her stubby arms to the sky, she closed her eyes and hummed. Similar to the humming I'd used to soothe humans, another gift from Mother Earth. Her calm expression caused envy. Would I ever appear so at ease with my own abilities?

I stood and followed her flowing movements. Arms to the sun and then down to the toes, stretch to one side and the other. I found it hard to hold the poses as the prickling on my back continued to get worse. Wiggling my shoulders, I tried to scratch an itch I couldn't reach.

From the platform outside the cave entrance, I saw the steep drop into a green valley with a wide river running through it. Watu said the river came from as high as the Aristos Sanctuary. A small trail led down from the entrance of the cave. The precipitous path went behind a waterfall and narrowed down to room for one. As a troll, she must be strong. How else had she carried me here on her own?

She stood at the ledge, sniffing with her large nose. "Reanimate the Androsace Alpina flowers."

"The what?"

She pointed to a small plant with tiny purple buds clinging to the rocks. "Also known as Jasmine Alpine Rock."

From what I'd learned at the academy, making natural things grow or flower was hard. Nature was not to be changed or altered. "Let's start with something easier."

She whipped around and pinned me with her gaze. "Why?"

My cheeks warmed. I didn't want to fail. "You know the saying, start small and work your way up."

"I know no such saying." *Can't do* was obviously not in her vocabulary. "You want to learn. You want to grow strong. You want to complete your mission."

"I do." I wiggled my shoulders again trying to get rid of the itch.

"Make the buds flower."

The difficult incantation was nothing I would've attempted before meeting her. I took a deep breath. She believed I could do this. I had to believe I could do this. She might not be magical, but she inspired confidence. She believed I had the power and the strength to do great things.

Be a leader. A princess. Someday a queen.

Zeroing in on the plant, I focused. I let the magic flow through me. Tingles started in my center and radiated outward. Each time she gave me a magical task, the power seemed energetic and substantial. Day by day, I grew stronger physically with the help of healing herbs and the Asian arts exercising, blending body and spirit. And each evening, we talked and discussed the kingdom and its possibilities.

The bud wiggled and glowed. The purple petals shifted and peeled, opening to the magic I poured into it and the sun. The tiny purple flowers bloomed, and they were beautiful.

My chest filled with elation. Without her mentoring and confidence, I never would've achieved and found my magic and my inner strength.

"Excellent job." Watu's simple praise spread a lightness inside me. She made me more self-assured. "Time for sustenance."

After washing up and eating a satisfying meal, we sat by the small fire and chatted. This also had become a daily ritual. She shared knowledge about life and the majiks, about how it used to be and how it was now.

"Did you know a fairy used to rule the land now called Alandaska?"

"No."

"When the humans took over, she retired and created Aristos Sanctuary. It's now where the elder royal rulers retire."

I tilted my head trying to recall what I'd learned about the isolated group. "I was headed to Aristos Sanctuary before being attacked by dragons."

Standing, I rubbed my back against the cave wall like a bear. Sharing my truth solidified in my bones. I trusted her with my health, and I needed to trust her with my mission. Maybe my history.

She nodded, already knowing my plans. "The Aristos Sanctuary is a good place to learn and grow. Even human rulers have gone to learn."

Guilt clogged my veins. She must not understand the true purpose of my visit there. It wasn't to learn. It was to retrieve the Divinity Orb. Plopping back on the log, I choked. Did this magical orb have any relation to the orb I saw in my dreams or the one Watu had conjured?

"The priestesses teach future rulers. They train and they meditate on the needs of others. They influence the kingdom." She filled her mug.

"How do you know so much about the priestesses?" A slight pain tickled my neck and back. I ignored it. I was learning too much to complain about discomfort. At least the itching had stopped.

Her hand paused while lifting the mug to her mouth. She stared at me over the rim. "I was one."

My mouth dropped open. "I didn't know a troll could become a priestess. No offense."

Her secretive smile hinted at other undisclosed information. "One of the many mysteries of the Aristos Sanctuary. All are welcome if they fit and are accepted."

Gardenia had told me you had to have royal lines to be accepted. "You're royalty?"

Watu gave a regal nod.

Now I understood her confidence and grace. Her knowledge and poise. Her Asian arts skill. She'd been a red-robed ninja priestess. I twisted my arm to reach my back, wanting to press against the throbbing. Clearly, I didn't possess any of those things. Although I was learning.

If she was royal, and knew you had to be royal to be accepted, did she know I was royalty?

Her mouth was closed, showing a hint of two pointy teeth. Her nose flared. She squinted back, knowing where my thoughts were leading me.

"You know I'm royal." It wasn't a question.

She nodded again and waited.

My pulse ticked like my dad's watch on my wrist. Sharing my biggest secret was a big step for me. I'd promised my fairy god-mother I'd tell no one, and besides telling Bee in a moment of shock, I'd kept the secret. I hadn't even told my best friend Arbor.

Swallowing, I spit the words out. "I'm the lost fairy princess."

An agonized spasm ripped between my shoulder blades. I cried out and fell off the log to the ground. Had Gardenia put a spell on me if I told someone the truth? Except I hadn't experienced pain when I'd told Bee.

Writhing on the floor, I craned my neck, trying to see what had brought on the agony. Something bulged beneath my plain cotton shift, resembling an alien. It was trying to get out of my body, out of my back.

"Take deep breaths." Watu stood and approached me. "I wish I had fairy clothing."

I didn't understand her mumblings. What was fairy clothing and why was this important at this time? I was dying. The torture was worse than any of my injuries. I was having a heart attack in my back. "Help me."

She ripped the shift off my back. "Only the first time hurts."

My numbed-by-pain brain didn't comprehend. "First time," I panted heavily, "for what?"

"The first time a fairy gets her wings."

Chapter Seventeen

My wings were beautiful.

Standing, I tried to get the full picture. They fluttered behind me in varying shades of blue and green. Purple edged the outline and flowed through the iridescent veins. I wished I had a mirror.

I ran a finger along the soft gossamer edge. Tingles spread across the sensitive wings at my touch. My shoulders pulled back and I couldn't stop the grin spreading on my face. Elation charged through my bloodstream. "I feel like a real fairy now."

"You trusted and believed in yourself as a fairy princess." Watu's sage expression filled me with pride. "It's what drew out your wings."

My step was lighter, and I didn't know if it was my happiness or the wings lifting me. "How do they work?"

"Clearly, I'm not a fairy." Her croaking laughter demonstrated as much. "It must be instinctual."

"Instinctual?" My wings drooped and folded behind me. "Most fairies have parents or siblings or friends to demonstrate."

"Mother Earth wouldn't allow her children to not be able to use their gifts." Watu's confident voice encouraged me. "Hop around a bit."

She helped me to believe in myself. I didn't realize how much I'd counted on her to have the answers, even if she gave the answers in pieces that I had to put together myself. Her process frustrated me, yet I learned more because of her methods.

Spreading my wings out fully, I took a small hop. The air brushed against the silkiness of the wings. Silliness and pride made my smile grow bigger and happiness danced from the tips of my toes to the edge of my wings—something I'd never said before.

I took another hop. My wings fluttered and pushed the air beneath me.

Sparks lit my insides. "I think I'm doing it."

I jumped higher. The air caught beneath the wings. My body floated for a few seconds. I hurried to the pallet and stepped on its platform. Spinning around, I leapt off. My wings fluttered and kept me up. "Aiea! Aiea!"

I knew it was an elf yell, Keltie's yell, but it suited the mood. Success, acceptance, strength.

Running out the cave entrance, I leapt higher and my wings lifted my feet off the ground. Watu followed me out and waved, wearing a big grin.

Taking a leap of faith, I vaulted off the ledge leading to the valley far below. My wings folded up and I fell. Panic seized my lungs and I couldn't breathe. I fell and fell and fell.

Think!

You're a fairy. You can fly.

My wings unfolded and flapped. Air brushed the sensitive surface and lifted me higher. I breathed again. My wings carried me up and up and up.

Watu's concerned face peered over the ledge.

She worried about me, which made everything go soft inside. She was more than a troll helping me out. She'd become a mentor and a friend, and my link to Mother Earth.

I waved to her. "I'm alright. I'm going to take a spin around the valley."

"Be careful and have fun!" She waved back.

Not since my father died had anyone told me to have fun. Sadness flowed across my skin even though I accepted his death. He'd always be a part of me, but I had a new life to move on to. One my mother had lived even though she wasn't here to teach me. One that would bring adventure and close connections with those I loved.

"Yippee!" I dove down with no fear. Accepting the naturalness of flight for a fairy. Knowing my body instinctively knew what to do. Enjoying my newfound skill and freedom.

The majestic mountains rose above me. The sheer cliffs plunged straight down into the valley below creating a circular wall of granite. To think I could fly with the dragons. My gaze skimmed around, checking the area. Fairies weren't as fast as them. They could catch up and fry me and eat me.

No, thank you.

Diving lower, I wove between the tall trees. A hoot of an owl and a howl of a werewolf greeted me. The evergreen scent wafted. The leaves brushed my skin and I reveled in the sensation. I was a true fairy now. A princess fairy. A fairy willing to fight for majiks.

I emerged from the trees at the river. Flying low, I dipped my feet into the water. The bubbling stream tickled, and I laughed. "I'm flying!"

Scooping down, I plucked a yellow flower from a bush and headed back to the cave. I landed on the ledge, out of breath and happy. Thrills traveled through the veins of my wings. Look what I'd accomplished and how much I'd grown. I was ready to head out and continue my mission. I'd get to Aristos Sanctuary on my own, for I could fly now, and from there get a message to my friends.

"Everything is beautiful!" I handed Watu the flower. "For you."

"Now, you are healthy and have your wings." She sniffed at the bloom. "The real training can begin."

Watu attacked me from behind.

Reaching over my shoulder, I grabbed her around the neck and flipped her onto her back as she'd instructed.

"Great job." She got to her feet slower this time.

We'd been practicing for hours, days really, and I was learning the ninja techniques and fighting skills. We trained at night, so I learned how to operate in the dark. We scaled the cliffs with nothing but our bare hands and feet. We swam in a nearby stream to build strength and stealth. We practiced being completely calm and quieting our breath to help camouflage ourselves and I did running sprints to build stamina and speed.

"Fifty jumps," she instructed.

"This." I jumped. "Feels." I jumped again. "Unnecessary."

She pushed a boulder by me. "Jump over this."

My wings emerged.

"No flying."

"Why not? I have wings." I preened between jumps.

"If you're trying to be stealthy in your escape, leaping may be required. Using wings will draw attention. Higher!"

I leapt higher, keeping my wings under control which was difficult. Since getting my wings, I wanted to use them all the time. They came out when I ran sprints and while I learned leg kicks to keep my balance.

"How do I best use my wings while fighting?"

"I can instruct. I can't know."

Which was true. I'd learned a lot from her, but she wasn't a fairy so she couldn't fully teach me fairy ways.

***

"We'll start with simple skills." Watu settled into a meditation position, sitting crossed legged in front of a small stream we'd hiked to. "Make it rain."

"Why do I need to make it rain?" It seemed a useless magical skill. Plus, it was a beautiful day. The sun was shining, and puffy white clouds decorated the sky. I wanted to go for a fly with my wings.

"You must learn what you need to know." Her answering without really answering rubbed against my practical nature. "Making it rain might come in handy if you need to cover your tracks in a forest, or if you're thirsty, or if a village is suffering from drought."

Or if you create an uncontrollable fire.

I understood our mentor relationship. She'd told me she couldn't teach me how to use my wings for an advantage in a fight. "How can you teach me fairy magic? You're not a fairy."

"Weather manipulation isn't fairy magic." Her lecture struck me. "It is a gift from Mother Earth."

Like when I'd called to Mother Earth to walk through the porous rock to get into the prison beneath Regent Theobald's palace.

"What about conjuring a snowstorm?" My friend Bee had used fairy magic to make it snow on our hike.

"Mother Earth magic, not fairy magic. Creating snow is similar to rain and one of the gifts granted to those who worship and understand Mother Earth."

My thoughts turned dark. Bee had lied about how she'd created the snowstorm. Why?

"Aim for a spot beyond the board." Watu held a wooden board firmly between her large hands.

On our fourteenth day of training, I believed I'd learned all she could teach me. Impatience itched at my skin. I was one hundred percent healed and I wanted to get on with my mission. I needed to find my friends and let Gardenia know I was alive. I had to be careful broaching the subject. I didn't want Watu to think I was ungrateful.

"Aiea!" I'd adopted Keltie's distinctive yell as my own. A way to honor my lost friend.

Flinging my arm forward, I swatted down at the board with the side of my hand. The board split cleanly in two.

"Nicely done." Watu handed me the two pieces of wood. "Throw those on the fire while I finish dinner."

After tossing the boards onto the fire, I took a seat close by. We enjoyed a simple stew dinner and she spoke of her time being a priestess.

"Why did you leave the sanctuary?"

"I had a different path to take. A different purpose." The way she stared caused me to grow restless.

I shifted my feet. Did her purpose include me?

Glancing around the simple home, I searched for a clue. She lived in a cave high in the mountains, alone and isolated. There was no way to communicate with another troll, majik, or human.

"What is your purpose, Princess Ellery?"

I gulped. It was the first time she'd used my title and the full effects felt like a crown of porcupine quills had been smashed on my head instead of a crown of jewels. I wasn't used to the title and didn't know if I ever would be. But the title was mine and I'd wear whatever crown proudly.

"Well, I um...need to prove to the fairies I'm worthy of being their princess." The reason for my mission and for disobeying orders and for running away. Did all those wrongs make my quest right?

"Worthiness is accomplished from within." Of course, she believed that when she reeked self-confidence and knowledge.

I hadn't started with either of those. I was learning. "In order to successfully lead, I need to show the fairies I'll be good at being royal."

I'd make a proper princess and a strong queen. I'd have their best interests at heart. And I was coming up to speed on history and training and magic.

"No leader starts off great. It's what they do while leading that makes them great." Watu proved her wisdom time and time again. "You must count on your friends and be aware of your true enemies."

All great leaders have good friends and teachers. She would always be one of those. As would Gardenia, Arbor, Stone, Bee, Tos, and Hokima. I missed them. The urge to leave now and find them rushed through my veins. "I've learned what I can. I'm healthy and have my wings. It's time for me to complete my mission."

"Is it, though?" Watu's tone sent a sliver of fear through me. "You have one very important lesson left."

Chapter Eighteen

"Instruction for your final lesson will be in the Beholding Grotto."

Startled, I couldn't believe this was my last lesson and Watu was inviting me inside her inner sanctum. This was the place I'd stumbled into one of my first nights and seen the orb and the vision.

While I'd practiced magic or went out flying, she would sneak into the grotto. I'd asked several times to go inside. Each time, she'd say I wasn't ready. I respected her request. Excitement pulsed. Finally, I was going to go in the forbidden place to learn what secrets it held. She believed I was ready, so I must be.

Entering the sacred walls, the grotto reminded me of a volcano. The walls went up at an angle and a round hole opened to the sky. Directly beneath the hole sat a pool of fresh water bubbling up from an underground stream. The air was thick and had an unusual scent of rotten eggs.

The mystical area gave me goosebumps. "How did you find this place?"

"A guardian has always lived here to tend to the sacred water and protect our interests." Her answer opened more questions.

"You're a guardian?" I furrowed my brow, trying to think of what I'd learned about majik history. "A guardian of what?"

"A guardian of Alandaska's future. As are all Aristos priestesses."

Wow. Big responsibility.

Inching inside, I trailed my fingers across the rock wall. "How long have you lived here? How long have you been a guardian?"

"All these questions." She tisked. "Remember, you can't ask and automatically receive. You must learn for yourself."

One of the tenants of her teachings.

A final question bubbled to mind, an important question. "How can I see the images you produced that night again?"

"You can't." Her words held no inflection, her face no expression.

My gut clenched. "I can't see them, or you can't create them again?"

Ignoring me, she took a seat by the small pool of water. "Both."

Resentment built in my firming muscles and roiling stomach. I wanted to demand, but I'd learned—no, she'd informed me—in time things would be revealed. Everything she'd done or taught had been for my sake and helped me. Just as I respected the privacy of this place, I needed to respect her answers and not pry. It was difficult.

"Sit." She pointed at a spot across the water from her.

I took a crossed-leg position. The four-foot round pool presented a calm blue today. The one night I'd been in here, varying colors had been reflected on the surface. Bending forward, I clearly saw my own face. I looked different than before. Sure, a few scratches hadn't healed, but searching beneath the surface I saw more. Dusky skin from the sun, hollowed out cheeks because of my recovery, strong chin, and a determined glint in my green pupils. I was ready to conquer and take my place in society after retrieving the orb.

"As a leader, you must draw power from everywhere. You must use more than your fairy magic and ninja fighting skills." Watu's lessons on ruling went deeper than royal rules or etiquette. She wanted me to be a good person while being a great ruler.

I wanted that, too.

Change had become part of my life and I'd resisted. First, by not wanting to recognize my half fairy side and then not wanting to acknowledge I was a princess. Now, I wanted to embrace who I was and who I could become. I'd continue to change for the better.

"Mother Earth's gifts are more ancient than fairy magic, for she was here first." Watu's ears twitched. "Other majiks and a few humans know how to access Mother Earth's magic. It is important for you to learn. Put your fingers in the water."

I kept my hand close to my lap. "I thought you said this was mystical water."

One of the reasons for not allowing me back here.

"Holy from Mother Earth." The serenity on the troll's expression showed she drew comfort from this spot. "How else to explain having fresh water high in a mountain and deep in a cave."

"True." I dabbled my fingers in the water, noting it wasn't too hot or too cold. It was perfect.

"You remember the orb I lifted out of the water?" Watu's expression went cross, remembering when I'd intruded. "It was a spectral orb. A representation of the real orb."

Adrenaline charged through me. I'd felt a connection to the object and saw myself fighting someone over it. "The Divinity Orb."

She nodded. "All priestesses, present and former, can access a spectral of the Divinity Orb from special water sources."

I wished it was the real orb, then my mission would be complete. I could return to Queens Academy in triumph and take my place as princess. I'd continue to train and now that I had my wings, I'd fight. "The real one is at Aristos Sanctuary."

"Correct."

"If you can access the spectral orb and see the future, why do you need the real thing?"

"Those who aren't trained as a priestess can't access the spectral orb. For example, someone like you."

Disappointment killed the earlier adrenaline rush. If what made the Divinity Orb special was its prediction powers then why not bring a priestess to the fairy castle and let her predict? I could bring Watu. My spirits lifted. It would be nice to have her mentorship in such an unfriendly atmosphere. "Why don't you come with me to Queens Academy so the queen can see through your sight?"

She chuckled. "I see visions that may or may not predict the future. I don't control what I see and can't force a vision."

The spectral orb didn't seem very helpful.

"When you possess the real Divinity Orb," Her voice went soft and spiritual, "you control the visions. You can ask to see something currently happening far away or ask to see what might happen in the future."

"Might?"

"Future visions are never for certain. If one slight thing changes, it can change everything else."

I understood why seeing something happening far away would be important. Especially now with war coming. We could see battles or enemy positions. Having the orb would be a great advantage. After the war, the orb could help keep the peace. For predicting the future, the orb sounded useless.

She stirred the water with her finger. Yellow, blue, pink, and purple spread out in a rainbow. "The real Divinity Orb can be possessed by those with royal ties."

Which was the reason Gardenia had sent me on the mission. Otherwise, she wouldn't have let me leave the castle. My imaginary shackles appeared again and my resentment built higher. When she sent the guards to bring me back, she knew Perry could continue and retrieve the Divinity Orb.

He was royal, not the next in line. No need to lock him up in a castle cage.

Anger flared at her treatment. Who was she trying to protect? Me or her precious position?

The real orb wasn't in this pond and I didn't understand the point of the exercise. Crossing my arms, I pinched my skin, trying to control my antagonism toward my fairy godmother. "What am I learning now?"

"You must learn how to use Mother Earth's gifts." Watu's reasonable tone chafed.

That wasn't important. "I know how to use Mother Earth's gifts. You taught me how to make rain. And I know how to walk through a boulder or rock wall. Besides, I have more powerful fairy magic."

"Power isn't always important." Watu sighed. "There are many more things to learn from Mother Earth."

I wasn't going to win this battle. Best to go along. "Alright." I spoke through tight lips. "What's the rhyme?"

"Excuse me?"

"The rhyme. The thing I say in my head to access Mother Earth's gifts." I remembered the words Arbor had taught me to go through the rock and the rhyme to make it rain.

"Accessing Mother Earth's gifts is more than saying a few words." Watu sounded offended. "It's an ancient art. Passed down through generations."

"Oh." That's why I needed to practice. "Okay. What do I do?"

"Close your eyes."

I did.

"Open your mind."

I opened my eyes. "What?"

Her jaw dropped and she tilted her head. "You must be accepting of her gifts. Let them stream into your body through your fingertips in the water."

Having fairy magic guaranteed I believed in a lot of supernatural things. But power was power, and it was there or it wasn't.

"What do you mean, open my mind?" I used my fist to knock on my very solid head.

She sighed again, sensing I'd reached my limit. "You must be willing to open yourself to new experiences."

I flexed my fingers into fists and released. "I'm still here, aren't I?" I had my wings and I could've flown away. Spending this time with Watu was keeping me from my quest because I thought she could help.

"Are you?" Frustration rumbled in her voice.

"What do you mean?" I spoke slowly, forming each word.

"I realize you want to be on your way. To get back to your friends and your mission." She firmed her lips. "This is important."

When Arbor had taught me how to walk through a rock, it had been simple. Recognize the right type of rock, place my hand on it, say the words. One, two, three. Watu was making this more difficult than it needed to be. "Tell me the steps."

"Step one," She sounded harsh, "put your hands back in the water. Step two, close your eyes."

"Step three, open your mind." I hurried her along.

"Step four." There was bite in her tone. "Forget everything else. Imagine the spectral orb." Her voice went languid, trying to put me in a trance. "Are you picturing it?"

Nodding, I made an effort to do as instructed. My mind distracted me. She was right. I wanted to head out and restart my adventure, especially knowing what I did now and with my wings.

"Really?" She doubted me.

And she'd be right.

I shook my head and rolled my shoulders. "Let me try again. I'm forgetting everything and picturing the orb."

"Good. Now pull the orb out of the water."

"You forgot to say what step that was."

"Ellery!"

"Sorry." I cringed. "I don't mean to be rude. Earlier you said I couldn't access the spectral orb."

"This is practice for the future. There's a prophecy..." She let out a long slow breath. "Please, try again."

Closing my eyes, I pictured the orb. I remembered the images from when Watu conjured the orb. Images of me dressed in the robes of the ninja priestess. Fighting a battle against my enemy, emotions helping and hindering my assault.

"I'm not seeing anything. Not a ripple in the water or an image of the spectral orb."

"Are you trying?" Her disappointment had me gritting my teeth.

"Yes, I'm trying."

"Are you focusing?"

"Yes, I'm focusing." Although it was difficult to focus when she was talking. "Maybe if you were quiet."

She gave a disgusted snort and said nothing.

Focusing harder, I squeezed my eyelids tight and tried to imagine the orb. Every time, the fighting images seared in my mind. I don't know how long I sat in silence. Trying.

I couldn't take it anymore. "This isn't working."

"Because you're not working." Watu's reprimand lowered my spirits.

Arbor had made it easy. She'd said I had natural instincts.

I glared. "Maybe because you're a troll and can't teach me very well."

Watu's face fell. Her gloopy eyes drooped, displaying her saggy skin, and her chin dropped.

My chest contracted. I hadn't meant to insult her. "I'm sorry. I didn't mean that to come out how it sounded."

Prejudiced and cruel.

I should know better than to judge. She'd done so much for me. Taught me so much.

She lifted her chin and gave me a slow nod. "Maybe you are right. Maybe someone else needs to teach you other aspects of Mother Earth's gifts. Maybe it is time for you to leave."

The blood drained from my head, pooling in apprehension and dread. "No." The one thing I'd wanted more than anything since getting my wings. But I didn't want it in this way. "I'm sure I can learn more from you. I'm getting anxious and frustrated and lashed out."

Watu stood and turned away. Her stiff back showed her upset. She left the sacred area.

Dragging my pride, I followed her. "Please, Watu. I'll try again."

"Trying and doing are different things." She lifted the lid of an old woven basket.

"I'm really sorry." My ungratefulness became an anchor. Was she going to send me packing?

Pivoting, she handed me a package wrapped in paper and tied with rope. "For you."

"What?"

"A gift from me to you."

The weight of the package seemed heavier than the item. Why would she give me a gift when I'd behaved badly? "You've given me so much already."

Watu had given me everything. I would've died on the side of the mountain without her coming to my rescue. She'd fed me and healed me. She'd taught me about leadership, Mother Earth, and my own magic. She'd witnessed me getting my wings.

She'd started with saving my life and ended with saving my future.

"Open it." Her lips pressed together in a pleased smile.

My chest contracted again, this time tightening around my heart. I hadn't received a real present since my father died. Unless you counted the gifts from Gardenia that came with conditions.

I untied the rope and ripped away the paper. A soft, rich red fabric caressed my hands. Holding the fabric up, I shook the material out.

Red leather leggings and vest, a red shirt, and short black leather jacket. Plus, a red-hooded robe.

Waves of emotions swept through me, making my knees weak. Fear and excitement. Pride and despair. Watu's emotions when she'd last worn the garment. Similar to my mother's things, I could sense Watu's emotions through her clothes. My eyes burned, and my body ached as if I'd fought a long battle.

I hadn't. She must have.

My gaze flew to hers and I wondered what the troll had been through. "These were yours. I can't take—"

"I've altered them to accommodate your wings." She pointed to the barely visible slits in the shirt and jacket. "You will represent yourself well."

She sounded proud of me. My body swayed, overwhelmed by everything. Her emotions and mine. "Thank you so much. I don't know what to say."

"Say you'll wear them proudly and be your best self while wearing them at the sanctuary." She grinned, showing her sharp, jagged teeth. "Go try it on."

Rushing to my palette, I slipped off the cotton shift and put each garment on. The leggings fit tightly and moved with my body. Black straps wrapped around my legs to hold weapons and buckled around the waist. The red overshirt hung low on my hips and the vest provided protection. The short jacket had holes for my wings and hugged my shoulders.

I twirled, and my wings spread out, creating a puff of air. "What do you think?"

"You look fabulous." She handed me slim-fitting boots and gloves. "To complete the outfit."

"Thank you." I put on the boots and leapt. My wings popped out with no obstruction and I did a short fly around the cave.

"And lastly, I'll return the Silver Snare." She held my whip in her hands.

The silver gleamed in the light. My fingers tingled and I reached out for my weapon of choice. "I don't know what to say."

Confidence soared with my flight. I was healed, instructed, and had my wings and my magic. It was time for me to continue my quest. The rest of Mother Earth's gifts I'd learn on the fly, literally. *Haha*. Once Arbor was healed, she'd teach me.

"You will say goodbye." Watu must be reading my mind. "And I will say good luck."

⇢⇢⇢ ⇠⇠⇠

The following morning, I'd packed my few things and some provisions and was ready to go. For someone who'd been so impatient to be on my way I kept finding ways to dawdle. Even though Watu had given me the gift of clothes, something felt off.

"Did I pack the gloves?" I lifted the blankets on my bed.

"Yes." She sounded indulgent. "Don't forget the gloves have a special stickiness for climbing."

"I can fly." I couldn't believe it and enjoyed saying it again and again.

She chuckled. "And as we've discussed, there will be times where you might need to climb."

"Hence the cliff-climbing." I laughed, remembering how much I'd complained about that particular training.

Biting my lip, I glanced around the cave, again noting the things that had changed since I'd arrived. The sparse furniture had been pushed to the edges so I had room to practice flying. There were two seats around the small fireplace. She'd made special accommodations for me. I was going to miss this place. And miss Watu.

"What if I don't remember what you've taught?"

She'd taught me so much. It would be impossible to remember everything.

Tapping her finger against her temple, she said, "Everything you need is in here," she tapped her chest, "and in here."

The head and the heart. Be smart and be caring. The pillars of her training.

"How can I communicate with you?" I asked the question, knowing the answer.

She shook her head. "You will be fine."

"Will I?" Resembling slugs, doubts nibbled inside my head. How could I count on those things when I already hesitated?

She walked to the cave opening and stood at the ledge peering out.

Shuffling my feet, I joined her. The sun wasn't directly above, but it was higher in the sky than I would've wanted. "Maybe I should leave tomorrow."

"Putting something off will not ever get it done." Her strange logic endeared me to her even more.

When I flew off this ledge, I might never see Watu again. I might never hear her wisdom. I might never experience the comfort she gave me. She was like the mother I never knew. My chest seized up in a fit of panic. Breath shattered in ragged puffs. "What if I fail?"

She put a hand on my shoulder. "The only failure is not to have tried."

My eyes burned and I sniffed back the tears. She was right. Of course.

Turning to her, I gave her a final hug, wanting to hold on forever, knowing I couldn't. I could do this. I had to do this. It was my legacy and my destiny.

I sniffed. "Goodbye Watu."

"Good luck!" She called to me as I spun and took flight.

I dipped my wing in a final farewell. I didn't know where this journey would take me next. I did know I was better for this delay. Stronger and smarter.

I was more prepared for what was to come.

⋙ ⋘

Stretching my wings, I considered the Kingdom of Alandaska from above. The beauty took my breath away.

Snowcapped mountains, green valleys, roaring rivers, blue sky. I knew the invisible dome keeping the kingdom secret from the rest of the world was up there. It didn't hinder the view. If we could live in such a beautiful place, and keep our secrets hidden, why couldn't the humans and the majiks get along? Why did we face this ugly war that could destroy the kingdom I loved?

I wanted to fly to Regent Theobald and give him a piece of my mind. And maybe see Rye too.

The roar of water falling caught my attention. Zooming lower, I spotted mountain goats and bighorn sheep, and even a snow leopard. The crisp air quivered across my skin and caressed my wings, billowing me farther. The smell of cleanliness and cold tickled my nose buds.

Flying boosted my confidence. I was now a true fairy. One with magic I knew how to use and wings.

Detecting a waterfall, I recognized it as the place Watu had described near the entrance to Aristos Sanctuary. I planned to fly to the entrance and get myself admitted. I would inquire about my friends and get a message to Gardenia. She must be worried.

I sniffed under my arms. First, a bath might be in order.

Watu's small magical pool wasn't for bathing. And the little water she had was for drinking, cooking, and quick sponge baths. Before meeting the priestesses, I wanted to look, and smell, my best. Especially before meeting my great-grandmother.

Landing by the waterfall, I peeked down into the deep, blue pool below. A perfect spot to get clean before announcing myself at the priestesses' door. I took off the boots and the rest of the outfit and folded them neatly in a pile. Wearing undergarments, I raised my hands above my head and paused.

Would I damage my wings with the water? But fairies bathed and swam. They got caught in the rain. My wings would be fine.

I dove into the lake.

My hands cut through the cold water, invigorating my body. The liquid sluiced across my skin, giving me chills. The clean alpine water went deeper than I would've expected. For as clear as the water was, I couldn't see the bottom. Kicking with my feet, I broke the surface and took a deep breath.

The waterfall poured from a spot higher up on the mountain. The falling water churned the pool beneath, making it impossible to see behind. I swirled around, taking in another beautiful view. Living in the city, I never appreciated the natural beauty so close by.

Wishing I had soap, I rubbed my arms and legs with the palms of my hand, hoping I'd get the smelly sweat off my skin. I dipped my head back, getting my hair wetter. It would become a tangled mess once it was dry. I could use magic to style the strands.

A splash caught my attention.

I swiveled toward the noise.

The flat surface didn't display evidence of a fish or water animal. Remembering the magical animals Bee had talked about, I shivered. Could there be magical fish or sharks in the water?

Better safe than sorry. Flipping, I started to swim toward the edge.

Something wrapped around my ankle.

My lungs clenched, squeezing the air out. I kicked with my other foot. Whatever had me wouldn't let go.

"Ahhh!"

Was I going to drown so close to my destination?

Chapter Nineteen

I thrashed and kicked, trying to escape whatever held my ankle. My pulse raced, shocking my heart into a rattled beat. Water rushed into my lungs and I couldn't breathe, couldn't get away. My wings wouldn't spread underwater. Panic shot a jolt of adrenaline through me.

Whatever gripped my ankle pulled me to the surface.

"Ahhhh!" My scream echoed around the lake.

"Elle?" The familiar voice caught me off guard.

Stone?

My thrashing stopped. My muscles became loose and flaccid. Twisting toward him instead of away, I took in my friend's wet face.

"I didn't recognize you with your wings." Long blond hair plastered to his head. Chiseled cheeks and chin dripped with water. His lips formed an *O* shape, and it was like he didn't believe he held me in his arms.

"Stone!" I wrapped my arms around his thick neck. I couldn't believe I'd found him by accident.

Hugging me back, he squeezed tight and brought me up against his hard body. His very hard body. My skin overheated, even in the frigid water. I could feel every toned muscle and hard surface. And I couldn't sense any clothes. He was naked.

My overheated skin boiled beneath the surface. I pulled back a little.

"You have wings." He swiped the dripping hair from his face and repositioned his arms around me, as if afraid I'd disappear. "Where the *hvitspyd* have you been?"

I opened my mouth to tell him of my adventures. "I—"

"I've been sick with worry. So has Gardenia and the queen." His face became fiercer, his blond brows going into angry slashes.

I didn't care because I focused on what he said. My mouth dropped open again. Queen Dahliadew was alive.

"Arbor has been trying to recover—"

"Arbor is okay?" The weight of worry I hadn't realized I carried, lightened.

"She's being treated by the royal healers." He cocked his head, studying me.

Blinking, I tried to focus on what was important. Not the desire in his green gaze. Not the beauty and strength of his square jaw and high cheekbones. Not his lips only inches from mine.

"What about Bee?" The last time I'd seen her she'd been huddled in a small crevice, trying not to be eaten.

"We found her wandering on the side of the mountain. She said you were taken by a dragon." His angry expression softened. His blazing eyes mellowed into rounded pools of concern. "What really happened?"

"I was taken by a dragon."

His strong jaw dropped. He hadn't believed Bee.

"And they let me go. Drago—"

"Drago?"

"The baby dragon I found under the human palace. I'm positive he was one of them, and he convinced the other dragon to let me go."

Stone swiped a hand through his wet hair again and placed each of his palms against the sides of my head. "Why didn't you come back?"

"I was injured and a troll took me—"

His eyes rounded so large I thought they might explode. "What troll? I'll kill him."

My muscles mellowed at his defense. He cared about me. "Her. And she was wonderful."

"Wonderful?" He tilted his head, exhibiting disbelief. "You've been missing for fifteen days."

"Watu, the troll, healed me and taught me and trained me." I straightened my shoulders, remembering what I'd learned. I wasn't a confused half fairy anymore. I had powerful magic. I had knowledge. And I had my wings. "I'm so much more capable and—"

His lips descended on mine. Hard and punishing and powerful. It was a kiss meant to prove dominance and control and I couldn't stop the thrill charging through my body. I'd thought his flirtation had been a way to keep me close while not divulging the fact he worked for Gardenia.

Maybe not.

I smiled under his assault.

"What's so funny?" He sounded grouchy as his mouth mumbled against mine.

"You kiss like you're attacking."

Leaning back, he glared and his lips smashed together in an angry line. "Are you an expert now?"

"I'm not saying I'm not enjoy—"

He cut off my words again with his mouth. This time his lips were softer, more persuasive than demanding. Another thrill, one tingling and tickling, traveling through me. I might not be an expert at kissing, but he was. Instead of pressing his hands against my head to hold me in place, his fingers ran through my wet hair. He cradled the back of my neck and I wanted to swoon.

This kiss meant something.

It wasn't flirtatious or desperate. It was touching and hinted at something more. What more could it be? And what about Rye?

My chest contracted. Would I ever see the prince again? And even if I did, he was the sworn enemy of my people. The fairies I would be leading. It was time to give Stone a chance.

Still holding my head, he broke off the kiss. "Something's different about you." He angled his head and studied me even more closely than before. "You were always beautiful. Now, you're glowing."

Fairy magic or confidence? Either way, I savored his praise.

"It's Elle!"

My name barely penetrated my fuzzy brain.

"Elle! Elle!" More voices joined the shouts.

"And she has wings." Tos' high-pitched tone went higher.

Stone dropped his hands away from me and swam back a bit to make room.

I shook off the daze, and twisted around to see who was yelling.

My friends stood near the edge of the waterfall. Tos jumped up and down, almost reaching the top of Perry's crossed arms. He wore a scowl. Hokima's mouth was open in a sort of smile, showing his jagged teeth and reminding me of Watu. Bee appeared pale. Probably shocked to see me alive.

My heart burst with love. They were here and happy to see me.

"What are you all doing here?" Had they decided to continue the quest without me using Perry as their royal with the priestesses? If so, they would've arrived weeks ago.

"Waiting for you, Princess," Stone whispered in my ear.

A tremble ran through me. Did he care more about my title than me? Was he trying to get in with royalty? What had the kiss meant?

The shock wave hit my stomach and changed to nerves, making me nauseous. I glanced back at my friends. "I'm not ready to tell them. Not yet."

"As you wish." Stone gave a slight bow of his head.

My fingers flexed into fists. I'd come so far, confessed to Watu, and accepted my destiny. Why didn't I want to tell my friends? My pulse pounded rhythmically. I just needed time and to find an appropriate way. I didn't want to show up after being missing and spit it out.

While I pondered, Stone had swam to the edge and climbed out. He'd quickly put on his pants and turned to face me. His bare chest had rivulets of water streaming between his broad shoulders and carved abs.

I blew out a slow breath and swam to shore, wondering how much to share of my absence and what the wood sprites I was going to do about Stone.

Bee waved her arms, indicating everyone should move back. What she wore resembled an old garment of Hokima's. Even if she'd lost all her stuff, why didn't she use her magic to conjure new clothes? "Let's give Elle privacy. Everyone, head back to camp."

They stepped behind a large boulder, and I climbed out of the water. With my wings still tucked in, I shivered. Even though the water was frigid, I hadn't sensed the cold with Stone by my side.

"Thanks, Bee." I gave her a big hug and picked up my leggings. "I worried about you so much. Whether the dragon had come back after dropping me and got you, or if you were injured, or even froze to death."

"If you got free, why didn't you come back to me? I waited a long time." Her tone had an edge, as if it was my fault.

I bristled and tried not to blame her back. She'd had me sneak out of the tent and run away. "I was seriously injured by the dragon and the fall when it dropped me."

"How did you get away? Survive if you were injured?" Bee questioned my actions and my loyalty.

I put on the shirt and strapped the belt around my waist. The clothing felt uncomfortable for the first time. Maybe because my undergarments were wet. "The dragon let me go."

"Why?"

I shrugged. For some reason, I didn't want to tell her about Drago. "I don't know."

"If you were seriously hurt, how did you survive? Heal?" Her questions didn't sound concerned, more like she wanted me to account for every day I'd been missing.

That was a form of caring, right?

"Where did you get the outfit?" Bee drew out the words, clearly shocked.

I pulled the jacket on to cover myself more fully. "Do you like it?"

"It's a priestess outfit." Her voice was accusatory. "Did you already go to Aristos Sanctuary? Without me?"

"No." I didn't want to share with her all I'd learned from Watu. It was my special time of growth. "A troll gave it to me. The one who helped me heal." I slipped on the boots. "I need to say hi to the others."

Slipping around the boulder, I saw them tramping to tents on a plateau further up the trail. My heart billowed. I couldn't believe they'd searched for me, and when they couldn't find me, they'd camped here, waiting. Hoping I'd return. They cared about me. And if they cared, surely the fairies would care when they got to know me. I had to believe.

"Hokima!" I approached the troll and gave him a hug.

He hugged me back, lifting me off my feet. "I can't believe you came back to us." Wearing a shift, he stood near a frequently used campfire.

"I can't believe you waited for me."

He jerked his fat chin at Stone. "We searched for you for days and hiked here to camp. That guy wouldn't ask for admittance into the sanctuary without you."

My shivers calmed with an inner warmth.

Taking Hokima's hand in mine, I squeezed. "I spent the time I was missing with a wonderful troll. She taught me so much."

His smile widened.

"Where did you get the fabulous outfit?" Tos bounced over to us and I bent down and gave her a hug with my two hands.

"Do you like?" I twirled around, modeling the way the robe flared. "Watu, my new troll friend, gave it to me. She used to be a priestess."

"Trolls can be priestesses of Aristos?" Tos fingered the cloak. "What about brownies?"

Perry came out of his tent wearing breeches and a silk vest. His wings fluttered and it didn't annoy me. "All majiks can join the priestesses."

Bee patted me on the back, right at the spot where my wings were located. "Show us your wings."

Heat hit my cheeks. Modeling clothes was one thing, modeling my wings seemed more personal. "Maybe later."

Hokima clapped his large hands together, causing everyone to stare. "We'll celebrate Elle's return tonight."

The group cheered, and I couldn't stop a grin. Their love and kindness soothed my heart and made the trials I'd been through worth it. I was better equipped to lead them now.

"Not too much celebrating." Stone had changed his wet pants and put on a shirt. He looked large and in charge. "We head to Aristos Sanctuary first thing in the morning."

That night, I used my magic to make a perfect fire. No anxiety and no strange bursts. Hokima told stories about how they'd searched for me with the castle guards and decided to wait for a few more days before proceeding without me. Tos sang songs. Perry participated, and still stayed apart. Bee was quiet, her gaze darting from one of us to the next, calculating a change in dynamics.

Stone stayed ever-watchful, expecting trouble.

"Everything okay?" I nudged his shoulder with mine, missing the closeness and attraction from the lake.

"It's been a long couple of weeks." A slight scruff on his face tried to cover his haggard expression. There were dark circles under his eyes. He'd worried about me and he'd probably disobeyed Gardenia again. Standing, he marched to the side of the encampment, away from the light of the fire.

I couldn't let it go and I approached him. "I'm sorry."

Twisting, he grabbed my upper arms with a hard clasp. "Why did you run away, Elle?"

He was referring to when Bee and I had snuck out of the tent. Shame blistered my reputation and excuses. I should've stayed and confronted the guards, argued with them about taking me to the castle. "I heard the guards say they were going to take me back to Queens Academy. I didn't want to go with them, and I thought you'd given me an opportunity to escape by delaying until the morning."

I wouldn't drag Bee into my problems. No one liked her as it was.

"I wouldn't have let them take you." His protective tone proved what he said was the truth.

He wasn't giving me time to sneak away as Bee had said. He would've fought the guards for me, except I hadn't given him a chance.

"You work for Gardenia. It was her direct order."

"Technically, I work for you." Sarcasm sneaked into his voice. "You're the princess."

My chest clutched. "Shh!"

"You're going to have to tell everyone soon. Perry already suspects. He might even know."

"I'm not ready."

Stone stared deeply at me. "When will you be ready?"

I don't think he was talking about sharing my princess secret with my friends. Clamping my mouth shut, I tried to give him an answer to only the single question. Yet, his mouth was so tantalizingly close. I remembered how his kiss had tasted so good and welcoming. I deserved a little love and attention and we'd been cut short in the water. When would I ever be allowed a flirtation again? Tilting closer, I took in his evergreen scent and pressed my lips to his.

His mouth didn't move. He didn't respond to my kiss.

He pushed me away. "We can't."

"What? Why?" Confusion and rejection rang in my head.

"Kissing isn't appropriate between us. You're the princess and I'm a guard."

The ringing got louder and revolved into a fit. "What was that in the lake? You kissed me."

"It was a mistake." His harsh tone rubbed my already raw nerves. His gaze narrowed into a glare and I knew he was mad too.

"It didn't feel like a mistake." It had felt thrilling and caring.

"Go to bed, Elle." He pivoted away from me.

"You don't give me orders." My statement proved his point. Flattening my lips, I fisted my hands at my sides. I was a princess and I probably couldn't carry on with a guard. He wouldn't go against the rules.

"Fine. I'll go to bed." He marched toward his tent, opened the flap, and disappeared inside.

Leaving me standing there, fuming. How could he say our kiss had been a mistake? Now that I couldn't have Stone, did that make me want him more?

The next day, the hike shouldn't have taken long, and yet it dragged on. Maybe because I was walking and not flying, maybe because we were so close, maybe because I didn't know what would happen when we arrived.

Maybe it was because Stone mostly ignored me.

Perry hiked behind me, and he stared daggers into my back. "Do you know how to do a rollback?"

"No." I didn't even turn around when I answered.

"It's a really helpful maneuver when flying and fighting. I'll teach you."

Angling my head, I wasn't sure if I trusted him. We'd never gotten along. He would've been the royal heir if I hadn't shown up, and I believed he knew it. But had he really tried to kill me when we'd sparred, or had he been proving his superiority? Since spending time with Watu, my instincts had changed. "What's so special about it?"

"The way you hold your wings helps keep your balance as you're fighting."

Good to know. It was one of the things Watu had tried to explain. Explaining and demonstrating were different and she'd had a difficult time instructing.

"Okay. Let's go." I unfurled my wings and fluttered. I could handle myself and I needed to learn to fly and fight.

"Ooh! Pretty." Tos clapped her tiny hands.

Stone did a double take. It was the first time any of them had seen my wings fully spread.

Bee's eyes grew wide and she frowned. She didn't seem pleased about my having wings. Hurt throbbed inside me.

Perry zoomed high in the sky and I followed on his heels.

"Don't get too far ahead."

Stone's order made me more reckless. I chuckled loudly. He wasn't the boss of me.

"I know a great place." Perry led me away from the group.

My stomach knotted. Sweat formed between my wings. I barely knew him, and he'd tried to kill me once. He knew my secrets. I'd been too rash. "Don't you think this is far enough?"

"Are you scared, Elle?" It wasn't really a taunt, and yet he baited me.

"I'm not scared."

"Good." His smirk appeared to be friendly and innocent. "Because for a new flyer you're pretty good."

"Did you say I was pretty good?"

"Yeah. And I can teach you to be better." He zoomed higher and I followed.

I admired how his wings barely moved while flying, taking little effort. His wings blended into the sky and created extra camouflage. I wondered if mine did, too.

Hurrying, I flew beside him. "Why do you want to help me?"

"Suspicious much?"

I needed answers before I'd trust him. "You tried to kill me at Queens Academy. I saw your hate. Why should I trust you?"

He flipped over and flew on his back. "I've come to appreciate you."

My gaze narrowed. Should I ask him outright if he knew I was the lost princess? He acted suspicious and Stone said as much. Knowing I outranked Perry might make him angry.

"This exercise will help increase your speed." He held his wings at a downward tilt and zoomed past.

Feeling awkward, I bent my wings to the same angle. It didn't seem faster, I only felt silly. And then, the air streamlined with my wings and I went faster and faster.

"Great." He didn't break a sweat. "When doing close fighting, you have to keep your wings out of the way and available in case you need them. Try this."

He yanked out his sword and pulled his wings back. Swinging the sword back and forth, he demonstrated how to fight and fly.

I took out my small dagger and tried to bring my wings to a similar tilt. Swinging the blade, my wings stuck back out. I bent them to the correct angle again and swung the dagger. My body dropped into a freefall. Yanking the dagger to my side, I corrected myself.

"May I?" He held his hand out to my wings. When I nodded, he held my wings in the correct position. "Swing your dagger."

I counter-parried and my wings didn't change position.

"Good." His praise made me try harder.

We spent the next couple of hours flying, with him teaching and me learning. Perry was supportive and instructive. Taking his time, he taught me an intricate maneuver he'd dubbed *The Perry*. He laughed with me, not at me. And I had to wonder if I'd misjudged him.

"We should head back to the group." He smiled and I believed we'd truly become friends. "The others will be approaching the gates of the sanctuary soon."

Worry twisted a knot in my gut. What would happen once we arrived? I'd loved the freedom and joy of flying. I wasn't ready to be shackled again.

Perry and I landed just ahead of the group.

Stone rushed forward. His angry expression showed in his scrunched nose and flat lips. "Where have you two been?" He sounded like a father scolding his children.

I leaned into him and whispered in his ear, "Flying lesson."

He whispered back, "How can I guard you if you don't stick by my side?" His expression smoothed out, and he spoke louder so everyone could hear. "Well, don't fly off again."

Rejoining the group, I hiked the rest of the way. Walking seemed so mundane compared to the freedom of flying.

"Places everyone," Stone ordered. "We each have to remember the role we're playing. Ellery, you need to be up front as our royal connection."

Bristling at his tone, I shifted into position by his side. From this point forward, he would be my personal guard and the others would be my servants. I had to treat them as such.

Having missed most of the hike behind the waterfall, I took in the area as we approached the door. A heavy dampness hung in the air and I could smell the scent of water mixed with citrus and mint. The roar of the waterfall was louder, and I could barely hear myself think. A small, wooden, rickety staircase wound through a dark shaft and appeared to never end.

My calves cramped as we climbed.

The large, wooden double doors of the Aristos Sanctuary were carved into the mountain. If we hadn't been searching for it, I would've passed right by. Which was probably the point. The priestesses were secretive.

Centered in the door was a large bronze gong. The metal blended with the door, again concealing it.

Stone lifted the hammer and banged.

The noise reverberated through my soul. This was the beginning of going undercover as a royal, except I was royal, so I really wasn't pretending. I shook my head. Even I was confused by the situation.

The doors creaked open and a tiny woman dressed in red robes stood inside the gate. "May I help you?"

Her snooty voice reminded me of Rye and caused the knot in my stomach to double tie. "Hello. I'm Ellery Kunglig. I was sent by Commander Gardenia of the fairies to see Mother Morningmist and collect the Divinity Orb."

The priestess peered down her nose at me, which was difficult to do since she was shorter and wore a hood. "You are late."

"Yes, and I'm sorry. We ran into a few difficulties. A fire, and dragons, and—"

"The Priestesses of Aristos don't take excuses." Her superior tone stomped on my pride. "You're late and we're not accepting guests for the competition."

The door slammed shut in my face and I stumbled back.

What competition? Did she have the wrong idea about me?

Chapter Twenty

Dazed, I stood for a second. I'd almost died trying to get here and the priestess had slammed the door in my face. The fire, the dragons, the hiking and climbing, the injuries—they weren't excuses. The tribulations I'd faced, *we'd* faced, proved our determination.

I glanced at my companions. Their expressions appeared confused.

Was the door slammed in our face because I was half fairy? I'd faced discrimination before. Seen it happen to others. Except I was a princess and I was on a mission.

Curling my hands into fists, I banged them on the gong again and again. I banged out my frustration and my anger and my worry. "Commander Gardenia sent me! She said you'd let me in! I'm supposed to meet Mother Morningmist."

Gardenia said they'd have no choice but to welcome me. Obviously, she'd been wrong. Which didn't happen very often. The only other time I knew her to be wrong was when she sent me to the human palace to assassinate the prince. And we know how that turned out.

"Help me." Determination jammed through my spine. I banged again and again. I banged so hard my hands hurt.

Stone, Perry, Tos, and Hokima joined me. They battered their fists against the door, making a ruckus.

The door creaked open and the same priestess glared. She narrowed her distrustful gaze at my group. "You'll wake the dead."

"We'll continue to bang until you let us in!" I snarled at the woman.

We'd come so far. I'd learned so much. I couldn't fail now.

Stone bowed to the priestess. "I beg your pardon. We'd appreciate being let in. I realize we were supposed to be here several days ago. We had a couple of emergencies. A wounded sprite, a dragon attack. I'm sure your kind heart will take pity on us."

Stone winked when he finished speaking. My lips sputtered and irritation ruffled my wings. He was flirting with the older woman.

The priestess' cheeks reddened. "Well, since none of us will get sleep if I don't let you in, you can come for the night and you will be interviewed at a later time to assess whether you can stay."

"Thank you." Relief poured through me. "You won't—"

"Don't thank me." Something in her tone told me I might regret this decision. Her red robe swirled around her feet. "Come this way."

There was a second locked gate beyond the first. The priestess used an ancient key to unlock the door and led us into a garden. The scent of flowers overwhelmed. Tulips and orchids and lilies. Flowers usually grown at lower altitude and a less cold and harsh climate. But anything was possible with magic.

"Wow!" Tos' exclamation echoed around the rock walls surrounding us.

The priestess halted and pivoted to glare. "Shush."

The edges of the garden were filled with less pretty, although impressive, agriculture. Corn stalks taller than me. Wheat and barley waving in the wind. Vines climbing the walls with plump grapes. Things that shouldn't grow at this altitude.

"You could have a feast." Hokima kept his voice low.

The priestess bristled her shoulders, choosing to ignore his comment. She swung open another gate, not locked this time, and led us into a courtyard.

The courtyard was surrounded by three walls. Where the fourth wall should've been, a lake led to the ledge of a tall waterfall and the valley below. The view was amazing. And the fall would smash anyone to tiny pieces.

"Good thing you can fly." Speaking quietly, Perry elbowed me in a joking manner.

"Yeah, good thing."

In the center of the patio was a bubbling fountain. Statues of priestesses forming a circle of defense were in the middle of the fountain. Peering more closely, the priestesses were different majiks representing fairies, trolls, brownies, giants, and even humans.

I sucked in a breath. I didn't realize humans were part of the Aristos Sanctuary. I'd found out about the other majiks being part of the priestesshood from Watu.

"Can you believe it?" Bee mumbled. She must've heard my sharp intake of air.

The three buildings in the courtyard were made of stone and cement, held together with large wooden beams. They must've used the best craftsmanship and magic of the majiks to build such an impressive place so high on a mountain. Smaller waterfalls flowed between the buildings. Onion-shaped domes and turrets reached high in the sky. Bridges glittering with magic connected some of the towers.

"The servants' quarters are through here." The priestess led us down a short set of stairs.

"Why are we being taken to the servants quarters?" Offended on my friends' behalf, I didn't know how much to push.

"Because they are your servants and we're overcrowded with visitors right now."

"You're late." An old woman stood, coming from behind a desk. Her red hood pulled low on her forehead shadowing her face. "We weren't sure if you were coming and were about to start without you."

"This is Sister Summer." The first priestess waved at the other. "I'll show the others to their rooms."

"You come with me." Sister Summer pointed at me. She advanced toward another doorway, her long robe trailing on the spotless floor.

I hugged my friends before they were led to rooms in the servants' quarters. The rooms better be nice. I didn't like them going off in a different direction. We'd already been separated for a long time.

Mirroring his name, Stone didn't move. "I'm Ellery's personal guard. I will go with her." It was the first thing he'd spoken in awhile.

"That's not appropriate." The priestess waved her hands in agitation. "The sanctuary is perfectly safe for everyone."

He crossed his arms. The glare he sent in her direction would've slayed most foes. "I will sleep in front of her door if I need to."

Anxiety swirled in my stomach. We were lucky they'd let us in. "There's no need—"

"There is a need, Princess Ellery." His words said little, while his eyes spoke volumes. He planned to carry out his duty as my pretend personal guard and my real royal guard.

Warmth comforted me. I felt cared for and protected.

The priestess tried to stare him down and hit a stone wall. Stone's wall. "Both of you, come this way."

She led us back up the small set of stairs and through another corridor. This one had gleaming wood beams, shiny floors, and floating lights to show the way. We passed several identical doors, reminding me of an expensive hotel. The doors didn't have numbers. How was I going to remember which one was mine?

"Here you are." The priestess opened a door in the middle of the hallway. "Your guard will have the room next door."

"Thank you."

She opened the next door and pointedly waited for each of us to go inside separately.

With the priestess watching, I waved to Stone and went into my room.

The round room was smaller than my room at Queens Academy, yet larger than my attic bedroom. The bed sat in the center of the room and was surrounded by a gauzy white material canopy. The chest of drawers and nightstand looked ancient with old fashioned brass handles. The atmosphere was welcoming and regal.

A quiet knock sounded. Before I could respond, the door opened, and Stone let himself in. He scanned the length of the room, checking everything out. "Everything okay?"

"Yes." I sighed. "I feel guilty for having such a luxurious room with so much space when everyone else is probably in cramped quarters."

"If it makes you feel less guilty," he winked, "we can share this room."

"Get out." I couldn't even summon the enthusiasm to toss him out or to take him to task for his flirting.

He'd barely spoken to me since he'd rejected my kiss. What had changed? He ran hot and cold, and I found it confusing and frustrating. And kind of attractive.

The following morning, the unfriendly Sister Summer brought me high into a turret to meet with another priestess.

A small office with shelves of books on each of the walls. Floating candles and colored reflections from the stained-glass window provided light. An antique wooden desk sat in the middle of the room and another priestess sat behind the desk.

"I am Sister Autumn." She wore a red-hooded robe the same as the other priestesses, covering her head and shadowing her face. Bits of her I could make out. The angular jaw and pert nose. The large blue eyes. I couldn't tell if she was fairy or not. What else could she be? She didn't resemble a troll or an ogre. She wasn't as small as a brownie or a sprite.

"Hello. I'm Princess Ell—"

"I know who you are." She snapped to a stand. She was tall for a fairy. Taller than me.

If she knew, why hadn't she bowed? Was it because everyone here was some type of royalty? "I'm here to meet Mother Morningmist."

A thrill of expectation went through me. Meeting Mother Morningmist was pertinent to my mission, plus she was my great-grandmother. A relative I hadn't known about until recently. Someone else who could mentor and help me learn the ways of fairy royalty.

"When you meet Mother Morningmist, you must be prepared to extract the Divinity Orb from the Reflection Pool." Sister Autumn's sharp tone told me she expected me to fail. She wanted me to fail.

"Excuse me?"

"Using the gifts from Mother Earth," her voice slowed and thinned with impatience. "You must extract the Divinity Orb—"

"I know what you mean." I spoke through gritted teeth. She approved of me less than Sister Summer. Maybe they were related. "Anyone can use the gifts of Mother Earth."

"Good. Then we understand each other." Sister Autumn's dismissal caused my stomach to churn.

Nausea rose in my throat. The skill Watu had tried to teach me, had counseled how important it was to learn, and I hadn't had the patience to keep trying. The troll must not have been able to tell me the priestesses' secret although she'd tried to guide me in what I needed to know. Failure choked me, and I found it hard to breathe.

"Why?" My question sounded shaky and dry, not demanding as I'd wanted.

"It is an ancient test to prove your worthiness." Sister Autumn steepled her long fingers under her chin and inspected me.

I tried not to squirm. "Worthy of meeting my own great-grandmother?"

"Ah. So, you know one of our secrets." She stayed calm, as if me knowing secrets was of no consequence.

"One of your *bazillion* secrets." I couldn't contain the sarcasm. What I was supposed to know and didn't and what I did know and wasn't supposed to stirred in my blood. "Between the fairy secrets and now the priestesses' secrets, I can't keep them straight."

Sister Autumn slammed her palms on the desk. She leaned forward, closer to me.

I didn't believe she'd threatened me. Clearly, what did I know? The woman hadn't liked me on sight. Because I'd arrived late or because I was half fairy? I straightened my shoulders. Either way, it didn't matter. I liked me.

"Listen, Princess Ellery." She spat my name. Clearly, not a fan of mine. "You might be a *different* type of fairy princess, nevertheless your royalty has no influence here. These are our customs and rules and you are obliged to follow them."

Follow them or get out.

I heard the warning beneath the surface. "Commander Gardenia sent me here—"

"She also has no influence here." Sister Autumn sat back in her chair and gave me a fake, pleasant smile. "Play by our rules or go home."

I couldn't go home without the Divinity Orb.

I nodded. I could do this. I had to.

Trying to sound unworried about the task, I asked, "When do I get to prove myself?"

"Try again," Stone commanded.

Commanded *me*. I was supposed to be the royal one.

"I've been trying." I was tired, and my muscles were tight and my anxiety about my worthless abilities added to my stress. If Watu couldn't teach me to withdraw the spectral orb, how were Stone and Bee supposed to?

The practice facility reminded me of the magic rooms in Queens Academy. Small, heavy concrete walls bare of everything but essentials. This one had a small, fake pool built into the floor, and we were on the third level. Magical. A current ran through the water, creating delicate waves and a colorful ball sat at the bottom.

We'd been practicing for hours. The time for the test kept drawing nearer and my abilities were still bad. If I couldn't learn to abstract an object, I'd never meet my great-grandmother, never get the Divinity Orb, and never prove myself to the fairies.

I'd be a failure before I began. The inner chide rubbed against my raw and weary nerves. I hadn't thought learning this from Watu had been important. I'd been frustrated and anxious to continue my quest. I'd been wrong. My entire ability to rule the fairies depended on it. The Divinity Orb would help me win the war against humans, it would prove to the other fairies I was capable to lead them, it would prove to them I would be a good princess.

"Come on, Elle." Bee had helped prepare the samples for my practice and continued to cheer me on. "I know you can do it."

"I'm trying." Frustration and helplessness tied the little abilities I'd had into knots. Arbor had taught me some very basic gifts from Mother Earth. I'd never practiced them. I'd used them in an emergency underneath Regent Theobald's palace and gotten stuck in the dungeon.

"Will you excuse us, Bee?" Stone might've asked but it was clearly an order.

Bee wrinkled her nose. "I'm her friend. I'm here to help."

"More pressure isn't going to help." He opened the door. "I'll let you know if we need you."

Glaring at Stone, she gave me a snarky squint before leaving. Our friendship had been strained since our fight on the side of the mountain. She'd commented on how Stone flirted with me and she didn't trust him. I wasn't sure how much I trusted her. Something had been off with her since we'd been reunited.

He shut the door behind her and approached me. "You need to relax. Using Mother Earth's gifts isn't something you can do when tense."

I understood. Every time I tried and failed, I tensed up more. Clenching my hands, I tried to control the frustration.

"You need to relax and be comfortable. You need to coax the object from the water." His lips twitched. "It's similar to coaxing a kiss."

I choked. Is that what he'd done to me? His deep suggestive tone had me thinking of kissing. Kissing him, and his rejection. "Why did you reject my kiss the other night?"

His mouth dropped into a straight line. "You're a princess. There can't be anything between us."

"You knew I was a princess before I did, and yet you kissed me with no remorse."

"True." He paced toward me and his expression went serious with flat lips and hunched eyebrows. "My flirting started as a way to keep you close. Then I saw how brave you were. How beautiful. How fierce."

My bones softened at his compliment and I leaned toward him, wanting to soak it in.

"I became attracted to you." His voice dropped low and his whispers tickled my ear. "When I saw you in the lake, I was so relieved, so overcome, I couldn't stop myself from stealing a kiss."

"You didn't steal a kiss." I'd returned it willingly. My knees quivered.

"I shouldn't have done it." Anguish crossed his expression, apparently battling with himself. "I'm a warrior, not a romancer. I flirt, and I have fun. You deserve more and warriors don't get involved with the person they guard."

My body drained of energy under the pressure. The pressure and the panic once everyone learned the truth. Watu had taught me a lot about myself, but I still had weaknesses and still needed a friend. "You're right." Even though I wanted him to be wrong. "Right now, I need to know you'll be there for me."

"I'll be there for you." His expression hardened into straight lines and harsh angles. "Now, try to get the orb out. You can do it."

If Stone believed in me, I had to try. Watu had believed in me, too. Gardenia must believe in my abilities or she wouldn't have sent me. Of course, if I failed Perry could take my place.

Placing my hand in the water, I blew out a breath and slowed my pulse.

Stay calm. Stay relaxed. Coax.

The water vibrated against my palm. Excitement trickled through my bloodstream. Something heavy landed in the palm of my hand. The practice orb. I shut down the instant tightening of my excited muscles. The orb was in my hand. I still had to withdraw it from the water. Closing my eyes, I concentrated. I rotated my hand palm up and slowly raised the orb to the surface. Water dripped from my skin, and I opened my eyes.

The practice orb was in my hand above water.

"I did it!" I jumped up. The orb disappeared, sinking to the bottom of the pool. I didn't care. I'd done it. I'd used Mother Earth's gifts to get the orb. "I'm going to get the Divinity Orb!" I swung my wet hands around Stone's neck. A smile burst on my face. "I did it."

His arms wrapped around my waist and he swung me around in celebration. "Great job."

His caring tone unwound something inside me. *Like coaxing a kiss, huh?* Gaining bravado from his touch, I leaned into his hard chest. His head tilted toward me. His mouth was so tantalizingly close. I could see the greenish tint to his skin, reminding me of our differences.

And our similarities.

He bent his head and his lips brushed mine. Softly, persuasively, caringly.

This time, I returned the kiss with passion. Last time I'd kissed him it was more of a reaction. This time, I wanted the kiss. I needed the release and he was attracted to me. I didn't care what happened in the future because right now he was here for me, he was helping me, he was protecting me.

The door burst open.

My lips froze against Stone's.

"Bee." He pulled away first. Pivoting, he blocked me from view of the doorway.

I could see around his broad back and spotted Bee wearing a smirk, standing with Sister Autumn. She entered the room with someone following behind.

Lightheadedness put me in a fog. She knew I was the princess and she'd seen me kissing my royal guard. My skin heated. What were they going to think of me? They were the ones making the decisions at the sanctuary. Blowing out a breath, I tried to cool my body. Until I saw the person standing behind her.

Rye.

My knees gave way, alerting everyone to my presence behind Stone. I pressed my palms against the damp wall to hold myself upright. Rye truly was alive. My heart stuttered and went into a full loud beat. My ribcage squeezed against my lungs. Relief and love pounded through my veins. He was alive.

I mean, my stepsisters had said he'd signed that terrible law, except I hadn't seen any evidence of his person. Not in news vids or gossip. Although, since I'd been staying at Queens Academy and come on this mission, I'd received no news of what was happening in our kingdom.

I had to remember, he wasn't Rye. He was Prince Zacharye.

Because he wore the full regalia of his station. Double-breasted jacket with gold buttons and a sash. Medals with colorful ribbons hanging from his chest. Dress pants with stripes on the side and shiny shoes. Even a hat with gold braid. What was a human prince doing in a majik sanctuary?

My gaze clung to his frigid, silver irises. He'd changed in the month since I'd last seen him. His pale skin exhibited a dullness as though he'd lost the joy of living. Shadows blackened beneath his eyes. His lips were flat and smile-less. The stress of attempting to win his throne must've aged and matured him.

Unless the rumors were true, and he now believed what his uncle espoused.

Even with the changes, I wanted to go up and run my fingers across his chest, to caress his skin, to see his megawatt smile. The scar I remembered at his hairline had healed and only a single tiny line showed. A couple of newer scars were scratched into his handsome face, making him less perfect and more rugged. A shiver passed through me when I remembered my vision of him being locked in a tower. Obviously, the vision wasn't true. So why was he wearing an ugly expression as if I was the last person on earth he wanted to see?

He was alive. I was healthy and alive. And I'd been kissing...

Stone.

He stood at a diagonal, half facing me and half facing the newcomers. A shadow had fallen over his face. His eyebrows gathered in a thundercloud and his just-kissed lips pouted in a frown. What did he think of my reaction to seeing Rye? We'd kissed and now I reacted like a schoolgirl. My cheeks heated.

Rye had seen me kissing Stone.

My stomach fell and my cheeks grew even hotter, as if I had been dipped in one of the priestesses' steaming baths. No wonder Rye's face was cold, and he didn't greet me. We'd shared something special, including my first kiss, and now he'd witnessed me kissing another.

Not that it was any of his business. He was my enemy even if at one time I'd had feelings for him.

Pushing off the wall, I forced my knees not to shake and waded forward. Was he angry I'd been kissing Stone? I know if I'd heard rumors of Rye being with another girl, I would've been mad. But it didn't matter. We could never be together.

"You're alive." A miracle stood before me. He was the miracle.

Sister Autumn gestured toward him. "This is Prince Zacharye of the human faction."

Ignoring the introduction, he appeared shell-shocked. His eyebrows rose forming a question. "You have wings."

Another of our differences.

Shifting my wings back, I tried to put two words together. "What're you doing here?"

This was a majik sanctuary ruled by female priestesses. He had no place here.

"Elle's not royal." His contempt had me standing taller.

Was I not allowed in a room with him because he was a prince? How much had he changed? He treated me as a peon. Of course, he thought I was a peon. He didn't know the truth. To be fair, I hadn't known I was a princess when we'd met before. That shouldn't matter. We'd had a connection, been friends—more than friends, worked together for a common goal.

How dare he?

The priestess' glance swung back and forth between us. Her gaze twinkled. "You two know each other?"

Stone glared at the prince, trying to kill him with a look. "They've met."

My overprotective guard knew there was more to it. Either Stone didn't want to admit it, or he didn't want to discuss it in front of the priestess. Or ever. I'd be okay with that.

"She is royal." Sister Autumn shook her head trying to clear up her own confusion and ours. "Princess Ellery—"

"Princess?" Rye jerked his head forward. His eyes enlarged, and his expression showed betrayal. The harsh lines of his face contrasted with the surprise in his gaze.

Raising my shoulders, I lifted my palms up and spread my wings. "Surprise?"

"She's the lost princess of the fairies." The priestess rushed through her statement afraid of getting stopped. "Princess Ellery is competing for the Divinity Orb. Just like you, Prince Zacharye."

My skin tingled, and I felt a heaviness in my gut. "Competing?"

CHAPTER TWENTY-ONE

My mind went into a tizzy. Rye was here. He'd seen me kissing Stone. I struggled with the test, and now I find out it's a competition. Against Rye. "What do you mean by competing? How?"

Rye's nose titled in a superior way, even though I was the one with magical powers. His sleek smile said he knew more than me.

I kept my huff inside.

Sister Autumn sneered, her lips twisting in disgust. "Everyone of royal blood knows about the Divinity Orb and how it works."

Pulling my thoughts and objections together, I pointed out the obvious. "Ry—Prince Zacharye is human. The orb is magical."

"Magical through Mother Earth's gifts." His objection pointed out an important fact.

One I knew and should've comprehended. Anyone could access Mother Earth's gifts. Even a human. Even Rye.

My stomach dropped as another realization hit. I narrowed my gaze at him. "You knew when we went through the rock together." When I'd first met him.

His lips lifted in a slight, knowing grin. That's why he hadn't pushed for an explanation the night under the human palace when I'd used Mother Earth's gifts to let us walk through a porous rock. I'd thought I'd gotten off easy not having to explain.

A burst of anger plunged through my bloodstream, and I held back my true thoughts. I refused to get in a shouting match with a prince. It wasn't dignified. I tilted my chin and glowered.

"Easy, Ellery." Stone put a hand on my arm sensing my anger. He tensed, ready to defend my honor, which soothed me.

Sister Autumn brought her hands together in a peaceful prayer position. She bestowed a smile on Rye. "All peoples, all races, can access Mother Earth's gifts. One merely has to know how."

Advantage, me. Rye might be familiar with the concept, but he didn't know how to call on Mother Earth's gifts. He didn't know how to open himself up to her gifts.

"Why are we being given this test? Why now?" I didn't care if my questions were stupid. I wanted to go in with knowledge.

"The Divinity Orb has been hidden in the Reflection Pool for decades. Protected. The priestesses have been able to access the spectral orb for our purposes of forecasting the future."

Watu had said she'd accessed the visions through a spectral orb.

"With our kingdom in turmoil, the full power of the orb is needed more than ever." The priestess slanted a glance at Rye. Did she understand it was humans who'd started this war? "There's a prophecy and the royals of each contingent will compete to bring the Divinity Orb out of seclusion and control its powers."

I stood there, shocked. Gardenia had explained it differently. I'd get here, my great-grandmother would hand me the orb because of who I was, and I'd waltz out and back to Queens Academy a hero. Watu had tried to warn me in her own way. And then I'd learned I had to extract the orb from the Reflection Pool. I didn't know anything about Rye competing, too.

Rye nodded. He understood the power and the importance of the orb. Why hadn't Gardenia told me? Or Arbor and Stone? Did they know? It would be me against Rye. We were on opposite sides. My blood slowed into a song of sadness of things that could never be. We would always be on opposite sides. My emotions didn't matter.

I didn't even know what my feelings were for him or Stone.

Stone's expression was cut from the rock he was named after. Nothing blinked or twitched. He stared at my opponent.

Rye stepped closer to me and leaned in a confiding manner. "You didn't tell me you were royal. A princess, no less."

I didn't appreciate his quiet tone. He spoke as if he didn't trust me. "You didn't tell me you were the prince."

"You learned soon enough."

"Only because you walked in on me and Stone..." Heat flamed in my cheeks. I should've continued my sentence. *Only because you walked in on me and Stone about to blow up the auraguillotine.* But Rye had also walked in on me and Stone kissing. Floundering, I didn't know what else to say or how to cover the gap.

Rye flattened his lips together in disapproval. His eyes narrowed, and he glared from beneath slitted lids. Even antagonistic, his aristocratic bearing and ruggedness shined through.

His anger had me taking a step back so I didn't punch him, and right into Stone, who put his arm around my shoulders.

Rye's eyebrows raised, and he gave me another dark expression. He believed he knew everything.

Well, he didn't.

Shaking off Stone's protective gesture, I didn't need any more misunderstandings. As politely as possible, I thanked the priestess and started to parade out of the room. Brushing past Rye, a zing of the old connection reached out and tried to stop me. I pushed through.

In a daze, I plodded back to my room with thoughts running wild and my heart beating as fast as a mockingbird. When Stone shut the door behind us, I swiveled and confronted him. I hadn't even realized he'd been following me. "Did you know?"

Stone hadn't seemed shocked to see the prince or learn that this was a competition.

He avoided my gaze. "Know what?"

My crazy thoughts and throbbing pulse stirred into anger. If he wanted specificity, he'd get it. "Did you know Prince Zacharye was here?"

Stone regarded the ground. He was hiding something.

"*When* did you know?"

No response came. I pushed on his arm, physically pressing him for an answer.

"Found out when we arrived."

"You knew the prince was here." I slapped Stone's arm and stepped away.

The nerves in my stomach twisted into a tight knot. Stone had known and yet he'd kissed me. I paced to the other side of the room and took off my jacket. Maybe he'd done it on purpose so we'd get caught. I paced to the other side and my anger built with each tensed muscle. Who could I trust now? Everyone was lying or keeping pertinent information from me.

I had to take one issue at a time. Pacing to stand in front of Stone, I asked, "Why didn't you tell me I had to compete for the orb?"

"I thought if you knew it was a competition, you'd put more pressure on yourself." He raised his hands to touch me. I backed away. "You needed to relax."

Which is what he'd said before I'd succeeded and we'd kissed. My blood pressure swooshed, shooting anger through my veins. Was he manipulating me? I was so tired of people pretending to be something else. Including myself.

"You knew Rye was here. Did you know I'd be competing against him?" I shouldn't think of him so informally. "Prince Zacharye."

Stone's expression closed down. "Why does it matter who will be competing?"

"You knew I'd be competing against Rye." That was clear. "How did you know?"

"It's common knowledge royals compete for the Divinity Orb." Stone shoved away from the wall and stalked to the other side of the room.

"Common knowledge to everyone except me." My body drooped. Watu had tried to explain the importance of the skill. She should've been more adamant, although that wasn't her way.

"My understanding was because your great-grandmother is in charge here, you'd be given the orb." Stone volunteering information skewed my thinking.

That's what I'd been told. There had to be more.

I needed to take him off guard. Stepping up to him, I placed my hands on the lapels of his jacket. "Why did you think I'd be handed the orb? Who told you?"

"Commander Gardenia said..." His gaze snapped from my hands to straight ahead. He'd said more than he was supposed to.

Gardenia. The name should've been soothing but it spiked my blood pressure.

I pushed against him and he stumbled back. Everything pulled together in my head. Had Gardenia known about his flirting and his kisses? Had she ordered it? He'd confessed he'd done it to keep me close, and then said things between us had changed. But had they?

He knew about the competition and hadn't told me. True friends didn't keep friends in the dark. I needed to be in control of my own destiny.

He'd known about Rye being here, competing against me, and Stone hadn't shared. He hadn't been surprised when we were interrupted while kissing. Had he kissed me on purpose knowing we'd be found out?

I wiped the back of my hand across my lips erasing our last kiss. Kisses I'd willingly returned. Now, I understood why Rye had been so frosty. As a royal, you couldn't trust anyone.

Stone grabbed my small fist and held it in the palm of his hand. "Elle, I'm sorry." He sounded raw and husky.

Snatching my hand back, I pushed away. I wasn't buying his remorse.

"Don't touch me." Hurt cascaded through my nervous system. My skin felt tender and bruised. "I thought you were my friend. I thought we..." My finger pressed against my once-kissed lips.

I'd never thought he'd use me and betray me similar to how Rye had. I had to learn to protect myself and my emotions. I couldn't count on Stone all the time.

"Did Gardenia put you up to this?" I huffed knowing my fairy godmother suspected my affection for the prince. "Were you just doing your job when you kissed me? Protecting me from danger. From Rye." The hurt spread, making my heart ache. Stone had tried to distract me from my attraction to Rye by making me look twice at him. I didn't know who to believe or who to trust. "From myself."

I was sulking in my room when the door opened and a blur of color flew in.

Arbor.

Joy rushed through my bloodstream and I flew to her. I wanted to hug her, although I didn't want to smash her. I held out my hand so she could land on my palm.

"You got your wings!" She hovered above my hand.

"I did." I spread my wings and fluttered them, prancing around the room.

She landed on my palm. "Congratulations. I'm so happy for you."

Inspecting every inch of her, I tried to spot any wounds or scars. Her shorter hair had been shaved into a military style and there was no flamboyance to her outfit. Her tiny wings had ragged edges. Sorrow slowed my excitement. "I'm so sorry, Arbor. I really screwed up with the fire. Are your wings damaged?"

Worrying about her reminded me of the strange burst of power when I'd started the fire. I hadn't experienced the issue again. Maybe I'd learned to control my magic better.

"I'm fine." She wiggled her wings. "I even got extra strength added for long distance flying. Now, we can fly together."

"You look wonderful." Joy filled my veins, making me less angry. "I'm so glad you're here."

I stroked her wings, enjoying this happiness of having my best friend back. We'd been friends for almost a year, which was about the time my fairy aunt, the former princess, would've died.

"Me, too."

"Did the priestesses let you in?" I remembered how difficult it had been for me.

"Stone spoke to the guards at the door, letting them know I'd be coming." Arbor buzzed around the room, peeking behind the drapery and peering in the closet as if checking for hidden combatants. "Quite the digs."

My grumpiness returned at the mention of Stone. Another thing he'd kept from me. "Too bad it comes with an overprotective and lying guard."

"A hunky and handsome guard." She waved her hand in front of her face. "You're lucky to have Stone protecting you." Did she know all the guards at Queens Academy?

"Enough about him. So much has happened while you were gone." I plopped on the bed, wanting to tell her everything and wanting to know if she'd truly healed. "What happened to you after the fire?"

She landed on my shoulder. "Nothing exciting. The guards brought me back to the castle and the healers healed me."

For someone normally so talkative, she didn't say much. What had the healers done to give her stronger wings?

I swallowed a lump in my throat. "How's the queen?"

"Holding her own, or so the official reports say."

"What do the unofficial reports say?"

Arbor shrugged. "I don't hear much gossip. Not like your friend Bee."

The change in Arbor's tone told me she still didn't cherish my new friend. I didn't want to get into a jealous argument. Now she was here, I wanted to get serious and confess. She was the only one who never lied to me. "I have to tell you something."

"By your anger and flushed skin, I'd guess you kissed Stone." Arbor could always read my body language.

"I did, but that's not what—"

"You did!" She flew into the air. "I was joking. I'm so jealous."

She didn't sound jealous, she sounded encouraging. If she knew my truths, she wouldn't be. She wasn't fond of the strict rules of the guards.

I got to my feet and paced across the room. "It was a mistake. I never should've kissed him. He lied to me."

"About?" Her wings didn't flutter as fast.

Twisting my hands together, I needed to tell my best friend the truth. "First, I need to tell you something no one else can know."

"Okaaay."

"It's a secret of the highest security. I'm not pretending to be royal." I took a deep breath. "I don't need to pretend because I'm the lost princess."

Arbor's wings didn't flutter. Her expression didn't change.

I'd been expecting a big reaction. "Aren't you shocked?"

Why isn't she shocked?

"Surprised, definitely yes." She took a twirl around the room. "I mean when we met you were a servant in Sybil's house." An awkward laugh came out of Arbor's tiny body.

Something was off. Why point out what I used to be?

I had too many other things to focus on than her reaction to one of many things I needed to share. "And I told you about what happened with Rye under the human palace. I mean, Prince Zacharye." My sole purpose for being under the palace was to rescue Arbor. She'd missed most of the adventure until the very end. "He's here."

"I heard when I arrived."

"I thought Rye and I had a connection when we met." I gripped the bedpost and swung around, practically swooning remembering. "He was my first kiss."

And I'd probably blown it out of proportion in my mind. I didn't even like the new version of Rye I'd met today.

I'd told Arbor about the kiss. She knew about my feelings, and hadn't reacted with giggles the way my best friend normally would.

She didn't react. Had her injuries taken away her fun attitude about life?

"Are you sure you're okay?" I didn't want this to be about me if she wasn't one hundred percent healthy.

"I'm fine." She gave me a big grin. "Go on."

I covered my cheeks with my hands. "Rye saw me kissing Stone."

"Was he jealous?"

Tilting my head, I remembered every detail of Rye's reaction. "He didn't display much emotion. More contemptuous than anything."

Which could've been the way he showed his anger. Maybe he'd met someone since we'd been apart. Maybe his uncle forced him to commit to a human girl and to get in his uncle's good graces he was going along with it. Maybe I'd made up the connection thing in my head. Or maybe it was because we were competitors.

"*Prince* Zacharye," I emphasized his title, "and I are competing against each other for the Divinity Orb."

She fluttered her wings. "Do you know what the competition is?"

At least I wasn't the only one who didn't know about the competition. I tightened my locked hands, trying not to exhibit my agitation. "Gardenia never told me I'd have to compete for the orb." Pulling my hands apart, I pulled them into fists, wanting to punch something for the deception. For all the deceptions. "She never told me about a lot of things. For example, the fact that Stone works directly for her."

My head jerked up and I considered Arbor. She wasn't surprised about this news. "Did you know Stone worked for Gardenia?"

"Doesn't everyone who will be fighting on the fairy side work for the commander?" Normally, over-opinionated Arbor didn't see a problem with the lie.

I'd forgiven him for knowing about me being a princess before I did. I'd forgiven him for pretending to be a human guard when he was a spy. This was different. "He kissed me before I knew about his connection to my fairy godmother, kissed me to keep me close.

He's lied about his real purpose. Lied about knowing Rye was at the sanctuary."

"Sometimes lies are necessary. Doesn't mean Stone doesn't care. I mean, sometimes when you're working on a job you really become friends, or um more, with your coworker, right?" She spoke with passion, but I couldn't trust him with my kisses.

Stone had kept too many things from me.

And now Rye was here, I didn't know what to do. The beat of my heart pounded in my head, hammering at my confusion.

"I'm so glad you're back, Arbor." I could rely on her. "I can't trust Rye because we're competing and I can't trust Stone because he lied. I can trust you."

Late that night, I strolled in the magical garden, trying to get away from the pressure and my own thoughts. While I had the opportunity of no one following me, I snuck out wearing pajamas.

The full moon shed an alluring light over the garden. The scent of lavender calmed. Exotic flowers mixed with run of the mill agricultural plants. A colored waterfall fell from one of the rock walls, leading to the lake, and a second, larger waterfall plummeted hundreds of yards down.

"Nice night." Rye's deep voice reached out and caressed me.

I thought it was my imagination or a dream. Pivoting toward the words spoken, I spotted him standing between a corn stalk and a eucalyptus tree. He wore the pants with the stripes. The jacket with medals and sash was gone. An untucked white shirt fluttered in the quiet breeze.

I couldn't stop the leak of suspicion entering my bloodstream. Too many others had lied to or betrayed me. "Why are you here?"

"I must've had the same thought you did." He took a step closer, not menacing but it worried me all the same. His dark hair had grown longer, and a shadow of facial hair gave him a careless and athletic air. "I needed to get away from everyone."

"Do you have an overbearing protector, too?" I wanted to kick myself for bringing up Stone.

Rye nodded. "Between my guards and my uncle and his spies, I'm never alone."

I understood what he meant. The servants, the friends, the pretend-friends, and the pretenders were something I was learning about. He'd dealt with it his entire life. My blood flow crawled to a slow, sad tempo. My life, my friends, and my enemies would never be the same.

The silence stretched. We each found peace in the chirping crickets and the occasional hooting owl.

"What you saw earlier..." I wanted to explain. How did you tell someone what they saw wasn't what they saw? Even when it was. "Stone was kissing me under orders."

"What?" The prince seemed offended on my behalf.

"Stone is my royal guard and he was trying to keep me close without telling me why." A short pang shredded through my chest. "You see, I didn't know I was a princess until recently."

It was important for Rye to know I hadn't lied.

"Your guard kissed you to protect you? He should be shot."

I couldn't tell if he was joking. "Stone needed an excuse to keep me close to guard me without telling me the truth."

Rye's lips lifted in a genuine smile. "He didn't need an excuse. You're beautiful."

My knees went weak and I gripped the bench positioned along the pathway. I didn't feel beautiful. I felt weak and stupid and gullible. I refused to show it. *Fake it 'til you make it, right?*

"Your wings are beautiful, too. And impressive." He stared past my shoulder with a curious-intense expression. Not disgusted or turned off. "Did you have wings before when we met?"

Turning my back slightly, I let my wings spread out. They were beautiful. "No. I got them days ago. I'm still getting used to them."

"Tell me something." He grabbed my arm and applied pressure. Sparks of pleasure circulated from contact. His expression went grim and thunder flashed in his eyes. "Did your guard force his attentions on you?"

His protective tone and questions made my knees go weaker and I sunk down onto the stone bench, taking him with me. While we talked about my wings, his mind must've been deciding whether to ask the personal question. If I answered truthfully, I'd reveal what an idiot I've been. I couldn't lie though. "No."

He pulled his shoulders back and let go of my arm. "I see."

"No, you don't." Frustration gnarled in my belly. I took his hand and held on tight. "What does it really matter? Stone can't be with me because I'm a princess and...and...you and I are enemies."

Meaning we couldn't be together.

Rye glanced down at our clasped fingers. He didn't remove his hand, which gave me hope. Raising his head, he looked me straight in the eye. The blaze of anger, or was that jealousy, I'd seen earlier disappeared. The silver in his gaze calmed, resembling an icy lake, except they weren't cold, only melting.

"I don't think enemies is the right word." He squeezed my hand. "Friends who happen to be working on opposite sides of a war, and yet our goal is the same."

"We're competing, although it won't be much of a competition because I'm a fairy and am used to using Mother Earth's gifts." He was trying to smooth things out between us, and I was running my mouth. "I mean, you went through one porous rock with me under your palace. Other than that, you haven't been exposed to these sorts of things. Humans have lost touch with Mother Earth."

He licked his bottom lip and bit down. "Elle, I've been trained in Mother Earth's gifts."

My eyes widened. "What?"

"I've been trained. When I was gone from the palace last year. The training was part of my secondment."

I remembered when Prince Zacharye had disappeared from news reports and didn't attend any royal functions. It was a time when his uncle, Regent Theobald, had tightened the reins against majiks.

"I know how to use Mother Earth's gifts." He wasn't bragging, only stating facts. Letting me know I had competition, telling me the truth. "I can withdraw objects from natural elements and walk through rocks and other things."

Air scraped out of my lungs. I had no advantage because I was half fairy. I was at a disadvantage because he'd been training and I'd just found out about the competition. I slumped against the back of the bench.

"Elle, what's wrong?" Concern entered his tone and because of his real emotion, I couldn't hold back the truth.

"I'm going to lose." I sniffed. If I didn't win the Divinity Orb, the humans would have an advantage in the war. The fairies would blame me and never accept me.

"Don't say that." He used a finger to wipe away a tear I hadn't realized escaped. His tender flick sent my heart into overdrive. "You have as much a chance as anyone."

"You don't understand." I couldn't believe I was going to admit my weakness. Still, I needed to talk to someone and he'd understand. "I've struggled with this skill. If I don't retrieve the Divinity Orb, the fairies will never accept me, a half fairy, as their princess."

He put his arm around my shoulders and tucked me in close. "It will be alright."

Even knowing we were competing against each other, I soaked in his comfort. "You're going to win, and I won't be able to face the fairies."

"You don't know I'll win." His soothing tone made me want to curl into him more. "It could be any of the others."

My head jerked up. "Others?"

CHAPTER TWENTY-TWO

I couldn't sleep.

There were so many things I didn't know. Either through ignorance or secrets being kept. At least Rye wasn't keeping anything from me. He'd told me about his training, and he'd told me there would be others competing.

One majik from each of the royal families in existence.

An elf, a troll, a goblin, and a human, Rye. Plus, me.

After sending a single firefly message—which is a Mother Earth gift I didn't have trouble using—I left my quarters and met Bee in a service closet. Of all my friends, she knew how to scout information and gossip. I could count on her to tell me everything.

"Did you know the competition includes one royal representative from every group?" I whispered to her when she arrived.

The room's walls had shelves with sheets and towels. The acidic smell of cleaning supplies filled the area reminding me of Milford house. A large maid's cart sat in the middle of the room.

Bee kept her voice low. "The servants don't gossip here as much as at the castle."

Something I'd need to fix when I returned home. Gossip was helpful to spies.

"Stone and Arbor made it seem common knowledge." And the reason I hadn't known was because I hadn't been raised in a fairy environment. But Bee had been raised by fairies. "You didn't know?"

She shook her head. "I did hear Hokima say the troll competitor is his cousin."

I scrunched my shoulders, remembering the sash he'd worn when he'd first arrived at the fairy castle. He was part of a royal troll line.

"Can you trust his loyalty?" Doubt hung in her tone.

"He's my friend. We've been through a lot together."

He'd been there for me and he came when Gardenia asked him to help on this mission. Unless he'd had ulterior motives. Frustration balled in my gut. Before, I never had to question how those around me really felt. My stepsisters were very clear about their hate. Was I going to spend the rest of my life worrying about the loyalty of those beside me?

Bee scrunched up her face. "Still, you might not want to share your training results with Hokima."

"What results?" I sagged against the shelf with the puffy towels. "One time I managed to pull the orb out of the practice pool."

I'd spent hours practicing during the afternoon and evening. Arbor had made me try again and again. She'd encouraged and cajoled and shouted. Every time I'd failed.

"That bad, huh?" Bee sympathized. "Are you sure Arbor's a good trainer?"

"Better than Stone." When Stone and I had argued earlier, he'd admitted to knowing about the competition and the prince. He'd said nothing about others competing. His deception slashed through me. Everyone kept secrets, even those I believed close.

"Worse." My throat constricted, and my mouth went dry. "I thought I'd at least have an advantage over Prince Zacharye." I was careful to use his formal name. "I've since learned he's been trained in Mother Earth's gifts."

"He has?"

"Yep. He told me earlier tonight."

"You saw the prince?" Her voice filled with surprise and dread. "How? Why?"

The questions being thrown at me were gauntlets and I side-stepped around them. "I happened to bump into him by accident."

"And you talked to him? He's a prince."

"We've met before."

"Really?" Her tone was high with suspicion. "Are you sure you really want to win? Are you really trying?"

I slammed my foot down. "I tried to learn from Watu. I've practiced with Stone and Arbor since learning of the competition. I've repeated in my mind what I'm supposed to do. Nothing works."

Bee leaned in and her expression went serious. "There is one way to guarantee the win."

I chortled darkly. "That would be nice."

Grabbing my hand, she pulled me upright. "You can steal the orb."

Her earnest and conspiratorial gaze gleamed. If I stole the orb, I wouldn't need to compete and I wouldn't be defeated. I was a fairy who should have control of my magic, all my magic.

I broke her mystical hold on me. "That wouldn't be fair."

"What's fair? Especially in war." Her voice went hard and cold.

Where was her sympathy for my plight? I remembered her complaints about me from our midnight escape. What did she really think of me? My lungs compressed. I hated the doubts I had about everyone.

"Commander Gardenia expected you to be handed the orb because of your great-grandmother."

Stone had said something similar. Everyone must know our relationship.

"Rightfully, it's yours." Bee hammered home her point.

My great-grandmother currently hosted the Reflection Pool imprisoning the orb. She had access to its powers, as did the other priestesses. Watu believed the orb was mine as well—it's what she'd seen in the vision, although I'd had to fight for it. If I didn't go home with the orb, Gardenia would be furious because she'd planned to cancel the mission. I'd gone off anyway and would most likely fail. Once the fairies learned I was the lost princess, they wouldn't believe in me as their future leader.

But if I came home with the orb, all would be forgiven and the fairies would believe in me. They'd follow me into battle.

"How would we find the Reflection Pool?" Seeing the location of the Reflection Pool in advance might make me more comfortable during the competition.

"It's in Mother Morningmist's chambers." Bee's knowledge didn't surprise. It was one of the reasons I'd come tonight. To get answers. "Do you have a plan?"

She meant a plan to steal the orb.

Uncomfortableness slithered across my skin. Who was Bee really that she'd suggest stealing from our hosts? Shaking my head, I refused to cheat. "I'm not going to steal the Divinity Orb."

The following morning a firefly buzzed my nose, waking me. I went to shoosh the bug away and spotted the message the bug had spelled in the air.

Will you meet me at our place? R

I sat up straight. The message had to be from Rye. I clutched my hands together. He thought we had a place. Our place. My heart swooned and I wanted to race to the designated spot.

"Oh." I flopped back onto the bed reading way too much into seven simple words. "I'm being silly."

Sending a message this way exposed his talent at using Mother Earth's gifts. At least he wasn't hiding the skill from me.

I shouldn't meet him. Although, what if by meeting him I gained valuable insight? Maybe he had important information to share. After all, he was the one who'd told me about the others competing and he had experience with Mother Earth's gifts. He'd been truthful with me, unlike so many others.

Throwing back the covers, I hurried and got dressed, putting on the outfit Watu had given me to bolster my confidence. I left a message for Stone that I'd be practicing with Arbor and scrambled to meet Rye. Guilt shivered across my skin. This time, I was lying. Was that right?

If liking Rye was wrong, I didn't want to be right.

Arriving at the garden, I paused my rapid stride. Rye paced in a small section, his arms swinging at his side, his head down. His slim-framed body appeared narrower, although his shoulders were wider as if carrying more burden. His hair feathered in the breeze making him seem less tense. His profile showed strength and assuredness. Things I wished I obtained.

"Why is it no one else is ever here?" Scanning the area, I spotted a butterfly landing on a large purple flower in the garden. The fragrance of the flowers lightened my step. The babbling creek tickled my eardrums.

"Who cares as long as we get to be alone?" Rye swung his arm and reached for my hand.

I clamped my arms to my sides, not willing to take hold. Flitting from one guy to the next wasn't my style. When it came to guys, I had no style. "Why did you want to meet?"

"I thought we should become reacquainted as our true selves." Sincerity shined on his face. "No lies. No masks. No pretending we're someone else."

My gaze darted around, and my pulse fluttered. I didn't know if I was ready to be honest with him. "We probably shouldn't be meeting. We are enem—"

He arched a brow, causing me to stop and change my wording. He'd known what I was going to say.

"Competitors."

Nodding, he stepped closer and I took a deep sniff of his sandalwood scent. "Competitors working for the same goal."

"Are we?" I fisted my hands. He wanted honesty, he'd get it. "Did you sign the law restricting majik movements?"

"My uncle forged my signature." Rye looked away and another scraggly scar shined on his forehead. "He did it when...he sent me away."

Rye's hesitation had my pulse wobbling. Is that when he'd received the additional scars?

He grabbed my hand and peeled apart my fingers. "Can you say the other majiks competing are working for the same goal?"

"I haven't met them. Have you?" I frowned. Another thing I'd been kept in the dark about. The one thing I knew was one of them was related to Hokima.

"I've passed them during training." Rye tilted his head to study me with his eyes, and I fell into their silver depths. He saw to my soul. "I never pass you."

"I'm thinking we were kept apart on purpose."

By Stone. I tensed, angry at him.

"Could be. Although Sister Autumn doesn't like you much. She purposely might be leaving you out of things."

I'd sensed the same thing. Although sensing and having it pointed out struck completely different emotions. Paranoia versus panic. Why wouldn't she approve of me? A question to be pondered at a different time. "Why did you ask to meet?"

"Besides wanting to see you again?" Rye's voice dropped lower.

Something about the way he spoke stretched deep inside me. The way his lips lifted in a mischievous half smile called to my playful side—a side I'd long ignored. I went soft inside, remembering our time together, wishing we could be together again. Two teens getting to know each other with none of the pressure from the outside world.

An impossibility. We both had responsibilities now.

I lightly punched his shoulder. "Stop."

"I thought about what you said, and I think I can help you." He'd gone from flirting to serious in seconds and my head spun.

"Help me what?"

"Help you access Mother Earth's gifts." He rushed through the words showing eagerness.

I tilted my head, trying to figure him out. "Why would you want to help? We're enem—competitors."

He chuckled reminding me of the babbling brook nearby. "Well, I wouldn't want to beat you out right. I enjoy a real competition."

Hmm, he wanted competition. Did he consider Stone competition? Competition for me? I couldn't go there now. I was too confused about both guys. Each of them pulled me in different directions.

Shaking my head, I thought it best to reject Rye's help. Who knew if I could trust him?

He pressed my palm against his chest. His heart hammered at a fast pace and I didn't know if that was from the fast movement or from me being close. "Because I care, okay? I care about you and I want to help you."

His tough tone didn't sound caring, and yet the words and the gleam in his eyes had me melting. "You do?"

"You said you needed the Divinity Orb to prove to the fairies you're worthy. I understand." His cheeks flushed a bright red. "Come this way. Please?"

He tugged on my hand and for a second I worried this was a trick. Helping the competition? Confessing he cared? I mean, I thought there was something between us. Was that connection in the past?

If it was, why did I race to meet him? Sure, I'd convinced myself it was a way to gather intel. Deep inside, I knew that wasn't the real reason.

Pushing a branch aside, he ducked under and entered a small clearing with a hidden roaring creek leading to the lake feeding the large waterfall. Grass surrounded the bank creating a perfect spot to sit and relax.

He took a seat on the grass at the edge of the creek and patted the spot beside him.

I sat down farther away than the spot he'd indicated. The surreal moment had me dreaming we were on a date. And yet, Rye and I could never have anything as mundane as a date.

"Look into the creek." His gentle command had me peering down.

The clarity of the water reflected my image back. Mine and Rye's. He was handsome and distinguished. And I appeared regal. I sucked in a breath, trying to get oxygen into my surprised lungs. Could this be a prophecy?

"What do you see?"

A trick question? "Water?"

"In the reflection. What do you see?"

"Me. And you."

"Put your hand in the water and disturb the image."

"Why? I enjoy the image." I lifted my gaze to his, finally brave enough to call out how I felt.

He stared back, his silver eyes morphing to an intense gleam. "So do I."

My skin heated as if we'd been sitting out in the sun forever. My cheeks flushed and I couldn't look away. What was this power he held over me?

"When you disturb our image, replace it with a new image. An image of the Divinity Orb below the surface."

I pictured the glowing orb at the bottom of the creek. It glowed and shot off colored lights, similar to the image Watu had produced. Visions formed and unformed, blowing away in what appeared to be smoke.

"Imagine your hand going deeper and deeper and grabbing the orb."

My hand wrapped around the crystal orb. The weight felt heavy in my palm. The power throbbed through my skin. Excitement palpitated inside me.

"Now, bring the orb to the surface." His voice dropped lower, sexier, more hypnotic.

I started lifting the weight. The orb grew bigger, got closer. It became more real than the one time with Stone when I'd lifted the practice orb out.

A thrill zoomed through me. "I'm doing it!"

The image crashed. My hand was near the surface and held nothing. "I lost the orb."

"Doing it in the natural creek is more difficult than trying in a practice pool." He lifted my hand out of the water and kissed the empty palm. "Great job. You had the orb in your hand."

"An imaginary orb, a spectral."

"That's how you access Mother Earth's gifts. You see one thing and imagine another, and you trust." He cupped my cheek with a tender cradle and leaned toward me. "Like me. Like us. Trust."

Anticipation tingled. I wanted his kiss, remembered the kiss from before, missed his lips on mine. I tilted toward him. His breath smelled minty, as clean as the creek beside us. His lips were full of promise and trust.

He pressed his mouth to mine, testing and waiting for acceptance.

I accepted. Moving my lips against his, I reveled in the contact and caress. The touch was familiar and exciting at the same time. I heard music in my head and in my heart. Losing myself, I rejoiced in being with Rye, even though it was completely inappropriate. We were competitors.

The music jangled with my intruding thoughts. Why was he willing to help me? Why did he want to kiss me? Or was it a distraction, the same as Stone's kiss? I couldn't switch my mind off and enjoy Rye's kiss.

Was this another way of being played?

When I returned inside, I'd sent out my own message to my team to meet me in a practice room. If Rye was truly helping me, I wanted to practice while the instructions were fresh.

Not the kiss. I needed to forget the kiss. My first loyalty was to my mission.

Stone hauled to the prescribed meeting spot with a desperate, accusing expression. He must've discovered I'd not been in my room. Before he could accuse me, the rest of my team had arrived. He continued to glare.

Perry flew in using the fairy skill he possessed. Skills he'd taught me how to use. Why? What were his ulterior motives? Did being royal mean not trusting anyone? I hated always feeling on edge.

Stomping in behind him was Hokima. I regarded him, trying to decide if he regarded me oddly or questioningly. Did he believe in my mission or would he be more loyal to his cousin?

Tos skipped in with Bee. I trusted both of them. They'd had my back.

And of course, there was Arbor.

She fluttered beside me at shoulder-height. My best friend and someone who I knew I could rely on. She'd been with me when I'd been a servant in my own home, a half fairy who planned to stay human and whose magic didn't work.

I trusted the girls on my team. The others, I'd use their assistance but wouldn't rely on them. Watu's instructions about great leaders needing great people to help them came to mind. Well, I wasn't leading yet. I'd sort through and find the people I could lean on when I was in charge.

"I need to practice, and I need your help," I began the meeting.

Arbor ruffled her wings. "Bee wasn't supposed to be part of the team."

Bee slashed a glance. "Perry was put on the team without Elle's knowledge."

How did Bee know? I hadn't told her. "Let's not quarrel."

"Perry was ordered to be here by Commander Gardenia." Arbor displayed respect for my fairy godmother even though she knew I was mad at the woman.

Arbor and I used to agree on almost everything. Now, it seems we disagreed plenty.

"And you always listen to Commander Gardenia, don't you?" Bee pursed her mouth in a snarl.

I reeled back. Why couldn't my two best friends get along?

Arbor flew in front of my other friend's face. "Who are you loyal to, Bee?"

The way Arbor drew out the question, I understood there was more meaning than I knew. What the elves bells was going on? I was tired of their infighting. They were both my friends.

With a stern expression, Stone faced Bee. "Who are you loyal to?"

I'd never seen Stone and Arbor act together. Why would Stone get involved in a jealous dispute between my two best friends? He should know better. Unless he wanted to stir up trouble. Did he think I'd turn to him if Arbor and Bee were fighting? *Ha!*

Bee's gaze darted back and forth. Her gaze screamed panic until a calm cruelness settled over her. "I'm loyal to the lost princess."

"Bee, sto—"

"Princess Ellery."

Bee's pronouncement went through my team akin to a wildfire. First confusion, then questioning, and then realization they'd been lied to.

By me.

Slumping, I staggered back and almost fell in the water. How could I be angry at their deception when I'd been untruthful too? Although mine was a state secret, not a lie.

"You didn't tell us you were a princess." Tos didn't jump up and down with her usual excitement.

"I thought you kept us informed." Hokima lifted his chin in rejection. "We are your team."

A smile played around Perry's lips. He'd figure out the truth and hadn't said anything.

I froze, too surprised to speak above their loud comments. Too shocked Bee would betray me in this way.

"How do you know about Ellery?" Arbor's suspicious tone told me she wouldn't appreciate whatever answer was given.

Bee smirked. "Elle confided in me back at Queens Academy."

All the air evacuated my body. I didn't want Arbor to find out the specifics. She was so suspicious of my new friend and she'd be mad I'd shared the information before I told her. Although, Arbor hadn't been around.

She buzzed in front of my face. "You told Bee? It's supposed to be confidential."

Holding up my hand, I hoped Arbor would land on my palm. I understood why she was angry and I needed to explain. "I needed to tell someone when I found out. I was going to burst. You weren't around."

Contemplating Bee, I realized my explanation had made her mad. "Look, Bee. I know Arbor a lot better than you."

"Do you?" Crossing her arms, Bee backed toward the door. "Tell Princess Ellery why you weren't around for her to share the news with you, Arbor."

Arbor visibly paled. Her smoke changed to a sickly yellow color. "I was, um, running an errand."

"For whom?" Bee asked the question, but by her voice, she already knew the answer.

"What does it matter?" I tried to play peacemaker. "Arbor and I don't have secrets from each other."

"Really?" Bee's superior tone rattled me. Her wings flapped with a slight whir.

I didn't understand the panic on Arbor's face. We'd been friends since right before I turned sixteen.

Bee pivoted to face me with a sharp nod. "So, you know Arbor works for Commander Gardenia? That she's a spy? And her most recent assignment was to befriend the lost princess."

Chapter Twenty-Three

All the blood drained from my face.

Arbor worked for Gardenia.

Disgust twisted in my stomach, causing my brain to pound. Realization scraped through my lungs. Our friendship had been fake. Just like Stone's attraction had been phony. Adrenaline shot through my limbs and I took off at a run.

The calls of *Elle stop* went unheeded. I couldn't stand to be around anyone right now. My face heated. What a fool I'd been. Everything became clear. Arbor befriended me as part of her assignment. She'd come into my life near the time the last princess, my aunt, had died. When the fairies needed me. She'd known all along I was the lost princess.

Taking a corner too fast, I scraped my hip against the stone wall. The dull pain was barely noticed. Too much internal torture, emotional agony, ratcheted through my body.

She'd been sent to protect me and influence me. She'd talked about how being part of the fairy world was great. She'd besmirched the human world. She'd taught me little fairy things, similar to following a trail, in order to change my way of thinking. To change my mind about pretending to be human.

Sliding to a stop in a familiar hallway, I flattened my palms against the wall, trying to let the dampness cool my raging emotions and overcome embarrassment. Torment stabbed through me, and I couldn't tell if it was from the run or from the death of my naïve self.

The deserted corridor seemed darker than usual. Or was that my outlook?

I was alone. All alone. Another loyalty bites the dust.

Bee had shared my princess secret with everyone, and now everyone would hate me for not telling them. Stone had lied and pretended he wanted to kiss me. Perry wanted to take my place. Hokima probably preferred his cousin. And Arbor had lied, lied, lied.

My throat constricted as I forced the tears back. I refused to cry.

I battered my fist against the wall. The movement didn't make a noise, didn't release any of my distress. There was no way to become stress-free. I had no one to talk to. And I was failing.

Watu's words of wisdom reverberated in my head. If I wanted to succeed, I needed to be a leader. I couldn't let the fact that I was half fairy and I'd lived in the human world for most of my life affect my belief in myself. I was the princess, and I was worthy of winning the Divinity Orb.

I let the thought cleanse through and purge my negative emotions. Inner strength built inside me block by block. Watu had shown me how to do this with the meditation and yoga. I experienced the change in myself and in my attitude. I was strong, a warrior princess, and I would take charge.

First, I'd go back to my team and apologize about keeping the princess secret. Not knowing about my royal status put them in additional danger. I'd tell Stone we could never be more than friends and I'd apologize to Perry for how I'd treated him with distrust in the past. I'd hug Tos and Hokima and ask them to stay on my side. I'd have to find a time to have a deeper conversation with Arbor, to learn what was real and what wasn't about our friendship. Lastly, I'd chastise and forgive Bee for outing me and Arbor.

Bee, one of the people in my thoughts, scampered around the corner and stopped. Her flushed face made her appear to be in a hurry. Her clothes were mussed.

"Bee?" Guess, I'd have to deal with her first. "I want to talk to you about—"

She grabbed my arm and bent it to a painful angle. If she knew I was mad at her, why would she attack me? I hoped we could clear things up and end as friends.

I struggled to free my arm. She couldn't be serious, yet she wouldn't let go.

"Bee! What're you doing?" I yanked at my arm, thinking how ridiculous we looked. "I'm mad, but I'll forgive you."

"Forgive *me*!" Her lips twisted into an ugly sneer. "You think you're so high and mighty."

Furrowing my brow, I didn't understand where this was coming from. We were friends. She should know the last thing I thought of myself was high and mighty. I broke free of her restraint. "That's the last thing I believe."

She panted. "Your poor little princess act doesn't work on me."

What was she talking about? I never pretended to be the poor princess. Did I? She'd stated something comparable right before the dragon grabbed me.

She wiggled her body and her hand went into a flap at her waist. The object she slipped out from the hidden pocket resembled a small mechanical doll.

I remembered seeing something similar at a human hospital. It helped paralyzed patients move and walk. The hi-tech device had been a miracle cure.

Bee fiddled with the doll and several beams of light flared out in sizzling bolts of electricity.

Zapping me.

The lines of light jolted, mirroring touching an electric socket. My skin tingled and my veins lit up. My body went numb and I released the hold I had on Bee.

"What did you do to me?" My lungs seized. Not from the effects of the doll, but from pure panic.

"Took control." Her quiet giggle morphed into a snarl. She ripped off her wings and the holster attaching them to her body.

I winced, thinking of the pain, until I realized, "Your wings are fake!" Shock pitched my voice high. I didn't even know they could make fake wings.

"You're so observant."

"Are you a fairy?" I didn't know what to believe anymore.

"Unfortunately, yes. But I don't have wings." She pushed the legs on the mechanical doll. "Let's go."

My right foot went up and stepped down again. The left foot did the same. She was forcing me to walk, to move where she wanted. Horror scratched up my throat and I wanted to scream.

"Don't." She snapped the mouth on the doll closed, reading my mind. "This way."

She opened a servant passageway and waited for me to shuffle inside. "If you scream, I'll make you crawl through the passage. Which would be fun to watch but would take way too long." She opened the doll's mouth slightly. "I'm sure you have a million questions. Ask away. Just keep going and don't scream or I'll make this worse."

Swallowing a couple of times, I realized Bee had never been my friend. She'd used me to go on the mission and tricked me into leaving the campground. She'd lied about changing weather being fairy magic. She'd killed castle guards and who knew where she'd been leading me as we scrambled over the mountain. Rage poured through me with each of the realizations and uncontrolled steps. *Calm yourself.* I needed to ask questions that would help my situation, and I didn't want to make her angrier.

We lurched down the same passageway she'd wanted to take the other night when she'd mentioned stealing the orb.

"How did you get the medical device?"

"Artificial Exoskeleton sends electrical pulses through the spine and brain. Human hi-tech is superior to fairy magic," she patronized. "It doesn't need patience, or calm, or any emotion."

She referred to how I'd failed to harness Mother Earth's magic and fairy magic. I was learning.

My muscles tensed. I used to believe technology was superior to magic. It was emotionless. Now, I realized it was gutless, too. A fighter didn't need bravery to battle. "You grew up in the fairy world. Where did you get human gadgetry?"

"I did grow up in the fairy world, as an outcast. Fairies distrusted me and treated me poorly because I didn't have magic or wings."

Surprise shot through my system. Everything about her made more sense.

"So where did you get the device?" I needed to know if someone worked with her.

"I was in a terrible accident and the humans gave me a better offer." She smirked again. "When I first started my secret mission, I thought I'd feel bad for you. After all, we are both half fairies. But you're treated special, like a princess."

My mouth dropped open. "I am a princess. But in the human world, after my dad died, I was a servant."

"Boohoo, you." She pursed her lips in distaste. "I don't feel bad for you. I don't like you."

Another person pretending to be my friend. I snarled. At least Bee didn't work for Gardenia. I couldn't think of that hurt now. I had to stay focused on the present. On getting out of this situation.

"Being half fairy is great." I forced enthusiasm into my tone, even as my feet continued to clomp in a direction I didn't want to go. "You understand both worlds."

"Not when my fairy mother rejected me as a child." Bee's dejection added an edge of reckless cold to her voice.

Her anguish delved down to my core. I understood not being accepted. I was lucky both my mother and father loved me, even if they hadn't been around for long. From what she told me of her life, Bee had grown up with fairies. Since she wasn't a Fire Fairy like me, she should have gotten her magic when she was young. And not getting magic in the fairy world would make her stand out in a negative way.

If she hadn't grown up with her fairy mother, who had she been raised by?

"Things are changing in the fairy world." She might accuse me of being high and mighty again, but I had to say it. "Now that I'm princess, half fairies will be more accepted."

Her earlier giggling went louder and crueler. "You're so stupid."

Huffing, I held back a response. She already hated me, why give her another reason?

"You didn't know Arbor and Stone both worked for Gardenia. You didn't know Perry was the male heir. You didn't know much of anything."

"You knew quite a bit." How? Who was she working for?

"I know *everything*." She pushed her way into a room and drew a heavy velvet curtain, revealing the pool of water in the ground. "And I know you're going to get the Divinity Orb for me."

The water glimmered from the sun shining through the round window. The surface lapped gently as if a breeze blew, although there was no wind. Gold spots flickered beneath the tiny waves. The rocks surrounding the water held a sparkly shimmer. The Reflection Pool.

The water tugged.

"No. I refuse." For me to get the orb out, she'd have to free me from this bind. No way could she force my hand into the water and force my thoughts to conjure and extract the orb. Ignoring the pull, I searched for something to use as a weapon. Once released, I'd fight. I'd use my ninja training and my fairy magic, and I'd win the battle against Bee.

"This is how it's going to go." She spoke slowly to make her point. "I'm going to free you from the binding, and you are going to pull the orb from the Reflection Pool."

I shook my head. "You've seen me practice. I'm not very good, especially under these stressful conditions."

"Then, you will die right here." Her chilled intonation told me she meant every word.

A frisson of fear rocked my numb body. How did I miss her loathing toward me? And if I was killed, I'd die with my friends mad at me, with Stone and Rye not realizing how I felt about them.

Because I was still confused.

"Not on my watch." Perry burst through the same passageway we'd used. His wings spread wide and his magic glowed around him.

My pulse skittered. He must've followed us and hopefully planned to help me. He wasn't my enemy. He was my protector and friend. He'd known for a while I was the lost princess.

He stood in a heroic stance, his sword thrust out and ready for action. His nostrils flared with determination and he held his chin in defiance. He was willing to fight for me, his fairy princess. Even though if I died, he'd inherit the throne. I'd misjudged him at the beginning.

I'd learned my lesson and would be very careful about making snap judgments.

"You stupid weasel." Bee raised the Artificial Exoskeleton and took a defensive position. "I should've killed you when I had the chance."

"I suspected something wasn't right with you." Perry jabbed with his sword. "And I've been keeping tabs on your whereabouts. I followed you when you left."

He hadn't been following me. He'd been following Bee. Because he was smart enough to recognize her duplicity. He'd be a good advisor when we returned to Queens Academy.

I wanted to tell him how much I appreciated him. Now wasn't the time. "I can't help you fight. I'm bound by this gadget."

"I'll defend your honor." He lunged toward Bee.

The hiking and the flying lesson must've given us a bond. We were distant cousins and close friends. He recognized I was the true heir and worthy of the title. And I'd recognize his service with knighthood.

"Defend her honor by killing her." Snickering, Bee used the gadget to make me step in front of her and toward Perry. "Or she'll kill you."

She tossed a dagger and my hand automatically grabbed the weapon. Bee didn't know I wasn't very good with a dagger. I wouldn't tell her about the Silver Snare always hanging from my belt, which I was very good at using. She might control my body, but I controlled my mind.

I lunged at Perry with the knife. Horror leeched down my spine. I didn't want to fight him. My teammate, my cousin, and my friend. He might've spoken unkindly, but he'd been honest.

He used his sword to block my dagger. A defensive move. He didn't counterattack.

Tension stretched my muscles tight. "Sorry, Perry. I can't stop myself." I hacked with the dagger at his face.

"I know, Elle." Raising his arm, he blocked the slash. He protected himself while trying not to hurt me. Using his wings, he hovered off the floor. "We'll figure something out."

"There's nothing to figure out." Bee used the mechanical doll to force me to attack Perry again and again.

Breathing heavily, I jabbed and sliced at Perry. Repulsed, I tried to hold back, to fight the contraption Bee operated.

"Either you'll kill her, or you'll get tired from fighting her and she'll kill you. Or I will." She'd enjoy any of those scenarios.

She didn't care who got killed. She just wanted the orb. Disgust threaded through me. She needed me to accomplish the goal. She'd fooled me from the beginning. There'd been small hints about her lies. I'd ignored them because I empathized with her situation of being half fairy and working to pay for school.

My arm tired from the constant charge and assault. A jab, a dig, a slash. My weary bones kept bustling.

Perry twisted and ducked and flew toward the ceiling. He used his sword to block and knock my blade away.

Good thing the doll didn't have wings or Bee would force me to fly and attack Perry.

I stepped closer to him and stabbed my dagger at his neck. Cringing, I said, "Sorry."

He swiveled out of the way and flung his sword forward to block me. The tip of his blade caught my arm and sliced. "Sorry right back at you."

Blood poured from the gaping wound. A stinging sensation throbbed around the injury.

"Not your fault." I gritted my teeth and attacked harder. "It's Bee's fault."

"It's never your fault, precious princess. *I was a servant. No one likes me. I have to earn the fairies' trust.*" Bee raised her voice in a poor imitation of me.

I didn't sound that way. At least not anymore. I took responsibilities for myself and my actions. Even for my mistakes. I glared in her direction.

The main entrance opened with a bang.

I blew out a puff. Finally, maybe someone who could help. Anyone.

Rye stood in the doorway, wearing full regalia. The sash, the medals, the ornamental sword.

My heart pounded to a different beat. A love beat.

His intense expression assessed the situation in seconds. His mouth firmed into a line and his gaze worried for me.

"Perry." Prince Zacharye used his royal, demanding tone. "Cease attacking Princess Ellery."

My pulse skyrocketed. He cared about me but didn't understand the situation.

"She's attacking me." Perry blocked another assault. "Bee's controlling Elle."

I tried to stop my forward momentum, tried to pull back my arm, tried to fall on my face. Nothing worked. Bee had complete control of my body and I was helpless. "She's forcing me to attack Perry. She's the evil one."

"How?" Rye withdrew his sword and stepped toward us with care. By his darting gaze, he was trying to figure out how to best handle the situation. "If it's a spell, I can't help with a spell."

Rye tread between Perry and me. He used his sword to block my dagger, assisting Perry. My dagger bounced off the hard metal and shattered up my spine.

My lungs screamed with exhaustion and panic. "It's an Artificial Exoskeleton."

"My uncle has one of those." Rye's brow furrowed and he blocked another blow from me. Then he twisted away, dropped on the ground, and rolled past me. He resembled a ninja, as if he'd been trained by one of the priestesses. Maybe he had. Jumping to his feet, he attacked Bee.

"Ah!" Bee let the arm holding the doll drop to her side. She pulled a second dagger out from near her waist.

My arms unfroze and I controlled my limbs again. Numbness zinged through my arms and legs. Rye's attack on Bee had distracted her and she no longer controlled me. "Perry, I'm okay. Help Rye."

Rye forced Bee into a corner by a window. He swung his broad sword down at her. I cringed. She held the dagger out, blocking the blow. Perry flew above them and attacked from above. Bee grabbed the velvet curtain and swirled inside.

I didn't want her dead. I wanted explanations.

Grabbing my whip, I advanced toward the group. I slung the whip back and forward, gripping the curtain and twirling it around. Bee had climbed up the curtain and clung to the top. The mechanical doll was held tightly in her hand. I didn't know if she could work it from there or how far its reach was, but I wanted my hands on the device.

Flinging the whip, I uncurled it from the curtain and cast it forward. The silver tip wrapped around the exoskeleton. "Yes!" I yanked it back and the device flew into the air.

"No!" Dropping his sword, Rye jumped up and caught the device before it crashed to the ground. "It's attached to you. It can still torture you."

"And so can I." Bee lashed out with her dagger at Perry. From her superior height, the blade punched through Perry's upper torso.

He tumbled to the floor.

A knife plunged into my soul. A sharp and stinging pain went through my chest and radiated outward. The agony carried through my veins to the rest of my body. I could sense my limbs, yet I couldn't move them. Paralyzed because of the torture. "Perry, no."

Hanging onto the curtain, Bee kicked off the wall and swung forward. With a wicked grin, she saluted us and smashed through the glass window. She plummeted down because she didn't have wings and we were hundreds of feet from the ground. Could she survive?

"Perry?" I sank to my knees beside him. My eyes burned. "Perry."

The wound gaped open around the dagger stuck through his breast. Blood poured from the injury and trickled down his shirt. His breathing was shallow and his face pale.

"Call for a healer. I'm going after Bee." The sorrow on Rye's face changed to grim determination. He dashed out of the room and toward the stairs.

I knew not to pull the knife out because it could cause more damage. However, I needed to stop the blood loss. Using the dagger Bee had forced me to use, I slashed a portion of the velvet curtain and applied pressure around Perry's wound. I tried to stop the flow of blood. "You're going to be okay. I'll summon healers."

Without thought or effort, I used Mother Earth's gifts to summon my team with the urgent message. I told them to bring a healer.

Perry coughed and blood trickled from between his lips. "It's my time to die. And it's your time to lead."

I couldn't breathe. "No."

"Yes." His body shuddered. "You need to have confidence in yourself." He coughed again and I used the edge of the curtain to wipe the blood around his mouth. "Believe in your abilities with Mother Earth's gifts, with flying, with your magic."

"Magic!" There must be some magic I could use to help him. "Tell me a healing spell or a potion I could make." My rushed voice pitched high with grief. "Anything."

"You'll be great." A cough rattled through his chest. "Take care of the fairies."

"Don't." I sniffed, not wanting him to give up. "You're going to be okay. I want you to help me rule."

His body seized up and stiffened. He stopped breathing. And he was gone.

My heart squeezed so tight it became flat as pressed flowers. My head pounded with pain. Tears slipped down my cheeks.

I didn't want the tears to stop.

Perry had been my friend and flying instructor. He was smart and funny. The kingdom would be a worse place without him.

CHAPTER TWENTY-FOUR

"Elle!" Stone ran through the open door and halted. Horror etched on his face in stark lines.

He was followed by Arbor flying above his shoulder, Hokima carrying Tos, and a group of guards. They came to a screeching halt when they saw Perry lying in blood.

A healer flitted forward with her bag of magic potions and put her head to his chest. Her lips moved silently in what must be a fairy prayer. She conjured a red blanket and laid it over his body, covering his face. "He's gone."

The words, no, each individual letter, dripped through me in a slow, painful flow. My bloodstream carried the emotional affliction like fire, burning through my entire body.

Sister Autumn dashed in behind them. Her head stuck out in a caricature of shock. "What happened?"

Energy fizzled out of my body and drained any fight inside me. I didn't know what to say. Forcing myself to my feet, I held out my bloody hands. Nausea whirled in my stomach. "Bee took control of me with this human device. She wanted to steal the Divinity Orb. Perry tried to save me." Right now, I couldn't relive how Bee had taken control and forced me to fight against him. "Ry—Prince Zacharye arrived and helped us. Bee killed Perry." My arm trembled pointing to the broken window. "She crashed out the window to get away. Prince Zacharye is trying to follow her."

Stone and Arbor sprinted toward the exit, ready to nab Bee. The two of them had never liked her.

A stomping echoed up the stairs, stopping them on their quest.

Rye thundered into the room, his gaze set on mine. His lips were flat and his eyes dull. Blood splatters decorated his chest. "Bee wasn't lying on the ground. She's not dead. She got away."

My veins twisted around my heart. How could she survive the fall? "Her wings weren't real."

"The rest of the guards, scour the grounds and find Bee. I will get to the bottom of this. Prince Zacharye and Princess Ellery stay here." Sister Autumn gestured to the rest of my team. "You know her best. Help find Bee."

Everyone hustled into motion at once. The guards rushed down the passageway. Tos, Hokima, and Arbor filed out. Worry for my team sank in my belly. I thought I'd known Bee. How could I have been so wrong?

"You are dismissed." Sister Autumn used her harshest tone with Stone.

He stayed in place, standing with his arms crossed and a glare on his face. "I'm Princess Ellery's personal bodyguard. I'm staying."

"I'm Mother Morningmist's second in command." The priestess mimicked his slow pronunciation. "You will do as I say, or you will be escorted out of the sanctuary."

Stone didn't blink and didn't budge an inch.

"She'll be safe with me." Rye regarded Stone and a promise passed between them.

They both were going to look out for me, even if they didn't trust each other. A calmness went through me. Stone and Rye were going to be okay with each other, and I was going to be okay, too.

Stone gave the priestess one final glare before heading out to help with the search.

"Get me some wet cloths, please." Rye ordered one of the guards standing by.

The guard immediately brought wet towels to him. He strode to my side and started using the cloth to wipe the blood from my hands. His gentle caress showed he cared about me and my lost friend.

My eyes prickled. I refused to cry. Now wasn't the time to mourn Perry.

"How did you know I'd be in this chamber?" I whispered to Rye. He hadn't known about the fight with my team or where I'd run or how Bee had forced me into the passage, yet he'd found me.

"I didn't." He shuffled his feet. "I came to visit Mother Morningmist."

My stomach hollowed out. He could visit *my* great-grandmother, but I hadn't been allowed to meet her. "You know her?"

His cheeks flushed and he lowered his head to remove a stubborn stain on my hand. "We got to know each other when I was here during my secondment."

The time when he'd mysteriously left public life.

"What exactly did you do during that time?"

He'd told me about learning how to use Mother Earth's gifts. What else had happened?

"Do you want to know what my uncle thought I was doing or what I was *actually* doing?" Lifting his head, he winked.

The answer-with-a-question and the wink confused me. "Both."

"Regent Theobald sent me on a dangerous training mission. He'd planned for me to die." Rye's wide grin told me he knew he'd be fine. "I'd brought guards loyal to me. I started at Aristos Sanctuary and through Mother Morningmist and Sister Autumn's connections, I met representatives from each of the majik races and forged a bond."

Rye wasn't a spoiled prince. He faced danger every day and was stronger mentally and physically because of it. He possessed ethics and morals the opposite of his uncle. He respected and had good relationships with majiks.

"Even the fairies?"

"Even the fairies, through Mother Morningmist." He winked again. "She didn't share with me the fact that the lost fairy princess had been found."

"Everyone doesn't know." I beamed. "Only a select few."

His lips twitched in a secretive smile. "I'm glad to be part of the select."

Warmth penetrated the numbness until I caught a glimpse of Perry. New horror struck and I collapsed to my knees at the side of his covered body. My eyes burned, and my throat closed. "Perry was the closest male heir."

Rye kneeled at my side and placed his arm around my waist. "You were lucky to have someone so strong and brave."

"He was a courageous fairy." It was the first time I'd heard anything but disdain in Sister Autumn's voice. She'd stood aside while Rye and I had talked. "Perry will have a burial befitting his bravery."

She took hold of my arm and helped me to stand. "It's time for Princess Ellery to meet Mother Morningmist."

Good thing the priestess held me because my knees knocked together. This was the moment I'd been waiting for since I learned my great-grandmother was alive.

⇝⇝⇝ ⇜⇜⇜

The three of us didn't have far to go. The room with the Reflection Pool led right to Mother Morningmist's chambers. Blank white walls. A functional sitting room with a couch, two chairs, and a coffee table. An austere and efficient desk. The sitting area and office were spartan compared to Queen Dahliadew's.

A curtain rustled and an older, petite woman appeared. She wore the red cloak of the priestesses, but this one had simple gold trim around the edges. Her dull-colored wings fluttered behind her. Bright green eyes shown from beneath the hood.

She had my eyes. Or I had hers.

My feet froze to the spot. Finally, I was meeting my great-grand-mother. I didn't know what to say or how to act. I wanted her to like me. No, I wanted more than liking. She was family. I wanted love and respect and tenderness.

"Prince Zacharye." With a serene expression, she held out her wrinkled hand.

He bowed and pressed a kiss to her knuckles. When he stepped back, she held her arms open for a welcoming hug. They must know each other well. Rye had said he'd stayed here.

A spurt of jealousy shot through me. He knew my great-grand-mother better than I did.

Her steely gaze switched to me.

With shaky knees, I made an awkward bow, worrying she wouldn't approve. Twisting my hands together, I was glad Rye had wiped them clean. I might be half fairy, but I was a princess and I was strong. "Mother Morningmist."

"Finally, I get to meet my great-granddaughter." Her pleasant tone soothed.

Maybe she'd always wanted to meet me. I glanced at Sister Autumn. Maybe the priestesses had kept us apart.

"It's nice to meet you." I sounded steady, even though I quivered inside.

"Nice?" Mother Morningmist gave a throaty chuckle. "You are my only great-grandchild, Ellery, and all I get is nice?"

She held open her arms. I hesitated a second, partly out of emo-tion and partly because blood stained my clothes. Then, I sailed into them. Her arms were strong and welcoming. She smelled of vanilla and cinnamon. I belonged here.

I held back tears. "I'm ecstatic to finally meet you."

"Family is good, child." Her warm voice sent a ripple of comfort through me. Her hands trailed across my back and I wanted to curl into them.

"Family is good." The thought settled in my gut. My parents were a great example, as were my current true friends who'd become family.

She gripped my arms and held me back. "You resemble your mother Lily."

The comparison had me glowing from the inside. "Thank you."

"She was a rascal." Mother Morningmist's lighter laughter was filled with happy memories. "Lily always wanted to do things her own way. If she was asked to conjure a butterfly, she conjured a toad. If you asked her to join you for dinner, she ate dessert first. She was an original."

I heard the affection. Hearing positive things about my mom made me stronger and closer to her memory. My father had wonderful stories, although not about her childhood or her life as a fairy.

"Which is why, of course, Lily chose to fall in love with a human." Mother Morningmist didn't appear upset. Maybe she had been back then, which was why I was never told stories about my mother's side of the family. Or maybe it was because they were fairy, and royal too. Her gaze switched from me to Rye and back again.

Rye had a slight smile on his face and seemed happy for me.

My stomach knotted. I didn't want to hear bad things, but I needed to ask. "Were you angry with my mother?"

"Of course not. Love is more powerful than fairy magic." Her eyes twinkled as if remembering a past love. She took hold of my hand. "We didn't think your mother's marriage would complicate fairy succession."

"My mother wasn't supposed to rise to the fairy throne."

"Fairies need more than an heir and a spare." She surveyed Rye.

The human standard was an heir and a spare for their throne, but Rye was the only one in line. Actually, he should be sitting on the throne right now.

"You'd think with two other daughters Queen Dahliadew wouldn't have had a problem. Alas, neither princess had children of their own." The sadness in Mother Morningmist's voice sent a shaft of melancholy through me.

I hung my head, not wanting to ask personal questions about my aunts that might bring more sadness to my great-grandmother.

"It was good your mother left the fairy world because she had you." She brightened once more. "And she was happy with your father and her life."

My parents had been happy together and I missed them every day.

Sister Autumn cleared her throat. "I'm sorry to interrupt this family reunion, but we have many things to discuss."

Mother Morningmist released my hand and rubbed her forehead. I fisted my free hand, embarrassed I'd clung so hard.

"What will happen to Perry's body?" I needed to take care of him.

Rye rubbed my back, sending tingles across my skin. I was grateful for his support.

"Perry's family will be informed, and we will adhere to their wishes." Sister Autumn was businesslike.

"What about Bee? She killed Perry. She was trying to force me to steal the Divinity Orb."

The two women exchanged a glance. Clearly, a message.

"We have guards scouring the entire compound. It will be very difficult for her to escape, especially without wings." The priestess sounded confident and efficient.

I wasn't buying the act.

"Which begs the question." Mother Morningmist was all grace. "If you had gotten the orb out of the Reflection Pool, what would Bee have done with it?"

Scrunching my brow, I didn't understand the question. "What do you mean?"

"The orb will serve any royal. It makes a special connection with the person who withdraws it from the pool." Sister Autumn's explanation was addressed to me.

"Bee didn't tell me her plans." My terse statement caused my muscles to tense. I'd misjudged my ex-friend and new enemy.

"Someone must know what her plans are though." Rye's eyes flashed. "We need to find out who she's working for."

⟫⟫⟫ ⟪⟪⟪

"The search for Bee won't change the competition dates." Sister Autumn stopped in the middle of the garden. Guards and volunteers had searched Bee's room and found nothing. They continued to search the sanctuary and Rye and I wanted to help. The priestess insisted on chaperoning. She must suspect our feelings for each other and wanted to discourage us.

Originally, she hadn't wanted Rye and I to help with the search because of our royal status. I'd convinced her I was a soldier and a warrior. Bee was my mistake and I planned to correct it.

"Princess Ellery, you take the hothouse where the orchids grow. Prince Zacharye, take the peace garden beside the lake. And I'll take the area around the gazebo." Sister Autumn pointed to a white wooden structure with a large clearing. "Call out if you see anything peculiar."

We headed off in three different directions to search and I was glad Rye wasn't far away. Bee was dangerous, even though she must be injured. She didn't have magic or wings, and I had both. Rye was a fighter and more capable than I'd ever given him credit.

Entering the hothouse, I paused for the wall of humidity. The rich earth scent overpowered the sweet scent of vanilla. Misters filled the space with a gentle dew. Row upon row of plants and flowers filled the glass structure. Placing my hand on my whip, I stalked between the plants and searched under shelves for a place that Bee could hide. She wasn't in here.

Through the glass, I spied Rye searching the peace garden with its ornamental flowers surrounded by benches and statuary. The beauty of the green shrubs with tiny buds, rows of larger colorful flowers, and the tall trees was set off by the calm blue of the lake.

Glancing my way, he waved. Had he sensed me watching him?

Jogging over, he opened the door of the hothouse. "Are you done searching your area?"

"Yes." I moved through the open door and into the crisp air.

"Come help me." He advanced toward a hedge and held a branch out of the way, and I stepped into a hidden garden.

The quiet paradise had a small patch of grass surrounded by succulent plants. The tall bushes hid it from the outside and a small, fast-running creek added to the peacefulness of the place.

"Finally, I've got you alone." He tugged me closer and his warmth wrapped around me, followed by electrified spirals. "I've wanted to comfort you since your friend's death."

The mention of Perry's murder crushed the thrills bursting through me at Rye's caress. "Being with you is comforting, knowing we're both on the same side."

He ran his knuckles down my cheek, sending new sparks of excitement across my skin. "Are we?" He cupped my chin and winked. He'd been the one insisting we weren't enemies.

"Yes, of course." The contact sent my heartbeat into a tizzy. I leaned into his palm, enjoying the toughness of his calloused skin beneath. He wasn't a do-nothing prince.

"You told me your guard pretended to like you." Rye's expression went serious and his lips dipped into a frown. "At the risk of losing you to him, I have to be honest. I don't think it's pretend on his part."

Confusion rattled my brain. If Stone's flirtation was real, what did it mean? I appreciated his friendship and loyalty, he was attractive, but with Rye, I'd always had this instant connection, a link going deep into my soul.

"How do you feel about your guard?" Rye's silver eyes held a sheen of hope. "How do you feel about me?"

"Confused." After this time at the sanctuary, we'd never see each other again. This moment in time would be lost forever and also branded on my heart. "With you, the risk is too high."

"I'm a risk-taker. At least, when it comes to you." Leaning closer, his voice dropped low. "How about you?"

With my slight nod, he placed his mouth fully on mine. My lips trembled and I responded. It felt so good to be cared for and cherished. To know it was honest and real. Not forced or ordered. The gentle kiss communicated a depth of emotion. Something meaningful and poignant passed between us. This wasn't just a meeting of lips, it was a meeting of minds and emotions. Our bond went deep.

One thing held me back. Stone. He was a friend and meant something to me, too. If his attraction was real, I'd need to let him down gently. Until then, I couldn't pursue things with Rye. I let the disappointment sink to my toes.

I placed my hands on his chest and mumbled against his mouth. "Stop. We need—"

"Prince Zacharye! Princess Ellery!" Sister Autumn's frantic tone reached through my fogged brain.

Rye's chagrined expression held a hint of humor. "I knew she'd find us. She's a bloodhound, even though she's human."

"Sister Autumn is human?" Is that why she favored Rye?

"Yes, and a great aunt on my father's side."

A priestess had to be a royal, and since she was human it made sense she was related to Rye. Her nature-based name was only a name.

The bushes, near where the creek roared, shook. Branches cracked, and the priestess pushed through. It was the opposite way we'd come into the small clearing.

"That's not a good spot to come through." Rye tugged on my hand to get us moving. "Sister, stop! We're coming out."

Before we could sneak under the branches, she crashed through the bushes on the side by the creek. Her body tumbled. Leaves scattered, and branches lay on the ground. Her large foot caught on a limb and she went flying.

And not magically.

Her body jerked and her hands wind-milled. She fell forward and landed in the deep, swiftly flowing creek.

Rye and I charged toward her. Panic blocked out thoughts of our kisses and confessions.

"Can she swim?" I didn't even know if that would help when the current was so strong.

He got to the edge and put a hand out trying to grab the woman. "I don't know."

She crashed into a rock and headed in the opposite direction from him. Her body tumbled like flotsam.

"Sister Autumn!" I searched for a solution, darting in every direction trying to find a low hanging branch or a large boulder to cling to.

Rye scrambled along the edge of the flowing creek and I followed. There wasn't a good spot to grab her.

She emerged above the surface in the lake and sputtered. Her heavy robes dragged her under again. Appearing, her arms flailed, and she tried to swim to shore. For every foot of progress, she'd lose two more. The rapid water was too strong for her.

"The waterfall!" Rye pointed to a spot beyond where she attempted to swim. "She's going to go over the waterfall."

Chapter Twenty-Five

I couldn't breathe, I was drowning with Sister Autumn.

She slapped at the quick-rushing water. Being tossed over a one-hundred-foot waterfall would kill her. Her arms became sloppier. Her head kept dipping under. Even her muscles couldn't compete against the force of the water pulling her closer and closer to the edge.

Rye ran along the creek. He tugged off his shoes and tossed them aside. Then, he pulled his shirt over his carved abs and shoulders. My pulse drubbed. I appreciated he was going to jump in and save her. He was more than a prince. He was a hero.

He dove in and swam toward the priestess. His strong strokes advanced his body swiftly in the water. He'd get to her in no time. But with the strong current and the waterfall tugging at them, they both could go over the edge and die.

My lungs stretched to take in oxygen. I needed to help. How?

My gaze darted around in frantic search for something, any-thing, to help. I spotted a tall tree near the spot where the water tumbled into the waterfall. "Rye watch out! I'm going to bring the tree down."

I hoped. And I hoped he heard.

Soothing my panic, I took a few deep pants. I had to focus. Concentrate on upending the tree. The roots must go deep into the earth. That was it! I'd use a combination of fairy magic and Mother Earth's gifts.

Rye grabbed Sister Autumn. He held her head above the water. She sputtered. The current was carrying them faster toward the edge. Rye's strokes weren't as strong now because he held the woman in his one arm and stroked with the other.

Stretching my fingers, I mentally rocked the trunk back and forth. The entire tree swayed, dancing to an internal rhythm. Then I focused on the roots, calling on Mother Earth to loosen them, and let them go free.

This better work. I didn't want to kill the tree and have Mother Earth angry at me if it didn't work.

The tree rocked harder. The earth quaked. The tearing and ripping of the roots bursting out of the ground scratched through my ears.

The tree tilted and hung for a second.

I held my breath.

Rye stopped swimming and kept the two of them afloat. His eyes widened as he gaped at the tree.

The tree plunged *down, down, down.*

"Forgive me, Mother Earth," I whispered.

The leaves and limbs and trunk hit the water with a huge splash. The lake lowered with the displaced water and then curled and advanced, creating a wave. The wave hit the shore and soaked me. I didn't care.

Running toward the roots of the fallen tree, I shook off the wetness. "Rye! Grab on!"

The tree lay at the edge of the lake where the water met the falls. I was lucky the trunk hadn't floated over the edge making the situation worse.

Rye grabbed on and held Sister Autumn against the trunk. His hair plastered to his head. Water ran down his face. Droplets of water glistened on his shoulders.

Sister Autumn's long gray hair clung to her head. Her hood had fallen off and I finally got a good look at her. An older woman with wrinkles. Definitely human. Her soaking wet robes must weigh a ton.

I approached the upended roots and climbed onto the two-foot diameter trunk. The water plummeted in a sheer drop to the right. My stomach lurched. If I took one misstep, I'd tumble. Although, I could fly. Rye and Sister Autumn couldn't. The tree had blocked them from the waterfall. Now, they needed to get out of the lake.

Shifting to a sitting position, I held out my hand. "You're both okay."

"Thanks to you." Rye flashed a quick grin, melting my heart.

"Use the tree trunk to work your way to the side of the lake." I scooted forward on the tree, heading back to shore beside them. If something went wrong, I planned to grab them and pull up.

"One hand in front of the other," Rye coached Sister Autumn.

She planted her palms on the trunk, shaking the tree and me. She must be exhausted. I gripped the trunk beneath and held on while they worked their way to the edge of the lake. Once both were on dry land, I jumped to my feet and edged across the trunk to shore.

They both collapsed on the grass. I fell in a pile next to them. We were wet and tired. And relieved. Rye and I made a good team. And I'd learned something about myself.

I could handle pressure. I could access Mother Earth's gifts when stressed. And I'd combined her power with my magic.

Sister Autumn rolled on her side to face Rye. "Thanks for jumping in and saving my life."

"With Elle's magical help." Rye winked at me and I didn't sense the cold of the water through my clothes.

The priestess gave me a regal nod. "With Elle's magical help."

Back in my room, I dragged off my wet clothes and cleaned up. The search assignment hadn't turned out as expected. We hadn't found Bee, and Rye and I hadn't gotten to spend much time alone. Although I'd learned I could do magic and use Mother Earth's gifts under pressure. I'd seen the reluctant respect from Sister Autumn. Maybe she wouldn't hate me so much anymore.

My bedroom door flew open and Arbor flew inside. "I heard you almost drowned."

"As if you care." I couldn't stop the snark.

"I do care." She buzzed around my face, revealing her fierce expression.

"Because you were ordered to care." I couldn't forget our fight.

Losing Arbor as my friend had felt like losing a limb. The impact had been more powerful and hurtful than when Bee had betrayed me. Because Arbor meant more. I held back a sniff.

"I really do care." Arbor's eyes glistened with tears. "Gardenia sent me to tutor, guide, and protect you without being obvious because it would be dangerous if humans found out you were the lost princess. The best way to do those things safely was to become friends."

"Exactly." My eyes burned as she spelled her crime out for me. "You're not a real friend."

"I like you Elle. We truly became friends and I want to continue being friends." Her words and tone resonated inside.

I wanted that too. How could I trust her? Sure, she'd protect me and be loyal to the crown. What about to me? To my personal secrets? It was similar to my situation with Stone.

Crossing my arms, I tried to hold my anger together. "What about Gardenia? Does your boss want you to continue to be friends with me?"

"Once word is out you're the princess, probably not." Arbor's sarcasm displayed a flippancy toward the commander. "I'd still enjoy being your friend though. Now and always."

She seemed sincere. Her tiny pursed lips showed contrition. Her hands pressed together in a plea.

My resistance weakened. I loved hanging out with her. I wanted to joke around with her again. I needed a female friend, someone to giggle with and confide in.

Arbor flew up and landed on the bedpost. "I can't change the truth of what happened or how we met. Gardenia sent me to watch you, and if she hadn't done so, we never would've become friends."

Remembering the day we'd met, sent a pang through my chest. I'd been so lonely and desperate for friends. Arbor had probably laughed behind my back.

"I must've been an easy target." My voice quivered, trying to control my embarrassment. "Desperate and lonely."

"You were lonely, not desperate." Smiling, she swung her arm forward in a fist. "You were so gung-ho on passing as human. You could've done it too if I hadn't gotten arrested."

"Arrested for magic I did."

"You could've let me die for the crime. Instead, you came after me. Risked your human identity and your life to save me. Do you know how that made me feel?"

Her statement ended on a high note. Full of promise and compassion. Full of emotion, charging the silence between us.

She fluttered from the bedpost to my shoulder and landed. "It made me believe you were my real friend. Someone who would risk everything to save me."

Her tiny toes gripped through my shirt and somehow reached around my heart. Her stubbornness told me she wouldn't bend from the statement. She was my friend, whether I wanted her to be or not.

I enjoyed her company and needed her friendship. Besides the Gardenia thing, Arbor had been helpful and loyal. She had even gone against the commander's wishes by taking me back to my human house.

"I am your real friend. And you were my real friend, right?" Arbor's tone trembled with worry.

Shaking my head, I saw her expression change to one of dejection. That's not what I'd intended.

"Not were." I picked her off my shoulder and brought her around in the palm of my hand so she could see my face. "Am. I *am* your friend."

She squealed, and I squealed, and we hugged.

All was forgiven, and we'd be friends forever. I hoped another relationship would be as easy.

Competition day.

I bolted out of bed the second the thought hit. Today was the day I'd be able to prove to the fairies, and myself, I was capable. Except hadn't I already proven that to myself?

I'd made the trip to the Aristos Sanctuary. I'd trained hard with Watu, and others. I'd gotten my wings and mastered my magic. I'd foiled Bee's plot, although she hadn't been found. I'd led my team and made up with Arbor. I'd reconnected with Rye. I'd gained the approval of my great-grandmother.

Surely, I could withdraw an orb from water.

Of course, there'd be others competing. Rye. Hokima's cousin. And others I didn't know. Possibly an ogre, an elf, a brownie. I wasn't even told the format for the competition. Would we stick our hands in the Reflection Pool at one time? That could create a hurricane with all of us using Mother Earth's gifts against each other.

While I got dressed, my stomach created a hurricane of its own. Churning acid, swirling bile, and internal pounding.

"Good morning." Arbor flew into the room. Her happy greeting was completely lost on me.

"What's good about it?" Besides the competition, I'd be saying goodbye to Rye. He'd already mentioned his uncle was impatient for him to return home. With the orb.

"Today's the day you'll prove the superiority of fairies." Arbor flapped her wings and made a nosedive for the bed.

Unease rumbled in my midsection. "Superior to who?"

She landed with a soft thud on the mattress. "The other majiks."

I shook my head, trying to soothe my growing upset. "This competition shouldn't be viewed in that way. The majiks are on the same side."

Of course, that meant Rye was on the opposite side. But I couldn't think of him as an enemy. He'd convinced me.

"The majiks will need to work together to win the upcoming war." I was positive about this. And this would be my platform as princess. I'd treat the other majiks as equals and gain their respect.

"Yeah, but I want you to win," Arbor groused.

"I want to win, too." Which would guarantee the Divinity Orb wouldn't be used against other majiks. "Whoever wins, we'll congratulate them and try to come to an agreement about usage."

Assuming it wasn't Rye who won. I could never come to an agreement with his uncle. How could he win though? The one with the strongest connection to Mother Earth would win. And Rye was human, even if he'd been taught how to use her gifts. Majiks were just more connected to nature.

"Are you ready?" Arbor flew toward the door.

I jerked my head down in a determined nod. "I'm ready."

Picking up the Silver Snare, I marched out of the room, down the hallway, and to my destiny.

Stone, Hokima, and Tos waited for me in the room with the Reflection Pool.

Stone's eyebrows were drawn together, concerned. Did he have doubts about my abilities?

"I understand you're good with water." His dark undertone told me he'd heard about my escapade by the lake. So not doubt, but jealousy.

I gave him a stiff smile, not wanting to explain things to him now. At some point, I'd have to talk to him about why we could never be a couple.

Tos appeared pale, as if she'd seen a ghost. I had to wonder if I looked sickly. Hokima stood solidly, his goopy gaze went back and forth between me and the other competitors.

The other competitors were huddled in groups with their guards and servants—their teams. I couldn't figure out which one was related to royalty and competing. One group had greenish-tinted skin resembling goblins. They were shorter and huddled together, holding sticks and spears. A second group wore all brown and had the pointed ears of the elves. A third group hunched their backs and kept their heads facing toward the ground. There was the human group standing tall around the prince. His guards wore dress uniforms and stood at attention.

Rye gave me a sly wink, surrounded by his guards. He seemed relaxed. His clothes weren't the formal suit with sash he'd worn before. Instead, he donned casual pants and an untucked shirt. I appreciated how he looked both ways. *Any way*.

Finally, there was my ragtag group. A half fairy competitor with a troll, a brownie, a half giant, and a smoke sprite as her companions.

"Alright, everyone." Sister Autumn clapped to get everyone's attention. "We will introduce the competitors first." She held a hand toward Rye. "Prince Zacharye from the human world."

He waved and the guards surrounding him clapped.

I put my hands together to clap and stopped myself. We were competitors now.

"Princess Ellery from the fairies."

Holding up my hand, I tried to focus on the competition until Rye blew a kiss toward me. My cheeks heated, and I bent my head. He was so open with his emotions. While I hid behind mine.

"Next, we have Napuka from the troll contingent."

He stomped out from his circle with clawed feet and shot me a contemptuous glance. His large hands had long pointy nails and he clenched them, ready to kill. He didn't remind me of Hokima and didn't act like him either.

"Wios from the goblins."

His skin was darker green and a gold ring pierced his large pointy ear. He shared a look with Napuka and bared his teeth at Rye.

I jolted. Had the two majiks formed a partnership? I'd stated how the majiks needed to work together in the war, but this competition should be each one of us one our own, based on our own abilities and merits.

"From the elves is Dareltie."

...tie, tie, tie. The end of her name echoed in my head and I squeezed my eyes closed and opened them again, fearing I was seeing the dead.

The female elf had bright red hair tied in a braid. Her pointy ears were delicate and her olive eyes reminded me of Keltie. She was identical to my friend.

My knees gave out and I stumbled back. Stone grabbed my arm to steady me.

"Keltie?" I whispered across dry lips.

The elf acknowledged Napuka and Wios, and glared at me. Her gaze pierced through to my soul with an evil leer. Her scowl revealed her hatred for me.

This wasn't Keltie. I'd seen her die saving Arbor. I still heard the elf's scream in my sleep. Plus, this one obviously hated me.

"Will the contestants step forward so I can explain the first contest." Sister Autumn used a come closer motion.

Keltie's twin stepped by me. Her glare cut through me, familiar and not. "Princess Ellery. I've heard about you. Heard how you got my sister killed."

Sister?

No wonder they resembled each other. Keltie had talked about her brothers and sisters constantly. She'd volunteered for the mission to destroy the auraguillotine so none of her siblings would die from the terrible machine. I hadn't known Keltie was of royal birth. She'd said her father was a lawyer. Then again, I hadn't known that about myself.

How was I going to compete against the guy I was wild about and a girl who looked like my lost friend and blamed me for her death?

CHAPTER TWENTY-SIX

"The competition will take place during the next two days,"
Sister Autumn announced after the introductions.

The gathering of a couple of dozen, including competitors and their teams, murmured. It was the first detail I'd been given about the competition. Had others been told more? Had Rye? My shoulders dropped. Two more days.

My gaze caught Rye's gleaming silver eyes. He didn't seem upset by the announcement. Of course, the sooner this ended, the sooner we'd each go our separate ways.

"The first two events will take place today and will eliminate two competitors."

Eliminate? So I might not get the chance to draw the Divinity Orb out of the Reflection Pool?

More murmurs as others came to the same conclusion.

"Your first task is easy and involves your team."

A sanctuary guard shoved me forward, separating me from my team. Nerves buzzed in my stomach. If it involved our teams, why were we being separated? I thought I'd have their emotional support and advice, even if I had to compete alone.

"Your team will vacate the room for my instructions to you."

The guards started pushing the non-competitors out of the room. Complaints rose from various members. Wheeling around, I searched for my friends and realized I was short two. My heart pinched, and I tried to get a grip on my wildly swinging emotions. Anger because Bee had betrayed me. And grief over Perry's death.

"You've got this." Arbor flew close to my head, tangling my hair. Hokima and Tos nodded their agreement.

Stone sent an encouraging salute and shot a sharp glare at Rye, telling him to take care of me. Smashing my lips together, I huffed. I could handle myself.

The priestess clapped her hands. "Your teams are being led to the meditation room and I will begin your first instructions."

Rye stepped next to me and brushed his hand against mine. The contact frazzled and calmed my nerves at the same time. His touch brought peace and comfort while eliciting a strong attraction. I scanned the area hoping the other competitors didn't notice because I didn't need more enemies. Raising my head, I studied Sister Autumn. She stared right at me and glanced down at our hands. She'd noticed.

Swallowing, I wondered what she thought. Since saving her from the waterfall, she hadn't looked at me with as much disdain. And she'd encouraged Rye and I to spend time together. Had she become my champion too?

Two servants swished a set of curtains aside and Mother Morningmist glided into the room, distracting my thoughts.

Everyone bowed. The respect my great-grandmother received had my chest swelling. They loved her. Someday I hoped to command at least a fraction of that love and respect.

"Communication is a key element in ruling. This task will demonstrate your ability to communicate with your team in a nontraditional manner. No magic necessary." Giving a slight nod to Rye, she held up a wrinkled hand. "In my hand, I have envelopes with items spread throughout the sanctuary. You will each pick one and using Mother Earth's gifts, you must communicate with your team to bring this item to you here."

I glanced at Rye and the others. They were inspecting each other, appearing confident. It wasn't a hard task. I'd communicated with fireflies before. They'd always been simple messages to help or meet me. The tricky part was the specificity.

"The last competitor to have the item in hand will be knocked out of the competition." Sister Autumn swished her robes and advanced toward my great-grandmother. "Each of you will pick an envelope from Mother Morningmist. Don't open it, yet."

Dareltie hurried forward and snatched an envelope from my great grandmother's hand. She gave me a nasty glare.

"Ladies first." Rye let me step in front of him.

My hand hovered above the envelopes, wanting to pick an easy object. My great-grandmother's expression gave nothing away. She wanted the competition to be fair and so did I. Picking the one on the left side, I held the envelope between my tingling fingers.

Rye took the one on the right.

Wios and Napuka pushed into each other, snatching their envelopes.

"Alright." Sister Autumn drew our attention. "Open your envelopes and begin."

I ripped open the seam. The noise of paper tearing was the only sound in the room. Unfolding the piece of parchment, I read the sentences:

Instruct your team to bring back the item cultivated in a humid environment for its pods.

So, some kind of a plant.

It has a distinctive scent in both natural and produced form and is used in cooking.

Peppers? Hot peppers?

There were peppers in the hothouse when I'd searched for Bee. A plant also used for cooking. Except the overwhelming smell of vanilla was inside. I squeezed the piece of paper. Vanilla was a flowering plant and the priestesses grew it in the hothouse for cooking. That had to be it.

Napuka dropped to his knees and started a small fire. He must plan to send smoke signals. Dareltie dashed to the window and started whistling. Wios closed his eyes and furrowed his brow.

Rye went to the Reflection Pool, put his hand in the water, and swirled his fingers. I didn't realize water could be used to communicate.

Which meant I should stop focusing on the others and concentrate on my message.

I focused on the fireflies from the garden. I needed them to show my team the object and tell them they needed to bring the vanilla plant here and not panic in the process.

Buzzing sounded in my ears. The fireflies gathered together in a swarm. In my head, I whispered my message. I pictured Arbor in my mind, knowing, as a fairy smoke sprite, she'd understand the message. The other teams would have it easier because they were all human or all elf or all troll or all goblin. Communicating with various races made my task more difficult. Similar to real life.

But being a team, we'd prove majiks could work together.

Smoke filtered into my lungs and I coughed. My concentration broke. Smoke from the troll's fire filled the room.

Rye wiped his wet hand on his pants. Dareltie leaned against the wall with a smug expression. They both must be done. Wios stomped around on the ground, doing an angry dance. His message must not be working.

Knock. Knock.

Could someone's team already be here? Holding my breath, I waited while the priestess opened the door.

The troll's guards and servants hustled into the room. They were covered in soot, as if the smoke message had attacked them. They carried a scroll.

Sister Autumn examined the object. "Napuko is first."

The trolls celebrated with a stomping dance and the floor shook.

The elf team scurried in, carrying a broad sword that had hung on the wall in the main room. Dareltie grabbed the sword from her team and held it up high without showing her team appreciation. The priestess announced her team second.

My nerves frayed. I paced the room, avoiding the other competitors. The waiting was the hardest part. I didn't know if I should try and send a second message or not.

Knock. Knock.

Arbor flew in. Tos and Hokima scurried forward. None of them carried the plant. Deflated, I hung my head. Had they misunderstood the message? Stone marched in behind them, holding a ball of dirt with the vanilla orchid in the center.

Elation zinged through my veins and pushed my legs into motion. I ran to them and we hugged, jumping up and down. "You guys did it!"

"We did it!" Tos jumped high on my leg.

"We did it!" Hokima grumped.

Stone smiled in satisfaction.

"Ellery is third," Sister Autumn announced.

That left Wios and Rye. While he might've studied Mother Earth's gifts, his guards probably hadn't.

Knock. Knock.

Whoever was behind the door would indicate the final competitor moving to the next leg of the competition.

Human guards stood behind the door, holding a feather pen. Rye had gotten into the next round. He congratulated his team with pats on the back.

I couldn't stop a grin.

Wios pursed his flabby lips and his skin turned a sickly purple. His eyes bulged out of their sockets. He screeched, a bloodcurdling scream.

My shoulders hunched, trying to block the noise. Too bad for the goblin.

Sister Autumn pivoted to Wios. "I'm sorry. You are out of the competition. Please pack your bags and leave Aristos Sanctuary."

He pounded the wall, putting a hole through it. His feet stomped and the ground shook. "No. No. No."

With the distraction, Dareltie sidled up next to me. "Aren't you worried your troll might defect?" Her snide tone didn't cut into the confidence in my team.

"No." I knew I could trust my team.

And I'd learned how to distinguish real friends from fake ones.

The second contest wasn't about speed or communication. Each competitor needed to demonstrate something positive using Mother Earth's gifts. The demonstration would be judged by a panel of priestesses, including Sister Autumn and Mother Morningmist.

"I'm going to replant the large tree I tore out of the ground in the garden by the top of the waterfall," I informed my team.

Teams had a break to rest and plan and then they'd be called to compete in the afternoon. I'd chosen my bedroom, believing it was the most secure place to talk.

"I feel terrible for uprooting the tree and killing it." I'd stopped by the secret garden to check on the situation. The tree still lay across the water.

Stone placed a large, comforting hand on my arm. Comfort from a friend, nothing more. "There's a good reason it's down. You saved a life."

"Which is a good excuse for jeopardizing a tree and for wanting to fix it." Hokima's reasoning went along with mine.

Smiling, I remembered Dareltie's question and swatted it aside. I believed in Hokima and I believed in my idea.

"A difficult task." Tos didn't express her normal enthusiasm.

"I know." Reanimation was difficult. I had the will and the determination. I'd done something similar with the alpine flower at Watu's request, although that had been much simpler. My bones strengthened. This was something I needed to do. And Mother Earth would appreciate my efforts.

When I was called to the panel, I brought them to the secret garden. Besides Mother Morningmist and Sister Autumn, three other priestesses were part of the judging panel.

"What happened here?" Mother Morningmist sauntered by the uprooted trunk of the tree with a frown on her face. "Wasn't this one of your favorite trees, Sister Autumn?"

I stiffened. I didn't know it was the priestess' favorite. I should've picked a different tree for her rescue. If I couldn't save it, she'd dislike me more.

A patch of color showed on Sister Autumn's cheeks. "Even more so now."

Because the tree had saved her with my help.

The other priestesses murmured.

I scooted to Mother Morningmist's side. "Um, someone fell in the creek." I decided to keep who fell in a secret. I didn't want to embarrass Sister Autumn more. "She was about to go over the edge of the waterfall. She would've died." I spoke louder, realizing the explanation was part of my demonstration. "In order to save her, I used my fairy magic and called on Mother Earth's gifts to fell this big tree so she had something to grab on to and save herself with Prince Zacharye's help."

Horrified gasps came from the other priestesses. Obviously, Sister Autumn hadn't told them about her near drowning. Why? The priestesses understood the danger of the waterfall drop.

Mother Morningmist stayed silent, a secretive grin on her face. Had she known the story?

"I felt terrible for uprooting the magnificent tree and I asked Mother Earth for forgiveness." I twisted my hands together. "Now, I want to repair the damage. To stand the tree back up and sink its roots back in the ground so the tree can live and thrive, so birds can nest in its limbs, and others can enjoy this majestic tree's shade."

Sister Autumn sniffed beside me. The other judges nodded slowly. They understood my reasoning and knew the challenges.

Mother Morningmist's gaze gleamed, and she smiled, which told me I was doing the right thing.

Even if it would be difficult. If I was successful, I'd prove I had a strong handle on Mother Earth's gifts. If I wasn't successful, at least I'd tried to right a wrong. Hopefully, they'd give me points.

Clearing my mind, I couldn't think about the competition or the politics or the eventual prize. I couldn't worry about the other competitors and what they'd chosen to do, whether simple or difficult. I had to focus on this moment, on this task, on this tree.

First, I pictured the tree standing tall the way it had been. Then, I closed my eyes and focused. I reached out to the roots dangling in the wind and imagined them digging back into the freshly turned dirt.

Back into Mother Earth.

In my mind, I saw the roots stretch and grow. Similar to worms, they dug back into the soil. The roots pulled on one side of the tree as they searched for the right environment. Nutrient-rich soil, moist ground. Home.

My nerves sizzled, and my muscles grew taut. This was more than communicating with Mother Earth. This was asking for her help and assisting her to beautify earth. It was tiring, and exhaustion worked its way through my system making me weaker and weaker.

Opening my eyes, I couldn't give up. I sensed the progress. Things were happening. I had to push harder.

The tree's limbs began to shake. The leaves shivered and caused ripples in the water. The tree began to tilt and rise.

Exultation filled my lungs. Not for me. For the tree.

The roots dug deeper, pulled tighter. The tree stood taller. Limbs lifted, stretching toward the sky. The leaves shimmied and whispered in the slight breeze.

My weary bones wanted to collapse. I dug my feet deeper into the ground, keeping my stance and my focus and my connection to Mother Earth. Instinctually recognizing the roots relaxing, I knew

I was almost done. With my mind, I pushed the dirt around the trunk, cushioning the base to resist a strong wind.

The tree sighed and settled and stood tall.

Satisfaction made me stand as tall as the tree. I'd done well. I'd repaired what I had broken using my strengths. Facing the bright sun, I let the pent-up guilt seep out of me. Guilt about the tree, about being wrong about Bee, about the deaths of Bim, Keltie, and now Perry. Like photosynthesis, the sun synthesized my guilt into strength. I regenerated and grew as strong as a newborn tree.

The priestesses applauded. Sister Autumn gave me a hug. My great-grandmother had tears flowing down her cheeks.

Nothing topped my own joy and contentment of doing a task well, of saving something valuable, of being true to myself.

⟫⟫⟩ ⟨⟨⟨

Dinner had a celebratory mood. Lightning bugs buzzed around the table, providing flickering lights and a jubilant atmosphere. A few robed priestesses sat on a raised dais, playing musical instruments. Several long wooden tables were festooned with festive tablecloths, fine china, sparkling silverware. The chandelier was adorned with flowers and vines. The priestesses had gone all out and served a mix of human, fairy, and elf food to honor the three remaining competitors.

Me, Rye, and Dareltie.

I tapped my feet to the music beneath the table I shared with my team. I'd used my ever-expanding magic to create a soft cotton dress in a green floral pattern. I wanted Rye to see me in more than a soldier's outfit. Tos and Arbor discussed the day's events in an excited tone. Hokima ate with abandon, trying what was to him exotic delicacies. He wasn't upset about his cousin's loss.

Stone stayed silent and a tension emanated from him. His abrasive attitude rubbed me the wrong way. This was a celebration and I wished I could find a way to convince him to join the party. He rarely let his guard down.

The group at Rye's table were eating and talking excitedly. He'd dressed up for the occasion wearing his more formal suit. He shifted his head as if sensing my interest.

My heart squeezed. Trying to sound casual, I asked, "What did Prince Zacharye do for his task?"

"He cleared the gardens of weeds." Arbor fluttered her wings, hovering above her plate of corn and bacon bits.

I tilted my head. "Magically?"

"No. Using his toned muscles." She waved her hand in front of her face in a dramatic gesture. "Shirtless."

The breath caught in my throat. That would've been a sight to see.

Stone growled. "The prince didn't use Mother Earth's gifts."

"Maybe the prince is not as familiar with Mother Earth's gifts." Arbor kept waving at her face, probably more to annoy Stone than any actual flush.

"He is. He's been trained." In fact, he'd helped me.

"Well, Prince Zacharye used manual labor for the task." She continued to fan her face.

I understood and appreciated manual labor. "And by doing so he helped the priestesses with one of their food sources."

Arbor picked up a kernel of corn. "Most of this food is from the garden."

He did a good task to help feed us.

"Dareltie expelled the rats from the sanctuary." Tos shivered. "Do you think I could learn? I hate rats."

"Brownies can access Mother Earth's gifts." Although getting rid of rats might disrupt the ecosystem. "I wonder why brownies weren't represented?"

I glanced at Rye again. He was laughing with one of his guards. They were friends. He wasn't standoffish or boorish. He was real.

"Our royal line died out in a war against the trolls." Tos peered at Hokima.

Hokima lifted his arms in an apologetic shrug. "Sorry."

"Not your fault." Tos wrapped her arms around his thick wrist.

Even though we were from different places, we made a great team. We were getting along and working together. This was the future of our kingdom. And by winning the Divinity Orb with my ragtag team, we'd prove to Alandaska how things could be if we got along and worked together.

"What did your cousin do resulting in his loss?" I hadn't heard what Napuka had attempted.

"I heard..." Arbor buzzed by me and lowered her tone. "He forced the sanctuary's cats and dogs to clean the bathrooms."

"You're kidding?" Animals weren't slaves. Just as majiks weren't slaves to humans.

I glanced at Rye again.

"Stop doing that." Stone nudged me with his elbow.

"Stop doing what?"

"Looking at *him*." He used his chin to point at Rye.

"I'm not." It wasn't a strong denial because I had been peering all evening.

"You are." Stone scowled. "It needs to stop. Tomorrow, you'll be competing against him and Dareltie."

I understood. My gut churned. I'd wanted Rye to continue in the competition, even though if we both were finalists, we'd be up against each other, head to head. The thought had been in the back of my mind the entire time. I'd kept it locked away, not wanting to face the truth.

"If you and Dareltie move on to the finals, it's guaranteed a majik will win the Divinity Orb."

I swallowed. I hadn't thought of that. If a majik won, the orb would be with our side during the war.

Stone crossed his arms and glared. "You need to work with her to assure one of you wins."

Meaning work against Rye.

CHAPTER TWENTY-SEVEN

The following morning, I dragged myself to the gazebo as instructed. The gazebo was near the hidden spot where Rye and I had met, and by the lake pouring into the waterfall. The tree, my tree, stood tall and strong and I couldn't stop beaming. Mother Morningmist sat on the bench circling the inside of the gazebo. Sister Autumn and the same three priestesses from the day before stood by her side in a semicircle.

I knew I had dark circles under my eyes from a rough night sleeping. Nightmares of Dareltie telling me I owed her because of Keltie's death confronted me behind closed lids. And Stone saying majiks needed to stick together was whispered in my ear. I'd barely spoken at breakfast with my team and was glad I could leave them behind.

Leaving Dareltie behind was impossible.

Strutting toward the designated meeting spot, she caught my attention as if she knew the thoughts running inside my mind. She wore an outfit matching what her sister had worn on our adventures under the human palace. Brown breeches and a tight top with a short, flowing cape.

Rye strolled to the gazebo seconds later with a confident stride. His casual pants clung to his muscular thighs and the untucked white shirt spread across his broad chest. His springy step showed he'd had no trouble sleeping.

Sighing, I tugged on the black belt circling my waist. I'd been wearing the outfit Watu had given me for each leg of the competition. The outfit gave me confidence and was a reminder of what was at stake. The majik side of the war.

My fairy future against Rye, the guy I cared for and connected with in a special way.

Conflict tore me in two. I had to pick a side, the fairy side, my side.

"Controlling the weather is an important gift given by Mother Earth in combination with your emotions." Sister Autumn's gaze connected with mine before shifting to Rye and Dareltie. "Using this gift should be limited to desperate need. For example, making rain in a drought. It's not to be abused."

My mind flickered. Watu had said something similar when she spoke of Mother Earth's manipulation of weather. Watu had pointed out weather was a gift from Mother Earth, and it's when I'd realized Bee had lied about making the snowstorm. Why hadn't I questioned her loyalty then?

"This competition is to demonstrate how you'd work with Mother Earth and her weather without letting it take control away from you." Sister Autumn flung her arms wide in a dramatic fashion. "To exhibit control."

My lungs filled with oxygen. I could do this. Watu had taught me how to use my emotions to change and control the weather. I could do something major, a real show of force. This was the last test before the final two competitors would get to try and retrieve the Divinity Orb. I needed to make it through. This was my chance to shine.

Or rain, as the case may be.

Or snow or hail. I should think bigger to really make an impression on the priestesses. A tornado or—my gaze caught on the smooth lake—a hurricane. An extreme weather manipulation to demonstrate I was strong enough to possess the orb.

Rye's forehead furrowed in an adorable way, showing he was thinking. Dareltie wore a superior smirk. She must be familiar with weather manipulation.

She was picked to go first. Stepping off the edge of the gazebo, she bumped into me in the process. A strong, calculating bump.

I stumbled and Rye grabbed my elbow, stopping me from falling. Sister Autumn glowered at me, believing I caused the ruckus.

Heat flamed my skin. Dareltie had bumped into me on purpose to embarrass me. It had worked. Her hatred for me would help her with the task. It also fed into my mortification. I could use the emotion when I manipulated the weather. In a way, she'd helped me too.

She marched about twenty yards from the gazebo and rotated around to face us. Her lips were smashed together in a determined frown, her eyes were slits, and her nose flared. She raised her hands toward the sky and stared upward. Then she dropped her hate-filled glare to lock with mine.

I refused to react, refused to glance away. She blamed me for her sister's death, but I'd let go of my guilt when I'd repaired the tree. Her sister had been a brave warrior and I was thankful I'd called her friend.

Dark clouds gathered in a fast-motion storm. The unique smell right before rain tickled my nose. The clouds burst and rain poured from the sky. Large drops pelted down and picked up speed.

Dareltie stood, not reacting to the rain, keeping her hands raised and her gaze intent on me. Her hair lay flat on her head and her clothes clung to her body. Her expression grew darker with the clouds. Her glare became fiercer. Her cheekbones more strained and her lips grew thinner and grimmer.

Her animosity roared in my direction. She fed off her anger and hatred for me, and in turn the storm got worse. She fell into a trance.

I took a step back and bumped into Rye. He placed a comforting hand on my shoulder. He'd seen how Dareltie had leered at me and must understand she drew her negative emotions from me, while pulling energy from the earth.

A clap of thunder shook the small gazebo. Lightning flashed close by. The storm went from wet and raging to magnificent and dangerous. Another crack of thunder, closer and louder. A lightning bolt struck an outbuilding and exploded with noise and light.

The priestesses murmured their concern.

The hair on my arms stood at attention. I'd planned to use my anger to display my strength. Now, I knew it was the wrong approach. Dareltie didn't seem strong. She seemed unstable.

"Dareltie!" Sister Autumn edged toward the boundary of the gazebo. "Dareltie!"

The elf didn't flinch, didn't move. At this rate, we'd stay huddled in the gazebo for hours. She'd lost control of herself and the storm.

Rain pounded the lake. Small waves crested and poured over the waterfall. The current became stronger than normal. A lightning strike hit the weathervane on top of the gazebo and crackled through the wood structure.

Everyone inside jumped, including me.

"Dareltie, stop!" Sister Autumn gripped a wooden beam with white knuckles and leaned out into the storm.

The other priestesses gathered around Mother Morningmist protecting her. I wanted to help too, but I wondered if I could assist better by stopping the elf.

The sizzling of electricity traveled through the wooden structure of the gazebo. A burnt smell filled the air. If lightning struck the wooden structure again, it would be toast.

I was next in line for the challenge, and I wasn't going to wait. I had to do something to stop Dareltie and protect the others. Waiting for the storm to subside wasn't an option.

Stepping out into the pouring rain, I ignored the wet and cold. My hair clung to my head like a helmet as if anticipating the battle ahead. My clothes hung heavily. Lightning struck a few feet away. I jerked but didn't stop.

Dareltie's eerie stare started a shiver from the tips of my toes to the top of my wet head. I forced the quiver to stop. Taking a deep breath, I soothed my nerves. I'd let go of my guilt. It was time to let go of my fear and my anger for being in this predicament. I needed to stop blaming Gardenia or Sister Autumn or Bee and count the positives. My old and new friends, Watu's mentorship, my wings. My fairy realm.

It was time for me to take charge.

And bring out the sun.

Here, in my fairy realm, in the Kingdom of Alandaska.

"Aiea!" I used my dead friend's signature yell.

Thinking these positive thoughts, I raised my face to the pouring rain and grinned. I closed my eyes and thought of the heat of the sun. I thought of my mother and father and their happiness. I thought of Arbor, Hokima, and Tos, and their friendship. I thought of Mother Morningmist and Queen Dahliadew and Watu, and even Gardenia for their guidance. I thought of Stone and Rye, and how they both warmed my heart in different ways.

I pictured the dark clouds losing their strength. The thunder silencing and the lightning not igniting. With my eyes closed, I pictured the sun beaming stronger through the clouds, breaking the gloom apart.

A glow tickled my cheeks. Steam rose from my clothes. The storm rumbled nearby, even as the sun became stronger.

Opening my eyes, I stood in a slash of sunshine. The sun peeked through Dareltie's clouds. The gazebo shined in the light. Mother Morningmist, the priestesses, and Rye were safe. A lightness filled me and a smile broke out on my face.

Rye smiled back at me. Mother Morningmist glowed with approval.

Splashes of red, orange, yellow, green, blue, indigo, and violet shined in a semicircle.

A rainbow.

The perfect end to my test.

Mother Morningmist started clapping. Rye and Sister Autumn joined in. The other priestesses added to the applause.

Satisfaction and happiness filled me up inside.

Dareltie stomped her foot and a loud clap of thunder accompanied her. "A rainbow isn't real. It's a mirage."

I stiffened. This battle wasn't done.

"My rain made half the rainbow." She flung up her hands.

The storm grew back with instant intensity. The rain came at me sideways. A bolt of lightning struck the gazebo. Wood splintered off. The priestesses tried to cover themselves with their cloaks and their arms. Mother Morningmist sat and stared as if watching a vid drama.

I hung onto my sunshine and my positive outlook, even as the storm agitated around, even though nerves thundered inside me. I stood in the only bright spot.

Rye lunged from the gazebo and fought against the wind and the rain to take a stand beside me. The heat from his body warmed my soul. He was here to help.

He wiggled his shoulders and pursed his lips and blew.

Wind swirled around us. The force increased and I grabbed onto him to stay in one place. His feet tethered to the ground. The gale force caused the leaves to shake and the trees to bend. The current in the lake picked up in intensity. Debris scattered in the wind.

As did the dark clouds.

Rye's wind blew the storm away.

Relief sweltered, relaxing me. I gave him a big hug. He wrapped his arms around me and twirled me around in celebration.

"Working together is a hallmark of a good leader," Mother Morningmist proclaimed in a loud and strong voice. She got to her feet and waltzed off the damaged gazebo. "We have our final two competitors."

I let the news soak into each of my brain cells. I was one of the final two.

And so was Rye.

The guy I was currently hugging.

"Heard how you and Prince Zacharye worked together to stop Dareltie." Stone entered my room as I was drying my hair off from the rain.

A priestess had brought me lunch on a tray and told me I had an hour until the final test at the Reflection Pool. I'd forced myself to eat to gain my physical strength back. Making sun took a lot out of a girl.

"She kind of lost it." I hung the towel on a chair and stared at Stone. "Aren't you glad I didn't pair up with her?"

He shifted his feet and scanned around the room. "Not sure I approve of you pairing up with the prince."

My lungs hitched. Was that jealousy? I needed to talk to him about the prince.

"You've always known how I feel about Rye, even when I didn't know he was the human prince." I didn't want to hurt Stone, but I needed to make him understand my strong attachment to another.

His lips pursed into a frown and he scowled. "I did."

"I'm sorry if you thought I led you on when I returned your kisses. I thought I'd never see Rye again and he might be dead."

"I'm sorry I led you on."

I jerked back. He'd admitted he flirted with me to keep me close and protect me, and then said he'd fallen for me. He'd seemed sincere. Was this how he thought he could protect me or was he protecting his own emotions now? "So, you really don't have feelings for me?"

I wasn't sure whether to be angry or grateful at his deceit.

"For you?" His voice rose and something flashed in his gaze. "You're like a kid sister, a friend." He punched my shoulder.

Furrowing my brow, I wasn't sure if he told the truth before or now. I rubbed the spot on my arm where he'd punched. Boyfriends didn't punch their girlfriends. "Really? You won't be upset if Rye and I get together?"

Although, he'd never said anything about a permanent arrangement.

"If it was anyone, I'm glad it's him. I respect him." Stone tilted his chin. "How can you and the prince be together when you'll be living in separate palaces and on opposite sides of a war?"

How indeed?

CHAPTER TWENTY-EIGHT

The Reflection Pool glittered brighter than before, catching my attention.

The final test.

The quiet chamber sent a wave of tension through my system. Everyone's eyes drilled through me. Probably because they were staring at me and Rye. I smoothed the same outfit I'd worn earlier in the day. It had finally dried and the gift from Watu boosted my courage.

Rye appeared confident approaching the pool. He'd changed into black pants and shirt. His hair was messed up, either from running his fingers through it or from the wind and rain.

Our steps echoed each other. We closed the distance, one on each side of the water. The priestesses lined around the edges, and our teams stood in the back to act as witnesses.

Quietly, I blew out a slow breath. This was the moment. The reason I'd journeyed to this place. Gardenia believed the orb, with its powers, belonged to the fairies. I had to believe it, too.

"You may begin when I say go." Sister Autumn stood on the edge of the pool, halfway between me and Rye.

This was a race without any running. To withdraw the orb, one needed calm and concentration. Not speed, but definitely endurance.

Raising my head, my gaze connected with Rye's. My heart fluttered, wanting to be released from its cage made of ribs and fly across the short strip of blue water to him. His silver eyes spoke to me, answering my unspoken confession. Did he feel the same?

And what did it matter? We couldn't work together on this final test because a winner needed to be declared. We couldn't spend time together because we'd both be going home separately. We couldn't be together as a couple because of the war.

Whoever won would be the Keeper of the Divinity Orb.

Protector of Mother Earth.

Guardian of the Future.

And if I lost, destroyer of my royal reign.

"Go." The priestess' barked instruction jerked me out of my fantasy.

Confessions could come later. After I won the orb.

I bent down and put my hand in the pool. Rye did the same. The small waves we created rippled out and greeted each other, inter-mingled, and became one. The enchanted water must recognize our bond. Getting to my knees, I focused on what hid beneath the surface.

The temperate water smoothed against my skin. I wiggled my fingers, trying to pull some fairy magic into my veins. The magic wouldn't help get the orb—only joining with Mother Earth's gifts would assist with the task—but the power thrumming through me would soothe my nerves. I didn't know how long this would take and forcing the sun through the clouds had drained me.

Tired, my gaze glazed, and I spotted something in the water—an Autostereogram, or magic eye picture. Bright and shiny. My pulse quickened, and I leaned forward. The Divinity Orb shone in my fingers, mystically materializing. I held my breath as I started to lift the orb out. The water rippled. The current moved against my hand, taking the orb away, disappearing into the water.

Had the orb been real or a figment of my hopeful thinking and imagination?

Rye's fingers splashed in the Reflection Pool. Had he created the current that stole the orb from my fingers? Stone respected Rye but didn't trust him. Arbor thought he was cute but didn't know him. And I...what did I think?

There'd been instant attraction the moment we met. Then, I'd discovered his lies, thought he'd died, and learned of the terrible laws he'd signed into existence. He'd explained his signature had been forged on the documents when we'd met again at the sanctuary. We'd gotten a second chance. He'd teased and taught. He'd cheered me on. He'd kissed me yet hadn't confessed his love.

Had he gotten into my heart to screw with my head?

Rye took on a purposeful expression. His hand stilled in the water. The orb was now in his hand. A ripple distorted the image and the orb disappeared again. Similar to me, he'd had the Divinity Orb in his hand and lost it.

Was the orb playing tricks on both of us? If so, why?

I shoved my hand deeper into the water. Determination made my bones steel. This was no time to be wishy-washy with emotions. This was about war, and possibly avoiding war if Rye took control of his throne. Because if there was one thing I'd confirmed on this journey, Rye wasn't against the majiks. He cared about them and he'd demonstrated his beliefs while at the sanctuary. If he ruled the kingdom, we could work things out. Still, I couldn't let him win the Divinity Orb because Regent Theobald would get his hands on it and that would be a disaster for the majiks.

Concentrating on the pool, I willed the orb to materialize again. My own image reflected back. Mine and Rye's. Not how we appeared at this moment. It was how we looked in the garden. My mouth softened and formed a mew. In the image, he cupped my cheek and peered at my face. I stared back. He inclined forward, and I tilted to meet him. My body heated as he brushed his lips against mine and I wanted to melt into a puddle on the ground.

I pursed my lips together. Why was I thinking of this now?

Rye sat at the edge of the pond with his hand floating on top. His eyes were closed, and his expression appeared calm and peaceful. Holding the orb and losing it hadn't upset him.

Swishing my hand around in the water, I tried to break Rye's concentration. It wasn't fair he was relaxed while I was not. That he was prince no matter what happened, while the fairies could reject me. Maybe not outright, but they could revolt or make things difficult. I squeezed my eyelids closed and pictured Watu calling the orb. If I could picture the Divinity Orb, maybe I could conjure it out of the water again.

My fingers brushed something alive. Tingles spread up my hand and my arm. My fingers brushed against it again. The tingles grew stronger and sparked to my heart. Rye's fingers threaded with mine. I gawked at him. He peered intensely back.

Our connection intensified becoming a live wire, a connection distance and prejudice couldn't break.

Water splashed and my hand felt heavier, as if a weight had been placed in my open palm. Half the weight. Rye held the other half of the Divinity Orb. Together, we lifted our hands out of the pool.

Emotion welled in my chest and throat. Tears prickled, changing the colors of the orb into a prism of light. We both held the orb in our hands. Our eyes connected like our hands. The Divinity Orb connected us.

Slowly, we raised our entwined hands, holding the orb higher.

The orb flashed in colors of purple and orange and green. There was more though. The hues went deeper, glowed with light from within and created a prism of color in the room. The glowing throbbed. The orb was a living thing.

"The prophecy is true." Mother Morningmist's reverent tone echoed around the room.

My wonder drained from within. "What prophecy?"

Rye seemed just as confused.

A single tear streamed down Mother Morningmist's cheek. "The Connected Crown Prophecy was revealed by one of our guardians, Watu."

I gasped. My mentor had foreseen whatever this was and hadn't told me. Had she known I was involved? Remembering her superstitions about the future, I understood why she couldn't inform me. The prophecy might not have come true if she had.

"What does the prophecy say?" And did I really want to know?

My great-grandmother stepped closer. Her head tilted one way and then the other, studying the orb. "The prophecy foretold the way to raise the Divinity Orb was with two royals of different blood who were united."

I stared at Rye. United? Were we? His brows were raised, and he appeared as surprised. He must not have known about the prophecy either.

"The best part." Sister Autumn inched forward. "The Divinity Orb belongs to both of you. Its power will work for *both* of you."

"We live in completely different places and are on different sides of the conflict." Rye's frustration showed in his clipped tone.

"That could be a problem." Stone's voice held a smile.

Tension filled the room. This was a major problem. Mother Morningmist froze. Sister Autumn's expression changed to considering. Stone's lips twitched while Arbor fluttered about. Hokima appeared stumped and Tos' mouth was tight trying to hold in her excitement. The human guards' fierce expression added an intimidation factor. They'd fight for Rye and the orb.

Rye used his other hand to press the orb firmly onto my palm as he slipped his other hand from beneath. "I'm giving the Divinity Orb to Princess Ellery."

The announcement reverberated in my head. My pulse scampered out of rhythm. I couldn't have heard right. He'd competed against me. This didn't make sense. "Why? Why compete and then give the orb away?"

His gaze stayed steady on mine. His enigmatic pupils communicated a message of their own. He trusted me. He believed in me.

"My uncle sent me here to compete. I don't know if he thought I actually had a chance to win or thought I'd die competing against majiks." Rye's lips ghosted upwards.

My lungs scrunched. "If you weren't going to keep the orb, why continue in the competition? Why not drop out?"

"Well, I wanted to stay because of you." He wiggled both his eyebrows and his lips trembled into a cryptic smile.

My heart melted. I wanted to reach out and hug him. Scanning the interested expressions, I understood I wasn't brave enough to share my emotions in front of others.

"When the competition came down to the two of us, I tried to drop out." He glanced at Sister Autumn. "Now, I understand why I wasn't allowed."

I sucked in a breath. "Because of the prophecy."

"The orb will unify the fairies behind you. It will help you lead. It will help you defeat my uncle."

I'd confessed to Rye why I needed to win so badly, and he'd listened. He'd paid attention to me and must care about me. I cared about him, too.

"What about you?" Fear choked my voice. What would his uncle do to him if he came back empty handed?

"I'll be on the inside fighting against him, too." Shrugging, he tried to dismiss the fearful task he'd set himself. "Humans aren't all bad and they don't all think like my uncle."

My heart started beating at a normal rate for the first time since we'd pulled the orb out of the pool. The Divinity Orb tingled the palm of my hand, as if welcoming my presence. "Everyone knows we won together."

"Not everyone." He waved around the room, indicating everyone present, everyone who knew what happened. "The priestesses will not speak of it. My guards are loyal to me. Your team is loyal to you, right?"

"Yes." No doubt in my voice or my soul.

"They will keep our secret." Rye's confident tone soothed my doubts.

Mother Morningmist viewed us with a pleased expression as if she'd known the outcome all along. Sister Autumn smiled at *both* of us. I couldn't help smiling back. The other priestesses' expressions were calm. Rye's team stood by silent and dignified, supporting the prince's decision while my team held back obvious joy.

I bit my bottom lip, needing to ask the question I'd ruminated about. "What about Regent Theobald? He'll be furious if you survived and don't come back with the orb."

"He will believe I failed and be furious with me. I don't care." Rye scowled. "I don't want to help my uncle. I want to help you, which will help everyone in our kingdom."

"That's a dangerous game you play."

"For you, for Alandaska, I'd risk everything."

Sparks shot through my bloodstream and surrounded my heart. He cared for me, wanted to help me. He understood what I needed, and he was there for me.

Tucking the orb under my arm with one hand, I reached up and ran tender fingers along his cheek. I didn't care who watched, who would know. No one would gossip about this in the fairy or human world. Our love for each other would stay secret.

I was thankful to Rye and I cared for him. Loved his roguish charm and his gallant antics, appreciated his honor and commitment. And couldn't define this strange connection as though we were meant to be together. Maybe the Divinity Orb had made the decision.

"Rye." His name came out deep and full of emotions. I didn't know how to tell him, a prince from the other side, how much I loved him.

The word love didn't punch me in the gut or make me sweat. It soothed me, strengthened me, made me happy.

He cupped my hand against his cheek. "Just as you made a sacrifice and didn't assassinate me under my palace, I'm making this sacrifice for you. I'm helping to build your reputation and respect among all majiks."

He'd known about the assassination mission.

I glanced at Mother Morningmist and her smirk told me everything I needed to know.

Rye's decision was similar to mine in the past. I'd risked the majiks fighting by my side's contempt and Gardenia's wrath by not going through with the assassination, even though he might've died when the bomb exploded and the auraguillotine was destroyed.

"I don't know what's going to happen in the future. I don't know if we'll ever see each other again." He stepped right up to me and tilted in close. "I don't want us parting without you knowing exactly how I feel. I love you, Elle."

He pressed his mouth to mine. I sighed and a tingle slid from my lips to my toes. Leaning into the kiss, I took in his scent, his warmth, and his touch. He wrapped his arms around me and brought me in closer. My knees gave in and his strength held me up. I never wanted him to let go.

Alas, that was not to be.

Someone clapped their hands.

Our kiss stopped and we separated. We didn't step away from each other. We'd formed an alliance, even if it was only through the two of us.

"Attention, everyone." Sister Autumn clapped again, not only to separate mine and Rye's lips.

Stone's expression morphed into pinched hard angles and planes. He smashed his lips together. His arms were crossed, and he leaned back in a too-casual stance.

Sadness wove around my otherwise happy heart. I hoped we'd stay friends and he'd come to understand I was destined to be with Rye, even if I hadn't returned words of love.

Hokima and Tos stood tall, taking everything in. Arbor winked at me.

Mother Morningmist glided toward us. "I have something for you, Prince Zacharye." She pulled a red covered box out and handed it to him. "It's a replica. I had it created after I saw the prophecy and believed the two who possessed the Divinity Orb together might be separated." She winked at both of us. "At least for a while."

He opened the lid and unwrapped the object inside. His mouth bloomed into a smile. "Amazing. Thank you."

The orb in my hand palpitated and I swished closer.

The box held an orb identical to the one I carried. The same size and shape. The flashing colors weren't as bright and didn't have the same depth.

Mother Morningmist's royal laugh sounded deeper, more mischievous. "The replica's only power is communication. Your uncle won't realize that."

Maybe the fake orb would help Rye escape punishment.

"Thank you for this and your hospitality." He hugged my great-grandmother and Sister Autumn goodbye.

The woman wiped away tears. "Good luck."

She knew he would need luck, and lots of it.

"Walk with me before I pack up and leave." He took hold of my hand and pulled me out of the room, away from prying eyes. He held out the box with the fake orb inside. "What do you think?"

I clutched the real orb in my hand. Nerves spiraled in my gut. He'd given the real orb to me and he'd suffer for it. "I don't think it will fool the regent for long."

"Don't worry." He grinned whimsically, with a twist to his strong lips.

It didn't fool me. I could spot his anxiety. His mean and spiteful uncle would seek revenge once he discovered the orb was fake.

"Besides, my uncle wouldn't know how to use the real orb. Regent Theobald has no connection with nature or Mother Earth. He wanted the orb so your side wouldn't possess it and the competition got me out of the way. Permanently, he'd hoped."

Pointing out the fact we were on different sides sent a slice of anguish through my midsection. "There's going to be a war."

"They've been saying that for months." He tried to sound breezy, but the underlying note of determination scraped against my worries. "I've tried my best to dissuade and undermine my uncle."

I didn't want his uncle to take revenge on him and I didn't want us to be apart. With my new royal powers, I could protect him. "Don't go home. Come back with me. Your knowledge would be an asset to the majiks."

Our gazes connected, and I willed him to do as I asked. His silver eyes warmed and then flashed with fatalistic determination. The image seared into my memory. My chest heaved and mourned. This was the real goodbye.

"I wish I could, Elle." He took my hand. His chin dropped, and he slowly shook his head. "My people, the humans, are going to need me. And I have ways to oppose my uncle. A secret revolt behind the scenes is being planned. I must be there to overthrow the regent."

A dense pressure pushed against my chest. I understood his responsibilities because I now had my own.

CHAPTER TWENTY-NINE

Our transport landed smoothly on the grounds of Queens Academy. Crowds rushed forward to greet us, having heard of our arrival when we'd messaged from the bottom of Drage Mountain after our four-day hike down. They must know about the Divinity Orb. The only reason fairies would come out to welcome me.

Licking my lips, I tried to control the lurch of my stomach.

My companions appeared as concerned. We hadn't left under the most auspicious circumstances, sneaking away in the middle of the night. And we'd returned with two less: one having killed the other and escaped imprisonment. One of my first orders would be to find Bee.

We'd had successes, too. I looked again at the weary faces of my friends. We'd been through so much together. We'd grown and changed.

I'd grown and changed. Learning my strengths and recognizing my weaknesses, training with Watu, and gaining my wings. My friendships had grown stronger, although my love life was a mess because of the separation from Rye. I accepted my new position and responsibilities. Recognized that every fairy wouldn't love me. As long as they respected me, I could deal.

Pulling my shoulders back, I peered out the windows of the podship. Fairies fluttered their wings, rising higher in expectation of getting a better view. The Divinity Orb throbbed in my pocket sending a shaft of extra confidence through my bloodstream.

The podship door swished open.

Cloudy skies blustered above the castle. Noise from the crowd gushed into the vehicle overwhelming me. In the past I would've staggered back, hid from the crowd, not anymore. I was ready to face the fairies, even in my dirty hiking clothes.

Gardenia climbed the small set of metal stairs and entered the vehicle. She wore a glittery dress and held a sparkling wand. "Welcome back, everyone."

"Welcome home, Princess Ellery." She gave me a hug. The maternal hug didn't hold any anger even though I'd disobeyed her more than once. "You got your wings!"

"I did." I pulled back and twisted to display my wings. "What's going on? Why is everyone gathered?" My gut knotted into a tight bow. But I could handle facing a crowd. I would handle it.

"They're here to celebrate winning the Divinity Orb." She took my hand and tugged me to the top step.

I quirked my head. "How do they know?"

Gardenia's lips curled at the end in a tease. "We're fairies. Sometimes we know."

My entire body grew hot when the crowd erupted in applause and cheering. "Then you know I didn't win it by myself," I whispered to Gardenia as we descended the steps.

"I'm the only one who knows that. Besides, the Divinity Orb should've been yours outright." Her tone went sharp. "After you left, the competition was foreseen."

My mouth dropped open. "Why didn't you tell me?"

"You'd already left."

The crowd cheered again.

Turning, I saw Stone and Arbor emerge from the transport. At least I wasn't the only one getting the attention.

Gardenia pulled me toward the building with a decorated balcony. Ribbons festooned the balustrade and garishly dressed members of the fairy court stood at the rail. I'd met none of them, just recognized them from paintings on a wall.

"You will learn," she took pleasure in reminding me I still had much to be taught, "the future isn't set, and learning and growth was one of the purposes of your mission."

"Are you and Queen Dahliadew mad at me for leaving?" Remorse tightened around my chest because of the circumstances of how I'd left. "How is the queen?"

The crowd erupted again. This time it wasn't cheering. Boos and hisses spewed.

I jerked my glance back to see Tos and Hokima emerging from the transport. Tos hid behind Hokima's massive bulk. His scowl of disgust hid the hurt I knew must be beneath.

Rage spiked and burst inside me. This belief that fairies were superior had to stop. Tugging my hand free from Gardenia, I snatched her wand and flew to the podship. I hurried up the metal stairs to stand at my friends' side.

Using a broadcasting spell, I held the wand toward my mouth. "Tos, the brownie, and Hokima, the troll, have fought valiantly by my side to bring home the Divinity Orb." Emotion clogged my throat and tears threatened. These two had been more loyal than the crowd. "They are part of my team, and more importantly, they are my friends."

Hokima stood in a superhero pose, holding his arms up. He was a superhero. Tos scooted from behind him and raised her hand in a wave.

I gawked at the crowd simmering with hate and distrust. How were majiks going to work together against the humans if we didn't trust each other? Spotting Arbor and Stone's nods standing on the balcony, I had to continue.

Tilting my chin up, I mimicked Rye's regal tone. "I expect you to treat them with respect and hospitality."

"Who are you?" someone in the crowd questioned.

"A halfling," another fairy jeered.

My head swam with embarrassment, frustration, and rage. Swallowing, I held back the scream building in my lungs. Everyone wasn't celebrating my return. They continued to show prejudice toward half fairies and other majiks.

"Why should we listen to a majik-want-to-be?" someone else yelled.

Before I would've hidden away and not confronted my attacker. No longer. Standing taller, I slipped my hand into the pocket holding the orb. "I might be half human and half fairy, but I've risked my life for you. I've trained, and I've fought. Just like the rest of my team. Just like Tos and Hokima."

The murmurs from the crowd changed, sounding less negative. The fluttering wings calmed. The upraised faces listened.

"I've brought back the Divinity Orb." My voice grew stronger. I pulled the orb out and held it up.

The orb flashed bright colors and palpitated in my hand.

The crowd *ooh*ed and *ahh*ed. Because they'd grown up around fairies, they understood the orb's history and importance. At least they weren't booing anymore. And while I had their attention, I was going to tell them one more thing.

Something big. Something important.

Gardenia stood on the balcony now, and she tilted her head understanding my intent.

Nerves jumped in my stomach and vaulted up my throat. Nausea swirled. I sucked in a big breath and let it out slowly. "And...and." I waited for the crowd to quiet. "There's one more reason why you should, *why you will*, listen to me." Perspiration slid down my back. My palms were sweaty and my pulsed raced. "I'm..." I licked my lips. "I'm the lost princess."

The crowd went silent.

The non-noise was more threatening. They'd heard my claim. Did they believe?

"I'm Lily Kunglig's daughter." My voice rang across the court-yard. "And Queen Dahliadew's granddaughter." I stood taller and stronger. "I'm your fairy princess."

The crowd murmurs grew louder and louder. They must be discussing my right to the throne. My muscles twitched, and my belly rolled. The fairies shuffled unhappily, their wings fluttering and creating a stir in the air. Would they overthrow me before I was crowned?

"We don't want a half fairy as our princess." A male fairy spread his wings and flew above the crowd.

The slur would've shut me down in the past. It didn't now. I could handle insults and slurs. "Well, I'm a half fairy and your princess."

"I don't believe you!" a woman shouted.

"IT'S TRUE." The robust voice crackled across the atmosphere. The tone was regal and wouldn't accept anyone talking back.

I glanced around. So did the crowd. I didn't know what to make of it, except the voice was on my side.

Queen Dahliadew apparated onto the decorated balcony. Even though she was tiny, she stood tall. Her face glowed with health and her mossy green eyes appeared sharp.

My twitchy muscles calmed. Queen Dahliadew was alive and well. Her voice was certainly strong. I was glad I wouldn't have to start ruling right away. And I'd have my grandmother to guide me. My chest filled with love and gratitude, and hope.

"She is exactly who she says she is. She is my granddaughter and your future ruler. The fact she has not lived among the fairies her entire life is a good thing. She is acquainted with our enemies and has made contact with our majik partners." The queen waved a stiff, royal hand. "Princess Ellery, you and your friends will join me on the balcony."

She was recognizing me and my friends.

I stepped down from the transport with Tos and Hokima at my side. The crowd parted. Their expressions were a mixture of disgust, disbelief, and delight. Stone and Arbor met us halfway. His ever-protective gaze scoured the crowd, searching for someone who might impede our progress. He finally understood my relationship with Rye, and we were now on solid friendship footing.

Together, we arrived at the stairs to the balcony. Guards and attendants bowed as I passed. Showing off my new wings, I flew to the top of the stairs and crossed to where Queen Dahliadew stood.

The queen bowed low and held out her hands.

Wiggling my shoulders, I was uncomfortable with her act of respect. I placed the Divinity Orb in her capable hands, and she displayed it on a pedestal near the queen's chair.

Queen Dahliadew nodded her head. "I meant to do this with more formality, but I believe the time is right now." She conjured a tiara made of shiny purple gemstones shaped into flowers and faced the crowd. "Fairies of Alandaska."

The crown glittered and winked. My eyes burned and I struggled to hold in a shaky breath. I had family and good friends.

Queen Dahliadew stepped toward me. "As your sovereign, I present to you, Princess Ellery."

My body froze. I didn't know what was expected.

"Kneel," Gardenia whispered.

Dropping to my knees, my skin dug into the stone floor of the balcony. I didn't care. Triumph swirled through me and pulled my shoulders back with pride.

"With the power vested in me..." Queen Dahliadew tapped my right shoulder with her wand. "And through the succession of the fairy royal family," she tapped my left shoulder, "I now pronounce you, Princess Ellery Kunglig, princess of fairies and ruler of the forest and fauna."

The queen placed the tiara on me.

The circle of gemstones tightened around my head. An electrical charge jolted through me. A strong tingling sensation vibrated from my head to my toes. The experience was similar to the first time the queen had touched me. Only stronger. I didn't sense the coldness of the stone ground or the tiny rock digging into my knee. I didn't hear the murmuring of the crowd, just the rush of the wind. I didn't see the present, and yet couldn't detect the future.

"Stand, Princess Ellery, and greet your subjects." Queen Dahliadew made it a request, not an order.

That's when I knew how different my life would be from this point forward. No more sneaking off on missions. No more visiting human cities. I'd have responsibilities and I'd take them seriously. Now, I understood Rye's devotion.

Standing, I locked my knees so I wouldn't fall.

"Princess Ellery, may you long live." Queen Dahliadew took hold of my hand and held it up. "Greet your new sovereign princess."

My scalp prickled, and I shivered. Coldness invaded my heart. How would the crowd react?

The fairies stared eerily from below. Their eyes rounded. Their mouths closed. Their wings shuttered in protest.

My throat constricted. They weren't going to accept me.

Beside me on the balcony, Stone bowed. "Hail, Princess Ellery."

Warmth spread from my frigid toes to my cheeks releasing the tension I'd been holding. Stone showing respect would go a long way because he was an admired member of the royal guard.

"Hail, Princess Ellery." Arbor flew in front of me and down to the crowd, encouraging them to join in.

My pulse pattered with her wings. She was a true friend, and not because Gardenia had ordered her to be.

"Hail, Princess Ellery," Tos and Hokima added their greetings.

"Hail, Princess Ellery." The mean girl who'd smashed the pudding cup on my shirt bowed and raised her fist in the air.

If she could accept me, there was hope the others would as well.

"Hail, Princess Ellery." More and more fairies joined in. Soon everyone greeted me and the chorus became jubilant.

I could float on the happiness of the crowd. They welcomed me. Celebrated me. Sent me good wishes. Most of them believed I was worthy, and I'd continue to prove myself. I wouldn't be a helpless princess. I'd work hard and learn everything about my heritage. In the long run, I'd be an admirable ruler.

Glasses of summer wine appeared in every fairy's hand. Music poured from invisible speakers. People danced and sang.

Arbor landed on my shoulder and did a jig. Hokima picked up Tos and twirled her around. Stone tapped his booted foot and

Gardenia's normally-deep worry lines dissolved. Queen Dahliadew sat on her throne with a peaceful expression.

For once, everyone was happy.

I took the queen's hands and leaned in for a hug. "How did you recover from the poisoning?"

"We have the best healers and I am strong in health." She smiled at me. "Like you."

A messenger fairy flew to Gardenia and handed her a parchment. Opening the note to read, her worry lines reformed. She bent over Queen Dahliadew's chair and whispered.

My lungs clenched. I didn't know if it was a princess fairy's premonition or what, but something terrible had happened.

The queen gripped my hand and my soul darkened—a knock on my grave. I didn't have a grave and I wasn't dead. I was supposed to be happy. Something had changed. The news was bad.

"I'm sorry to interrupt this auspicious occasion." Queen Dahliadew used a spell to broadcast her voice. "I've received word our negotiations with the humans have failed. Regent Theobald has attacked our delegation. Hundreds of fairies and our fellow majiks have been slaughtered. We have no choice except to declare war."

Icy tendrils reached out around my neck. My body went cold, but not numb. No, I experienced every dreadful thought. War against humans. Against Rye.

The crowd cried out. Fairies jerked in frantic motions, hugging their friends and loved ones. Most of them were students and in training to join the army. They'd experience the devastation firsthand. They could die, and they knew it.

"I will be sending a delegation to confer with other majik leaders." Queen Dahliadew made her decisions quickly, not lightly. Someday I'd be in charge and make the tough choices. "We've been preparing. We must step up our efforts. Immediately."

Her pronouncement rang across the courtyard and echoed in my chest. I'd known war would be inevitable. I'd believed I would have time to adjust to my new role.

None of that would come to pass.

Pain wrapped around my heart like a steel band. I found it difficult to breathe. Prince Zacharye would be in trouble because he'd helped me. I had to return the favor.

My gaze caught on the Divinity Orb, my only link to Rye. The bright colors disappeared, and cloudy, dark colors made the surface murky. Was the orb mourning the start of war, or something else entirely?

CINDERELLA SPY

Are you ready for the exciting conclusion to Ellery's story?

**Cinderella Spy
A Glass Slipper Adventure Book 3**

She only wants to be with the prince. But love is impossible between enemies.

Elle Milford has finally accepted her position as princess, destined to be the future leader of the magical world. But that hasn't stopped her from falling in love with the prince of the opposing forces. After communication with the prince is cut off, Elle convinces her fairy godmother to let her travel with a peace delegation to the enemy's headquarters. In exchange, Elle must promise that if the treaty fails, the kingdom's elite will be dethroned.

The reluctant negotiator's mission turns against her when Elle discovers a plot at the highest level to topple the government and take away the prince's right to rule. But she can't risk the treaty for one person—no matter how important he is to her heart.

Can the tenacious half-fairy princess find a way to unite the kingdom or will she destroy it?

Cinderella Spy is the third book in the charming Glass Slipper Adventure YA fantasy series. If you like determined heroines, star crossed lovers, and royal pageantry, then you'll love Allie Burton's spellbinding story.

Buy Cinderella Spy to reveal the truth about the royals today!

"OMG! I loved books one and two, but this third book just blew me away!" – Reviewer

A Glass Slipper Adventure Series continues with an exciting new trilogy: Snow Wicked White, Snow Warrior White, and Snow Witching White. Read on for more information.

Excerpt:

"What? Why?" This was my favorite time of the day. Or should I say night? I could be myself and say what I wanted with Stone. "Has someone discovered us?"

My question sounded like we were having a tawdry affair. With my spirits already at a low point, I didn't want anyone thinking that or for him to get in trouble.

"No one has found out." He pursed his lips together and stepped closer to me. "I'm leaving for an undercover mission."

Anxiety scraped down my spine. "Where? When?"

He shook his head. "Things I can't disclose."

"I'm the princess." I never pulled rank with him, however I needed to know where he was going and whether he'd be safe.

"Sorry, Princess." He smirked the last word reminding me of when I'd thought it was a nickname. "Let's continue training while we can. You have a lot to learn."

"Ha." I raised my sword and charged.

He easily blocked each and every attack. His teasing and encouragement kept me going. Someday I'd be as good as him.

A branch cracked.

We both paused and froze. My pulse hammered in my ears.

An owl hooted and crickets chirped. Wind stirred through the branches.

"What was that?" My tense muscles scrambled for release. I should run. I couldn't get caught the night before the Grand Council meeting and my wand test for entrance into the Guild of the Wand Supreme.

Stone hunched and his gaze darted around. He waited for an attack. "Wait here."

His whispered words triggered my nerves. He edged toward the edge of the forest and stood by the trunk of a tree. It was too dark. He wouldn't see anything.

I tiptoed behind him. Flicking my fingers, I created a ball of light.

"Elle, no." He covered the light with his large hand.

Stumbling, clattering, pounding feet ran. The light alerted whoever watched. "Elves' bells."

Stone sprinted after them.

It had sounded like one person or an animal which he could handle. If we found them, I needed to explain why I was out here in the middle of the night. Putting out the light, I tried to follow behind. I came upon Stone one hundred yards away from our original spot, bent over and panting.

"Who was it?" I landed next to him, bringing my wings to my side.

"I don't know, but they were fast."

"Only one?"

"Yes."

I didn't appreciate his short answers. "A deer or a brown hare?"

"Nope." He lifted his head to stare at me with incredulity. "She was blond."

Jolted, I teetered not knowing what to think. He meant a human. A really fast human if Stone couldn't catch her. And so close to Queens Academy when we were at war against them. "She must be a spy."

SNOW WICKED WHITE

**The exciting new trilogy in
A Glass Slipper Adventure Series...**

**Snow Wicked White
A Glass Slipper Adventure Book 4**

**She chooses to stay out of the fight. But when she's forced
to help the enemy, her betrayal wakes a sleeping giant.**

Destiny Snow is the last known banshee in the kingdom. Or she
fears she is because her grandfather has disappeared. Humans and
majiks alike discriminate against her because of the banshee wail
of death. That's why she and her grandfather have always lived
as hermits and never joined the majik resistance movement. Until
royal guards knocked on her door.

Under the regent's orders, Destiny is held in an overcrowded cell with seven other criminals while she's forced to track majiks to steal their power.

Except she's never been trained and has no magic. When she makes a major mistake, several important resistance leaders are captured, including her childhood crush, Stone.

Can the bad news banshee convince her cellmates that she can be trusted and help them escape the dungeon before they're all tortured to death?

Snow Wicked White is the first book in the Snow White trilogy and the fourth book in the captivating fairytale series A Glass Slipper Adventure. If you like feisty heroines, twisted fairytales, and secret identity stories, then you'll love Allie Burton's spellbinding novel.

Buy Snow Wicked White to escape with the daring rebels today!

"And that ending, oh my I need the next book!!" – Reviewer

And don't miss the trilogy's exciting conclusion!

A Note from Allie Burton

I hoped you enjoyed Elle's continuing saga in Cinderella Soldier. Her story concludes in Cinderella Spy, but the fun doesn't end! To get information about the rest of the series, A Glass Slipper Adventure, join my newsletter and receive a free book. You can join at www.allieburton.com.

Please consider giving this book a rating or review at your place of purchase. In this brave new book world, the only way for a good story to find its way to other readers is if the people who loved it let others know. I appreciate any little bit you can give, and reviews encourage me to write faster.

I love to hear from my readers! If you have any questions or comments, or just want to say "hi" please feel free to email me at allie@allieburton.com or connect with me on social media at www.instagram.com/allieburtonauthor, www.facebook.com/AllieBurtonAuthor, and www.twitter.com/allie_burton.

If you're interested in my other young adult series, additional information follows. Thanks for reading CINDERELLA SOLDIER!

Allie

Atlantis Riptide
Lost Daughters of Atlantis Book 1

When a girl runs away from the circus...

For all her sixteen years, Pearl Poseidon has been a fish out of water. A freak on display for her adoptive parents' profit. Running away from her horrible life, she craves one thing—anonymity. But when she saves a small boy from drowning, she exposes herself and her mutant abilities to Chase, a budding investigative reporter.

Now, he has questions. And so do the police.

Once Pearl discovers her secret identity, she learns she's part of a larger war between battling Atlanteans. A battle that will decide who rules the oceans. A battle raging between evil and her true family. Will she find a way to use her powers in time to save a kingdom she never knew existed?

This is the start of a young adult fantasy action-adventure novel series. "Sweet summer young adult paranormal with death-defying underwater rescues." Reviewer

Other books in the Atlantis series: Atlantis Red Tide, Atlantis Rising Tide, Atlantis Tide Breaker, Atlantis Dark Tides, Atlantis Twisting Tides, Atlantis Glacial Tides.

ALSO BY

A Glass Slipper Adventure-Young Adult
Cinderella Assassin
Cinderella Soldier
Cinderella Spy
Snow Wicked White
Snow Warrior White
Snow Witching White
Lost Daughters of Atlantis Series-Young Adult
Atlantis Riptide
Atlantis Red Tide
Atlantis Rising Tide
Atlantis Tide Breaker
Atlantis Dark Tides
Atlantis Twisting Tides
Atlantis Glacial Tides
Warrior Academy Series-Young Adult
Warrior's Destiny
Warrior's Chaos
Warrior's Prophecy
Warrior's Curse
Warrior's Rising
Castle Ridge Series-Contemporary Romance
The Romance Dance

The Christmas Match
The Flirtation Game
The Playboy Switch
The Billionaire's Ploy
The Heartbreak Contract
Find all of Allie's books on her website

https://www.allieburton.com

About Author

Allie Burton has always been a reader and writer. She wrote her first novel at the age of twelve when she was stranded at a hospital by a snowstorm. Receiving her first romance from her grandmother, she fell in love with the genre. As an adult, she read young adult books with her own teens and was excited to find something fresh and new. Now, she writes both.

Having so many jobs as a teen and adult became great research material for the stories she writes. She has been everything from a bike police officer to a mascot escort to an advertising executive. She has lived on three continents and in four states and has studied art, fashion design, and marine biology.

Allie is a member of several writing organizations. She loves to ski, golf, and run. Currently, she lives in Colorado with her husband and two children.